XVII

THE
Book of Wanda

SEVENTEEN
VOLUME TWO

Mark D. Diehl

THE BOOK OF WANDA
SEVENTEEN: VOLUME TWO
Copyright © 2018 by Mark D. Diehl

ISBN: 9780692158227

AUTHOR'S NOTE

As resources are depleted and power is concentrated in fewer hands, hierarchical organizations are evolving into the world's only consumers. We, as individual human beings, are merely raw material to be processed and utilized, and our survival depends almost entirely upon our employers' judgments of our worth. Our organizations are claiming absolute dominion over us. Though some human bodies may ultimately survive this process, other aspects of what we now consider to be our humanity will disappear.

"The individual cannot compete for resources against the colony, so in a world of colonies the individual cannot survive."
—Eric Basali

"Human events are never as linear as people imagine."
—Gregor Kessler

XVII

↕

VIXI
(Latin)

↕

"I have lived."

I

1

Zone IA1.24, formerly part of the Des Moines metropolitan area, now referred to colloquially as the Zone

Hey!" a voice said. "Break his ribs all you want, *after* we see what the pink shit does. Don't fuck up my experiment."

Daniel "Mr. B" Martel became aware he had been kicked. His side ached.

"Get up, Mister Bitch," a different voice said.

Spattering liquid. First it was a sound, and then a feeling. Warm. A fine, sour stream into his face.

He shuddered awake and attempted to deflect the urine with his hands, but they were tied, spread apart near his head. "Tsshuwha!" He wiped an eye against a shoulder but that was soaked, too.

Alfred.

His memory was coming back now.

It was Alfred, the manufacturer who sold bactrosynthesized street drugs to most of the gangs and dealers in this part of the Zone. Relatively average in build and smarts, the man managed to survive among the vast local criminal population simply by being one of the more psychotic ones.

Mr. B was bound hand and foot with plastic rope, lying sideways on a shipping pallet in a loading dock.

"Aw, see?" Alfred said, showing brown, rodent-like teeth beneath his mustache. "Mister Bitch likes that. You like that, Mister Bitch? The bactrohypnotics should be outta your system now." Alfred zipped up. "You told us all about how you and Spooky were gonna set up shop, makin' your own shit 'steada sellin' mine. Now he's gonna get a big surprise just like you did. You shitheads really thought you could just cut me out? You go around askin' for a strain, it ain't gonna stay a secret."

Someone twisted Mr. B's arm, veins-up, tying a rubber tube just above the elbow. The tip of a needle made its way along a vein as it was laid flat, and then punctured, stabbing up, shuddering along inside. He tensed and straightened his spine, pulling against the bonds.

"I gotta tell you don't break the needle?" Alfred said. "Hold still, Mister Bitch."

The needle and tubing disappeared, or maybe they only seemed to because the new sensation drowned out anything else. The dose stalked up his vein, its causticity giving the impression of thousands of tiny insectile legs. His vision filled with gray perhaps as much from terror as from the effects of the drug. Sounds became distant and distorted.

"What the fuck?" Alfred's voice seemed to echo to Mr. B from thousands of kilometers. It might have been seconds or hours since they'd shot him up. Someone may have been slapping and shaking him. "It just fuckin' knocks him out? Maybe it's not injectable. We'll try the powder on Spooky Brian, see if it does anything when it's snorted."

Mr. B tried to force his eyes open wider, but nothing came into focus. Some little part of his mind thought the conversation was important, but it couldn't get other parts to listen. He realized he was not recovering from the dose. Rather, he was still in the process of succumbing to it.

"What're we gonna do with this shit if all it does is drop 'em into a fucking coma?" Alfred said. "Anesthesia, maybe? Hey, do we know anybody who traffics human organs?"

Dobo Protein Refinery, The Zone

"Someone's here, sir."

Mikk Evans sat up, groggy but wary. It was his wife and office assistant, Kym, on the speaker. She knew better than to wake him without a good reason.

The office had been a gas station at one time, a little glass island at the back of a concrete slab. Now the space was fenced off and piled high with dead roaches, shit, cadavers, pets, and other assorted waste, waiting for its turn to be fed into the extractors and exported out as the raw amino acid building blocks used to make sterile nutrients for bacterial synthesizers.

"Chips?"

"Yes, sir."

"How much in total?"

"They're claimin' four hundred, but I only saw two."

He'd started making Kym confirm that potential buyers actually had casino chips after an unpleasant incident occurred that taught her a lesson about junkies and their fucking drama. Kym picked it up quickly. Not once had she failed to check for chips via camera since the day she'd watched Mikk beat that begging, sobbing idiot to death.

Two hundred. Hardly worth lifting his head for. He checked the screen: Two little punks. They'd just been here last week.

Still, if these kids moved small quantities with a fast turn-around, they could be worth something to him. With a few more in the chain moving product like that, he'd be able to pull in more serious weight. He stood and cracked his neck, stuffing his handgun into the front of his pants and shuffling out past Kym in the slightly bigger glass box attached to his office, and out to the gate. Shells for the clunky, old-fashioned .44 revolver were worth their weight in gold coins, but it was handy for dealing with nuisances.

The whole place was surrounded by electric razor-wire fence with auto-aiming guns, and the gate was a thick piece of steel. He checked the screen next to it to be sure there were still only two of them out there, and then slid open the gate to peer out. A knife blade shot in through the opening, obviously trying for

Mikk's throat but cutting deeply across his forehead, instead.

He snatched the gun and turned toward the screen again, but he could barely see. He tried wiping the blood from his eyes with the back of his hand, but it continued to stream from the wound. He managed to block the flow a bit with the web of his hand against his eyebrows. The two kids, maybe late teens, stood glaring at the gate. He remembered the patches. Apparently showing membership in whatever piss-ant gang they'd formed, the kids had sewn on capital letter *D*s cut from old printed fabrics, turned rounded side up. There was one hoodlum with lighter hair, who looked scared, and one with darker hair, who looked angry. Scared ones were often the more dangerous, and Mikk noted that one was holding the knife.

"Hey, fucker! We want our fuckin' chips back for this!" the angry one shouted. He held up a baggie of powder. "Stepped on so much it's worthless. We got nothing out of this bag, asshole! Nothing!"

Mikk had wondered whether this might happen. His supplier, Mr. B, had disappeared. To squeeze as much profit as possible from his remaining stash, Mikk had cut it almost to half-strength. These two had bought a good-sized bag of the most stepped-on shit he'd ever sold.

Using the screen to aim, he fired once through the steel gate, hitting the knife-wielding one squarely in the chest.

"I don't give refunds. Get away from my employer's property."

Amelix Integrations, Central Business District

"Dr. Chelsea, ma'am?" Wanda Kuon called. "I have an important observation to report!"

Wanda waited as the younger woman turned slowly toward her. Chelsea had the same dark hair and the same grayish blue eyes, which were now looking Wanda up and down, but she wasn't the person she used to be. When Wanda had first known her, she'd been Zabeth Chelsea, eight years Wanda's junior and eager to be trained in biochemical lab work. That had been before her reconditioning and subsequent status as an Accepted, which had unlocked the doors to promotion and further education. Upon earning her Doctor of Corporate Sciences degree a few years ago, Zabeth Chelsea had become Dr. Chelsea, Wanda's supervisor.

"Wanda!" Dr. Chelsea huffed. "How many times do we have to go over it? The lab is not a place for excited outbursts. Your choice to stay stagnated forever at Tech Two is no excuse for childish behavior in our place of business." Her voice had the Accepted speech pattern, enunciating every syllable in a haughty and hypnotic roll.

Wanda stood rigid and straight but averted her eyes, as Dr. Chelsea always insisted she do. "I'm sorry, ma'am. I have what I feel is an important observation about your *special* project."

Dr. Chelsea stared a moment, apparently utilizing her Efficiency Implant, the interface between her brain and the Amelix network. She spoke, using the EI's communication link. "Dr. Synd, do you have a moment? Wanda has something to share. We'll come to your office." She gestured to Wanda in the direction of Jeremy Synd's door. Jeremy and Wanda had gone through undergrad together at Zytem University, so he would always be "Jeremy" in her mind, even though he, too, had changed after reconditioning. They made their way through the busy laboratory to a pair of smaller labs along one wall, each cordoned off with walls of transparent bioplexi. In the far corners of each office were piles of equipment shielding from view the most unsettling project Wanda had ever seen.

Wanda had grown up hoping a science career might allow her to work with animals. She loved the parts of her job that let her care for the rats, watching their little personalities interact as they wrestled and chased each other. Some were shy, while others were fearless. Some were affectionate to other rats, and others were stand-offish or even hostile, even though they all had the same background, having been born in standardized laboratories like this one. She could swear some of them actually giggled when she tickled them. The rats in every lab, even those who were suffering, all displayed more variation in personality and were infinitely more relatable than the Accepted humans she worked with.

Wanda had learned as much from her grandmother long ago. Her grandmother was non-Accepted, but had been allowed to share a corporate housing unit with Wanda and her parents. Wanda had many strong, warm memories of her. The last such memory was especially vivid. Her grandmother had secretly borrowed rats from the lab she cleaned and brought them home for Wanda to play with. "Accepted are nothing but machines, you know, and that's all we have around us, anymore," she'd told Wanda. "I brought these rats home so you could have the chance to connect with a real life form, to experience natural play, and maybe we can balance out the machines' influence just a little. These are the first I've been able to access that don't have to be isolated and sterile. Remember that they're small but they're alive, and they've had a tough life. Be very gentle and let them decide when they are ready to interact with you. I've worked quite hard to teach these little ones that not all humans will hurt them." Wanda had sat with the animals for almost an hour (an unheard-of stretch of unoccupied time for an eleven-year-old at Integrations Elementary), letting them approach each other and learn to play, and then finally, slowly, they had come to her and poked tentatively at her fingers. Eventually she'd been able to gently touch them back, feeling their warm, soft fur and long, twitchy tails. Then Wanda's father had come home unexpectedly, and her grandmother had swept the rats back into the crate before he could see them. As an Accepted, her father would have been compelled to report her grandmother if he'd known of her actions.

After that day the world looked much different to Wanda. She felt she understood now what it meant to truly be alive, to be one unique organism in a dynamic universe comprised of different types of organisms, all interacting with each other. Her outlook began slowly shifting, in all parts of her life, leading her to recognize how sterile and un-alive her Accepted parents seemed, and her friends, and everyone else around her. Her grandmother soon disappeared. The memory of her, and that of the little rats freed from their cages for that single hour, remained as the only examples of natural, independent minds Wanda had ever known.

Those had been ordinary rats. The rats in this project were different. In fifteen years as a lab tech, she had never seen anything like them.

This entire end of the office suite radiated a sinister, chilling energy. Every step closer to the animals made something inside her recoil and squirm. They were locked away, sealed behind multiple encapsulations of bulletproof bioplexi, on a sealed air source, and she knew they couldn't touch her. Still, her breath shortened, and her lips and fingers went numb.

Jeremy came up from some other part of the lab and accessed the security mechanisms to open his office door. The machine took his iris and palm scans and required a code entered mentally through his brain's EI. Wanda and Dr. Chelsea were admitted separately, via EI identification only, once he had unlocked the door. It closed and locked behind them as they entered. Wanda's eyes reflexively turned away from the corner where, sequestered behind equipment, cordoned off and sheltered under a fume hood, were the sealed bioplexi cages of the Rat Gods.

Wanda had been here the day Roger Terry had treated them with the symbiotic fungus, forever changing them into … whatever they were now. After that, the project had quickly disappeared to a clearance level unreachable for her job description, though as the Senior Tech Two she was still sometimes brought into proximity with the animals.

"What is it, Wanda?" Jeremy asked. There was an edge of annoyance to his voice.

"Well … " Wanda sought the words.

Dr. Chelsea's head cocked slightly and her eyes widened. Her lips formed an increasingly thin line.

"I brought the requisitioned chemicals into the project workspace in Dr. Chelsea's lab," Wanda said. "As you know, the cages are transparent but at opposite ends of the two labs; the rats can't see each other around all the equipment."

"Yes," Jeremy said.

"The chemicals were still sealed in Mylar bags," she said. "As I entered the area, the rats there both stood on their hind legs, at exactly the same time. They froze, staring at me, which isn't unusual. But the reflection in the Mylar showed the same thing was happening over here, in your office, Dr. Synd, sir. At the instant Dr. Chelsea's rats stood, Dr. Synd's rats did, too. Exactly the same motion at exactly the same time."

"They heard you come in, and they stood," Dr. Chelsea said. "There is nothing strange about that; you said so yourself."

"Yes, ma'am. But the others, the rats here in Dr. Synd's office, couldn't have heard me. The offices are separated by ten centimeters of bioplexi. They might have caught a glimpse of me between pieces of equipment, but by the time I reached the back corner there had been plenty of time and opportunity for them to react to my presence over here."

"You think they're communicating," Jeremy said.

"Yes, sir. And there's more. After I observed the phenomenon I turned to look at the ones in your lab, sir. I had to bend down to where the Mylar had been because that is the only spot in Dr. Chelsea's office from which they can be seen. There was a pause, as if maybe the rats were trying to decide what to do. Then they dropped down to four legs and started doing what I can only describe as a little dance. They were lifting and lowering each of their legs, one at a time, proceeding in a counter-clockwise direction: front leg, front leg, back leg, back leg, and then around again, both rats lifting the same leg at the same time." She swallowed and blinked, struggling to keep her voice steady. "I turned back, and the ones by me were doing it, too. The same feet, touching down at the same time. Counter-clockwise."

"Well," Dr. Chelsea said. "You've certainly made a detailed and potentially important scientific observation, Wanda. I will go note that in my journal." She stood.

"There's something else," Wanda said. They'd probably have her evaluated for mental instability for saying it, but she was duty-bound to do whatever was in Amelix's best interest. Her voice was softer than she would have liked, but she got it out.

"They made me sick."

"Sick?" Jeremy asked.

Wanda nodded. "Yes, sir. I know they're sealed up. I know there's a chance I was just over-stimulated. It was a disturbing thing to witness, after all. But still, I think it was connected to that dance they did. Somehow it felt *invasive,* like some sick energy was radiating from them, targeted right at my brain. I became dizzy and nauseated, and an incredibly strong impulse kept flashing through my mind, telling me to attack and destroy the rats any way I could. They're an Amelix priority, precious to our institution and dangerous to the world, but all I could think of was how I might kill them. Only my sense of duty to Amelix helped me resist sealing the air filters and suffocating them. I even felt an urge to push the cage over the burners and cook them to death. It was a desperate, terrifying feeling, and I came so close to actually doing it. I ended up running out of the lab." She gave her superiors a shallow smile, gesturing toward the other lab, the casualness of the act making Dr. Chelsea's nose wrinkle. "You can see I left the cart there. I'm sorry about that."

Dr. Chelsea had already taken two strides toward the exit. "You needn't worry about the cart," she said. The door opened on her EI command, and Wanda watched through the transparent wall as Dr. Chelsea went through the security steps to open her own office door.

"Wanda!" Jeremy's voice sounded flustered. Desperate, even. Her eyes met his, and her EI, scanning his iris, told her he'd flagged a page for her. She let her EI follow it, opening what turned out to be the page for Amelix Retreat, the reconditioning division.

"Sign up. Now!" Jeremy said.

Wanda cleared her throat. *This again? Now?* "Look, Dr. Synd, I appreciate—"

"What do you think she's doing over there?" he said. "You just told her that you have acquired intimate knowledge of a project beyond your clearance."

"It was just an accidental observation, sir. You know I did nothing wrong, don't you, sir?"

"Your eyes were where they shouldn't have been. You know that's classic nonconformist behavior. She's communicating with someone right now, firing you." His eyes met hers again. There was no flagged page connected to them this time, just an expression slightly resembling human concern. "Register for voluntary reconditioning right now," he said. "Making the request means all your mistakes are forgiven. Otherwise she'll complete the process, and once the Unnamed Executives come for you it will be too late. They'll disable your EI before you even see them. They'll grab you, and you'll be gone."

"I..." she said.

Should she tell him his reaction was crazy?

It wasn't entirely crazy. It was how the corporate machinery functioned, and even among the Accepted, Chelsea was certainly a zealot. But that she would be cast out just for this observation was too far-fetched an assertion; Wanda wasn't about to turn over her brain and become, as her grandmother had said, a machine. As both of these doctors were fond of pointing out, Wanda had sacrificed her career, and even her daughter Nami's future, to hold onto what little spark of individuality she was still allowed. Uniqueness had brought her endless punishment and torment, but she had struggled on.

Jeremy thought the threat was real and immediate this time, but he had been pressuring her to surrender herself for reconditioning for years now.

Maybe he's right. I'm so tired of fighting it, so tired of being looked down on and held back. Maybe it's time.

The thought reverberated through her mind, unwelcome but unsurprising. *Succumb to reconditioning.* The benefits and virtues of the process had been pounded into her head every day of her life, always delivered with the implication that reconditioning was inevitable in the modern world. Maybe it was.

No. Nami's still too young to have her mother disappear into the structure so completely.

Accepted became more efficient and dedicated to the company, but also cold and often brutal to anyone they deemed a potential drain on corporate resources. Family members were generally the first casualties. Wanda's grandmother had been her only contact with a genuine, independent personality, and the only source of love that machines could not provide, yet her mother and father had been cruel to the woman because she had never progressed beyond the company's lowest stations. Wanda had repeatedly incurred her parents' wrath once they recognized her intention to follow her grandmother's warm and caring example rather than their own cold and ruthless one. She had chosen a path that not only contradicted the will and expectation of her family, but that of everyone she knew. Even so, Wanda had fought for her individuality, to remain her own person as she knew Grandmother would have wanted, and had been able to be a natural, loving mother to her own daughter. Nami deserved that. For Nami Wanda continued the fight.

All Accepted had a conditioned compulsion to make their coworkers submit to voluntary reconditioning and become Accepted, themselves. This was obviously what was motivating Jeremy right now, but she couldn't say that to him.

"Whatever inexplicable aversion to reconditioning you've had, it's time to lose it, now," Jeremy said. "You allowed your juvenile pride to derail your career. Fine. But don't let it cost you your life. You still have a chance to serve Amelix and the Lord." His voice dropped to a shaky whisper. "Don't end up *Departed*."

Wanda felt the familiar chill that overcame anyone in the corporate class at the mention of the Departed. It was a topic of hushed conversations between CBD workers intoxicated enough to broach the most taboo of subjects. The Horde of the Departed was the setting of nightmares, where former corporates huddled together and slowly succumbed to starvation and disease in the city's sprawling, hyper-violent ghetto, the Zone. It was almost certainly where her grandmother had ended up, probably because she'd brought the rats home for Wanda.

"Thank you, sir, for your concern," Wanda said. "But Dr. Chelsea understands that I'm valuable here and that I had no intention to go beyond my job duties or my clearance. She wouldn't react so strongly to a simple report, made out of a sense of duty to the company."

Jeremy closed his eyes for a moment, but his eyeballs darted around under the lids. "There is no time to discuss this. No time to convince you and I can see your heart is still closed to the truth." He opened his eyes again and her EI followed a new link to another page: a list of names. Roger Terry was one of the names. Alma Traxler, Wanda's grandmother, was another. On the list of maybe three hundred she recognized three others, all people who had Departed during her time with the department. A closer inspection would probably show a few more she had known, but she shut the page again.

"Store that," he said. "They won't permanently disable your EI, just cut you off from everything inside the building here. That list I gave you is of people who Departed from here. If you can find any of them, maybe they'll be able to help you somehow."

"Thank you, Dr. Synd. I know you gave me the list out of concern for me and I truly appreciate that you care. But I just cannot bring myself to believe that the things you're warning me about will actually come to pass." Through her own EI she searched greeting cards, finding one with a pink cartoon rabbit with one ear flopped down, reading, "Thank you."

She was halfway through her command to flag it for him when the site vanished from her mind. She tried to recall it and discovered it wasn't available. Links, communications, codes, and everything else were all gone. Her EI had been disabled.

Zone IA1.12

Len Jurphy's last meal had been two days ago, a bowl of synthesized goo intentionally left bland because prisoners didn't deserve patented flavorings. There were only two meals after a conviction, anyway: one as intake orders were processed, and one, like Len's two days ago, upon release. Len's intake into the penal Brain Trust had been months earlier. In between he'd been unconscious and fed only with minimal intravenous supplements, connected to the Federal computers that kept his brain processing government data for the duration of his sentence, like the thousands of other offenders all around him. Such was punishment on this depleted, dying planet of seventeen billion people.

Len lay sprawled, weak and wasted, on the concrete outside a club called Babygirl in the Zone's entertainment area, his body weight half what it had been before his sentencing. His metallic tattoos, once menacing decoration on the taut skin of a strong and dangerous ghetto male, now sagged and hung awkwardly from his skeletal limbs and torso.

There was no possibility of work. He'd never again be considered for the manual labor jobs he'd gotten when his arms had been triple their current size. Begging had proved futile. While Zone people might be sympathetic, might understand how a decent guy could end up with a larceny conviction and find himself on a slab, Zone people had no money to give. Golden salarymen from the Central Business District had money, but to them Len's emaciated frame meant that he could be nothing but a criminal, an obvious menace to society, undeserving of their charity. Two days as a beggar had led only to Len being constantly chased off the street by abusive bouncers. His only donation had been a dirty linen napkin some drunken rich guy had carried off from a restaurant by mistake.

Len's landlord had evicted him halfway through his sentence, selling off everything inside his decrepit room to pay back rent. Aside from his buttonless pants and a shredding t-shirt, the napkin was his only possession. He had tucked it across his chest under the shirt to keep warm, and he liked to imagine it made him look just a bit bigger.

There was motion off to his side. Someone was coming at him.

" … think you're doin' here, slabbie? Huh?"

Another bouncer. They always came whenever he sat down. The giant hand grabbed Len at the chest and made a fist, lifting him off the ground and throwing him farther down the sidewalk. Len's shirt disintegrated in the air and the napkin fluttered to the ground as he hit hard, brittle bones sliding under loose, shredding skin across the gravel. The bouncer approached, checking the distance to the edge of the building to judge whether he'd thrown Len far enough. He gave Len a threatening look and picked up the napkin, stuffing it into his back pocket as he returned to the club.

Federal Administration Building

Federal Agent Daiss leaned forward in his seat, watching Instructor Samuelson write with a finger over a map of the Zone that appeared to be projected against one wall. In truth, the wall was blank and the map was projected only in the Agents' minds, as were Samuelson's diagrams that appeared as glowing lines, all via an application that worked through their EIs.

"Two years ago," Samuelson said, drawing a small green circle around maybe fifteen blocks, "this was the area known as Fiend territory. The label was misleading. Really, it was simply a part of town nobody but Fiends would want to go, or for that matter, could survive in at all. And this," he said, drawing a circle around an area nearly ten times larger, "is Fiend territory today. It is no longer a misleading name. Nearly all Fiends are now organized within a real army called the New Union, which holds and patrols the area as a military force."

The map disappeared. It was replaced with an image of a man with a close-cropped beard walking alongside a building that had been blasted to bits. "Top Dog, he calls himself. Be sure to note that while he appears to be walking alone, there are four others in the picture with him."

Daiss squinted. It was a habit he couldn't break even though he was aware that the image wasn't entering through his eyes. This was far from his first briefing on the Fiend threat, and he had encountered them in person on a few occasions; by now he should be able to spot them all immediately, especially in a picture taken with Zeta's best tech. He found one, crouched behind some rubble in front and to the left of Top Dog, but only by noticing the rifle barrel poking up above the debris. Without that clue, it was almost impossible to distinguish the actual Fiend.

"For those who haven't yet mastered how to pick them out without resorting to IR and UV scans, the other four are here, here, here, and here," Samuelson said. He drew circles, first around the Fiend Daiss had found, then around a shadow at the edge of the building, and another around what Daiss could now make out as the eyes and hat and plastic-wrapped rifle of one otherwise submerged in a mud puddle. Finally he circled an indistinct, shadowy form protruding just above the roofline. Samuelson overlaid the picture with an EI enhancement using infrared and ultraviolet spectra, and the Fiends came clearly into view.

Fiends were hard to see and harder to hit, and every encounter with them had proven that they were getting stronger all the time. Daiss personally had seen one Federal Agent killed and three others seriously wounded in clashes with Fiends, yet no strike had yet been ordered to eliminate the threat.

"Top Dog took them over, kept them from fighting amongst themselves, and turned all the Fiends' desperation and rage outward, calling his army the New Union," Samuelson added. "At first they merely continued their small-time operations in the Zone, robbing, kidnapping, and killing, but then they expanded their operations to include raids in the suburbs. This brought them corporate attention, which, as you know, led to the establishment and funding of Task Force Zeta.

"The New Union publicly claims just over five thousand soldiers, which it calls Elements, but that claim is significantly lower than the actual number," Samuelson continued. "It is imperative that our official estimates remain consistent with their claims for now, but equally important for us within Zeta to know exactly what we're dealing with. We want the public to equate the suburban damage so far with just the five thousand Fiends he acknowledges. When the actual numbers are released as startling new statistics showing dramatic growth, the politicos will demand that Zeta get anything it wants. What we've pieced together from satellite footage and the Zone's remaining cameras puts the actual number of New Union Elements some-where in the range of twenty-five thousand."

Zetas knew this already, though Daiss supposed there might be new brothers and sisters attending today who hadn't heard it before. He had first learned of Top Dog's deception and actual strength in a meeting just like this, himself.

"Every New Union Element we've interrogated has claimed they had around five thousand total, and that's clearly inten-tional," Samuelson continued. "They don't believe the number, but every last one vehemently insists on it. There are several reasons Top Dog might be trying to mislead us as to his army's numbers. For example, Fiends outside the New Union are quite wild, typically running in small gangs of around ten to forty, and could well be put off or intimidated by the idea of such a large organization. It may be easier for him to recruit and retain soldiers when he tells them it's a smaller group. But we think the main reason is that he knows the New Union's actual size warrants Federal attention. At this time we are pri-marily observing without engaging. This will remain true for the near future, not only to keep Top Dog in the dark as to what we know, but also for the strategic reasons I mentioned a moment ago."

The map appeared again. Samuelson drew a star on a square standing for one of the buildings. "This structure here currently serves as New Union headquarters," Samuelson said. "Top Dog is usually somewhere in this building, and about a quarter of his forces stay in close proximity, in these buildings." He circled each one, resulting in a "T" shape with the star at the intersection of the two lines of circles. "The rest of them are out churning around in the wasteland, accumulating resources and fighters. If left unchecked, Top Dog will completely take over the thirty-three hundred square kilometers known as the Zone within the year."

Italy, 73 BC

Centurion Septimus Furius curled his lip in disgust, but the legionary in front of him kept talking.

"Decimation is not intended for this purpose! It's supposed to punish legions with deserters and legionaries who refuse to fight. Crassus commands that we ten percent die today at the hands of our own brothers at arms, simply because the battle was lost. He's culling soldiers so he doesn't have to feed so many! Where's the honor in dying for that? We can run!" he shouted, turning to address the men around them. "We can still escape if we go now. We need not die just because of this madman's order!"

Crassus was the wealthiest man in Rome, which meant he was the wealthiest man in the world. When the rebel Spartacus and his army of escaped slaves and gladiators had become a threat to the Roman Republic, Crassus had used his own funds to build this army and fight them, becoming praetor and absolute ruler over all soldiers comprising it. His cruelty and brutality were legendary, but that was what Rome needed to defeat such a threat to the social order.

"We certainly must die because of this order, Legionary," Furius said. "Our lots were drawn. Crassus is our general, our *praetor*, even, and we swore the *sacramentum*, making us instruments of his will. Remember all those raids? The people we slaughtered? The *sacramentum* meant Crassus was responsible for all that, not us. The blood stained him, alone, because our obedience is absolute. This is no different, and you disgrace us all by pretending otherwise. Decimation may be a shameful death for a soldier, but it's still a soldier's death. Abandon the *sacramentum* and you're just filth. They should crucify the likes of you, to make a proper example." Furius turned away, pushing to the front of the livestock pen where they were being kept. He straightened his spine, stepping up to face his soldier's death, and took off his armor before wading out among the men with whom he'd campaigned all these years.

A fist split his lip. A bronze forearm brace smashed his collarbone. A kick to his lower back nearly took him to his knees, but he struggled to stand. It was the last fight of his life, after all; why go down easy? A few blows to the gut doubled him over. Another kick took out his knee, and he went down hard. Then feet were everywhere, smashing his face, his spine, his groin. They found his head and began stomping repeatedly, and Centurion Septimus Furius ceased to be.

Amelix Company Housing

Wanda sat at the only table in their tiny corporate housing unit, stroking Nami's hair. The table folded away to provide sleep space, but neither of them would ever sleep here again. Nami would soon be off with her father, and tomorrow a new family would be living here. Tears cascaded down Wanda's cheeks and soaked the front of her Corporate Green uniform. She felt a bit hurt that her daughter hadn't cried. But no eight-year-old has the capacity to understand all this, Wanda reasoned, and it was nice that they could share the last of their time together without hysterics. It would make for a better memory.

She realized now that this terrible, wrenching pain was the other side of natural life, balancing the strength and comfort of real love. Insulated by the system and their beliefs, Accepted never had to hurt like this. *I got love, and I was able to give love. The chance to experience that was worth it. All of it, even this.*

"Jenni's dad Departed last year," Nami said. "Dr. Kim told the class not to tease her, but everyone did. Even me."

"Why did you tease her, dear?" Wanda asked, numbly turning the girl's hair around her finger.

"Her dad had to leave the company because he was bad, Mommy. We wanted to show we hate things that are bad for Amelix. Even though Dr. Kim said not to tease her, we saw how he liked that we were loyal to Amelix. But now *you're* bad and I'm the one who's going to be teased."

Wanda's eyes stung. "Yes, honey. I'm sorry for that." She pulled Nami's head to her own and held it tightly. "And I'm so, so sorry that I won't be able to be with you when that happens."

"But Father will be, so it's okay."

Her Accepted ex-husband Davi had strategically divorced her following his promotion when Nami was three. He had a new wife, at a grade in the company one level higher than his own, and together they were raising that woman's daughter, now four. Davi and Nami had only seen each other a few hours a month since the divorce.

Accepted parents were ten times more likely to raise Accepted children, according to various persecutors she'd had over the years. Wanda, as an Accepted couple's failure, was among the few inconvenient and embarrassing outliers that prevented a perfect one hundred percent succession.

"Why are you bad, Mommy? Have you always been bad?"

Wanda sniffed. "Do you remember the story we read together when you were a little girl, about Laurel the Chicken, honey?"

"Chickens aren't real, Mommy."

"Laurel the Chicken didn't want to lay her eggs, remember? And she went squawking and squawking, and irritating the other chickens who were working hard to make eggs."

"I remember. Then Laurel turned into soup."

"That's right, honey. Well, in my case, I didn't mean to squawk, or even to make noise at all. But somehow it was decided I was squawking, even though I didn't know it."

"Amelix is our provider, Mommy," Nami said seriously. "Amelix does not make mistakes."

That was the dogma. Though admitting it made Wanda's heart hurt, Nami's personality was terribly similar already to that of someone who had been reconditioned. The educational system was even more effective now than it had been in Wanda's childhood. What would be the point in arguing against the system now? If Wanda said she thought otherwise, that Amelix was capable of error, she might plant a seed of dissension in Nami's mind, a doubt. Nami would have the roots of a notion that perhaps the company wasn't as infallible as it was made out to be. That might grow into discontent and then even to full-fledged nonconformity, which would get Nami Departed.

Like her mother. Like her great-grandmother.

"You're right, honey. Amelix doesn't make mistakes. I made a mistake. And I'm so, so, so sorry."

It didn't matter whether I Departed or got reconditioned. Either way, she would have turned out the same. I knew that. I didn't fight in the hope that she would be a different person in the end. I fought for the right to love her, truly and completely, as her mother. As myself.

Wanda squeezed Nami as tightly as she could, pressing her forehead against the girl's silky golden-brown hair. "How can I put a lifetime of real love and affection into this one moment?" Her whisper became increasingly high-pitched. "How can I load you with the care and advice you'll need, put it into a little package for you to open up someday when you need it? Is there any way to make you see that you are my only love in the world, and that you are so special and wonderful and precious, even when you're being teased, even when you feel all alone?" She kissed Nami's head and sniffed, tightening her stomach to keep her own quiet crying from erupting into sobs. "Just keep me in your heart, and know that you are always in mine."

The apartment door opened and Davi entered, his eyes widening. "You didn't pack a bag? You didn't get anything ready?" Behind him were the two Unnamed that had escorted her here. They had waited in the hall while she sat with Nami, but now they were inside and no longer willing to wait for anything. Davi had just begun to dig through a closet when the Unnamed tore Nami away, the girl putting up not even the slightest resistance. They hoisted Wanda to her feet and yanked her toward the door. Davi dropped whatever he had clutched from the closet and grabbed at something in his jacket pocket, shoving it into her hand as she passed. "Casino chips, as much as I could collect from around the office. I'll take good care of her, don't worry."

Wanda tried to turn for one last look, but they held her too tightly. "Nami, I'm so sorry," she called out, her face toward the ceiling. "I love you so much."

The elevator shot down into the basement where the Unnamed kept their offices and vehicles. They squeezed her into the back of a black truck where four others were already seated: one woman and one man, both of whom were also Departing, and two Unnamed guards. The two Unnamed who had dragged her down here got in up front, and the biocat engine began its low growl as they started moving.

The Unnamed sat stiffly with blank faces, their black suits stretching over their chemically enhanced bulk. There was no reason for them to think about her at all. She was cargo, just garbage to be dumped. They did this every day. Each of the four Unnamed was more than twice Wanda's size and carried what she supposed was some kind of mini machinegun. Each had been conditioned for automatic, unquestioning obedience to superiors, and each had probably thrown a hundred moms like Wanda out of this truck.

They slowed, approaching one of the entertainment streets next to the Central Business District. She didn't know which numbered zone this was. There was almost no way to tell. Towns and villages had been collapsing into the collective Zone ghetto for decades, and there were too many of them for anyone but the Feds to keep straight.

There were people standing around on the street, even though the day was cold. They seemed to be watching and waiting, like she supposed they did every day, for an opportunity like this. Her eyes welled with tears, but the rest of her body was numb and unresponsive.

She had to shake herself out of the shock, and fast. When she got out of this truck, the Zone dwellers would see her being unloaded and know she was newly Departed, defenseless fresh meat, carrying as much as she would ever again own.

The truck stopped. The Unnamed next to her opened the door and stepped down, pulling Wanda out by her hair and flinging her behind him as he climbed back inside.

She fell to the gravel, landing hard on her side. She forced herself to her feet as the other two newly Departed landed near her, all three of them practically glowing against the Zone's grit in their Corporate Green office uniforms. As the black truck sped away, Wanda sprinted in the direction with the fewest people. Her legs burned and her chest hurt, but she didn't slow down. Maybe the Zone toughs running at them would catch the others instead of her.

Amelix Integrations Offices, Central Business District

Gregor Kessler, DCR, answered his EI intercom. "Yes, Issac?"

"Keiko Piccola is here to see you, sir. She says she has an urgent matter to discuss."

Kessler found himself gripping the edge of his Grown wood desk as if he were about to break off a chunk of it. Perfect Golden-skinned Keiko Piccola had already been directly responsible for four Departings from the Corporate Regulations Division since her new Accepted status nine months ago. Before that she'd been double promoted over her peers, and she was only twenty-five. Whatever evidence she was here to discuss today would probably lead to a fifth Departing. Saving Amelix all those salaries was good, but the division still had to meet deadlines and the extra demand was pushing the remaining employees to the edge of endurance. If his group wasn't able to keep pace with the growing corporate regulations workload, Kessler himself could be the next to go.

Keiko was proof that being too zealous an employee was as destabilizing as being too jaded or too lazy. Reconditioning could fix jadedness and laziness, but there was no cure for ones like Keiko.

"Have her wait," he said. "I'll tell you when to send her in."

At least Kessler still had authority over her and could still make her wait. Seeing her right away may have started her thinking of him as someone with too little to do.

He made Keiko stay out in reception for more than half an hour, hoping she'd just go away, but knowing that she wouldn't. Eventually he let her in and she stood, hands on knees and head down, with her back just straight enough to point her firm little breasts up at him from the scoop neck of her uniform.

"Hello, Dr. Kessler, sir," she said. "Thank you for seeing me today, sir."

"You know I'm busy, Keiko," he said. "What do you have for me?"

The girl raised her chin, briefly meeting his eyes. His EI recognized and opened her flagged page, playing a recording she'd made looking over the shoulder of a coworker: Eric Basali.

Why she cared to attack this poor idiot, Kessler couldn't fathom. He was no threat to her and he'd probably Depart soon without her help, anyway. Basali always turned in substandard work and was consistently reported by coworkers as being difficult and antisocial. In the video, he was writing with a pen in a little paper notebook. The angle made it hard to read every word, but Keiko had dubbed it with her own voice as he wrote, making it easier to follow.

> "...Why do we hide the most basic human traits like compassion and creativity? Why must we pretend to be nothing but machines in order to survive? It's because while we ourselves are not machines, the organizations we form are. In order to function within them, we must surrender anything that makes us unique and alive, becoming fungible and disposable elements of the whole..."

Like nearly everyone left in the company, Gregor Kessler had been reconditioned. Reconditioning had brought him to the ranks of the Accepted: those who were graced with true understanding that the work of Amelix was the work of the Lord, and trained to recognize the Lord's work through all its manifestations within the company. Like all Accepted, he had occasionally been confronted with so-called arguments against that truth, but they had always been online and always from Accepted at other organizations trying to insist that their companies were closer to God. Those claims were ridiculous; Kessler was here because the Lord had created him for a purpose. He served Amelix, so Amelix, obviously, was his purpose. Therefore it must be true that Amelix was the Lord's one true corporation.

But Basali's words here were more general, and they didn't allow Kessler the luxury of an automatic defense. Instead of sliding through the passages in his mind the way speech from other Amelix Accepted did, what Basali said abraded his mind, trying to force it into unnatural patterns. How could basic human traits fail to conform to the Lord's plan here at Amelix? Who could possibly believe the organization was nothing but machinery, when it was clearly the Lord's most perfect creation?

Kessler's pathway amplification kicked in, compounding the already disturbing feelings the words had created until he felt his very existence seem to unravel into cold, empty, endless, meaningless space. He shuddered violently, leaning against the desk to keep himself upright. He swallowed and gritted his teeth, repeating one of the mantras from his training, to counter Basali's blasphemous whining. "The Lord provides through Amelix. The Lord provides through Amelix. The Lord provides through Amelix."

The writing went on. Kessler stopped the video and closed the page. "How did you do this, Keiko? How did you review such toxic material and make this recording without becoming ill?"

She came close to him, snuggling her breasts against his arm. "Does this please you, sir?" she asked in a voice slightly above a whisper. He nodded and she relaxed slightly, letting her body settle heavier against him. "Waste is a companywide crisis, sir," she said. "For whatever reason, the Lord has seen fit to guide me in attacking it. This individual is wasting time and other resources. By pointing it out to my superiors, I am helping Amelix rid itself of dead weight. But even more important is the fact that what he's writing is subversive and dangerous to Amelix, and possibly to our entire way of life."

"But *how* did you review it, specifically? How did you keep it from affecting you as you worked?"

"I translated it, sir. I made myself analyze it in terms most supportive of Amelix's position, rather than accepting the frame he used."

Kessler narrowed his eyes at her. "Give me an example."

"Well, sir, for this one I chose to see what he said as an acknowledgement of the company's true strength. What Basali calls humanity and uniqueness and life are really just flaws, burrs that need to be polished off the pieces of God's plan before they can all fit together into cosmic perfection. After they are removed, we are still human, unique, and alive, and those traits are confirmable by scientific evidence. Therefore, his assertion otherwise is clearly foolish." She cocked her head slightly, obviously proud of her ability to do this, though her chin was lowered and her eyes were wide. "My recent reconditioning process gave me all the tools I need to work with this material without being poisoned by it, sir."

The sickness abated. Now his pathway amplification was back doing what it was supposed to do, reinforcing his commitment to the company and the Lord's plan. "Amazing work, Keiko. Your devotion to this cause is quite evident. Very impressive. And I suspect that what you call translation can be useful in helping others who might be infected with these sorts of misguided constructions. I hope you saved those interpretations, as well."

"Thank you, Dr. Kessler," she said quietly, close to his ear. "I didn't record any translations, but I can do it quite quickly, if it pleases you. I do hope we can review more of this material together. You are so clearly my superior, sir, and I greatly value your guidance, on absolutely everything."

Kessler's breath caught. With an ordinary employee this dynamic was obvious and expected: a simple trade of sexual submission for career advancement. With Keiko, though, there was always the threat of her turning on him, setting him up just to experience the thrill of watching his collapse.

He was still her superior, though. He didn't have to fear Keiko. The girl was newly reconditioned! He knew how to push buttons she didn't yet know she had. He could take the deal she was offering, accepting her submission in exchange for his guidance, but only if he used every tool at his disposal to keep her completely under his control.

"I'm happy to guide you, Keiko. Waste is a companywide crisis, as you say, but we wouldn't want to condemn Mr. Basali unfairly and thus deprive Amelix of his skills. What if your interpretations are the true intention behind what he wrote there? Perhaps his real meaning has been skewed by poor writing ability, and he is actually doing the Lord's work after all. Acting rashly could divest Amelix of what, with more consideration, would have proven to be a fully functional employee. I'll tell you what. Let's watch another clip, and I want you to translate it for me; interpret it as a comment favoring Amelix."

"Whatever you think is best, sir." She stayed in physical contact with him and looked up into his eyes. His EI found another bookmark she'd tagged for him: another video of Basali writing, with Keiko's voice reading along.

> The individual cannot compete for resources against an organized group, so in a world of organizations the individual cannot survive. Did the first colony-forming ants and bees mourn the inevitable loss of self? Did they train themselves to see the formicaries or hives as heaven and the outside as hell, or did the new societal structures create a hell from which they were the only escape?

The words, generated by Kessler's EI, hung before him as if suspended. He gestured as he spoke, though Keiko's EI was probably projecting the words at a completely different angle. "Okay. How about this one?" He put an arm around her shoulder. What can we make out of it? Translate it for me."

"Easy one, sir," she said, running her palm along his thigh. "Inside Amelix is heaven, where we thrive. Outside Amelix is hell, where we suffer. It's true, no matter how it came to be so. The ants and bees had their heaven, and now we have ours."

He sat down in his chair. "Very good. Start a document. We have his wording here, and you're going to keep track of all the interpretations where it could be argued to benefit Amelix. That will be number one: Inside Amelix is heaven, outside Amelix is hell. We flourish in paradise or wither in the desert."

"Yes, sir," she said. He watched her face slacken as she performed the mental machinations to create a document through her EI. "Done, sir."

"Good. Now do the first example again. How did you put it? Our surrender to Amelix polishes off the burrs and allows us to be perfect pieces of God's plan. Match these first two with their original quotes."

"Yes, sir."

Kessler kept talking while she worked. Sometimes it was better to have her conscious mind distracted when he really wanted concepts to sink in deeply. "I hope you can see why you need my guidance. I am your superior, and as such, to you I am Amelix and Amelix is me. Disobedience to me would be disobedience to Amelix. This is a serious matter, and I know you can go right on being a good girl for me, can't you, Keiko? You can keep on doing just what I say?"

"Oh, yes, sir. I would like that very much."

He touched her knee.

"Done, sir." Her eyes met his. No pages were flagged.

He ran a hand along her hip. She tried to sit on his lap. He pushed her off and she stood with her head bowed and her palms crossed over her upper thighs. Sighing, he hooked a finger in her belt, bringing her to her knees beside him.

"Do you see how difficult it is to be fair?" he asked. She kept her head bowed. "Can you tell how inefficient these processes protecting fairness make us? Yet they are our duty to Amelix, to make sure no resources are wasted or discarded irresponsibly. You brought this question to me, which necessitates lots of review. You're going to help me with that."

Oh, thank you, Dr. Kessler, sir," she gushed.

"It will take a while," he said. "You should bring a cushion for your knees."

"Yes, sir. I want to do whatever you say."

"I know you do. Relax for me, Keiko. Feel yourself give in to my will. Close your eyes and let it wash over you, let it compound through pathway amplification. I am Amelix and Amelix is me. I'm older and more experienced, better educated, and higher ranked. You already obey me completely, don't you?"

"Yes, sir. Completely."

"And so when I tell you to close your eyes and relax even deeper, you automatically comply with that order, don't you?"

"Yes, sir," she said. Her head briefly lolled to one side and then rolled back again, tilting her chin slightly upward.

"That was a gift of your reconditioning process, wasn't it, that you always obey your superiors? It's easy for you to obey me and just sink deeper and deeper down, isn't that right? Reconditioning tore away the barriers and made it easy to let me in, didn't it? So easy to just open up to me, because I am Amelix and Amelix is me, and you love and trust and obey Amelix with all that you are, isn't that right?"

"Yes, sir." Her voice was a reedy whisper. "So easy. With all that I am."

"That's even true when I order you, like I'm doing now, to relax deeper and deeper and deeper, more fully down inside yourself than you have ever been before. You want to open your mind to me like a beautiful flower, waiting for me to pollinate it. Isn't that right?"

"Yes, sir. Like a flower. Waiting for you. To pollinate."

2

Evans Household, the Zone

Kym tiptoed from the sink to the cabinet, carefully wiping a plate with a ragged towel and slipping it quietly into place. Mikk was in a bad mood this afternoon, having just been nearly murdered. Kym was in a bad mood, herself. She had watched her husband be nearly murdered, but she'd ended up disappointed as usual. All the bastard had gotten was a cut across his forehead.

She washed another plate, slowly dried it and put it away, as carefully and quietly ,making as little noise as possible. The little apartment vibrated with a familiar tainted energy and she knew what it meant: He wanted an excuse to get angry.

That Mr. B guy had been due with more product over a week ago, and in the last few days Mikk had cheated a lot of people. Some were now coming back angry and ending up like the body she'd had to dispose of today. Shit like that kept Mikk pissed off, and Kym had taken beatings twice already this week. The first time she'd just gotten some hard slaps and been slammed into a wall. The one yesterday had been a real beat-down, though, leaving throbbing bruises all over her face and stomach. Now he was stalking around the apartment and watching everything she did, waiting to pounce on the slightest mistake.

She tried to steady herself, but the impending violence was making her legs shake. Her fate was out of her hands.

I won't survive another week if Mr. B. doesn't show up.

Mikk didn't care about Kym's life or anyone else's, even his own. He had hired her at the protein refinery and then coerced her into marrying him. His proposal had been: "You're gonna marry me and sign over your checks. If you don't wanna do it, find a new job." Now everything was in his name. If she tried to leave she'd be jobless, homeless, and broke, which in the Zone meant she'd soon be dead. It took constant, dizzying effort to convince herself that life like this was somehow better than no life at all.

Her vision went black around the edges from a combination of stress and exhaustion. She grabbed the countertop to steady herself, forgetting the knife in her right hand. Her left hand clenched around the blade, which sliced into her index and middle fingers. Her sharp inhalation and the clatter of the knife into the sink were sudden and loud.

Oh, no.

"What the fuck is wrong with you, throwing shit around?" Mikk was now centimeters from the back of her head, his breath hot on her scalp.

"Nothin', sir. I just…I just dropped it. That's all."

"That's all? You know what I gotta do to buy all the shit in this place? You know what I go through? Then you go throwing it around like it's free, and you tell me it's nothing."

"Nothin's broken," she said, picking up the knife and running it under the water again. The fresh cuts on her hand burned and stung, but she ignored them; it was best to avoid giving him anything else to criticize. "Just dropped somethin' in the sink. Sorry it bothered you." She quickly wiped the knife dry and slipped it into the drawer, out of his sight and hopefully forgotten. Though it had from time to time crossed her mind to attack him, she always thought better of it. Mikk was physically huge and he enjoyed causing pain. Nothing good would come from introducing a weapon into the mix.

"I'm supposed to be happy that you didn't break shit this time?"

"Accidents happen. Just let it go, please, sir?"

"Accidents happen? You giving me a lesson, now? You think you gotta tell me *accidents happen*, because maybe I'm too stupid to figure that out?"

She turned, facing him, and backed up a step, instinctively raising her palms between them.

"What the hell is this? You can't even wash dishes without cutting yourself all up?"

She risked a glance at the hand. A trail of blood ran down her palm from the cut on her index finger.

"I'm sorry, sir."

"You're sorry." Mikk said. "First you insult me, telling me *'accidents happen,'* like you're gonna wise me up, and then you're too stupid to even wash dishes." He slapped her, not angrily, not even particularly hard.

He was warming up.

There was always a pattern. His rage built in stages, and she had to watch them develop, knowing what was coming. That was almost worse than the beating itself. It started out light, with Mikk making little excuses to criticize or insult her. Then he'd react to whatever she said, or, if she tried not to say anything, he'd respond to her lack of response. Whatever she did, or didn't do, made him angrier than he'd been a moment before. Step by step, it built from words to slaps to harder hits, shoves, and worse, like it was all written into a script. Watching it happen to her, Kym felt detached and dizzy, even before she started to feel the blows, like she was seeing it happen in a puppet show instead of experiencing it herself.

Another slap followed the first, then a shove against the wall and a few more, then punches to her midsection, and after she collapsed, to her back and head. Kym felt completely disconnected, like just another puppet in show after show.

The fists stopped raining down as he started kicking.

This was going to be a bad one.

(?)

Consciousness returned slowly. Was this Hades, the underworld?

Centurion Septimus Furius rolled slightly to one side. His hands were tied apart!

Crucifixion!

His last memory of Roman life was the beating he had taken, the decimation. Had he survived it, only to be crucified like some seditious insurgent enemy of Rome?

Gods, please, no.

Death did not frighten Furius. It had been his career, after all, bringing death. It had become familiar, like a companion, even. But *this*! Nothing horrified him like the thought of such shame, such public disrespect of one who had devoted his life to honor and discipline. To die in this way was so much worse than death itself. Always he had supported Rome and obeyed his orders; he deserved better than this disgrace, to be slowly tortured and left to rot as an example.

But why tied here, not nailed?

The rope was yellow. The room was called a loading dock. He knew these things, but he had not yet opened his eyes.

Furius was not being crucified. His head rolled to one side as he relaxed.

Inside his mind were memories of Rome, of his death, and even hazy images after that, full of mist and light, but there were other memories, too, now, of a different life, one that he could not have imagined. He was still Centurion Septimus Furius, but he also remembered being tied here, and pissed on here, which were not things Furius had actually experienced as himself.

He opened his eyes and struggled to bring his vision into focus. A ceiling. Gray. Most settings for his newly acquired memories were gray.

He now lay cruciform on a square wooden shape just large enough to support his weight from shoulders to hips—a shipping pallet, he realized was the term for it. His hands were indeed bound with yellow rope at the corners level with his neck, leaving his head tipped awkwardly backwards over the edge of the pallet unless he fought to hold it up. His bare feet were lashed together, cold against the concrete floor.

A short distance away three men sat working at a table, packaging a white powder into plastic bags and wrapping them with tape. This building was a small warehouse, and he was on the side where trucks came to be loaded.

Trucks. Furius pondered the machines that moved on their own, without power of man or beast. *How strange.*

These memories, of oddities like trucks and plastic and tape, were those of another man, who had called himself *Mr. B.* The name had been a rather ineffective attempt at becoming known for selling *base*, a form of cocaine, a drug similar to the one those men were packaging. These men had called him *Mr. Bitch.*

It had been more than two thousand years since Furius had suffered that decimation beating and died. Now he'd been brought back, in what felt like no time. He wasn't sure exactly what had happened or how, but the new memories indicated that it had occurred after administration of one of these drugs. The men here had called it *Pink Shit*, and when they'd injected it into Mr. B, they'd permanently removed that personality from this body. Furius was fairly certain it was Pink Shit they were packaging now. They had taken B's dose from that same pile.

He would have to kill these three men, and soon. Surely Dis, the god of the underworld, had not allowed Furius back again to be kept in this dungeon.

The wooden shipping pallet to which he was tied was quite old. B had not seen much wood in his lifetime. It was apparent that wood was rare here, and had been for a long time. He tugged at the ropes. They were made of *plastic*, a material softer and with more give than proper Roman ropes, but his arms and legs were held quite securely, nonetheless.

He tried to retrieve the hazy memory of the decimation and his subsequent brief and strange journey through mist. He faintly recalled a metallic taste in his mouth. Perhaps it had been the coin his legion brothers had placed there to pay Charon the ferryman, though he couldn't remember actually meeting Charon or crossing the River Styx, or even what had subsequently happened to that coin. The other memories, the memories that could not possibly be his, were apparently interfering with his recollection.

So, then, Pink Shit had brought him here. They called it that because tiny germs floating around in water produced white powder but also turned the liquid pink. B had worked in this business, and now through him Furius understood that these people had germs to produce all kinds of things, including drugs. Still, the Pink Shit germ was something new. They hadn't intended this one, and now they were trying to figure out what it did, what it was. Furius knew. The gods had made Pink Shit, to bring him here.

The men had *guns,* the concept of which Furius found fascinating. They enabled a shooter to kill from a distance like an archer, but more accurately; one did not have to lob shots in an arc. They were loud, though, guns. B's memories showed that this building was owned by Alfred, who controlled perhaps five or six such henchmen besides these. With no idea where the others were, Furius had to be sure he didn't alert them. He would have to kill these three without using guns, and without allowing them to fire theirs in defense.

He remained still, closing his eyes while he thought about his predicament. There was no sense in keeping them open and risking that one of the men would notice.

Why had the gods brought him here? What purpose did they have in bringing a lone centurion to this place?

According to B's memories there were no Roman legions anywhere around here for him to join. What use was Furius in a place like this, where *Feds* and *Unnamed Executives,* twice the size of ordinary men and armed with guns more powerful than any Mr. B had ever touched, worked in legion-sized armies? What use was any Roman soldier alone, without his legion?

Yet perhaps his isolation didn't have to be permanent. Maybe Pink Shit could bring others, as it had brought Furius. The bags the men were packaging were kilos, and each kilo had enough for thousands of doses: multiple legions of soldiers. Alone he was worthless, but with an army like that he could conquer this place for Rome. Even now, even here, his mission was the same as it had ever been: He had to conquer these foreign nations and bring them under Roman rule. He would form new Roman legions in this place!

Furius let his eyes open again, just a bit, taking in the table at the other end of the room and the door next to it. He strained against the ropes with his hands, slowly so as not to draw eyes with jerky motion. While the edges of the pallet were thick wood, the slats he lay upon were thinner, though still solid. With enough force Furius might have been able to pop the nails out, but enough force was unlikely, tied as he was.

His feet were bound tightly together at the bottom of the pallet, but the plastic cord didn't bite like real rope would have. It was a bit stretchier, too. Furius bent his knees, testing the flex and grip of the bindings. There was enough play for him to be able to slide one foot along his other ankle. Working slowly but diligently, he was able to increase the amount of slide there until he could rotate the whole foot at the ankle. Pointing his toes all the way down and pushing off against the other leg, he slowly dragged the bottom of the foot along his ankle. The rope dug deep into his flesh all around, numbing his feet and misting up his eyes, but he felt it stretch just slightly. Eventually he got his toe under one of the loops of rope and, gritting his teeth, pulled it down and over the other foot's toes, creating slack. By pushing his feet against each other he was able to work the slack into the other coils, and eventually he was able to pull his right foot free. The tensionless rope dropped loose around his left ankle, and his cold feet coursed with blood again. He waited for the thousand-needles feeling to subside, taking the opportunity to calm his mind for battle.

He pushed off the ground with his legs, rolling over his shoulder and grabbing the pallet with his hands. Lifting it as he stood, he charged at the men and swung the entire pallet over his head and down in front of him, ducking as the pallet slid down his shoulders and the ropes bit severely into his wrists. It crashed onto the two closest henchmen, the ones seated with their backs to him, slamming their faces against the table. He had hoped the pallet would shatter or at least pull apart, but it didn't. One man went limp and the other sputtered in the

powder. This body was too weak to lift and use the entire pallet as a weapon again. His bowed head was turned to the side,
and he saw the third man rising from his chair to snatch a gun
from the table. Furius squatted but straightened his back so the
pallet slid down behind him, and as the bottom edge hit the
floor he pushed off, slamming into the guy's face with both
feet. The gun clattered to the floor but did not fire.

Furius dragged the heavy wooden frame and, raising his
elbow, pulled its edge up under the dazed henchman's neck.
Grunting with effort, Furius jerked his own body downward
until there was a crunching sound. These were clearly ordinary
men rather than the enhanced ones called Feds and Unnamed;
this neck had broken as easily as any other he'd encountered
in his career.

When B had been dosed with Pink Shit the effect had rendered him unconscious almost instantly, but the sputtering
henchman who had inhaled it in the attack was still awake. He
stood, wiping powder away from his eyes.

Furius dove for the gun, bringing the pallet with him, and,
careful to avoid touching what Mr. B's memories said was the
trigger that made the weapon erupt, snatched it up. He pointed
it at the last conscious henchman, the one with powder all over
his face, who raised his hands. Holding the man at gunpoint
with one hand, Furius squatted to wedge a chair leg against
the pallet slat to which he was tied. Finding the right angle for
leverage, he popped the slat off its nails and slid the rope off
its end, repeating the process at the other corner.

Going through pockets, he found several strange coins he
knew were casino chips, and a knife that sprang open when
he touched a button. There was also a rig for injecting drugs,
complete with a syringe and rubber tube, which he kept but
couldn't imagine ever using, given Mr. B's recent memory of
the activity. Over one chair hung a long black coat, which he
put on.

There was one kilo of Pink Shit packaged up already and
no time to waste wrapping up another one. Furius could
come back to get the rest of it, as well as the apparatus for
making unlimited quantities of it, as soon as he'd created a

few thousand more Roman soldiers. He tucked two guns behind his belt and carried the third in his right hand, stuffing the kilo, knife, and rig into the coat's big pockets. He took a handful of powder in his left hand, to throw into faces and blind his enemies if he needed to fight. Thusly prepared, he flicked the gun toward the door. "You first," he said, momentarily taken aback by the sound of his new voice and this strange language. "If we're quiet, we both get out alive." The man nodded, but staggered as he opened the door and stepped outside.

After leaving the building the two marched for a few blocks, with Furius making increasingly graphic threats to keep the man focused. Eventually, the drug took over and his human shield collapsed. Furius left him where he lay and ran off into the night.

Back Street Off 46th Street, the Zone

Mikk Evans still hadn't cooled from the encounter with Kym, which was a good thing now that he was out on the street making his real money. This sort of work, dealing and keeping his girls in line, required an edge like he was feeling now.

Kym didn't know how good she had it, running the refinery for him and thus allowing him to hold onto the corporate benefits package, including limited access to a synthesizer and at least some freedom to move around the city. These girls had to work much harder than Kym did, and their corrections had to be crueler, too.

Addi, here, was a good example, in her purple mini dress that stopped a hand's width above her stocking tops and hair that looked and felt like old-fashioned pink fiberglass insulation as he tightened his fist in it. Keeping her eyes pointed up at him was a necessary part of her training. He spat into her face to punctuate his pep talk.

"I hope you're this late because you had a customer. Gimme the money."

"I'm sorry, sir," Addi whimpered. "I worked harder on my makeup to get more business tonight."

He gave her a light slap, not hard enough to bruise, and then wiped the snotty spit off his hand with the part of her dress hidden under mess of hair. "CBD shifts get out between one hundred and two hundred GMT," he said. "Those hardworking corporate men and women bring those credits straight to 46th so whores like you can service them. You get 'em off, they go home. If you're not here, someone else's whore gets 'em off, and I'm standing out here for nothing."

She opened her mouth to say something. He yanked her hair, turning whatever word it was going to be into a pained groan. He spat again, this time landing most of it in her mouth.

"Last night you brought in fuck-all nothin' and the night before that, too. Now tonight you're late. Three nights of fucking up!" He pushed down at the back of her neck, bringing her thudding to her knees. She misjudged and kissed his shoes. He pushed her the rest of the way to the gravel and put his shin across her back, flipping up one of her feet and knocking away the shoe. There was no need for fanfare or further explanation, no need to remove the stocking. He pulled the shears from his back pocket and grunted slightly with effort, lopping off her smallest toe. Her shocked and desperate gasp turned into sobs, a typical response when he had to do this with one of his whores.

He stood, avoiding the blood that gushed down her calf to pool behind her knee. "Get cleaned up. You got one hour to find a customer and bring me the chips. Don't make it in an hour, we do this again. Two hours, we do it twice more." He kicked her lightly in the ribs, careful to keep it soft enough that she didn't bruise. "Keep your shoes on when you fuck so you get better tips."

Amelix Executive Quarters

Dr. Zabeth Chelsea had already synthesized herself a second glass of wine by the time her husband Alin came home. He was her first husband and she knew she should be taking advantage of her youth to marry up in the organization, but she enjoyed the fact the Lord had made her the ranking executive at home. Alin was Accepted, but hadn't yet been given much chance to prove himself at Amelix.

Upon seeing her, Alin carefully set down his bag and placed his hands open on his thighs, facing downward as she had taught him to do. "Good evening, ma'am. I hope your day was productive and pleasant."

"It was a stressful one, actually," she said. "A talented tech Departed today. She will be difficult to replace." She took another sip of her wine. "God's will. I'm going to need to punish you tonight, or else I'll never get to sleep. It won't be anything too terribly hard on you, I shouldn't think. A few bruises, maybe, but that will show others in the company what kind of service you give, won't it?"

"Yes, ma'am," Alin said. "I am always proud to serve you, ma'am."

"If I work out enough tension I might like to let you serve me in other ways tonight, as well." She nodded and he dropped to his knees. "You're going to be brave and good so that we can have that happen, isn't that right?"

"Yes, ma'am."

"Let's get warmed up, then."

She opened her robe and spread her knees to make room for him.

The Place B's Memories Called the Zone

His escape had been so easy! Furius supposed it made sense that he should have help from the gods; they had brought him here, after all. Now his mission was to get Pink Shit into as many of these people as possible and begin training the resultant legions.

But how to distribute the stuff?

It was a drug. Drugs had been Mr. B's business. Furius just needed to find others in that trade and engage in a few transactions, and unknowing end users would dose themselves for him. He would have to collect them all and train the newly hatched Romans later.

One contact came to the forefront of his mind: the Garbageman. Mr. B had moved more product through him than anyone, and that he had been overdue for a meeting with the man. At this time of night the Garbageman would be pimping his girls over on 46th Street, not terribly far from where Furius was now.

His palm still held the handful of pink shit as he turned onto one street and then another, following Mr. B's understanding of the city as if he had lived here himself.

A Zone Back Street

Len was too weak for real tears, but his tiny, ruined body shook with sobs. He was lying sideways near a building, but on a side street this time. Nobody would bother to force him away from this spot. There was no business being done here, and the few people that passed clearly had nothing to give him, even if he begged.

A pimp had just disciplined one of his girls, cutting off a toe. It was pretty typical behavior for that guy, the one everyone knew as the Garbageman. Len had thought maybe she would hobble off somewhere or cry for help, or perhaps tend to her injury. Instead she just sat there, silently staring at the toe lying on the gravel, and apparently still bleeding, since she'd done nothing to stop it.

He told himself it was her pain that made him cry, that he felt sad and sorry for her shitty situation, but hers was actually less hopeless than his own. The girl and her severed toe were probably going to be the last images he ever saw.

"What's this, then, little man?" a voice said. Len would never have let someone get so close before he'd gone to the slab, but now his reflexes were shot to hell with the rest of him. A man stood over him, a silhouette with a straight, military posture, not looking particularly friendly but not actively hitting or kicking Len, either.

"Tell you what, son," the man said. "I'll give you this, if you promise to share it." He placed a vinyl bag in Len's hand and watched as Len opened it and discovered it was an injection rig. There was a little brown glass jar for dope, and it appeared to have a bit of powder in it. He unscrewed the cap and peered inside.

"Here you go," the man said, pushing his closed fist over the jar's opening and releasing powder that spilled all over everywhere, but also filled the jar to overflowing. "It'll make a man out of you." He laughed once, sounding as crazy as he now seemed. "Well, that, some legionary training, and the swearing of an oath. Be ready to report for duty the next time I see you."

With that, the man wiped his powdery hand on his clothes and walked off toward 46th Street, passing the bleeding hooker without a glance.

Fisher University Study Center Lobby

Edward Schiff, IV, known to family and friends as Li'l Ed, sat quietly on a bench, consuming his biosynthetic liquid meal. His friend Jack was still holding their table inside, but all members of the upper class were obliged to have dinner with their families and this was the Schiff family dinnertime. Like nearly every other family he knew, Li'l Ed's family met this requirement virtually, communicating in conference intercom mode through their Efficiency Implants. In fact, though in-person family dinners were supposedly the norm, Li'l Ed had only known one person who actually sat down with his family every day: his friend Sett, whose family owned its own corporation and could arrange its schedule however it wished. For those responsible to a higher purpose than the interests of their own families, there were schedules and dinners via EI.

Ed's current stepmother, Nolene, had muted her EI, as she was concurrently meeting with a few subordinates. She had been present to lead the evening prayer, so officially the dinner had now occurred. While Sett's family was rare for owning its own business entity, Li'l Ed's was rather typical among the upper class for having all its members and former members working within a single large organization: McGuillian Corporation, the same entity that owned and operated Fisher University.

"I know you're concerned, son," his father said. "You should be. Those who don't worry about the fifteen percent will find themselves part of it. But you have an advantage; you've grown up in a household with some of the most dedicated Accepted parents anywhere. You've seen the kind of devotion to the organization that's necessary, and you have what it takes to provide that."

"Thank you, sir," Li'l Ed replied. "I do work very hard. But then so does everyone I know, sir."

"Now don't get snippy," his father said. "I said you'll be fine, so that's good enough. Start second-guessing your superiors and you really will be pushed out. I've told you before: The company doesn't care about what you know. That fifteen percent who are kicked out of the university every year aren't necessarily the ones who learned the least. Some of them are quite gifted, academically. It's all about how you cooperate and how you obey. The complacent survive, the uppity Depart."

Li'l Ed shivered. How could anyone survive the horror of Departing and losing all corporate status? What point would there be in existing after your own organization had determined you were an unworthy parasite? "Yes, sir. Compliance with directives is what separates Golden workers from monkeys." Li'l Ed realized his fingertip was tracing the company emblem embroidered on his blue school uniform. Suburban students had their towns' logos, and those who lived in company housing, whether McGuillian or any other, had the corporate logo.

Real monkeys had been extinct for some time.

His mind was wandering again. He took another drink of his Synapsate, the McGuillian energy drink he consumed constantly to help him focus. When protein and nutrient levels were adjusted properly, Synapsate was a meal in itself. People always said Li'l Ed's platinum hair and half-closed eyes made him look sleepy, but thanks to this stuff he didn't ever actually feel tired. "Thank you for your guidance, sir."

"You'll be fine. I just hope your group is up to the task," his father said.

"Actually, sir, I do have some concern along those lines," Li'l Ed said. "It's Sett, sir. The eldest among us, if you remember me saying."

"The one whose parents work for Andro-Heathcliffe?" his father said.

"That's right, sir, I do have a friend whose parents are with Andro-Heathcliffe, sir. His name is Jack."

"And which one is Sett, then?"

"The chalk company, sir. Williams Gypsum."

"Oh, of course. Well, I can understand your concern. Those families who still own a business tend to be a little *out there*."

"Yes, sir. I'm worried. There's a waitress at the McGuillian Diner..."

"Ah!" his father said. "I remember that place from my time at Fisher." He laughed to himself. "And the waitresses."

"Sett *stares* at her, sir. He watches her, and he even seems to get nervous around her. It's disturbing to see someone of our class behaving that way, even to our own. To see how he is about this waitress... I worry that he might not be entirely sane, sir."

His father's laugh was warm, if a bit condescending. "Don't worry, son. It's perfectly natural. Men get that way around women. Some like to go straight for marriage material and others like to play around with inferiors for a while first. Why wouldn't he want a few practice rounds before he starts playing for real?"

The Place B's Memories Called the Zone

"The fuck you been?" the Garbageman asked. Someone had tried to open his head, leaving a wide scab across his forehead. "I been outta shit for more than a week. That's bad business, and bad business gets people killed." His eyes made it clear this was a threat, but Furius didn't care. The Garbageman's ill will was nothing compared to what the former Roman slaves had spewed, and they'd outnumbered him in most confrontations. In conflict after conflict, Furius and his professional, better-organized Roman military operation had wiped out more primitive fighting forces. Soon the legions would return, and the likes of the Garbageman would be brought to heel.

"I'm here now," Furius said. He followed the Garbageman into an alley, removing the kilo from his coat pocket. The man used a pair of shears to poke a hole in the plastic, tapping the kilo to knock some powder out onto the back of his hand to snort.

"Same price?" the Garbageman asked.

"Yeah," Furius said as the Garbageman snuffed it up. He felt impatient, but Mr. B.'s memories told him waiting for the snort to work was part of this business.

The Garbageman's eyes widened and his jaw set in anger as he realized the new drug was not what he'd been expecting. Furius dodged the shears flying past his head, but didn't anticipate how fast the Garbageman would draw the gun. Furius knocked the barrel aside with a forearm as if it were a thrusting spear, and the bullet blasted past him.

Furius snatched one of his own guns and yanked the trigger three times as he ran away. The Garbageman fired two more shots over his shoulder, missing both times. Furius dove to the ground, rolling against a building. Unsure when he could stand and chase again without being shot, he waited too long. By the time he got back to his feet, the Garbageman was gone.

Somewhere in the Zone

The dilapidated Partner Hotel smelled like old shoes and industrial solvents, but it was the first Wanda had seen, and she knew she wouldn't last long on the street at night. Her hands shook, rattling the little plastic bag of casino chips. Was there a protocol for this kind of transaction? Many of her colleagues had bought prostitutes and rented rooms in places like this, but she never had. Was she supposed to haggle about the price of a room? How dangerous would it be if she tried to do so and tipped her hand that she didn't know what she was doing?

The man on the other side of the counter was barely tall enough to look over it. He had facial stubble and frizzy brown hair down past his hips, whitewashed in the smeary gray dust that seemed to coat everything here in the Zone. "Wha'chu want, Golden lady?" he asked, peering over dark glasses with octagonal yellow frames.

A startling headache had formed at the base of Wanda's skull, as if a scalpel were splitting her brain stem. Her nausea and sweating indicated she'd probably vomit soon. It was withdrawal from all the synthesized medications she'd been on. There was no time to haggle. No matter how foolish she might seem for it, paying full price was better than collapsing and being totally helpless out in the open.

"Room," she said, placing a hand on the counter to steady herself. The wave of nausea passed and she was feeling better again, though she probably didn't have long before the with-drawal symptoms fully kicked in.

She counted casino chips onto the counter until they added to the room fee and key deposit. It was more than a third of what Davi had given her. The man slid them into his palm and dropped them into his pocket, placing an old-fashioned metal key on the counter.

"What..." Wanda's voice cracked and she cleared her throat. "What time is checkout?"

"If the sun's up, get the fuck out," he said. "But be sure to turn in the key here at the desk. You get your key deposit back and also we don't fuckin' kill you."

Out at sunrise. She had thought she'd be able to hide until late morning, especially at this price. She bit her lip, keeping her head down as she took the key and turned away toward the crumbling linoleum staircase.

"The freer you are, the harder you've got to fight, hon," her grand-mother used to say. She had taken great pains in teaching Wanda how to stay independent. Her last attempt, bringing home the rats, had apparently gotten her Departed. Had she once stumbled into this same hotel? How hard had she fought, here? How long had she survived?

Zone dwellers were drawn to weakness; letting them see her cry would invite no end of trouble.

Wanda, herself, was now a Zone dweller.

"6th and G," the desk clerk said.

She stopped, but couldn't make herself turn back to face him. "What?"

"That's where you're going," he said. "6th and G. The Horde of the Departed. Don't try to stay over in the morning. We have people for that and there's no reason to start out with serious injuries."

It was obvious. *She* was obvious. The nausea came flood-ing back, but she forced it down again, disgusted that she'd revealed enough to put herself in serious danger when she'd been trying to be so careful. "It's the uniform," she muttered, looking down. The Amelix logo, stylized DNA in shimmering black that glinted green, gleamed smugly up at her.

"It's everything," he said. "Uniform or no uniform, you'd stand out. But it don't help."

She nodded. A tear fell to the dusty floorboards.

"I'll sell you my jacket for another night's room charge," he said. He held up a threadbare brown sports coat with lapels, obviously from countless decades ago. She looked at him blankly. "You won't live long here in Corporate Green, sweetie."

She sighed. "I won't live long without money, either."

"I'll let you fuck for it," he said.

She froze. Was this really happening? Already?

She couldn't breathe.

"But none of this bullshit where you say halfway through that you didn't agree to something. I want it all, everything. Nothing's off limits."

She stared blankly. Without her corporation, what was she? She had been raised inside Amelix, and she had no valuable attributes beyond the small corporate niche for which she'd been trained. Amelix was the whole world, and she had been expelled. Exiled. Banished. She was…

Soup, just like Laurel the Chicken.

Was her pride worth fighting for? Her health? Nothing like that mattered as much as survival, right now. She retched a bit but she made herself turn around, slapping her hand down on the counter. She needed something to cover herself, she didn't have much time, and things would only be increasingly hopeless from here on out.

"*Everything's* off limits," she said. Her voice stuck and she cleared her throat. Tears ran down her hot face. "Except the basics. You put it in, you fuck, and you're gone. That's it."

Better now than after the corporate birth control wears off.

"All right." He held out the jacket and she watched her hands slowly grasp it.

"Smart girl," he said. "And a tough bargainer for a Departed. You might just survive after all." He put his arm behind her back and guided her toward the room.

3

A Zone Back Street

Len showed the hooker his rig and bottle of powder. "You probably know some cheap hotels around here, huh?" he asked. "I don't want anything but a place to sleep and maybe some food. I'll share this with you and whoever we need to bargain with, if you can help me."

The woman sniffed, looking away.

"Obviously I can't hurt you," he said, giving one pathetic breathy laugh at his own pitiful state. "We can have just... just a moment of peace, without pain," he said.

After a moment, she nodded. Len extended a hand and tried to help her up, but she was too heavy and he nearly toppled. They held onto each other for balance and he tried to start walking, but she seemed frozen in place.

Was someone approaching? Len pivoted his head quickly, expecting a threat. Following her gaze he realized she was staring at the severed toe. "C'mon," he said. "That's not a souvenir you're gonna want."

A Closed but Crowded Restaurant Outside Rio de Janeiro's Cidade de Deus Slum, 1977

Lucas Araújo lay curled on a sheet of plywood, which rested on a metal cart. Men tied his wrists together behind his knees. At sixteen years old, he was young and strong enough to have put up a good fight, but instead he remained compliant and still except for his body's uncontrollable shuddering. This was a small storeroom, set off from the main dining and kitchen area where the mostly white-clad crowd danced and chanted in the ongoing Macumba ritual. The thick wooden door slightly muffled the sound as the drums repeated their quick but rhythmic *do-DOONK, do-DOONK, do-DOONK.*

Just yesterday Lucas would have thought this man towering over him was an ordinary restaurant owner, whose establishment Lucas had attempted to burglarize. Today he had learned that this was the man known as *o Caimão*, the Caiman, famous as the most vicious gangster in the city. *O Caimão* had punctuated the lesson by repeatedly breaking the shinbone of Lucas's four-year-old brother Vinicius with a hammer, crippling the boy and further burdening their already impoverished family.

On the shelf near him were dozens of yellow cans reading "feijão," the same as the can of beans he'd had in his hand when he was caught.

"Let's give you another pill, okay?" *o Caimão* said, opening a small brown bottle. Lucas gobbled it greedily from his palm. Even with two of these powerful tranquilizers already in his system, his body shook so much he was nearly toppling the cart.

"You probably wonder why I give you these," *o Caimão* said. "If I want to make a point, demonstrate my power to the community, shouldn't I want you to scream and thrash? Wouldn't that make them fear me most?" He grinned, making the puckered, acne-scarred flesh of his cheeks crease, but leaving his eyes cold and flat beneath his close-trimmed black hair. "There's something more important than showing them I can cause you pain, boy. They already know that. But if instead I show them you're willing to die for my agenda, well, that's something else again. That's how we change their fear into devotion. Your example will teach them to fear me, but also that my agenda is worth sacrifice, commitment, even piety."

The glassy black eyes stared down pitilessly as his captor continued speaking. "If you thrash and scream, it looks more like you were forced. But if they see you alive, *submitting* to my power, then they see that even your desire to live is subordinate to my will. They see devotion."

"They know you gathered my friends, my family, my neighbors," Lucas slurred. "They know you caught me stealing from this restaurant, and you threatened to torture until death everyone close to me, before my eyes, unless I agreed. It is still fear."

"There is always fear in any dealing with true power," *o Caimão* said. "How could there not be? But fear alone would not get us to this point, would not produce such a volunteer as you. Today your entire life energizes my expanding power and authority, teaching everyone that it is proper, even natural, to willingly lay down their lives for me. Besides, after you're gone, there will only be me to tell the story. Your death stands for whatever I say, because I alone have the power to say it."

Lucas felt himself losing connection with his consciousness. All tension drained from his muscles.

"Yes! Good!" *o Caimão* said. "Your eyes roll up, just like the Macumba men when they say they're possessed by spirits. The guests will see this as some kind of sign. I don't care what their superstition tells them, as long as their minds accept that I am worthy of reverence and awe."

Lucas felt his face droop toward the plywood. They were wheeling him into the main area now and a Macumba man was waving a dead rooster over him. The man had cut or yanked the tongue out of the chicken's beak and it now sat in front of Lucas on the plywood. "You will speak the language of the dead," the Macumba man whispered, biting a piece off of Lucas's ear and lapping at his trickling blood. Lucas felt his own tongue swell in shock or disgust, but he was too drugged for much to register beyond that.

O Caimão laughed. "They listen to this man, yet people say *I'm* crazy. He says he can follow you, see what happens after your death, by tasting your blood first. I let him, why not? It's a community service." He smiled impassively down at Lucas.

The tempo of the drumbeats remained constant but they seemed to be hitting them harder: *do-DOONK, do-DOONK, do-DOONK*. The plywood levitated above the room.

No. Not levitated. Men had lifted it. Lucas jerked and twitched, but it was true: In this drugged state, he was rendered incapable of mounting even symbolic resistance.

The heat seared his eyes and lungs as they pulled down on the wide tubular handle and lowered the restaurant oven's pitted white enamel door. The rectangular opening was too narrow for him to have fit if he hadn't been bound this way. They pushed the plywood inside and slammed the door shut. Lucas was unconscious before his addled mind could make him scream, and then he separated from his body.

Amelix Integrations Secure Research Memo
Engineered Organism Division
Dr. Reni Donova, H.S., DCS, Vice President

AAA CLEARANCE LEVEL OR ABOVE ONLY

Re: Projects RT1117 and RT1118: Communication by Unknown Means

Dr. Donova, ma'am:

This memo is to keep you informed of recent developments with the animals in Projects RT1117 and RT1118.

The Generation 1 (G-1) rats were observed communicating with the Generation 2 (G-2) rats while in neither visual nor aural contact.

An experiment was conducted in which each generation was intentionally disturbed/agitated while physically separated from the other. Both generations evinced ability to sense the agitation of the other and respond instantly, standing on hind legs with straight spines and eyes toward wherever the disturbance was taking place. When the agitated animals were relocated to more distant parts of the laboratory, the non-agitated generation still became concurrently alert and instantly located the other rats and the disturbance, in multiple trials. Though the mechanism of communication remains unknown at this time, the outcome is identical regardless of which animal group is directly disturbed.

As you know, G1 was the first group of animals directly exposed to the symbiotic fungus now known among those with clearance as the "Deity Strain," internal catalog #616Tr3312s. G2 was exposed only to air exhaled by G1, not to the strain directly, for a period of sixty seconds before a complete flush with sterilized air. At no point have the animals seen each other or been caged in the same room. There appears to be no difference between the generations as to the sending and receiving of communications.

An experiment is being designed to further test the modes of communication, beginning with a screen for subsonic and ultrasonic waves and progressing to scans to detect any anomalous electromagnetic waves. Detailed laboratory notes are available for your review in the DEO archives.

Zabeth B.D. Chelsea, DCS

A Zone Hotel Room

Lucas gently stroked the face of the woman with whom this tortured, meatless body had checked in. That man had been Len, and he had been even poorer than Lucas had been back in Brazil. He had access to the memories of the man who had previously controlled this body, though that man existed no more in this world. Those memories showed that this body had injected a drug with the rig that now sat on the window-sill, while the woman had sniffed the same drug as powder through a tube.

Her eyelids were fluttering now.

She groaned and thrashed. "Shhh, shhh, shhh," Lucas whispered. "It's all right. Shhh, shhh." He stroked her hair.

Her eyes opened. He watched as she took in the room, the view out the window, the rig, and himself. He had done the same thing, matching his own perception of this world with the memories the other man had left him. She gasped suddenly and bent down to where her foot rested on a pillow, feeling the makeshift bandage fastened around the stump of her missing toe.

"You are from some other place, some other time?" he asked, raising a shockingly skinny arm from where her neck had previously rested upon it.

She nodded slowly, narrowing her eyes.

"I am Lucas Araújo," he said. "I am sixteen years old, from Brazil." He watched her as she processed the information.

"I ... am Inti," she said. "I remember that. But ... "

"It is confusing," he said. "I felt the same when I woke. This place, this body, this language, all different. But I woke maybe two hours ago. Since then, I have been sitting here as you slept, letting the memories come to me. If you stay quiet and listen, the memories will come to you, too, I think. It's good that you already remember who you are, your name. It took some time for me to see, because my memories are jumbled with someone else's." She wriggled and moaned. He gently touched her cheekbone with two fingers. "It is a pretty name, too, Inti."

"It means the sun," she said. She paused, thinking, staying quiet like he had suggested. "I am ... fourteen years old. Or, I was fourteen then. There are other memories, too. Other memories that are not mine."

"Yes," he said. "I have those, too. From another person who is not here now. If you practice, you can let them blend together.

What's in your head that you did not live, it can help you see your own life differently."

She was quiet again, for a much longer time. When she spoke again, her voice was quieter, her speech much slower. "I believe that my life was several hundred years ago, though I do not remember so many years." She fell silent, staring into space with a dreamy look. "I begin to see what you mean about letting all the memories work together. It is very strange. My home is the place these people would call Peru." She smiled slightly. "I can see … a map. Not from my world, from this one. It has my mountains on it. I can read it and see that I am from Peru, and I can see Brazil, too, Lucas. It seems we were … neighbors, almost." She turned on the bed they shared, to better face him.

"And in your place, Peru, did you die, Inti?"

She nodded again. "The village leaders said a maiden had to die, to please the gods and protect our home, our people. It was a great honor to give this gift to our people. I volunteered. They…they gave me strong drinks with alcohol and drugs, and they carried me up to the mountain." Her eyes settled on him. He watched them soften as she discerned his new body's extreme deterioration.

"You died willingly for an agenda," he muttered. He cleared his throat and continued in a clearer voice. "Now we're back, you and I, to see the world our sacrifices have built. You can remember things the other woman knew?" he asked. "I am the same. The man who had this body is gone, but I know what he knew. It is the same for you, I think."

She shook her head slightly. "This person is not gone. I can feel her inside me. She still lives." Inti gave him an amused smirk. "Perhaps we are different in this because while each man is just one man, every woman is many women."

He smiled back.

"She thought this was cocaine," Inti said, gesturing at the little jar of powder. "That's a preparation from leaves my people chewed and used for tea." She paused for a moment and then asked, "Do you know why we are here?"

Lucas shook his head. "Maybe it's because you and I both

gave up our lives for others. Perhaps we're back merely to live again, just to share this moment together."

The Place Mr. B's Memories Called the Zone

After he was relatively certain the Pink Shit had done its work on the Garbageman, Furius circled back to find him. Presumably, they would all eventually come searching for the new legion, but he was particularly looking forward to this man's absolute obedience once he swore the *sacramentum* and became a proper legionary. In this case it was worth the extra nuisance of collecting him while still unconscious.

Though, he supposed, like Furius himself, the legionary would be someone else, not actually the Garbageman. He would have already sworn the *sacramentum* a few thousand years ago.

The Garbageman was nowhere to be found.

While the Garbageman had ensured that Mr. B had no idea where he lived, it was relatively common knowledge that he had worked at the Dobo Protein Refinery. For now, he would just turn his attention to running down his list of B's contacts and moving as much Pink Shit as he could.

The Zone Hotel Room

Addi's foot throbbed, sending pain signals not just from the swollen part that remained, but even a phantom sensation from the missing toe itself.

The sun was up. The window was caked with so much grime it was hard to see through, but there was no mistaking the daylight coming in. Why hadn't they been thrown out yet?

She remembered the drug and the girl in her head. There was no better way to make a seventeen-year-old prostitute feel like shit than to have a fourteen-year-old virgin inside her head, dredging up memory after memory of degradation and abuse. The visitor was shocked at every recollection, but kept forcing herself to dig deeper, layering new associations of disgust and horror on top of the memories Addi had tried to bury. Worse, the girl seemed to have fallen in love with this slabbie, who had given her the drug in the first place.

The drug! She had used it to pay for this room. Charley at the desk downstairs probably had someone else in his head, now, too.

If the sun was up now, it had been several hours since the Garbageman had taken her toe. That was several toes he would take, now, and still she had no money. The girl, Inti, had warm and sweet memories of just talking and cuddling with the slabbie all night. There'd been no way he could've done anything more than that, anyway, in his starved and exhausted state. Addi had never known before what closeness and intimacy felt like. The many protective walls she'd built around her psyche kept her from experiencing such things. Right now, though, there was no time to be sentimental or weirded out. They had to get out of this room and hopefully slip past Charley, and then she had to evade the Garbageman or suffer worse pain and disfigurement.

"Hey," she said, nudging him, searching Inti's memory for his name. "Hey, Lucas. Time to go." She put a hand on his shirtless chest and shook gently. His skin was cold and the shrunken body was stiff.

"Sorry, Inti," she sighed. "Your new love is dead."

Little Guadalajara, "La Guada," the Zone

"Arrulfo, it's not good that you teach him to rely only on you," a voice said. "He needs to have others in his life he can trust.

This trip will be dangerous and if you go, he's going to go, too, because you taught him to be glued to your side."

"Rosa, we have talked about this. It is difficult for him to trust people, but he has learned to trust me. Because I'm the only one he trusts, he needs me, he relies only on me."

"He can't go with us."

"He can't stay alone. He won't."

The voices were in the hallway outside this room.

Ernesto Silva ran the ballpoint of a long dead pen cartridge around the bearing track of the rear wheel hub from the bicycle he was restoring. There were little pits there, evidenced by the pen point's wobbles and vibrations. He had a smooth stone with a nice corner that could fit into the track and gently abrade away the unevenness. The tiny bearings themselves were corroded and misshapen, too, but Ernesto could roll them against the flat part of his stone to smooth them. When he was finished the track would be slightly larger than the original manufacture and the bearings would be slightly smaller, but he could compensate by packing them with wax from a toilet seal he'd taken out of a crumbling abandoned building.

Someone knocked on the open doorframe behind him.

The bike's axle wobbled as he rolled it against the floor. Ernesto always worked in this spot because he knew the floor was smooth and level. The wobble meant the axle was bent. It was as wide as his palm and nearly as thick as his pinky finger, made of hardened steel. There was no way to bend it back straight, even if he'd still had his pliers, which had been stolen. He did have a fist-sized rock with a rounded point he could use to pound the axle against the floor. That could make it straighter than now, but it would also introduce new pits for him to have to smooth out again. Even after pounding it that way, the axle would never be truly straight.

"Ernesto?" a voice called in Spanish from behind him, gentle but strong. "How are you doing, *amigo*?"

The bicycle would never be fully fixed if the axle couldn't be truly straight. He was doing this work to fix the bicycle, but it would never be fully fixed. More wax would help, but the bicycle would never be like it was supposed to be. Ernesto's face felt hot. He was trying to make the bicycle work the way it was supposed to work, but the axle was bent forever and so the bicycle was broken forever. He could make it work well enough to be ridden, but it would always be broken inside.

Soft footsteps came up behind him.

"Ernesto?" a voice said.

The rubber seal around the bearings was cracked in too many places to salvage. The washers, spacers, and locknuts had corroded, and though he could abrade away most of that damage, the washers, spacers, and locknuts would corrode again without a new rubber seal. He could make one out of old plastic bags, but it wouldn't be durable so it wouldn't last long. The bicycle wouldn't stay fixed for long if he had to use plastic bags instead of a rubber seal, but the rubber seal was cracked in too many places to salvage, and the bicycle would never be fully fixed, not ever, because of the axle and the track and the bearings and the pits and corrosion.

Something touched him!

Ernesto gasped in shock, shouting and flailing to remove the hand from his shoulder. Ripping his attention away from his work was as difficult and painful as if his eyeballs had been in physical contact with icy metal. He turned his head and saw fingers and palms, not reaching for him but just empty palms pointed at him now.

"Easy, cousin," a voice said. Ernesto peered past the hands and found a face. It was narrow and smooth, with big brown eyes and a small tuft of beard under the chin. There were thick, bushy eyebrows and matching bushy close-cropped hair. The face was similar to the picture memories of Arrulfo that Ernesto carried in his mind. Picture after picture from his memory matched the face before him now, not exactly but close, close, one after the other. This was Arrulfo. Ernesto let his eyes return to his work.

"I don't like to be touched, Arrulfo," Ernesto said, testing the track again with the ballpoint. Ernesto was ten years and forty-four days old. Arrulfo was seven years and fifty-two days older than Ernesto.

"I know, *amigo,* I know. I'm sorry. This is important and I need to have you listen to me now. I touched you so I could make sure you're listening."

The stone was making progress on the track, wearing down the little pits, but the corner he was using was wearing out. He turned it to a sharper one and ran it around the track again.

"You can ask me questions," Ernesto said. "Questions are a good way to tell if someone is listening."

"Okay, cousin. You're right."

"You don't have to touch me."

"I am sorry, Ernesto," Arrulfo said. "I know you don't like to be disturbed when you are working, but I have something important to ask you."

Ernesto looked back down at the cracked rubber seal. It was too cracked to salvage. "I don't like to be disturbed when I'm working, Arrulfo," Ernesto said. "You know I don't like to be disturbed when I'm working."

"I know, Ernesto. I know. But this is an emergency. Mari is very sick and I need to take her to find a doctor in a different part of the Zone. There is a doctor there who can help her, but it is not safe for her and Rosa to go alone. It is dangerous for us to leave this area. If I go with them, there will be nobody to watch out for you here, so I'm going to have to take you along, also."

"I don't like fighting, Arrulfo. Dangerous means fighting, and I don't want to fight anyone. I'm not good at it. I don't understand fighting."

"I will try to do all of the fighting for you, cousin, if I can. Will you come with me?"

"Yes."

><)><()><()><

Corner of 6th and G, the Zone

The threadbare brown jacket hung limply, doing a decent job of concealing her Corporate Green uniform on the dirty Zone street. Wanda turned in a circle, looking all around. A few bums sat on the ground in different spots, leaning against crumbling walls of buildings with glassless window holes, but she saw no one else at all. Where was the legendary mass of former corporate humanity, the Horde of the Departed?

The stench here was like nothing she had ever experienced. It was the most powerful combination of urine, vomit, death, rot, sewage, and chemical smells imaginable, laced with a strange sort of electrical discharge and ozone scent she thought might just be her own terror. The sensory overload excused her tears, perhaps. This was her life, now: decay, desperation, and toxicity.

Her EI told her there was a signal here, and briefly an idea flashed of trying to send a message to Nami. Such a message would never get past the corporate firewall, though.

Down G there seemed to be a greater concentration of bums. Perhaps they had strayed from the Horde, or maybe the Horde had already migrated away from this location. In any case, there was no sprawling mass of desperate former corporates. She supposed the desk clerk could simply have gotten it wrong, and the Horde may never have been here at all. She walked farther that way, staying on the gravel in the middle of the street to avoid contact with the dirty and frightening people against the walls. Each face turned up to stare at her as she passed.

Wanda felt the Zone wearing on her already, making her paranoid. Of course these people would watch her go by, she told herself.

They have nothing else to do. It's nothing more than that, no reason to imagine it's a calculated, orchestrated observation for some nefarious purpose, even though…every single one of them is still looking at me.

By halfway down the first block she had passed half a dozen, and one by one they had all risen to their feet. They now stood where they had sat, no longer leaning against walls, still staring. At the corner of Fifth Street, a cluster of them stood silently, more than she'd noticed there before, each one unabashedly watching her every move. With every step past Fifth Street, they seemed to close in a bit nearer to her. By the midpoint between Fifth and Fourth, a new one approached, fast, coming straight up into her face.

"Hello, friend," the man said quietly, but with a strange intensity that made the hairs stand at the back of Wanda's neck. He was dressed in rags and had a long, scraggly beard, but he seemed to stand straighter than most bums she had seen, and to enunciate his words more clearly, too, though his voice was barely above a whisper. She hadn't noticed him before he'd appeared a few steps away. Now he stood directly in front of her, blocking her path, and a quick glance from side to side showed at least seven others just slightly farther than arm's reach, now, all standing, all peering into her face.

"Where are you going?" he asked, as quietly and intensely as before.

"I...nowhere," she said. "I think I made a mistake. Someone told me I should come here, but I don't think this is right."

"Yeah," he said. Wanda found herself leaning toward him, listening intently so as not to miss a word he said in that disturbingly quiet voice.

Where a moment ago there had been a small group standing and watching, there were now more than twenty. She gasped, pivoting her head from side to side to look over both shoulders.

"I...Yes. I should go back. I was looking for...I'm sorry to have disturbed you." She started to turn around and walk toward 6th again, but she thought better of it, stepping backwards rather than turning her face away from him.

"Are you looking for someone?" he asked. His voice was that of a person talking in a library or study hall, eerily out of place on a Zone street.

She turned then, angling away from him and taking a few quick strides. He matched her, step for step. She set her eyes toward the intersection where this had all begun, 6th and G, and tucked her chin, almost running. The number of people watching seemed to have doubled, crowding in as she ran past.

The man stopped following her. She ran the last half-block, finally looking over her shoulder as she returned to her starting point, breathing heavily, the stench stinging her nostrils and tongue.

The same small group of bums sat in the same spots they had before. Nobody else was around.

4

Evans Household, the Zone

Kym opened her eyes.
Eye.

She realized she could only see through one. The other still seemed to be there, though. It tracked achingly along with the seeing one from behind its swollen lid.

It was dark. *Still dark? Still the same night?*

No. She was lying in a drying puddle of her own urine and her stomach was empty. Probably a whole day had gone by. Maybe more than a day. She wanted to feel around, to get her bearings, but her body was too badly damaged to move. Her knee was wedged under something with a hard, straight edge … the kitchen cabinet beneath the sink. She was on the kitchen floor.

Need help. But how can I get to Dok's place when I can't even stand?

It was her last thought, and then she was unconscious again.

A Zone business

The door was made of many layers of plastic, wood, and particleboard, all glued and screwed together into a massive sheet. It slid in and out of a concrete wall so thick that the doorway seemed more like a tunnel. Scrawled in large black letters across it were the words "SYNTH INSIDE."

Wanda had been watching people coming in and out, trying to summon enough courage to try it herself. There was nothing else around here. As primitive as her surroundings felt, it wasn't like she could go forage for nuts and berries or spear a wooly mammoth. Whatever sustenance she got would have to come from a synthesizer, and the black letters on that door were the only evidence of one she had seen in the Zone.

She had figured out the pattern, insofar as it worked on this side of the door. There were two big goons standing out front, and customers approached with chips in their hands. The men would grunt at them and they would quickly open their palms to show they had means to pay. Then the door would be opened to admit them and quickly slid shut again after they entered. Wanda had positioned herself on the street at an angle that would allow her to see inside, but the interior was too dark to reveal anything.

How many chips should she present? The patrons all held them too tightly and flashed them too briefly for her to see. Presumably they wouldn't let her in if she showed too few, but would they demand she turn over whatever she did show? The company had always provided her with internal credits for such purchases and she had no idea how much things might cost out here.

Finally her empty stomach and increasing lightheadedness won out. She approached the giants and showed them all the chips she had. She could only figure out her next step once she got inside.

They slid the door open and she entered a dark room. Off to the left was a single light source, shining down onto the synthesizer. Wanda had only seen the interactive parts of them before, the dashboards through which users would order whatever product was wanted. The other parts had always been hidden behind walls and countertops. This one was simply sitting in a corner of the room, partially hidden by a battered cabinet and a man who was taking orders across it, but Wanda was still shocked by the sheer size of it. The synthesizer was at least three times the size of Wanda's body, formed of a flat gray material she supposed was a kind of polymer, its shape obscured by hundreds of translucent pink tubes and valves. The interface she recognized was only one small rectangle right in the middle, though this one was severely worn and coated in Zone grime.

Her eyes adjusted and she saw the line of customers, with three ahead of her. Someone else came in and stood behind her. Though synthesizers could make anything, everyone seemed to be buying patented energy drinks. It made sense, she supposed; they offered the most nutritional content for the money.

Pulsarin, the Amelix brand, was the only one she had ever consumed as an Amelix employee. It took a certain amount of mental preparation to get the stuff down, with its numbing sensation and metallic aftertaste.

But I'm not an Amelix employee anymore. I have no obligation to keep my credits inside the umbrella!

She would try Vibrantia, a competing product she had always been curious about, though she'd heard it was virtually identical. Her life was coming to an abrupt end here in the Zone; why not allow herself the pitiful luxury of a new consumer experience?

The person in front of her approached the counter and ordered.

Nami. That's why not.

Her daughter Nami was still supported by Amelix, and Wanda would always do whatever she could to support the company as long as that remained true. Pulsarin it was, and Pulsarin it would be until she died.

The man behind the counter nodded at her and she approached. "Pulsarin," she croaked. "Loaded." She presented her palm with all the chips, trying to appear bored with the process so that he would assume she knew how much it was supposed to be worth. He took a few chips and stared at her.

She looked around. Everyone was watching her.

"Cup?" the man asked, annoyed.

A cup. No, she did not have a cup.

Wanda dumped the chips out of the plastic bag Davi had given her and handed it across the counter. The man filled it with her dose of Pulsarin.

Somewhere in This World of Filth, Death, and Pain

Inti padded nervously down the gravel sidewalk. What had she done to deserve such a punishment as this? The memories she got from the other girl sharing this body showed that misery was nothing new here.

There were no trees or plants in this place. Since she'd arrived she'd not seen a single animal. The people here were not kind or even merciful. There was nothing but gravel and crumbling buildings and desperate, murderous crowds.

She couldn't make herself prostitute the body, even though it belonged to this other girl, Addi, more than to herself. Somehow Addi had blocked most of the memories, but the tiny fragments Inti saw of her experiences had made her numb with horror.

I am sorry to you, Addi. I should do it, too, so that you can be conscious for something not terrible once in a while. You feed us both, doing that. I will try to be strong for you.

Her missing toe felt as if it were still there, burning and cramping. Every step sent an electric pain up her leg and spine.

The bits of memory she found were enough to show her what to do and what she ought to charge for various tasks. Men and women wanted to use all parts of her body, and each thing was worth a different amount, paid in local casino chips. Those chips then bought things like food and clothes, and a shelf to sleep on in a windowless room shared with two other girls, the room itself so small that the shelves fit from wall to wall.

She kept her head down, ashamed to be what everyone saw, and yet even more ashamed to not be doing what they thought she was doing. She should do those things, to support Addi, to justify herself.

Nobody seemed to notice or care. Perhaps everyone was ashamed here.

Her mind went blank as she found herself suddenly immobilized.

Hands had grabbed her by her throat and scratchy pink hair. She wriggled and gasped, taking in only a fraction of the air she needed. The fingers tightened, cutting off blood into her head. She saw nothing but a section of brick wall across the alley above her, but now the image darkened and became spotty. Her feet dug trenches into the gravel as the hands dragged her off the main street and into a narrow gap between two empty buildings.

"Where's your boss, whore?" The voice was angry and male. The hands held her face against the wall, pointed up and away. Her heart beat faster and her breathing became shallower and faster. Her head was pulled forward, away from the wall, and then slammed back up into it. Her skull thudded hard against the brick. The attacker pulled her forward once more, faster and farther down, then back again, hard, against the wall. Her limbs crumpled, suddenly unable to support her weight. The voice got angrier, more threatening. "Where is your fucking boss?"

"I don't know! I don't know!" she whimpered.

The hands jerked her down the walkway and out the other side, onto some relatively empty back street. She could only see a bit of it with her head tilted the way it was. Inti struggled to keep her balance and avoid being dragged by her head. The man marched her quickly around a corner and then around another, and down a few more blocks. They went down a short flight of stairs and he kicked a door as if he were knocking. "Bridges!" He called. "Hey, lemme in, man! Look what I got!"

The door unlocked and he pulled her inside by her hair, which ripped out as she was thrown to the floor of a dark basement. "One of the Garbageman's girls!" her captor said. "We're gonna send him a message."

The one who had answered the door made some empty but enthusiastic comment.

From another side of the room a third voice spoke. "Awright, Magic! That fuck rips us off and kills our boy Murph? Fuck yeah the Bridges gonna make him pay!"

The one who had brought Inti here slapped her hard and began tearing her clothes. "Garbageman gonna know he can't fuck with the Bridges. He's too much of a bitch to show his face, fine, we can still hit him. First we fuck up this one, then every other whore he's got."

Amelix Building, CBD

"Hello, Dr. Kessler, sir," Keiko said, fumbling with her bag as she waited for his invitation to enter his office.

Kessler nodded his head and spread his arms, "Hi, sweetie. C'mere." She entered and slid against him sexily as she shut the door. "How are you today?"

"Tired and sore, sir."

He took her gently but firmly by the arms. "But ready to serve." His eyebrows were raised but he had not made it a question.

"Oh, yes, sir," she said breathlessly.

Their conditioned automatic obedience to superiors meant that these young Accepted workers were themselves the greatest perk available to management in any corporation. By pushing the boundaries of her reconditioning the way he had been, Kessler was able to stretch her definition of obedience, pushing ever closer to perfect submission, when she would unquestioningly obey his commands even to think and feel whatever he directed. But for now the charade of spying on Basali was still important: This one wasn't completely under control yet, and she'd proven she was dangerous before he'd begun working with her.

"I have a surprise for you, Keiko," Kessler said, looking into her eyes. Her EI loaded the page he'd flagged, full of Eric Basali's notebook entries, in Basali's handwriting, suspended one after another for her to read. "I had an intern use office security cameras to piece together and catalog every single entry he wrote in that little book. You saw only a tiny fraction of them. We have lots of work ahead of us tonight."

"I'm so happy, sir."

"Of course you are. It's what I want." He sat down in his chair, patting his thigh. She took a cushion from her bag, placed it on the floor beside him and knelt down, placing her cheek where he had patted, facing him. He stroked her hair. "Here we are, working. Notice how pleasurable it is to be working with me, now, Keiko. Let pathway amplification take it and build on it, always better and better and better. I am your superior and it is for me to judge what you deserve." As he spoke, Kessler made his voice deeper and softer. He stroked back from her forehead, over the top of her head, and all the way down, letting his whole palm gently smooth her hair and spread warmth and relaxation down her neck, over and over. "Right now I have decided that you should experience very, very good sensations, because you want to serve me —and Amelix Integrations—so well. Are you experiencing those good, good feelings, all through your body and all through your mind, those wonderful tickles you feel in your fingers and toes, your limbs, your eyes, ears and lips? Do you understand that I decide what you deserve, and that I have decided you deserve the ecstasy starting to build in you now?"

"Yes, sir," she said. Her breathing was slower and much heavier. Already her lowered eyelids revealed only white.

"Good. Let it keep feeling better and better and better, and relax for me. Good. Now let's work, because this is a working relationship, isn't that right?"

"Yes, sir."

"Let's look at the first one," he said. He pulled it up and into focus through his own EI.

The gods of the powerful serve only those who worship power.

"Do your thing, sweetie," he said. "Translate. Open up that brand-new Accepted mind and claim this one for Amelix."

"Yes, sir." There was a brief silence. Her eyes closed and her mouth opened slightly, forming a blissful expression. "There is only one God, sir. Amelix is the entity with legitimate power here on Earth, and we worship God because we acknowledge He is all-powerful in the universe. This is a fundamental truth, sir. Amelix serves the Lord's will."

"Excellent," he said. He ran his fingertips lightly along the bare skin of her neck and shoulder, back and forth. "Can you feel that you're serving the Lord's will, yourself, Keiko, right now?"

She shuffled a little closer up his thigh. He considered rebuking her, putting her back where he had patted, but that was probably too strict at this point. Instead, he lowered his chair a bit more.

"Oh, yes, sir," she said.

Bridges Clubhouse

"Naw, man, you do whatever," Rus said. "I guess I'm just too sad about Murph right now, you know. Magic catchin' that fuckin' whore brought it all back for me. I was right next to Murph when the Garbageman offed him." He rubbed one eye. "Could've been me. Now Murph's gone, and I'm here. It fucks with your head."

"Rus," Duke Q said, placing a hand on his shoulder. "I know you're feelin' bad, but you got to join the action, man. This is the way we make it right. Every cut you make in this whore, every load you dump in her, you're takin' cash right out of the fuckin' Garbageman's fuckin' pocket. I know Murph was your boy an' all that, but you gotta step up, now."

Murph had been a twitchy, hand-wringing little creep, so afraid of power that he would do absolutely anything to please his superiors. Because of this, other Bridges with more power than Rus had given Murph some rank, which he'd lorded over everyone he could. Rus was not too sad about Murph.

Duke Q was right. The Bridges had to build a reputation to make every thug in the whole Zone piss himself at the thought of crossing them. It was just the way things worked. Unless you made yourself totally fucking terrifying, you'd be wiped out by something that was.

He took a long drink from his sodje bottle. Maybe he could drink himself unconscious.

What the Bridges were doing to that girl was totally fucking terrifying. The sounds she made were turning his stomach and making his whole body shake.

Duke Q forcibly lowered the bottle again. "The Bridges are makin' a statement, here, brother," he said. "Are you in, or are you out?"

Out. Rus knew what it meant to be out, with nobody to watch his back, night after night on the Zone streets, exposed and helpless against whatever might come along. He had thought that nothing could be as frightening as living like that. Now he saw there was something far worse, and he was about to be face to face with it. Duke Q stood and offered his hand, helping Rus to his feet. Together they walked into the other room, to discover how far Rus was willing to go to prove his loyalty.

46th Street, the Zone

Wanda had found her way to another entertainment area, disconcertingly close to where she'd had the incident at 6th and G. This district looked rougher than where she'd started out, but hopefully it would be cheaper. She'd found herself a relatively secluded spot on the front steps of some building and had been watching the hookers, pimps, and johns.

There was a rhythm here, a dance of danger and protection, of cost and benefit. Pimps beat hookers to keep them in control. In exchange for that control over them and their incomes, pimps scared and often severely injured johns who got violent. They did this not out of altruism or respect for the girls, but as a means of ensuring their property would continue turning a profit. The girls weren't happy or secure, and they had no say in what happened to them, but they were alive. Whatever modicum of safety they managed here came from surrender to their psychotic guardians.

The last time Wanda had experienced a feeling of relative safety had been as an Amelix employee. She realized now that it was the same deal: Amelix had demanded complete surrender in exchange for protection from the life these Zone people lived, the way she lived now. When even the slightest reason for suspicion arose, the company had discarded her, the way she supposed these pimps might drop girls who gave them trouble. Obedience was paramount because her only value had been as property.

After her single Pulsarin meal this morning, her supply of casino chips was severely depleted. If she could brave the night outside, she would have enough for another serving tomorrow.

And then what?

She looked again at the whores and their pimps. How long would she last here, outside, with no income and no raging psychopath to own her and keep her alive? Was "life" here, like *that*, better than death?

Some deaths are probably better, some are undoubtedly worse.

She shuddered. That was all the Zone was, really, a collection of ways to die.

A man approached. Not a Zone man. He wore Corporate Green with a logo from one of the smaller data firms, and at first she felt the momentary rush of superiority she'd always felt in the CBD when brought into contact with those from lesser organizations.

He grabbed her breast without saying anything. His hand made two rough circles and then traced down her body to her crotch. "How much for your ass?" he asked.

She was alone. She had no company, no family, no pimp. There could never be any lesser organization than just one person alone.

But Wanda was so old. Why would she be approached in this way, when she guessed the average prostitute around here was maybe fourteen? Glancing quickly around, she realized why. Compared to these people, she was still quite attractive. For one thing, she had all her teeth. She also had no bruises or scars, no open wounds or scabs, and no bald patches where hair had been ripped out.

If she reacted to this man like the person she had been, he would see she wasn't a streetwalker. He would know she was fresh meat, newly Departed. The whole street would know, if they didn't already.

You're already a whore. Why not start walking the street? Isn't bleakness better than terror?

She gently guided the hand from between her legs and kissed it passionately, twice. "Sorry, baby," she made herself say, lowering her eyelids halfway as if lost in ecstasy. "My man's got me sidelined today. But you see that guy there, bald with the gold crown tattoo? He got two girls who love to give you the ass, an' you won't believe how good they are. She ran her tongue between two of his fingers, rolling her eyes up to find his. "But you look for me next time, okay, baby?"

"Why not you?" he asked as she released his hand.

"My manager says no, sugar," Wanda said. "I don't wanna cross him. Do you?"

The man's face went blank. No. Clearly he did not want trouble from her imaginary pimp. He turned away from her without a word and went to contact the bald pimp she'd pointed out. Wanda stood and walked the opposite direction as fast as she could.

It was scary how quickly she'd figured out how things worked here. She spat, scraped her tongue against her teeth, and spat again. At least she'd been able to fool him.

Did you fool him, really? How long until you're licking more than fingers?

Wanda wrapped her arms around herself and doubled her pace.

Two blocks further down 46th was the nastiest, cheapest hotel she had ever seen. It had once been a home, but now the front door was held on by hinges made of old car tires, and where its window had once been was a piece of decayed plywood with "HOTEL" written across it in drippy red paint. She pushed it open, fighting the hinges, and approached the front desk across the rough, dusty particleboard floor that shifted and creaked like it might drop her. The desk was a narrow door that had probably once closed a broom closet or pantry, balanced on columns of cinderblocks. The cadaverous man behind it had painful-looking red eyes with bushy gray eyebrows.

"How much for a room?" Wanda asked, careful to avoid the extra pleasantries like "excuse me" and "please," which would have tipped him off that she was new here. He flicked a thumb at the wall behind his head, where rates were written in charcoal for one hour, three hours, and all night. She could afford the all-night rate, but it would take all her chips.

These people haggled, didn't they? Would she seem out of place for not trying it, or would her inexperience be more pronounced?

"I...I think the three-hour rate should be good enough for all night at this point," she said. "It's pretty late already. All night wouldn't be that much longer."

The ghoulish man stared at the floor somewhere behind her. "If it's not that much longer, you can get your ass back out after three hours."

Wanda pursed her lips. *What now?*

After a moment of silence, the man spoke. "Tell you what. I'll give you a room all night for the three-hour price, but you gotta clean it yerself. There's garbage in it that needs to be hauled downstairs and out the back. The other desk clerk disappeared an' I gotta watch the desk. You clean it, you can stay 'till sunrise. Deal?"

She smiled openly, gladly showing him her gratitude as she counted out the chips. He walked her upstairs and unlocked the door for her. "I don't get a key?" she asked.

"Metal in the key's worth more than you got," he said, pushing open the door. He flicked on the light switch, which illuminated the room in a sickly yellowish brown glow. On the windowsill was a kit for injecting drugs. On the bed was a man: skeleton thin, shirtless, and dead.

"Just get him down the back stairs," the clerk said. "Someone'll drag his ass off to turn in for carbon recycling, make some scratch off him."

Wanda stared, dumbstruck. She took a deep breath.

Ugh.

She nodded. At least the corpse wouldn't ask anything of her for his non-Corporate Green pants.

"Get out first thing in the morning," he said, snatching up the drug kit. "You'll be lookin' for the corner of 6th and G."

Amelix Integrations Secure Research Memo
Engineered Organism Division
Dr. Reni Donova, H.S., DCS, Vice President

AAA CLEARANCE LEVEL OR ABOVE ONLY

Re: Projects RT1117 and RT1118: Communication by Unknown Means

Dr. Donova, ma'am:

Following is a summary of the most recent developments with the animals in Projects RT1117 and RT1118.

Both G1 and G2 animals were monitored with sensors capable of detecting visible and invisible waves ranging from 10-1 nm (x-ray range), through the visible light spectrum, as far as 1 cm (microwave range), as well as sound waves from 10 Hz to 1 MHz (including all known animal audible ranges from 100 Hz to 100 kHz). Evidence of communication was observed in that a response by one generation to a perceived stimulus (abrupt standing at attention when a researcher entered the space surrounding the cage) was mirrored by the other generation who had no exposure to the stimulus. Response mirroring was observed in 100% of trials, but **no communication through visible or audible signals, even at ranges far outside ordinary rat or human sensory perception, has been observed**.

Detailed laboratory notes are available for your review in the EOD archives.

Zabeth B.D. Chelsea, DCS

One of the Zone's entertainment areas

Furius had now done ten drug deals, moving maybe enough for thirty doses. He had pockets full of casino chips, and there were at least ten more people out there dosing themselves with Pink Shit, about to turn into useful Roman legionaries. Two of the buyers had been women. Whores would be helpful in forming a legion, certainly.

He watched this latest little punk scurry away from the doorway where they'd done the deal. It was Mr. B's word, *punk*, but it fit. Furius had seen many little punks, here and back in ancient Rome. It didn't matter; training and fear could keep any legionary in line. The point of concern now was how to find all these soldiers once they turned. None of them had appeared before him yet, even though the time that had passed should have been more than adequate.

Furius was about to step from the doorway when he stopped dead, staring across Tsingtao Street. It was Alfred, the man who had pissed in Mr. B's face and dosed him with Pink Shit. There were two men with him, pushing people out of the way. Furius turned his face toward the wall as they passed and then slipped across the street to follow them.

Alfred disappeared into an alley, leaving one man behind as a guard. Furius stayed back, behind the guard, watching.

If they'd left a man here, they weren't simply passing through the alley. They'd be coming back out. He just had to wait.

And do what, then?

He mapped it out in his head. He'd follow them, and, after letting them open the warehouse, he would kill them. He would take the means for producing Pink Shit, and proceed in building the new Roman legions. It was what he was meant to do.

Gunshots sounded in the alley. The man stationed as guard fell over, dead or nearly so. Someone came running out, stumbling and disoriented: Mr. B's memories said it was his friend Brian the Spook. Nobody followed him. Furius ran in, locating Alfred's slumped body, which still held a gun and a machine for weighing gold coins, possibly with one inside. In a pocket there were keys! The other one also had a gun and a plastic bag full of what was possibly Pink Shit, but Furius decided to leave that for someone else to find.

5

Amelix Building, CBD

Dr. Zabeth Chelsea stood frozen, watching the rats dance. These were the G-2 rats in her office rather than Dr. Synd's G-1s. The action was just as Wanda had described: Both rats put down the same foot, at the same time, moving in a rhythmic circle, counter-clockwise.

Her experience watching them, however, was nothing like Wanda's. There was no nausea, no desperate fight-or-flight response. Being present as these perfect unions of heavenly inspiration and corporate flesh performed this elegant display was the most rapturous experience of Chelsea's entire life. The rats did seem to connect with her mind, but the sensation was one of pleasure and relaxation. The longer she watched them the more open she became to the feeling, which was like float-ing downward in an endless spiral of warmth and enjoyment. Something in their motion made her feel like the yoke of man-agement responsibility was being lifted away, leaving her with the peace that came from knowing she was doing exactly what she was supposed to do.

She suddenly became aware that the rats were again going about their business in the cage, no longer dancing or paying any attention to her. Checking her EI's clock, she realized she'd been standing in front of their cage for more than twenty minutes. She had a vague recollection of having just fed them, but that wasn't possible, surely. Their next ration wasn't due for hours. There had been something different about the rats today, something she had thought worthy of reporting to Dr. Donova, but she couldn't remember it now.

Outside Alfred's Warehouse

Furius had been watching most of the night. Alfred wouldn't have left his building unguarded if he had any henchmen left at all. At no point had he seen any light coming from inside, but this place was short of resources and even powerful criminals would conserve what they could. It was also possible that there were lamps lit in an interior room.

A lone man emerged from the warehouse and stumbled toward the street, leaving the door wide open. Furius expected someone from inside to come and close it, but nobody did. Based on the man's shape and size he might have been the first one Furius had dosed with Pink Shit during his escape, though in the dark it was anyone's guess. Could the man have been unconscious in there the whole time?

Whoever it was seemed lost, looking around every corner and making seemingly aimless strides first in one direction and then another. Could this be his first legionary? This fellow showed signs of the disorientation involved with the process of coming over.

Then again, this was a place where disorienting drugs were common. This one might be on any of a hundred drugs, some of which B's memories said caused paranoia and blind violence.

Perhaps the henchman was just drunk, still able to draw his gun. Still able, even, to remember Furius.

Or maybe he wasn't even a henchman. Maybe this guy had just ripped off the warehouse, as Furius himself intended to do.

He hadn't been carrying lab equipment, so the means of Pink Shit production were likely still inside.

Alfred's warehouse was a trove of drugs and guns that was sure to draw looters, though, whether or not this guy had been one, and the next might not come alone. If the place really was empty right now, he had to get in and out before anyone else showed up.

The man seemed to settle on a street, wandering off without looking back. Furius pivoted his head back and forth from the man to the open warehouse door.

He had to get the Pink Shit. There were too many risks in confronting the man, and the potential cost of forgoing this opportunity to get inside the warehouse was too high. Gritting his teeth, Furius charged the door.

B's memories showed Alfred had commanded five or six henchmen at one time, which meant there could still be one or two here. Their weapons made them dangerous, but few men in this place had been forged in true battle. They did not know what it was to watch an opponent's eyes as a gladius point erupted through the back of his skull and knocked his helmet forward. The new warfare of this place was just blasting and hiding.

Furius slipped quickly through the door, with one gun in his hand and another tucked in his belt for easy access. B's memories told him he needed both hands to steady his aim. He heard no sounds inside at all. The door still hung open, leaving an angular shape of hazy moonlight on the floor.

His eyes adjusted to the shadowy interior. Furius was an easy target in this large and open space, especially this close to the light coming through the doorframe. He dove to a different spot, darker and farther along the wall. No shots sounded. Standing, he made his way around, feeling along with his empty hand in the darkest spots, and ensured that the warehouse was truly unoccupied.

From the loading area Furius spotted a large interior window high above him. A set of stairs led up to the door next to it. It was an office, from which the entire warehouse could be surveilled. Or fired upon.

He climbed the stairs as quietly as he could. This door was locked.

He had keys. Mr. B's memories helped him understand the way they worked. He tried one after another until at last the lock turned. He swung the door open and jumped aside, ducking, expecting gunfire. Instead, the room was so silent he could hear the grit he'd stirred up, as it settled down onto a plastic sheet beneath the landing.

The office was dark, illuminated only by light from the warehouse, which itself came from the one bright spot on the floor and a few little windows at the edges of the roof. B's memories indicated there was a good chance of electric light, and Furius found the switch.

It was an office and bedroom, with a large antique desk set back from the window and a bed in the corner big enough to host an orgy. Next to the desk sat a man-sized safe that probably held drugs, cash and weapons, but B's knowledge of such things told him there was little chance of opening it. He tried the handle anyway, finding it secured. It was a combination lock and there was no way to use a key. Across the foot of the bed was a dingy red throw that had probably been a bedspread for a smaller mattress. On a small stand next to the bed he identified a pair of handcuffs.

Taking the red fabric over one shoulder, he brought both ends around his neck and fastened them on the other side by forcing the handcuff tabs through the fabric. Looking and feeling more properly Roman, he descended the stairs again.

Corner of 6th and G, the Zone

Wanda had hoped that the streets would be abandoned so early in the morning. Instead, there were just as many people shuffling around as ever. Nobody here had anything else to do.

Even if it happens again, I survived, didn't I?

Her mind struggled with the idea.

What exactly was it that I survived?

It could be that the locals were especially aggressive because everyone sent the newly Departed here looking for the Horde.

There was nothing here except the unfriendly people and that horrible smell. Why would people keep sending her to this same corner when there was nothing here? Maybe the key was getting away from these predators at the corner; the Horde was probably just up some nearby street.

Her EI still showed a signal here, which was strange since there was apparently no industry or commerce of any kind to be found. Why an open access point here, in the middle of all this rubble and decay? She supposed it didn't matter much. There was still the corporate firewall, locking Wanda away from everyone she had known.

She straightened her spine and inhaled, gagging on the stench, and then strode down G Street again. This time she paid attention to the people on the street. On both sides, at least one bystander stared blatantly at her while at least one other went running off. Within minutes a crowd had appeared, with more people popping up out of nowhere with every step she took. At about the same point she'd reached last time, maybe half a block in, a woman approached.

"Hello, friend!" the unsmiling woman said, standing directly in front of her at an uncomfortably close distance. Her eyes were strangely wide open and her hands were held tensely apart, as if waiting for a pass in a Traverball game. Like that of the other accoster from the last time Wanda had been here, this woman's voice was disturbingly quiet and intense. "Where are you headed?"

"Just…this way," Wanda said.

"Why this way?" the woman asked. "Why not some other way? Is there someone you're looking for?"

"I…I'm just going to see some friends, way down past here."

"What friends? Who?"

"Nobody you'd know," Wanda said, stepping sideways to get around her.

The woman stepped sideways and backwards at the same time, keeping so little distance between Wanda's face and her own that Wanda felt the woman's every breath. "Try me."

Wanda stopped moving and met her gaze. "I'm just walking here. Leave me alone."

"You're not just walking. Not here. Tell me who you're looking for."

Wanda looked around. There were more people on the walkways than before. The street was a tunnel of faces.

Every cell in Wanda's body wanted to turn and run, back to 6th and as far beyond as she could go, to leave this weird, horrible place and this crazy woman and all these bums behind. But the Horde was home, the only hope for dispossessed people like Wanda. She didn't know how or why -- maybe it was only through strength in numbers -- but somehow, finding the Horde of the Departed enabled former corporates to survive, if only for a little while. Clearly she would never endure on her own in any other part of the Zone. From the stories she'd heard, living among the Hordesmen might be a fate worse than death, but she may as well try it. There would always be time later to die.

"I will not be intimidated," Wanda said, trying again to get past the woman.

"You don't know what intimidation is."

Wanda took another step to the left and forward and found herself matched once more by the woman moving backward. She lunged to the right, but the woman blocked her again. Finally Wanda shoved her and began running down G as fast as she was able. The woman stumbled back and pointed a finger as Wanda passed, shouting in the loudest voice Wanda had ever heard:

"ALL STAND AGAINST YOU!"

Instantly, every person within earshot pointed at Wanda and repeated the sentence. The resulting roar stopped her in her tracks.

"ALL STAND AGAINST YOU!" They all stood frozen, pointing at her, as another wave sounded behind them. *"ALL STAND AGAINST YOU!"* It seemed to echo after that, further and

further back, but the sound was really the voices of unseen people on other streets, repeating the words. Finally, the sound died down as the wave reached the outer edges, ending with a haunting *"you! you! you!"* from different places as the last speakers finished.

Turning in a circle, Wanda found perhaps two hundred fingers aimed at her. The street was silent again. The woman appeared next to her, using that same quiet voice she had before. "You'd better give me some names, friend."

McGuillian Diner

Li'l Ed couldn't help questioning his choice of study group, in spite of what his father had said. It was embarrassing, even painful, watching a grown college man lose control over some waitress from this throwaway caste. Wasn't everyone struggling, every day, to avoid people like that, or at least to keep separate from their fates? Still, Li'l Ed's father had insisted that there was no problem with Sett's behavior. By definition, then, there was no problem. Questioning a superior's judgment was wrong—was *evil*, even. Doubt cripples any organization.

There was no debating that the waitresses here were attractive. Li'l Ed's eyes followed one of them, her pink skirt hugging the curve of her tight little bottom as she swished away.

Yet here he was, shaky and uncomfortable at the diner with his study group again. His worries had potential to erode group harmony and success, but what could he do? The others didn't seem to understand how serious it all was.

"People say the new Departed don't last long," Li'l Ed said. Maybe it would help his classmates to remember that the point of school was survival. "The others in the Horde call them 'fresh meat.' They're all starving, anyway—I bet they really do eat the new ones."

Matt Ricker and his friends came into the diner. Like Sett, Matt was from a family that owned its own company. Like Sett, Matt often behaved in strange and wild ways.

Stop it. The matter has been decided. Sett's behavior is normal!

Li'l Ed and his friends sat straighter, demonstrating due respect for the Upperclassmen who had immediately taken notice of them upon entering. There were other Upperclassmen in the place; in fact nearly every seat here at this time of day was taken by a Fisher student who outranked them, but none of the others commanded this level of deference. Even Sett, with his own family's sovereign corporation, was nothing compared to Ricker, whose company had bought him future command as Chief Executive Officer of his own subsidiary. Talking to Matt Ricker was essentially the same as talking to an active CEO!

Li'l Ed's heart beat faster. Matt Ricker himself was standing next to their table. "Hello, Firstyears," he said.

"Hello, Upperclassmen," the three boys said in unison.

They zeroed in on Sett. He was the eldest and thus the de facto leader of the study group, but how had they known that?

Just good intelligence, that's how. Matt Ricker knows everything about the company because it's his job, already, to know.

After a bit of hazing to remind the Firstyears that they were subject to hierarchy and had better watch themselves, Ricker took the table from them to punctuate the lesson. Li'l Ed snatched up his drink and scurried away. He couldn't wait to tell his father that he had been face to face with *Matt Ricker himself!*

They settled in at another table. "I'm sorry I brought up the fifteen percent again, friends," Li'l Ed said. "We all know the situation. I need to learn to face it as gracefully as you, focus on my work and my duty instead of fretting over what could happen." The others muttered and nodded.

The Upperclassmen at their old table were now handling some waitress roughly. This was probably the kind of situation Li'l Ed's father had assumed was going on with Sett, but watching this would never have worried Li'l Ed. There was a clear hierarchy of purpose between the Upperclassmen masters and the lowly servant girl. What Sett did was more desperate and personal, more like trying to be her boyfriend. Even now he sat with his eyes locked on his favorite waitress, and not just on the flashes of white panties from beneath her short pink skirt.

The old man who ran the diner came out and bothered the Upperclassmen. Li'l Ed knew these people had no manners generally, but did the man truly not know any better than to harass someone like Ricker? They ignored the old codger, of course, but he still should have known his place.

The Upperclassmen let the waitress go and focused their attention on some drunken bum, smacking him around a bit, which Li'l Ed had already been thinking was necessary. Certainly, he'd know better after they taught him some manners. Why had nobody stood up to him before, the way he flaunted his filth and offended decent people in a corporate establishment like this? The upper class was constantly under attack from obnoxious agitators, but now these Upperclassmen were taking the fight back to them.

Sett's waitress came charging over toward Ricker. Sett would finally see how annoying and even dangerous these types could be. What was this girl thinking, challenging someone of Ricker's status? Surely Sett would see—

The waitress assisted the bum back to his feet. Ricker, understandably insulted by the interference, grabbed her and tried to instruct her in proper etiquette.

She kicked him!

The crazy waitress was trying to start class warfare, spitefully attacking her betters this way. The other two Upperclassmen grabbed her and roughed her up a bit. Ricker regained his composure and rejoined the struggle, grabbing the little bitch by the throat. She—*she smacked Matt Ricker in the face with her palm!*

He slugged her hard and she went down.

Finally!

Sett suddenly launched himself at Ricker and tried to wrap an arm around his neck. Li'l Ed's mouth hung open in horror. Ricker easily beat Sett about the body and head, putting him down to the floor almost immediately.

It didn't matter. The damage was done. Sett had, in one brief moment of insanity, doomed Li'l Ed's entire career, and consequently, almost certainly, his life.

Near the Corner of 6th and G, the Zone

Wanda blinked, focusing internally toward the list Jeremy had flagged for her in her last moments as an Amelix employee. Maybe a name from Jeremy's page would satisfy these people, whose fingers remained pointed at her as she began to read down the long columns.

She went on, reading name after name out loud. Not a single one brought even the slightest reaction. "Adam Kirton? Natalia Kopley?"

She stopped. Her eyes welled with tears. Her throat felt as if a sob had lodged in it, blocking all her words. Finally, she managed in a quiet voice: "Alma Traxler?"

Her grandmother's name.

Silence.

She cleared her throat and tried it again, louder this time. "Alma Traxler!"

The sob broke loose for a moment and then she recovered, reading on.

The woman who had accosted her stood watching a cluster of people behind Wanda, evidently looking for a response to any of the names. Quick glances revealed that they, like the first woman, had lowered their arms, though the rest of the crowd remained pointing.

"Judee Bayar?" she asked. "Berne Komena? Vanessa Reed?" She reached the bottom and stopped, glancing nervously around at the wall of accusing fingers. The woman in front of her did not change her expression, but her eyes flicked behind Wanda.

"What was the one you just said? Judee someone?" she asked.

Wanda found it again. "Judee Bayar?"

The woman looked past Wanda again and then gestured to someone. "Stand on guard," she said.

"Stand on guard," the closest people repeated. Those behind them repeated it again, and the words echoed off into the distance. The fingers lowered but the crowd remained, staring.

McGuillian Diner

Li'l Ed felt numb as he watched the fight. Ricker had a knife now. He cut the waitress whore and she went down again.

She sprung up in a sneak attack and cut him with a broken plate.

She cut his throat!

The thought seemed to have been screamed at Li'l Ed from some great distance. This was a terrible offence. A stupid waitress had seriously injured someone who was not only one of her own superiors, but one of Li'l Ed's own superiors!

Though Li'l Ed supposed his own status was lost, now. Since Sett had just ruined their careers, Li'l Ed and the waitress would likely be considered part of the same class.

No! I won't let that happen. There is no life without the company, and I will serve it even from the Brain Trust. I will fix this. I will find a way.

Li'l Ed stared blankly, trying to process what he was witnessing. The girl collapsed. Sett appeared next to her, helping her up again.

Li'l Ed willed his legs to make him stand, to conquer the shock that had taken him over. If he fought Sett now, he could demonstrate that he hadn't ever been a part of this. He just had to stand up now and kick Sett's legs out from under him. Instead he stayed frozen in his seat. Sett picked up Ricker's knife and *threatened the Upperclassmen with it!* Li'l Ed's head felt like it was floating away from his body. He nearly vomited.

"Can anyone help?" Sett asked, scanning the room. Li'l Ed averted his eyes, ashamed he hadn't been brave enough to stop this craziness. Only the bum came forward. He helped Sett and the girl out of the diner.

Jack shook his head, wide-eyed. "What was that? What did we just see?"

"Our friend just sacrificed us," Li'l Ed said. "For nothing."

6

W anda was guided by five people, two of them with fingers digging into her shoulders, shoving her roughly
this way and that, through so many convoluted turns she lost
track of where she was relative to the intersection of 6th and G.

She now found herself in an unlikely place: an old strip
mall, one with glass still in the windows and bright, fluorescent
electric lights inside. Three of her guides stayed outside and
two escorted her in through one of the many unbroken glass
exterior doors. They spoke at a normal speaking volume but
gave the impression of shouting.

"Judee Bayar!" they called.

Wanda realized the cavernous room was full of beds. Some
people had longneck bottles hanging above them, sealed with
plastic and wax, with tubes coming down and connecting to arms.

A hospital!

A woman who had been tending a patient in the corner
stood up and made a kind of bowing motion with her knees
together and her hands on her thighs. The guides brought
Wanda toward her and the woman took several quick steps to
shorten the trip for them.

"New arrival," one of the guides said, speaking in the same
creepily quiet voice as had been used by the Horde members

who'd challenged her. They released her and turned, exiting the building again without a look back.

"Hi," whispered the woman. Her voice seemed slightly less creepy than those of the others who had spoken. "Where did you work?"

"Amelix," Wanda said. Her voice betrayed her anxiety.

The woman nodded. "I'm Judee. Come with me." She headed toward a door off to the side, almost running.

Wanda followed as quickly as she could, given her level of astonishment and terror. They went through some swinging doors into what might once have been a storeroom but now contained surgical equipment. "It's a bit dark in here, but the light can only be used when there's a surgery. I think we can see each other well enough," Judee said. Her smile was clearly forced, appearing almost as if she were holding it in place with her fingers. She put a palm on Wanda's shoulder, too stiffly to be comforting. "I can see you're feeling confused and stressed." Wanda nodded. "What's your name?"

"Wanda," she said, proud that she'd managed to speak without vomiting.

"I'm sure you've figured out that names are a big deal around here," Judee said. "Someone gave you a list when you left Amelix, obviously. I don't know why they do that, but they always do. Every department in every organization keeps a list of its own Departed."

Wanda would never get used to thinking of herself that way, as Departed.

"Amelix, in the labs, right?" Judee asked. Wanda nodded. "Just like me. Coach V has been taking on women for this role from our labs since the beginning. We get men, too, but Coach is even harder on them and most either leave right away or kill themselves. Of course, some of them just die. That's a pretty common thing, here, just plain dying." Judee gestured out toward all the patients, then rubbed her eyes.

"Coach says our science backgrounds make us better at following her orders." She shrugged, looking surprisingly defeated. "Good thing someone gave you that list, in any case," Judee said. "That's how the Horde screens people who wander up. If you don't have a connection to at least one person here, we can't be sure you worked in the CBD, and if you didn't work in the CBD, you're not one of us." Judee's eyes locked on Wanda's. "If a name on your list matches someone who is still alive here, that person becomes your mentor, teaching you how to survive. You apprentice under them to learn whatever job they have."

Someone who is still alive here. Judee was at the bottom. The entire list is now dead, except for her.

Wanda couldn't bring herself to say anything at all.

"You'll work here with me," Judee said. "I'm your mentor and your boss. It's like a job and marriage. You do everything I tell you, always, without question, right away, just like I did for my mentor when she was still alive. Of course I am required to do the same for our boss, Coach V. You'll meet her soon, Coach V. She's … mean. And she's strong, and incredibly demanding and…well, I guess it's obvious you'll have to do everything she says, too. That'll be a lot. But with you joining us, that makes it easier for everyone. There are five of us: myself, Sula, Chi Sun, and Piyumi, plus you now, Wanda. You'll get to know us." She closed her eyes and exhaled sharply, seeming to fake a laugh. "You'll get to know us more intimately than you can possibly imagine, she'll make sure of that." Her eyes opened again. "We're all women, of course. You'll know why soon enough."

"So…I'm going to be a nurse?" Wanda asked. She recognized the incredulousness in her voice but was powerless to change it. At least the volume was as low as everyone else spoke around here. "In this hospital?"

Judee's smile was so sad Wanda felt her own eyes welling up as much as Judee's. "Don't ask questions. It's easier if you just accept. Asking questions here is bad, okay? Don't ever, ever do it again. But no, dear. You're a slave. Your choice, now and for the rest of your life, will either be to do what you're told, or die. She won't kill you, but if you displease her she'll kick you out of here." She sniffed forcefully as if to bolster herself. "No job means you're out of the Horde, just like it meant you were out of the CBD. But the good news is that while *we* are part of the Horde, Coach isn't. We live right on the edge of the territory because Coach insists upon treating everyone who comes in the door. Even so, about eighty percent of our patients come from the Horde. You'll meet so many people working here. Because our job is medicine, we need to see the body in order to treat it, and we need to talk with people to learn what's wrong with them. Life in the Horde gets lonely, as you can imagine. Everyone stays silent so the special words can work; it's like an alarm, and they all have to be ready to hear it and respond. Here, lots of people come in and out, usually thrilled to talk to you…or anyone." She gave a tight smile that quickly melted into expressionlessness. She blinked, steeled herself, and smiled again.

"Because we're outside the regular group and we work together to treat Hordesmen, our rules are looser than theirs," Judee said. "We can flush waste, for example, instead of carting it to the edge of the territory to scare away those who might wander in except for the smell. Or at least we *could* flush waste if we didn't use everything coming out of every patient. Everything can be of use in the labs, like for petri dish media or extracts of various chemicals. Anyway, we can talk to each other, which is wonderful, though it can only be about work, and we still have to use the quietest functional voice."

She paused again and her face went blank. Wanda suspected that Judee's habitual state was expressionless and empty. "Also, we are able to mind our tasks by ourselves without being subject to constant monitoring by everyone around us." She swallowed. "That's a big one." Her head nodded slowly. "And we're not obligated to swarm."

Wanda blinked, and even that action felt like it was in slow motion. "Swarm?"

"The Horde of the Departed exists for security," Judee said. "We're all safer inside than we would have been outside. None of us are the kind who can make it on our own out here, so we have to watch each other's backs. For that, we pay a price. The way we survive is by using our only resource: human beings who are predisposed to cooperate and acknowledge a hierarchical structure. You saw them use the special words, right? Don't say them, ever. Using those special words when we're not being invaded will bring the same fate upon you that they would upon an invader. But you saw what happens, right? I heard it right before you showed up. Did you try to push past your questioner?"

Wanda nodded.

"And after the words and finger pointing, you probably stopped and listed names, right? That's also what most do. If you hadn't, all those who'd been pointing fingers would have run to you and beaten you to death. Most of the time when that happens it's just some poor fool who wandered into the wrong place, but occasionally it's a group of Fiends with machine guns. When it's Fiends, two-thirds of that first wave can get cut down. But others do reach the invaders and pummel them, and the ones who pointed fingers from farther back come running up to take the place of anyone who already rushed forward. At the physical center of the Horde are those with the most experience here, and all the weapons the Horde has collected. As swarms occur, weapons are accumulated, and now some of the Horde is armed. For most, the swarm is the most important duty there is here, and failure to participate brings an automatic death by swarm. But we don't have to do that here at the clinic, because we belong to Coach V."

Wanda looked away, facing the floor but focused on nothing. "We *belong* ... "

Judee's strong fingers gripped Wanda's chin, tilting it up again. "We belong to Coach V. Never forget that. Coach V's will is our will, and that is the way it is. She'll tell you herself, but you might as well know what she believes: She's responsible for every life here, and that means she needs complete control. When mistakes are made, people die. It's better to let her be responsible."

Judee's smile was so sad Wanda began sobbing. "Just remember, Wanda," she said, patting her gently on the back. "It's better than what they call life inside the Horde proper." Judee placed her fingers against her forehead as if trying to massage away a headache, her Golden knuckles whitening as she pressed.

"You'll work with patients," Judee said. "But a lot of what you do initially will be back there, in the lab and storeroom." She gestured to a small door at the back of the room with a dim light showing underneath it. "We make almost everything we use. There are a dozen strains of modified bacteria we use to produce human antibodies, though by far the one we use most is the syphilis one. We're the biggest manufacturer of sterilized syphilis antibodies in the Zone. You'll be turning blood and stool samples into nutrient suspensions for some of the antibody strains, as well as doing everything that's required to support the drug-producing strains, distilling sterile water from urine and collecting urea from the remaining solids, sterilizing instruments, cataloguing stocks. Pretty much all the behind-the-scenes stuff that keeps this place running, is what you'll start off with."

At least some of those activities sounded like the kinds of work Wanda had been trained for in her long career as an Amelix lab tech. Maybe she could find a way to fit in here, after all.

"I'm going to introduce you to Coach V now, and to the rest of the team when it's appropriate," Judee said.

"But... I ... I don't understand," Wanda said. "What about—"

Judee slapped her so hard Wanda nearly lost her balance. She expected Judee's eyes to show anger, but instead they were wide in terror. Her body was stiff. "She'll punish me! You can't go behaving like that, questioning what you're told. I'm your mentor and she'll punish me as well as you." The shaking in Judee's hands turned into a full-body shudder, and then she slapped Wanda five more times, fast and hard. "Questions show a deficit of respect for Coach! If Coach wants us to know something, she will tell us. Asking questions is trying to substitute our judgment for hers. Just shut up and do as you're told, or else run away and hope they don't think you've already seen enough to be dangerous. Don't ask questions. Do you understand?"

Both women stood frozen a moment. Wanda's face stung and throbbed, and her eyes burned, flooded with tears. "Yes. I understand."

Judee straightened. "Now. You saw me bow before. Watch again. This is what you'll do when you meet her." Judee's knees came together and she placed her hands on her thighs, curling her head toward the floor. "You try."

After a few practice bows Judee led her back out through the doors and across the room to where a wiry woman with shoulder-length gray hair and thin metal-framed glasses was writing with a brush across a rough-hewn piece of stiff plastic. She let them wait a moment as she finished writing and hung the plastic on a hook at the foot of the bed.

"Coach V," Judee said. "This is Wanda, my apprentice."

Wanda put her knees together and bowed as the woman looked her up and down. "We have little to go around as it is," Coach V said. "Turn her out. What she would eat would be better spent on my patients."

"Coach, ma'am," Judee said. "She called me by name. It is a Horde rule, Ma'am, one of the most fundamental rules we have, as I'm sure you are aware, Ma'am."

The woman, Coach V, came to Wanda, grabbing her by the chin and crotch. "I don't want you here, but the Horde protects this clinic so I have to let you in," she said. "Understand this: My girls do what they're told. I am responsible for every life here and I will tolerate no deviations from perfect obedience. I will have full rights to every part of you: your labor, your body, your mind, your soul. I will watch you, make you watch my other girls for me, and use you in every possible way. I will educate you when education is appropriate to your duties, guide you in the provision of care, teach you how to satisfy me, and correct you when you fail me. I will drug you, interrogate you, inspect you, and analyze the composition of your blood, stool, and urine. You will have weekly confessionals with me where you will inform me under the influence of bactrohypnotic serum about every transgression. You will have no privacy, no rights, and no dignity. If you choose to stay, you admit you are dead without me and agree to exist solely as an extension of my will, as payment for saving your life.

"Most Hordesmen don't make it past about four months, while I tend to keep my girls for nearly a year. Without a job you're out of the Horde, and your life expectancy will be measured in hours. Only out of obligation am I offering you this job opportunity, and it's the last you'll ever get. The choice is yours."

Wanda surprised herself with her immediate answer. "I want to stay here with you, Ma'am." She bowed again as she had been taught.

Coach puffed up to say something but another woman had approached, Golden with auburn hair, bowing in the same way and freezing like that until Coach acknowledged her. "What is it, Chi Sun?"

"The Directorate, Ma'am," the woman said. Though her voice was as quiet as anyone's around here, it shook with a chilling desperation.

Coach turned abruptly to look at the door but there was nobody there. "How far away?"

"All seven are on the lot, ma'am.

Coach cursed, looking out across what had been the strip mall's parking lot, and then walked toward the door with her hands on her hips. Chi Sun followed her, one step behind.

"Let's find you a project," Judee said, leading Wanda away toward a back corner. She gestured to a patient whose head was wrapped with a bloody red bandage. He was relatively young and his face had a gentle, boyish quality. Sprouting just over the bandage was apparently well-groomed, short brown hair.

"How many of yours do we have today?" Judee asked the man.

"Not mine," he said. His was the most natural smile Wanda had seen in the Zone. "Each of us belongs only to the One."

"Wanda, so far we've triaged Porter, here, about third in terms of need for immediate attention. It's a head wound, but he seems able to walk and talk. See what information you can get from him that will be helpful when Coach sees him."

Judee shuffled away again. Standing upright among so many who were lying in beds made Wanda feel conspicuous and exposed. She sat on the edge of the bed next to Porter's, lowering herself gingerly onto the mattress so as not to disturb its unconscious occupant.

"You're new here," he said. He kept looking past her, his eyes darting around the room. She supposed that was common behavior in people of this area, given how traumatic life was here in the Zone.

"So... you're Porter," she said. There was nothing to write on so apparently she was expected to remember all of it. "How did you get hurt?"

"We were attacked by a small street gang. Just a fight. Hit with a stick. How long ago did you Depart?"

She paused, shocked by the question. It seemed so personal, so invasive, to be asked about the moment when her company had decided she was a disgrace and ended her life. It was probably unwise to answer, anyway.

"Let's see," she said. "Head wound." She tried to think of what might be a good check for brain damage. "Here. Grab my hands and pull them. I want to see whether you're able to control your limbs on both sides."

"No," he said. He had a hand tucked under a blanket in his lap. She was pretty sure it had the shape of a gun. Most Zone people who had guns probably had a hard time letting go of them.

"I can't help you if—"

"Ask me something else."

"Okay. How's your vision?" His eyes had normal-sized pupils and no apparent broken blood vessels.

"I see fine. I see that you're brand new here, for example. I never thought I'd be nostalgic for that time, fresh from the company, but life here has a way of evoking strange feelings."

At least he was talking. Perhaps by chatting a bit she could get him to participate a bit better in his own care. "How..." she started. She couldn't even make herself talk about *his* Departure, let alone her own. Her insides clenched at the thought, making it impossible to speak. "How long have you been part of the Horde?" she managed finally.

"I used to be part of the Horde, but I'm not anymore. Our group is separate. We're something new."

The Federal Administration Building

"Agent Daiss reporting, Instructor Samuelson, sir," Daiss said from outside the door.

"Enter, Brother Daiss," came the voice.

"Thank you, sir," Daiss said. "It is always an honor to see you, sir." In a world with so much gratuitous ass kissing, Daiss was happy to mean it this time. Instructor Samuelson was the finest Federal Agent ever to have lived, the one who truly justified the layman's parlance referring to their kind as Federal Angels.

"Sit down, Brother Daiss," Samuelson said, gesturing to a chair. "I have a new assignment for you." His eyes focused on the air between them as he read something via his EI. "Clayton Ricker's son has been killed. Now I know what you're probably thinking, and no, it doesn't appear to be politically or economically motivated. We've found no link to any legitimate corporate interest as a perpetrator, so this case remains under Federal jurisdiction. A waitress and some bum got uppity in a corporate diner. The waitress was the first to become violent, and then some student from Fisher Academy got involved ... we suspect he may have had some grudge against Ricker."

"Thank you for telling me, Instructor," Daiss said. "But there are no corporate diners in the Zone. Why would Task Force Zeta be interested in this case, sir? Outside the Zone is outside our focus area, isn't it, sir?"

"I volunteered you for this one," Samuelson said. "A waitress and a bum, so obviously they're from the Zone, which is certainly our focus area. But more importantly, it's Clayton Ricker's son, dead. It is crucial that you do everything to show him we're working on the case around the clock and expending all available resources."

"Yes, sir. Though I am surprised at this. Task Force Zeta has never strived to impress ordinary businessmen before, even at Ricker's level. Don't we usually let other Agents do the bowing and scraping to those people, sir?"

"If the point was to keep him happy, then yes. But in this case it's something quite different. We need Clayton Ricker, and everyone else, to believe he's getting special treatment because of who he is. What's material to us is the impression we give about our work, not his actual satisfaction with it. Then when he and the rest of the public have seen that the Zone forbids justice even to the likes of him, they will clamor to seal off its dangers."

"Brilliant, sir! And so what level of involvement shall I have?"

"Well, full involvement, of course. You will do everything you can to investigate the case, duty-bound as you are. And eventually you'll locate the waitress and bring her in, unless she ends up dead from the Zone's various hazards first. But you needn't be terribly efficient about it. And if she does end up dead, perhaps we'll keep that information to ourselves a while and let the tension remain high. This investigation will allow us to begin addressing other issues as we gradually claim total jurisdiction over the Zone."

"Yes, sir. I understand, sir."

Coach V's Clinic

"Okay," Wanda said. "I guess I got the information they needed. I should probably find someone to assign me a new job."

"Could you stay with me a bit longer, please?" he asked. "I want to keep talking to make sure my brain is okay."

Wanda glanced around the clinic. "I don't know what I'm supposed to do. They haven't given me another assignment but maybe I'm supposed to ask for one. I don't want to get in trouble."

"You won't. I promise."

"I don't know that I can afford to trust your judgment in this case. From what I've seen it's quite strict here." Wanda glanced over her shoulder toward the storeroom, where Coach was meeting with the Directorate. "I don't know what's going on in there now, but it looks serious."

"I'll tell you what's going on there," he said, leaning closer. His voice became a legitimate whisper, rather than the low but more forceful speaking tone these people used generally. "The Directorate controls the Horde, and the Horde controls this whole area. They used to control *me*. I made it into some of the inner circles, and they trusted me enough to make me kill for them. I ended up here in the clinic a few days ago, after getting shot on a mission to poison a water supply." He pulled his shirt collar away, revealing a bandaged shoulder. "The Directorate has always wanted control of this clinic, but Coach has made it clear that she won't treat anyone if she can't treat everyone. They've tried many times to convince her otherwise, and I'm sure they're running out of patience. This clinic is a strategic asset they want to control completely."

"A strategic asset?" Wanda asked. Her own voice had dropped to a whisper, too. It was uncomfortable speaking in a room with so many silent people all around, especially when she remembered Judee's desperate, slapping warning. If she were to survive here at all, though, she needed to understand this world.

"A strategic asset is something that helps win wars, like a port or a fortress."

"There's a war?"

"A war has been brewing for a long time. There have been skirmishes between the Horde and the Fiends, but it hasn't erupted into more than that because the Horde has so little the Fiends want. The Fiend army, called the New Union, preferred to enslave the wild people on their side of the Zone because they were better fighters than the Horde's CBD rejects. Now they've claimed all the wild types, and there's been some evidence that they're starting to capture Hordesmen. Controlled with drugs and fear, the captives become slave soldiers for the New Union. They're not in any hurry, I think because it takes time to get the new ones brainwashed and addicted, but once the Fiends decide to make a real push on this territory, the Horde will fall in a matter of days."

"I just encountered the Horde, not even an hour ago," Wanda said. "It was an overwhelming experience."

"The Horde is scary, that's true. Nothing like the Fiends, though. I was with the Horde for nearly two years. Lots of us

Saved come from it. There were a dozen of us in here when the One Who Returned appeared, and we all just stopped being Horde right then. We've been following him since."

"Since you were here getting that shoulder patched a few days ago?"

Porter nodded.

"You met someone here and just followed him out?" Wanda asked. "I can see how the idea of leaving the Horde has some appeal, especially if what you said about the Fiends is true, but how did you suddenly decide to abandon the only form of security available? The Zone is a dangerous place."

"When you meet the One, it'll be obvious why I chose this path. You'll see what we all saw that day: He has come to save us from the misery that is life here. Every day more come to join us, mostly from the Horde."

"So you started with twelve, a few days ago, and now you have, what, like thirty?"

"Nine hundred seventy something, as of last night. Probably many more now."

Wanda gaped.

"It's surprising, I know," he said. "But there are several reasons for it. Think about how many Zone people would have joined the Horde if they could," he said. "Every day the Fiends get a little more dangerous, a little more brutal. Regular Zone people live all alone out there. The Horde, with its thousands of Hordesmen, provides protection to former corporates, but even it is threatened now. We're different. We have a truly divine leader who promises salvation, and we welcome everyone who believes. The more who join, the more protection we're able to provide each other. Even those who have never seen him are coming to join us, and bringing family and friends."

A boy of maybe twelve came running up to Porter's bedside.

"United in faith we live," the boy said. It was strange to hear such formal words said with such a guttural Zone accent.

"United in faith we live," Porter replied.

"The other Disciples're ready," the kid said. "There's twenty-seven elite guard total, seventeen still standin' outside, so mus' be ten in here. Assault weapons an' body armor."

Porter laughed to himself. "Unbelievable," he said to Wanda. "The entire Directorate came to this place with not even thirty guards between them. You can see they've only had to worry about border skirmishes with a few Fiends now and again. Cockiness like that will get them in trouble, you'll see." Turning back to the boy, he said, "Tell the other Disciples to wait until they hear me."

The boy ran off.

The storeroom door opened and Coach V. appeared, holding it open and gesturing for the Directorate and guards to leave through it. "...not be intimidated!" she said. The Directorate stayed where they were.

Porter sprung up, making Wanda jump and slip off the edge of the bed, landing on the floor. Six patients sprang from their beds, aiming assault rifles into the still brightly lit operating room. From where she sat, Wanda could see one of the guards grabbing for his gun. Then all six attackers fired. Porter lunged toward the door, repeatedly firing a handgun.

The bandage lay on the bed where it had fallen off; there had been no head wound. Wanda could now hear the steady fire of automatic weapons outside.

Amelix Building, CBD

"Hello, Dr. Kessler," Keiko said.

"Hi, cutie," he said, looking her up and down. Her body curved nicely beneath her Corporate Green uniform. "Come on in."

"I guess our analysis of Eric Basali's writing may as well end now, sir, with Basali's suicide attempt today," she said. "There's no reason for us to determine wrongdoing if he's headed for mandatory reconditioning and a clean slate."

"No, no," he said. "Wrongdoing was only part of it. I've begun a new project for us, where you'll translate all his writing into those fundamental pillars of Accepted life you're so good at parsing out. It's powerful stuff you're producing, Keiko. When added to our supporting documentation for various regulations, that language will thoroughly discourage workers from questioning their applicability. We have an amazing opportunity to codify the moral and ethical basis for everything Amelix does. I think you'll be coming here for quite some time."

"That's wonderful, Dr. Kessler, sir," she said breathily. "But will Amelix allow such an investment of our time and energy?"

"Of course. Humanity itself is any modern organization's main raw input. Amelix is special among the corporations of today because as a biotech firm we still produce a high number of patented products, but it still holds true for us. Our most important business is processing raw personnel into a devoted workforce that exists solely to further the company's interest in every possible circumstance. This project has huge potential for streamlining that process, and I will make sure you are recognized for your contribution to it.

"Mmm. Thank you, sir. You're truly a gifted executive, Dr. Kessler, and I have so, so much to learn from you."

"Yes, you do. But tonight, we're going out. Let's visit a nasty little bar I know in the Zone."

"Oh, thank you, sir," Keiko gushed.

Kessler put his arm around her waist, escorting her out of the office and out of the building. His hand caressed her hip. They left the CBD on foot, through one of the gates that opened into the Zone's entertainment area. The smell of decay was still easily noticeable, but it seemed somehow more bearable than it was most days in the Zone. The gravel crunched under their shoes.

"Where are we going, sir, if I may ask?" Keiko said.

"It's a hidden bottle club called Lincoln's," he said. "Private. I'm a member there. It's safer than regular bars and we can have a room to ourselves."

"Welcome to the Roman Legions," a man wearing some kind of cloak or cape said as he passed, throwing a handful of powder into Kessler's face. Keiko screamed as Kessler coughed and choked and tried to wipe the stuff from his eyes.

Fisher University Campus

"I can't even tell you how glad I am that we have class together now!" Jack said. Li'l Ed wished he'd taken a different route. He pointedly looked away, at anything but Jack, and tried to increase the distance between them as they walked, hoping their interaction would be less obvious to observers. Jack kept pace and continued to talk. "People have stared at me in every class today. Nobody said anything about Sett or the waitress directly—they hardly said anything to me at all, actually—but they never seemed to look away."

"We can't sit together," Li'l Ed said. "If we separate, maybe they'll see our group that day as just a random gathering. Maybe they'll forgive us for having been there. It's unlikely but we have to do whatever we can."

"Come on, Li'l Ed!" Jack said. "I don't know how much more isolation I can take. If we sit together like always, it will be like we still have some status, some reason to be here."

"Precisely why we can't. If we act like we have no group, no status here at all, then we're not a threat. They can bully us and push us around, but in the end they will have no real reason to kick us out. If we seem to be a united front, though, a group with pride and a sense of belonging here on campus, they'll feel they have to destroy us right away."

"But they'll probably do that anyway," Jack said. "There will be some decision made, by the school and by the crowd. We know how the dynamic works. They'll probably decide we're out, no matter what we do."

"We have to try. A slight chance is better than none." Li'l Ed bounded up two stairs and then two more, causing Jack to fall a few steps behind. "Don't walk with me, Jack, and don't sit with me. Act like we're strangers who were caught in an awkward situation and now are trying to put it behind us. That's what we are."

Outside Dobo Protein Refinery

Furius sat leaning against a wall, appearing to be just another hopeless Zone inhabitant with no place to go and nothing to do. He'd been watching the closed refinery for about an hour. He supposed the red cloak around his shoulders might stand out a bit, but in this part of town, people had little choice but to wear whatever was available. His appearance didn't seem to strike anyone as unusual.

Collecting information about the Garbageman and his life had been surprisingly easy. The man had not been nearly careful enough, given the kind of work he did on the side and the number of people around here who hated his guts.

With the various deals Furius had done and the single-dose packages he'd exchanged for information, plus the random passersby he'd been dosing with fistfuls of Pink Shit on the street, he'd now put more than two hundred more doses into circulation. The new Roman army would soon rise to conquer this strange, desolate land.

According to its posted business hours this protein refinery was supposed to have opened hours ago. People had come carrying waste to turn in for payment, waited, and then left again. The Garbageman's continued absence made sense if he had been replaced by a Roman by now. Perhaps he was out searching for his superiors.

Or perhaps he is a superior.

Until now, Furius had assumed the army would consist of foot soldiers oath-bound to serve at his direction. It had not occurred to him that someone of higher rank might come through, a general or praetor with a clear plan of action. He was a bit surprised by his disappointment at the thought. Shouldn't he be happy to have a leader, someone to whom the blood would stick, someone who would be responsible for the carnage and misery the new campaign would bring?

Yes. Of course that will be better. My job will be as it always was, keeping discipline in the ranks and killing as I'm told. Let the generals make the decisions and carry the guilt.

If Furius remained the highest-ranking Roman in this territory, he would have to assume sole responsibility for advancing the Republic's interest here. It was his duty, and duty was everything to a soldier. Given the choice, he'd prefer to take orders and keep his mind clean, though.

A vision came to him: He stood in Charon's boat, regal and powerful in a general's armor crossing the underworld's River Styx. Then suddenly a thousand unseen hands grabbed him and threw him out of the boat and into the water.

Not water! Blood. Blood I have spilled!

It burned his flesh as if it were molten bronze. He sunk down into it, fast, burning, suffocating, and dissolving in it, yet he never died, never lost consciousness or moved on from it. In campaigns before, the *sacramentum* had protected Furius; the blood hadn't counted against him. This would have been his fate, had he been a general controlling those conflicts.

He shook his head and the River Styx faded away. Furius returned, shuddering, to the world of guns, drugs, and garbage.

Gods below, please let there be a general.

Dok's place

Kym Evans leaned woozily against Dok's office wall. It had taken her a few tries to lift herself off Mikk's floor, but finally she'd managed to change out of her stinking, blood-stiff clothes and head here. She had stumbled and shuffled along the street, stopping to rest and even sitting down on the gravel a few times, but now she'd made it here and everything would be okay. She was already feeling better, from just a single dose of bitter powder mixed into water. Dok was a great healer.

Some mother had brought in a boy with rotten teeth, and Dok was working on them now. He'd hypnotized the kid into feeling no pain.

A strange man sat next to Kym on the floor, bearded and dressed in rags even more torn up than hers. The harder she made herself look away from him, the harder he seemed to stare.

Another man trying to bully and control me!

Fed up, she turned to him, scowling.

"Hello, there," he said. "How are you feeling?" His gaze was flat and his voice was monotone, but it was a more pleasant exchange than she had expected, or, for that matter, had experienced in a long while.

"Better," she said, deflating. "Thanks." The man's eye was partially black and his lip was split and swollen. "Looks like you got some of what I got, huh?"

"Well worth it, I assure you," he said. "I was the first casualty in the General's war." He nodded toward the young girl with the long gash across her face. "She will end the kind of abuse you and I suffer in this society."

"Okay. Sure she will," Kym said.

"What we need is a leader to bring us together," he said. "To make us strong. The General's army has already begun to gather around her: The young student you saw before, for instance, and me. We're merely followers, but you can see she possesses the kind of true greatness that can bring together all the various elements of our society."

"Yeah, tough girl," Kym said. "Gonna take it all on, turn it around for us. Doesn't seem to be goin' so well just yet."

Crazy fuck.

"Actually, ma'am, it is. Think about your own experience and I bet you'll remember a time when you just didn't care what happened anymore, a time when your desire to fight was too strong for fear alone to stop you. Maybe you fought, or perhaps you refrained from fighting only because there was nothing to gain, but I'm sure you understand the feeling of power that comes from having nothing to lose."

"So what? Nothin' I do is gonna change anything."

"Of course you're right about that, ma'am," he said. "One's feeling of power is meaningless as long as she remains isolated. The General's power arises from her ability to inspire all those thousands and thousands of people who feel that way. *Individuals* with nothing to lose may fight a few small battles. *Groups* with nothing to lose, however, when rallied around the right leader, can become a revolution."

A teenager and her dirty hobo were going to take on the power structure, with its Feds, its guns, its Unnamed...

"Okay," she said. "Dok said I need rest. Nice talking with you." Kym closed her eyes.

"You still think as an individual," he said. She could feel him staring at her. "You see yourself alone, myself alone, even the General alone, and you see weakness. But coming together for a common goal can make us strong, and the General brings people together. Imagine joining us and gaining your own followers, people willing to support you. You might become an officer with us, maybe even the General's second-in-command, able to take the helm in her stead, perhaps eventually becoming a general yourself. I can see that you have true leadership ability, even when it is hidden by doubt, as now. I, for one, would be proud to follow you, ma'am." He slowly lifted himself off the floor. "Excuse me a moment, please, ma'am."

He went to talk to his *general*, giving her what was apparently some kind of warning, though cryptic and strange. The girl told him she'd consider whatever it was he was saying, and he bowed and sat back down.

He bowed?

Kym couldn't help thinking about it. An *army* of reasonable people who could truly support her and give her power to change things? In her mind she saw Mikk's sneer, the one his face always wore right before his first blows struck her, and then she heard her own voice commanding. The vision changed and a wave of people—*soldiers*—*justice!*—swept past her to annihilate him.

Even Mikk, with his gun, his physical strength, and his cruelty, was insignificant to a real army. What if Kym's weakness did stem from thinking she was alone and therefore had no power? Maybe this weird little bunch could change things, or maybe not. Probably not. Almost definitely not. But like the bum said, Kym had nothing to lose.

He was watching her again. She faced him, finding herself no longer disturbed by his blank stare. "I'm Kym," she said.

He bowed as he had done for the General. "It is very nice to meet you, Kym, ma'am. Perhaps one day we'll call you Colonel Kym, or even General Kym." He grinned slightly. Kym's bruised face ached as she clenched her jaw, suppressing a shiver. "And if you like, you may call me as others do. I am the Prophet."

Coach V's Clinic

After the gunfire had erupted outside the clinic yesterday there had been the predictable and terrifying Horde response, and then silence. Porter had gone out to speak to the mass of pointing fingers, and apparently he'd known enough of them personally to talk them out of a swarm. Many of the ones he'd spoken with had quit the Horde right then to join the Saved. Coach had growled that the clinic would go on as it always had, and now she and her "girls" were back at work, bustling between beds and triaging emergencies.

Wanda removed a bottle from the spiral of coat hanger wire that held it upside-down above a patient's bed. She checked the inked letter on the bottom. The sun was going down, making it harder to see the dark marker on the dark glass. This one read "Q," so she replaced it with another "Q."

The bottles were old longnecks that had once held beverages, but sealed with sterilized plastic putty, they functioned as IV bottles here.

"Q" was for Quanara, an Amelix patent that had now made it to the street. Wanda had learned about it in her lab tech training, but she'd never imagined she'd actually be holding a bottle of the stuff, let alone using it to treat patients. One of the sixth-generation engineered antibiotics, Quanara was mostly outdated and useless except against the deadly FLIEs bacteria it had been sold to combat. Amelix, always the world's most innovative company, had created and released the FLIEs strain, knowing that only Quanara could fight it. The monopoly had been a huge boost for the company economically as other organizations scrambled to license it, though Amelix soon found itself paying similar ransoms to other biotech companies who'd created their own lock-and-key diseases and cures.

The corporate class no longer used antibiotics. The drugs were too clumsy, and reliance upon them made corporations too vulnerable. Once the engineered antibacterial fungal strains had reached their twelfth generation, R&D had taken a new tack, producing a new generation of synthesizers that could test for specific pathogens and develop special hunter-killer antibodies for each one. Microbes mutated incredibly fast, especially when they were human pathogens in a world with seventeen billion people to attack, so companies now had entire departments of scientists and programmers whose sole function was to monitor and tweak the relationship between the synthesizers and all the targeted germs.

Wanda peered through the glass, hoping to gain a little insight into the situation outside. What was happening with the Saved and Horde? Would there be more shooting?

Nobody would count on Quanara to cure anything today. Coach undoubtedly added it to control contamination, as a prophylactic safety measure more than a treatment.

"Sister Wanda!" Sister Chi Sun called from the front of the room. Wanda dropped the empty bottle into her sterilization bin and scooted toward the area where they were admitting new patients. Her pace would have been a run, but one of the rules she'd learned here was that the girls were not allowed to take steps longer than a foot's length. Ostensibly it had to do with patient safety in the cramped space and the stirring up of germs. Wanda had noticed Coach observing her girls with a look of satisfaction as they minced around the place, though, and it was obvious that bullying and control were the main motivations for this constraint.

Sister Chi Sun handed her a thin dowel with a cardboard disc attached across one end. A spiral pattern on the disc would rotate when the dowel was rolled between palms.

"Show him this spiral and just keep quietly repeating to him that he needs to stare at it, that nothing matters but watching the spiral, okay?"

Wanda took the dowel and began rotating it, speaking softly. "It's okay. Just stare, right there at the center. Watch it go inward, down and down and down. And watch it come up, now, up and up and up, always turning. Which way does it seem to be going to you?"

"Look here, Chi Sun," Coach V. said, running two fingers in a light circle midway up the patient's calf. "See this indentation, the cavity beneath the skin?"

"Yes, Coach," Chi Sun said.

"Ruptured tendon," Coach said. "Let's get him into the operating room. If we were busy now we'd triage this down, but right now it's slow enough for us to address it. Wanda, help us move him."

"Yes, Coach," Wanda said.

Wanda moved the patient's hand to the dowel and got under his shoulder. "Your turn to work the spiral for yourself, now," she told him. "Just keep staring at it. Let yourself get lost in the pattern as it pulls all your pain away." Chi Sun put herself under the other side and together they lifted, half-dragging the man backwards to the room where Wanda had first spoken with Judee. The powerful light came on as they hoisted him to the table, helping him turn onto his stomach.

Wanda took the rod again. The patient lay with his head turned to the right, so she moved toward that end of the table and knelt down next to him. She held the spiral a short distance from his face, alternating from one hand to the other so she could keep it spinning in the same direction. "Stare at the center," she told the patient in a hushed, calm voice. "Is the spiral coming up, up, up, or going down, down, down?"

Coach and Chi Sun poured sodje onto the back of the man's leg, spreading it around with their hands. The alcohol was the best means of sterilization they had available in an environment like this, without soap or running water.

"Okay," Coach V. said. "See here? Look at the anklebone, and then see this slope in this direction and the curve in the other? In this case we need these muscles relaxed, so we're going to put one needle here, and the other up here on the other side, behind the knee. You see that?"

Wanda wished she could see, but the spiral was in the way. They were doing acupuncture, which she'd not yet been allowed to observe. Coach had made it clear Wanda was to learn only what Coach taught her, whenever Coach decided to teach it.

"This guy's Golden," Coach said. "So you can see where the ends of the snapped tendon are inside the flesh, from the borders of the dark red patch that formed on the skin, there. Now, I'm going to make an incis—"

"Stare into the spiral," Wanda said to the patient. He certainly didn't need to hear about the incision. Coach turned to get some equipment from the counter behind her and Chi Sun whispered in Wanda's ear. "Never stop talking when you do the spiral. Coach will punish you to help you remember that."

Wanda went blank for a moment but quickly recovered, saying the first calming thing that came to mind, a simple "Shhh, shhhh, shhhh." She discovered she could still see some of what was happening in the reflection in one of the glass cabinet doors. Coach cut but the man stayed surprisingly quiet, even as Coach prodded around with forceps in the incision, looking for the ends of the tendon.

"Wanda," Coach said. "This foil is ruptured so I can't use this packet. Hurry to the storeroom and ask Piyumi for a gut-threaded needle. Chi Sun, you take the spiral until she gets back."

Wanda handed off the dowel and passed through a little door at the back of the operating room. Sister Piyumi was there in the storeroom, standing on a stepstool to place a box onto a shelf.

"Coach said she needs a gut-threaded needle." Wanda said. "I guess that's cat gut?" Wanda had seen a live cat, once, when visiting the home of a schoolmate whose parents were much higher ranked than her own.

Sister Piyumi descended and moved over to a different set of cabinets and drawers. She opened a long, narrow drawer and examined various items inside as she talked. "Our job is to do and learn what we are told, Sister," she said. "We do not wonder. We do not speculate. Coach said a gut needle, so you will be given a gut needle. And we address each other as Sister, Sister. Coach will punish you to help you remember that."

"I'm ... sorry, Sister," Wanda said haltingly. "I have noticed that you all say that, about Coach punishing me to help me remember."

"What did I just say about wondering, Sister?"

"I'm sorry. Sister."

"Coach will punish you to help you remember that." She selected a small foil packet and closed the drawer. She spoke more quietly as she came up and placed the packet into Wanda's hands. "We are required to educate and remind each other of Coach's rules, and also of the fact that we are watching each other so that Coach can help improve us through punishment. Coach is responsible for every life here. Her gift to us is allowing us to do exactly as we're told. We absolve ourselves of ultimate responsibility through obedience to her."

"Yes, Sister," Wanda said. This was her life now: absolution through obedience. "Thank you, Sister." She hustled back to Coach, making sure her feet stayed close together.

Dok's place

Kym averted her eyes. General Eadie and the Prophet had run off just before this nasty fucking giant Fed had showed up looking for them. The Fed had been beating on Dok, asking him all kinds of questions. Dok had been shining him on, making him madder and scarier until finally the Fed had just thrown him to the floor.

He stomped on the back of Dok's head and Dok went limp. Then he focused his icy stare on Kym.

Mikk was weak because he was alone. Or rather, because he'd only had control of his whores and Kym. This Fed was just like Mikk, but there were thousands and thousands of other Feds like him, all armed and protected by an entire society. Kym had never hated anything like she now hated this Fed.

He reached her in a single stride and yanked her up by the arm, his thumb digging into a bruise. "How about you?" the Fed said. "Do you know where the waitress with a cut face might have gone?"

It had to stop.

Kym should have been terrified, but instead she remained steady. A rock. A tiny stone, flung by the General, straight into this clunky Fed's eye. She had nothing to lose and no fuel but hate.

"Didn't see any waitress," she said, truthfully. She had seen only a general.

The Fed's thick fingers hooked into Kym's shoulders and lifted her until her toes dangled. She tensed her neck muscles in a desperate effort to keep her head attached to her body as he shook her violently. He stopped and shifted his grip, taking her by the throat. This Fed could snap her neck with his thumb, and he could see she knew it.

"Tell me where she went, you dumb bitch," he said quietly.

Kym thought about what she should say. Should she be angry and insult him, proving she was innocent by her more extreme reaction? Or maybe she ought to be calm and meek, acting like she was impressed with his power? Or cower and whimper?

It didn't matter what she had to do, as long as whatever it was helped the General and her cause.

Behind the Fed, Dok slowly pulled himself up to a standing position and leaned against the counter. The thought flashed through her mind that Dok could kill him, smash his head from behind, but that would never happen. Dok wouldn't have the heart to kill anyone, even this giant demonically engineered Fed.

The Fed grabbed her shoulders, preparing to shake her again. It didn't matter. He could shake her, choke her, beat her, or whatever else. Mikk had beaten her all the time and she'd just taken it, mostly out of fear, and yet now she was facing this Fed and the power of thousands and thousands of Mikks, and holding her ground. There was no longer any fear. As the Prophet had said, Kym understood the power of having nothing to lose. The General was something to believe in, and Kym would not betray her.

A loud crack sounded somewhere outside the clinic: a door getting kicked in. The Fed let go of her and turned his attention to Dok again, punching him in the face for some comment he'd made.

Pivoting back to Kym, he said, "I have no further use for you. You may go. Now."

(?)

"Dr. Kessler, sir?"

It was Keiko's voice.

"Dr. Kessler, sir?" she asked again. Kessler sat up.

"Keiko," he said. "Where are we?"

"This is Lincoln's, the club you'd told me we were heading for," she said. "After that man on the street threw the powder in your face, you were okay for a little bit, and then after a few more minutes you became disoriented. The doorman recognized you and pulled us in, sir. It was lucky he did because this place has no sign and the door just looks like part of the wall outside."

He looked around, recognizing the private room Lincoln's had provided. The floor was raised to about knee-high and padded in black vinyl, everywhere but the space into which the door opened.

"How are you feeling, sir?"

He realized he probably looked foolish, repeatedly massaging his forehead and temples with the tips of his fingers. He imagined the action was working badly needed blood back into his head. "What time is it?" he asked. There was no way to know inside the windowless space.

"Twenty-oh-four GMT, sir," she said.

That was midafternoon.

"The office must—"

"I told them you had been attacked on the street, sir, and that I was caring for you. I know it's not the best story but I didn't know what else to say."

"They'll say it's still my fault for being out of the secured areas," he said. "But you stayed with me, Keiko. You cared for me."

She grinned. "Yes, sir, I stayed. I was very concerned for you, and I was also afraid to leave here alone."

Kessler made himself lower his hands to the vinyl pads. He realized he was leaning against a wall, also padded in vinyl, though he had no recollection of having leaned. "We'll square it away with the office. Don't worry."

"I have complete faith in you, sir. Are you all right now?"

He nodded. "It was the strangest experience, that drug. It was like…like I was a cup, and the drug was trying to pour something in. Like it was trying to make me into something else. A junkie, maybe, I don't know. But I was already full, so it just skimmed over the top and down the sides. I kept thinking of Amelix. I…I feel like I was saved by the fact that my heart was already full of my love for the company, as if reconditioning had vaccinated me."

"Reconditioning is truly a blessing, sir. Do you think you're ready to go back to the office now? I'm sure you're sorely missed."

"Yes, I think so. Better to walk through this area in the middle of the day, too, I think. Let's get back to work."

Approaching Dobo Protein Refinery

Rus led the way back to where it had all started, where that cheat fuck Garbageman had ripped him off, where Murph had gotten killed and probably carbon recycled, lining the Garbageman's pockets even more.

"Tonight the Bridges are doin' some payback!" he said, far too loudly for a part of the Zone this far from home. He'd heard there were some tough gangs around here. One called Plague was known to come running straight at you and beat you into the ground with no warning, no demand, no nothing. Another that called itself the Hueys was supposed to have more machine guns than any other street gang. This street, J Avenue, was said to be at the center of a territory dispute between the two, but Rus hadn't seen anyone wearing any colors at all here yet. It seemed like there were fewer and fewer gangs lately. In any case, it was better to be safe. There was no excuse for shouting like that, even if he was pretty messed up right now. He'd finished the sodje bottle and another, needing to clear his head after he'd—

A greasy coating of cold, black guilt and self-loathing settled over him.

I don't have to think about this bitch, not now, not ever. Unlucky property of a shitty guy, that's all she is.

He stumbled and went down hard to one knee.

"Damn!"

Too loud again.

Shouldn't one of his *brothers* have caught him? They made him into a fucking monster, a hateful fucking monster, and they couldn't even—

The image flooded his mind again. He was fucking the girl— *the whore*—and she opened her eyes. She'd been crying with her eyes shut all goddamned night, and then right when Rus was fucking her, she opened her eyes and looked into his, not sad, not afraid, but just like she was saying, *"I'm here and I see what you're doing."*

"Fuckin' Garbageman!" he said. This time he was glad it was too loud. Maybe some worse gang would come and kill them now. It was only a group of eight Bridges here tonight, since the entire gang was now down to twenty-four. How big a force could they fend off, really, with just eight? Four Bridges carried the whore, and the other four, including Rus, who had wanted to distance himself from her, walked at their sides as protection.

"Garbageman! We gonna fuck you up!" D'Wayn called out. Now Rus wasn't the only loud one. "When he sees this bitch, cut up and covered in blood and cum and bruises, he'll know he fucked with the Zone's hardest thugs."

Rus needed to be more like D'Wayn. The Bridges who truly ruled were always the hardest and the meanest. He had to grow the fuck up, but this shit with torturing the hooker had made him lightheaded.

They dumped her outside the heavy metal doors and gave the finger to the Garbageman's security camera, pulling out weapons. Everyone had a club and at least one knife, but Duke Q also had a .38, and Pawley had a .22 that would look like a bigger gun on camera, even though neither had any bullets. "You're fucking dead, Garbageman!" Rus taunted to the camera.

"We gonna ugly up every bitch you got, including you!" Duke Q shouted.

The Garbageman would never face the Bridges all together. Then again, he might just start shooting, too. In fact, he would probably do that, straight through the metal gate like last time.

The Bridges hustled away from the door, just slowly enough to avoid seeming scared. The laughing and backslapping trailed off quickly as they turned onto a back street. They walked without speaking, the only sound being that of their feet crunching over the gravel.

They wound from one back street to another. Rus's neck was starting to ache from craning in every direction. Just a few months ago the Bridges would have attracted the attention of serious tough guys here, but tonight the streets were silent. He would have been less on edge if they'd been confronted already.

The Bridges' footsteps stopped as the others came into focus, just standing there, frozen, each one of the six or eight silhouettes aiming rifles at the Bridges. Rus realized how easy it would have been for these shapes to remain hidden here, and how many might still be hidden there, with so many layered shadows. These silhouettes had intentionally let themselves be seen.

Blood rushed to Rus's head, making his lips and ears throb. This was no ordinary street gang. His chest tightened.

Fiends!

"Move and you meet Unity," a gravelly voice whispered, rancid spittle landing among the hairs on Rus's neck. A pistol barrel appeared there next, then a hand on his shoulder pushed him to his knees. The other Bridges landed next to him. Hands stripped the Bridges of their possessions. "Congratulations, kids," the voice said. "You're now property of the New Union. If any of you survive the training, you'll have glory, wealth, and power."

Outside Dobo Protein Refinery

Kym Evans still limped and wobbled a bit as she walked, but Dok's treatment had helped a lot. She'd already found a way to be a part of the General's holy mission, first by staring down the Federal Agent and not telling him shit, and then by recognizing her student follower on the street and filling him in on how to find her.

"Perhaps one day we'll call you Colonel Kym, or even General Kym."

The Prophet's words stuck in her mind. It felt right: Kym, herself, commanding hundreds or thousands of dedicated soldiers. More than that, it felt *owed* to her.

I'm Colonel Kym, you fucking Fed. You won't scare Colonel Kym into telling you shit, fucker.

It was dark now. Mikk never came here to the refinery at night because it was too far away from the action, so she'd be safe from him, though she'd have to deal with the stench of carbon recyclables all night.

She could leave at sunrise to avoid Mikk.

As she approached the refinery she discovered someone had dumped a corpse outside the heavy doors. Who would just abandon this much carbon? A full-sized adult body could bring enough cash for a decent meal, maybe two. Kym unlocked the door and grabbed the corpse by a wrist to drag it in. It writhed and moaned—the girl was alive! Kym got an arm under her and hoisted her up and through the door, heading for the office. Someone came in after her, closing the door behind them and locking it. "Where's the Garbageman?" a gruff male voice asked.

Kym felt as afraid as the situation called for, but the feeling was insulated by her rage and her new sense of power. "You did this to her so you could find him?" Her voice didn't even shake.

"No. A gang of punks dumped her here about an hour ago. Where is the Garbageman? I won't ask you again."

"Oh, you gonna kill me? Criminals like you are all going to disappear," Kym said. "The General is going to build a new society, and I'm gonna be fightin' too."

Even in the dark, she could sense the man deflating somewhat. His voice softened. "Which general did he become?"

The comment seemed strange, but she had too much real shit going on to worry about whatever particular way this guy was crazy. Kym turned her back on him, helping the girl toward the office and unlocking it. If he wanted to stab, shoot or rape her, there wasn't much she could do to stop him, anyway.

"There are a lot of us," she said finally. "And more coming."

She got the office unlocked and turned on the dim light. The girl was a teenager. Kym was surprised to find herself retching. She would have figured she'd be used to horrible acts like this by now. Two other of Mikk's whores had been dropped here after being raped and mutilated, but this was the first one she'd ever found alive.

The man standing here in the office was a basic Zone dealer type, slender, mid-twenties, with dark hair and facial stubble framing cold blue eyes. She'd probably seen a hundred just like him coming and going from deals with Mikk. This one wore some kind of red cape around his shoulders, which was fastened with handcuffs.

"I know there are more coming," he said. "I'm the one bringing them."

"You?" she said. "You serve the General?"

"Haven't yet met him, but yes. I'm here to form the new legions."

Kym knew better than to correct him about the General's gender. "Who are you?" she asked.

"Centurion Septimus Furius. I formerly served under Praetor Crassus and I look forward to meeting your general. Is it Crassus? There is much to be done if the legions are to be formed. If the General came from this place, I will wait here with you until he returns."

Kym lowered the bleeding, naked girl gently to the floor as he stood there in the doorway, looking out at the mounds of trash.

The attackers had cut the girl's nostrils out from inside and left diagonal slashes across her face, as well as across her breasts, midsection, and thighs. The cuts were all deep enough to leave nasty scars but none had cut any major blood vessels. Kym kept a bag of rags in a drawer for whenever they might be handy, mostly just clothes she'd stripped from corpses. She dug around to find one of the cleaner ones, an old plaid shirt, and ripped it into makeshift bandages for the girl's various wounds. The man who called himself Centurion whatever turned from the doorway and stood in silence, watching her work.

"This place is a protein refinery, so it takes all this garbage and turns it into food, right?" he asked finally.

"No," she said, a bit glad for the chance to condescend. "Synthesizers make it into food. Here we just break it down, back into amino acids that the bacteria inside synthesizers will make into proteins."

"So it goes from here to those things, the synthesizers, all over?"

She shook her head. "Goes to the factory that produces sterile nutrients. Sterile nutes packages have our aminos, plus other things like vitamins and phytonutrients, all combined. Those packages get shipped to the synthesizers all over."

"And how many people does one of those blocks you make here, the amino acids, end up feeding?"

"Dunno. Probably a few thousand, when it's mixed into sterile nutes packs. There's a backlog of amino blocks, though, so they've been lettin' them pile up here instead of paying us. Trying to use it as an excuse to lower prices, but a lot of us are just sitting on 'em, waitin' for the manufacturers to need 'em again."

"Waiting for a shortage of dead bodies and garbage," he said. "Bold move, that."

He stared out through the glass at the various steps of production, which were relatively well illuminated by moonlight. The hopper was huge and dirty, and from there the pipes traced the process of chemical disintegration and recombination, ratio control, and sterilization. Kym stopped working on the girl as he removed what appeared to be about half a kilo of white powder from one of his big coat pockets.

"Is there a final step in this process, right before it goes out from here?" he asked.

"Yeah," she said, without looking up from the girl's wounds. "The sterilizer. Doesn't look so clean on the outside, but that big, grimy blue machine sterilizes the aminos inside and wraps them into those big blocks you see on the shelf. They're sealed in super thick bioplexi film to keep out germs."

"This is how we're going to build the legions," he said. As she watched, he strode out to the sterilizer and dumped some of the powder into it.

Part of the Zone outside La Guada

"Arrulfo!" Ernesto said. "You're pushing me the wrong way! It's the wrong way, Arrulfo. We've already been there."

"We have to be quiet now, Ernesto," Arrulfo whispered. "Remember what I told you?"

"Yes. If there's a fight I should stay by you."

"That's right, *amigo*. What else did I tell you?" Arrulfo was pushing hard now, even lifting Ernesto's feet from the ground a little bit.

"If you get hurt in a fight so bad you can't move anymore, I should run and run and not stop running until I can't run anymore. And also this is a dangerous area for us so we have to be careful not to be seen."

Nine men and boys shouted from across the street. "Mex! Mex!" they yelled. English was a strange language Ernesto didn't understand very well, but "Mex" was clear enough. Their voices were loud. More of them came. Rosa pushed Mari against a wall. Marcos was swiveling his head around from side to side. Arrulfo had said Marcos was a psychopath and all psychopaths were dangerous, but Ernesto had said that Arrulfo didn't know all psychopaths so he couldn't say that they were all dangerous, but Arrulfo had said that was what a psychopath was, it was a person who was dangerous. Then Ernesto had said that people in LaGuada said Arrulfo was dangerous because he was so good at fighting, but Arrulfo had said that there were different kinds of dangerous people and psychopaths were just one kind, so someone could be dangerous and not be a psychopath. But Arrulfo had said he paid Marcos and threatened him because Arrulfo was even more dangerous than Marcos, and so Marcos protected Ernesto and Ernesto could be okay around him. Not safe, exactly, but kind of okay, with Marcos and Arrulfo around.

Now there were thirty-two other men and boys shouting. Arrulfo was fighting them but he was still moving, and that meant Ernesto didn't have to run away. Arrulfo gave Ernesto a stick. "Hit anyone who attacks you, amigo," he said.

"That's fighting, Arrulfo!" Ernesto said. "You know I'm not good at fighting!"

Someone hit him hard on the side of his face! His eye ached, getting worse and better and worse and better over and over as his heart pumped. He couldn't open the eye and he wasn't crying, but his face was wet and his mouth tasted salty. Now everything in the world was completely different because now *he* was completely different, with one crying, aching eye getting worse and better and worse and better, one broken eye Ernesto didn't know how to fix.

His stomach! A shoe was there, and then it pulled away. Now his stomach was hurting but not getting worse and better but just hurting the same all the time and making him fold in half. He was broken in two places and now he was different and unfixable and he lived with his eye getting worse and better and his hurting stomach folding him in half.

This was an attack! Hitting someone in the face was an attack, and kicking was an attack. Arrulfo had said Ernesto was supposed to hit anyone who attacked him. Keeping a hand on his stomach and turning his hurting eye toward his raised shoulder, Ernesto screamed and swung the stick back and forth as hard as he could with his one hand.

There were more attackers now, but Arrulfo was fighting them, protecting Ernesto. Arrulfo had said he would always protect Ernesto, but Ernesto had said he couldn't always do that, like if he were dead he couldn't protect Ernesto. Then Arrulfo had asked him how many fights he had seen Arrulfo protect him in and Ernesto said he had done so in one hundred forty-three fights before today.

This time there were thirty-two attackers, eighteen with weapons.

There were shouts around the corner where these had come from.

Ernesto ducked his head again, flailing and staggering. Whenever he watched Arrulfo fight, he saw how perfectly Arrulfo's motions counteracted and overcame his opponents. Now, being attacked himself, Ernesto still saw the hinge actions of his attacker's joints and the arc of the weapon. Arrulfo could push on one side of a joint and make the body fold and crumple, but pushing the same joint another way made a long, awkward limb he could use for leverage. He recognized the mechanics of what Arrulfo did, working those hinge actions and arcs to his advantage in grappling opponents to the ground, intercepting the blows before impact, and using cunning spins and shifts in balance to neutralize whatever attack came at him, but it didn't help. Ernesto couldn't move his body the way Arrulfo could. There were too many things happening when Ernesto tried to move his body, too much information to process, for him to be able to do it smoothly.

Ernesto did not like fighting.

There was someone next to Arrulfo, now. Not fighting him, just standing there next to him, fighting other people. He had long hair in a tube on top of his head.

7

Li'l Ed sat on a bench, staring at the untouched bioplastic container of Synapsate next to him, still in the spot he'd set it over half an hour ago. The family dinner had been in progress for the last twenty minutes or so via EI, but so far it had been silent except for a few preliminary greetings and the prayer.

"What will you do now, Li'l Ed?" his father asked finally.

"I don't know, sir," he said quietly. "The school situation seems to be in limbo at the moment. I'm sure everyone is waiting for some sign from everyone else, and then there will be a collective decision about us."

"I think the most likely collective decision is that you and Jack will Depart," his stepmother Nolene said.

"Yes, ma'am. I'm afraid you're right. But if I turn myself in for voluntary reconditioning now, I'll lose my place at Fisher. It would be highly unlikely for McGuillian to put any additional resources into me after that. I'd be reconditioned and Accepted, but I'd be at the very bottom rung of the company, probably for my entire career. I would like to attend for just a while longer, to see how it all plays out. I promise that at the first sign that the wind has shifted and they've turned against me, I'll apply immediately for voluntary reconditioning. I have a completed application form pre-saved, and I keep the site permanently open in my EI."

"It's a serious and unreasonable risk, Li'l Ed," his father said. "We can't condone that."

"It's so much to give up if I don't need to, sir. I worked so hard to get into Fisher Academy and take my place on the executive track. Life at the bottom of the organization is barely life at all, and I think I'd rather risk Departing, if I have even the smallest chance of staying at Fisher." He paused, then took a different tack. "What if the Lord's plan for me was to stay on track, to pass this test of my determination?"

"Li'l Ed, I'm surprised at you," his father said. "You are old enough to understand that the Lord and McGuillian are the same. It's fine to envision them as separate entities as long as you don't try to put them at odds, but it's time to grow up, son. The *company* is from whom all blessings flow. Your clothes, your food, your home, your health; everything about you is a gift from McGuillian. The company is our provider, and it alone judges our worth."

Li'l Ed sat without speaking, unable to respond. Finally, he cleared his throat. "Yes, sir."

"The risk is unacceptable, Li'l Ed," his father said. "There's nothing more dangerous than Departing; it's the endgame scenario every time. Any life at McGuillian is better than no life at all. You will surrender yourself for voluntary reconditioning."

Li'l Ed felt his stress melt away. It had been decided. His father outranked him at the company, and the company was God. His father's word was law.

"Yes, sir. I should probably let you get back to your work sir, and ma'am."

His EI suddenly slammed off! They would think he'd terminated the connection before they'd given him leave! Li'l Ed scrambled to reopen the function but found he was unable.

A black truck pulled up directly in front of him. The doors opened and two Unnamed stepped out. Jack was inside, wide-eyed and pale. "Get in," one of the Unnamed said.

Someplace dark and underground

"Yes, go ahead, one more!" Rus screamed. "Another!"

He was seated naked on bare concrete with his arms and legs bound around an oil drum. The hooded Fiends called Divinators were working him over. There was a plastic bag over his head that sucked against his face when he inhaled too fast, and the electrical cord whipping across his back made him involuntarily gasp and gag.

It didn't matter what they did to him. He deserved all the pain, desperation, and suffering the Fiends could administer. Let them torture him to the end. There was no life worth having in a world like this, anyway.

A hand roughly grabbed at his head, pulling the plastic off his face as it closed into a fist. It yanked him backward, pointing his face at the ceiling as his lungs tried to suck in the whole room's air supply.

A hooded face appeared above his, but Rus' unfocused eyes stared blankly into the space between them. The vomit-stinking breath stung his eyes.

"What are you?" a voice growled.

"Nothing," Rus said, meaning it. "I'm nothing."

The hand released his hair and the muscles that had tightened to counterbalance his tilted head flexed, slamming his nose and brow ridge against the oil drum.

"This one's ready," the voice said.

At a Hotel

Arrulfo said this was a hotel. Ernesto had never been to a hotel before. A hotel was a sour-smelling building with concave stairs and too many people in it. And noise, too much noise. Ernesto did not like the hotel.

"Arrulfo, let me take him instead," Rosa said. "He needs to learn to be apart from you."

Rosa took Ernesto's hand. He yanked it back away from her, holding the lighter close against his chest. "You see?" she said. "You see what he does? You protect him so much he's overwhelmed by everything."

Arrulfo appeared, smiling at Ernesto from a close distance. "It's okay, *amigo*," Arrulfo said. "Don't worry. It's me. I'm here." Arrulfo turned his face away again. "He is overwhelmed by everything, Rosa, and so, I protect him so much." Then the face was back in front of Ernesto, saying, "Let's go down the hall together to try and get some gas for the lighter, okay?"

Ernesto nodded. Arrulfo stepped back. Ernesto liked that Arrulfo didn't offer to help him up. People sometimes put their hands on Ernesto and thought they were helping, but that was terrible; it was not helping at all. Arrulfo never did that.

They went out into the hallway together. It smelled like ashes and rain. It was too narrow to walk next to each other. Arrulfo went first and Ernesto followed, seven and one-half steps from the door, to the closet where there was a toilet. There was still some gas in the lighter from before. That part had not been broken in the fight, the part holding the gas. So little gas was left that the lighter might not light for Arrulfo's friend with his big hair in a tube, but Arrulfo said maybe they could get some from this toilet.

Ernesto worked the tube and crank, trying to get some gas out of the pipe he could access through the toilet. The little piece on the tip had a membrane that let only gas pass through it and not water and the membrane had not been broken. He couldn't get the tube to where he wanted it because there was something inside the pipe that was blocking it. Ernesto found a tiny pocket and turned the crank, meeting resistance as the membrane kept out water, but finally a tiny bubble formed inside the lighter's internal tubing and then slowly worked its way to mix with the rest of the gas inside.

"You got it?" Arrulfo asked. Ernesto nodded. "Okay, good, *amigo*. Maybe you can give it to Kel, maybe practice talking to someone new, huh?"

Ernesto shook his head like he did when he was tasting something bad. He pushed the lighter into Arrulfo's hands, but Arrulfo didn't take it. "You can give it to him," he said as they walked the seven and a half steps back to the room.

Arrulfo talked with the new girl, Eadie, and had Ernesto show her the lighter and its gas level. "I don't want to give it to him, Arrulfo," Ernesto said. "You do it."

"She can give it to him, Ernesto. Just give it to her. It's good practice for you."

She took the lighter and said something to him in English. Ernesto went back and sat down. Now there was nothing to fix, nothing to do. People were talking and making too much noise.

Outside the door a voice yelled, "It's Dok! I'm coming in!"

Rosa opened the door and three people came in, slamming the door again behind them. Rosa worked the big metal rod through the loops and the door shook with some tremendous impact. Others ran to push against the door.

So loud!

Some huge noise sounded outside, painful and shocking. One of the people here, Lawrence, pulled an arm away from the door, dripping blood onto the floor.

Now the loud sounds were everywhere, and especially coming from the window. *Guns.* The sounds were guns. Someone was shooting guns. Sometimes the sounds were different from each other and sometimes they were the same, but all the sounds were much too loud, painful and shocking. Ernesto covered his head with his arms.

Arrulfo grabbed him.

"I don't like to be touched, Arrulfo!" Ernesto said, pulling back.

"We have to go now, Ernesto," Arrulfo said. "We have to run from the bad men."

Arrulfo had taught Ernesto to run from bad men. Bad men would hurt him unless he ran away from them. The change was so hard to do, as if he was tied up and trying to stand on his own, but Ernesto forced his arm and leg muscles to work, and he made himself stand. Arrulfo released him and he went into the hall with the others.

There were dead men there in the hall he had to climb over. They wore black suits and sunglasses. The word for the people who wore black suits and sunglasses was *Sinnombres*. Arrulfo said *Sinnombres* were bad men, but he only knew some of them, not all of them. These two *Sinnombres* were dead, which was what happened when their bodies stopped working and they went away to leave the bodies behind. Bad people did bad things, and these *Sinnombres* weren't doing anything bad; they were just lying there, or gone. These *Sinnombres* were not bad men. There was also a dead one who had no black suit or sunglasses. He had a little glass vial on a string around his neck. Those were called *Demonios*. Arrulfo said *Demonios* were bad men, too, but he didn't know all the *Demonios*. This one wasn't doing anything bad. He was just lying there, dead.

Coach V's Clinic

A few days ago, Wanda had become Coach V's "girl," and the Saved had assassinated the Directorate. Since then Wanda had been subjected to Coach's cruel punishments, and the Saved had converted a quarter of the Horde's members. The Horde had withdrawn, and now the clinic was a strategic asset for the Saved.

The job was just as she'd been told it would be. She was a slave, with every task, movement, and even thought, controlled and prescribed. The only rest she got was during lectures from Coach that were part of her "training," but even then she had to sit on edge, listening. Coach took so many bactrostimulants that her words came fast and often through a clenched jaw, and the punishments for failing to register and recall what she said were severe.

Coach didn't seem ever to sleep, and the schedule she kept her girls on already had Wanda begging, literally, on her knees, for pills of her own. The begging was Coach's idea. "Once you've become what I want you to be, then you get speed to lock it in place," Coach had said every time so far. "Keep begging for now. Keep trying to prove you're fine-tuned enough for me to rev you up." Quickly, desperately, and for perhaps the thousandth time today, Wanda forced her thinking back to the task at hand. She was with Sula in the sealed, windowless room Coach used as a lab, mixing up a suspension of blood and other fluids to sterilize for the production of bacteria. Nothing went to waste here.

"In our old world, the corporate one, people just go to synthesizers for their medical needs," Sula said. "For Golds in the CBD, a doctor is a computer network manager. The only real medical thinking going on is in labs like the one you worked in at Amelix, or like I worked in at Ipoh, where we work on experiments that result in new programming for the machines to diagnose and treat different conditions. That's why Coach gets her girls from the Horde, from each of the big biotech firms—we're the ones who still use scientific thought processes. Our minds still have the capacity that many have lost due to atrophy."

A capacity Coach fills up with her own agenda.

Wanda cringed. That thought would be revealed to Coach in her confession later, under chemically induced trance, and it would earn her a punishment.

This time, I will choose pain.

Would she be punished for thinking that? It was what Coach wanted her to do, wasn't it? Why else make her choose between a painful punishment and a humiliating one?

"Coach has decision trees mapped out in the books," Sula said. "We're not allowed to answer any question on the decision tree with anything but 'yes' or 'no.' If there's any gray area at all, that is, if there's ever a time you want to say, '*Yes, and,*' or '*no, but,*' it becomes an issue for Coach to decide. Coach does not allow anyone else's attempted logic to create interference with her practice."

Sula stopped talking and stood staring at the door, where a small group of Saved had entered. Three men and two women stood gazing, awestruck, at a central figure who had apparently led them to the clinic. He had a scab all the way across his forehead and bandages on his neck and under his shirt, but he didn't seem to be seeking medical attention.

"Coach said to stay away from that guy," Sula whispered. "She said he's actually a dangerous criminal they call the Garbageman, and we should not believe the front he presents. She told me to get rid of him if he came back, and I have authority over you. Go get rid of him. Just...tell him this clinic is too small and we can't have him in the way." She turned and busied herself with something on a cart, pushing it away in the opposite direction from the group that had entered.

"Yes, Sister."

As Wanda approached the man, his followers blocked the way with relaxed bodies and tranquil smiles. She had almost failed to notice them, having been so focused on the central figure. Now that she was close to him she felt giddy and nervous. His actions, and his presence here, seemed natural, correct, and ordained by something wiser than herself and more powerful than Coach. She found she couldn't make herself address him directly. Yet Wanda had to speak. She had been given a direct order.

The people between them were a blessing; she could talk to the group instead of the individual. "I'm sorry, folks, but you can't be here right now. We're busy and the clinic is just too crowded."

The followers held their same positions and facial expressions.

"We certainly don't mean to interfere in your important work," one of them said. "We wish to assist with it." The central figure turned slightly and bent down to one knee next to a bed, gently touching a patient's forehead and whispering to her. As Wanda watched between two of his followers, the woman's eyes widened and she smiled broadly, sitting up in bed.

The leader rose to his feet and took a step toward Wanda. The ones standing between them moved off. Her feet felt stuck to the floor. The man had a wide, bulging scab cutting across his forehead that could have made him seem ugly and dangerous had it not been for the look of peaceful benevolence on his face.

"I'm sorry, sir, but this is Coach V's clinic and she alone is responsible—"

He cut her off, not with words or even a gesture, but simply by looking at her. She tried again. "They said you're here to assist. Are you…are you a doctor, sir?"

He smiled slightly. Wanda's eyelids drooped.

Wanda felt a warm glow spreading out from the point where his eyes had met hers. "What…what may I call you, sir?"

He had gentle and knowing eyes. "These friends call me the One Who Returned," he said.

This was Porter's group, the Saved. How could she kick them out of their newly captured strategic asset?

Still, the order had been clear, and she would rather challenge these gun-wielding psychopaths than subject herself to more of Coach's punishments. Yet she stood transfixed, unable to form the words.

Wanda sniffed and shook her head. There truly was something different about this guy, but that didn't mean she should just let herself be taken in by it. The Saved had just assassinated the Directorate and all its guards, and now here he was, acting concerned about the patients here. His presence made her feel irresistibly compelled to do what was right and good, but his influence was clearly more complicated than that. How could she trust the feelings of virtuousness and compassion he exuded when the people he surrounded himself with were so brutal and callous? How many had they killed in his name to build their power base?

"Coach!" Judee cried from the back room. "Coach? Are you all right?"

Wanda stayed still, uncertain what she should do. The One returned to his rounds, touching patient after patient. "Piyumi, help me start CPR," Judee said.

"Sir?" Wanda said finally. "There's an emergency and I may be needed in the back. I need to ask you to—"

The One looked at her. She forgot what she'd been saying.

"You won't be needed there," he said. "Your Coach is gone."

"I…" Wanda said. "You don't…"

The One nodded, slowly and benevolently. "I know." He took her hands in his. "I am sorry you were separated from the love of your life. You will soon be raising a new child. I sense that you still have doubts, but you will raise this new child to believe. He will be Saved."

The One turned away again.

There was a commotion in the lab, sounds of glass breaking and items falling to the floor.

"Coach!" someone shouted. This time the voice belonged to Chi Sun. Wasn't Coach already back there? "Coach!" Chi Sun shouted again, this time sounding more distressed, even panicky.

"Sisters!" Chi Sun called. "Please come to the back. We need to figure out what to do. Coach is dead."

Wanda felt a wave of relief begin to build but she refused to let herself experience it until she was sure. Indulging in the belief that she had been freed from Coach's obsessive and tyrannical control would be catastrophic to her psyche if it were not actually so.

Wanda headed for the back. Someone followed her. Porter. Had he been part of the group surrounding the One?

"I want to help," he said.

Wanda's mind barely registered the comment. Could Coach really be dead? How would the clinic run without her? What would happen to the girls, now that the Horde no longer controlled the clinic?

She reached the door to the lab, held open by Sula leaning against it. Coach's pale, still body lay on the floor in front of the lab bench, her eyes staring at nothing.

"What now?" Judee asked.

"We can't run this clinic by ourselves," Sula said.

"She taught me more than she taught anyone, and I can't take her place," Chi Sun said.

Porter pushed past Wanda. "This is a hospital and it has to be kept clean. I'll take the body out so you can gather yourselves. I know what a shock this must be." He knelt and gingerly picked up Coach's frail remains, draping her over his arms. Everyone backed away to give him room.

"Each of us only knows a little bit," Piyumi said. "Coach made sure none of us could replace her. But together we did all of the work to keep the clinic running, and between us we've seen everything she used to do. Can we try to keep it open without her, just by each doing what we know how to do?"

"We have to keep it open," Wanda said. "There's nowhere for us to go."

"Don't worry," Porter said over his shoulder. "The Saved will help you."

The place called Dobo Protein Refinery

Inti lay on the floor, staring dully at the man who stood over her. Furius, he'd called himself, though he didn't seem particularly angry. This world's language often made no sense.

She hurt everywhere. There were no words for what her kidnappers had done to this body, neither in her language nor in this new, strange, often obscene one.

No. Not to the body. They did it to me.

Had it been just a body, they wouldn't have enjoyed tearing, beating and fucking it so much. What had really motivated them was that she was inside that body, experiencing the helplessness, the pain, and the shame. What they had taken, what they had been so thrilled to destroy, was the part that had not come from Addi.

Addi's memories showed she had been to this place, the protein refinery, before. She had been abused here. Both of the broken spirits sharing this body had suffered too much abuse to keep such memories sharp, but Inti was pretty sure this man talking was not the one who had abused Addi.

"Hey!" Furius said, leaning closer into Inti's face. He adjusted a red shawl around his shoulders. "You listening? Kym here says this Garbageman guy is now the General I'm supposed to follow. I'm bringing my things here to wait for his return."

The Garbageman! That was the abusive one. He was coming back?

Inti thrashed and moaned. The deep cuts covering her body throbbed as the scabs loosened but she couldn't stop.

"No, no, honey," the one he'd called Kym said. "I know you worked for the Garbageman, but he's not the General. The General is going to rid the world of his kind, don't you worry."

Inti calmed, letting the pain and exhaustion consume her. The man harrumphed at the interruption and kept on talking.

"Now, there's this powder that brings soldiers like me and the general here," Furius said.

The powder! Like Lucas, like me!

"We've got to spread the powder around, and I'm thinking of ways to do that. I figured a way you can help, if you want. If you don't, you can go and find your own way in life. This is the only use you'll be to me 'cause you're ugly like liquid shit, now. Got it?"

Inti didn't react, but he kept talking as if she'd agreed. "The guy who last used this body had a contact who makes this drink, called sodje. Popular stuff, seems like everyone here drinks it. I've seen groups of people all over the place sharing bottles of it. Anyway, I'm going to introduce you to the bottler and tell him pretty much the truth, that you can't be a whore anymore and you'll work there for one meal a day. This guy and my body donor used to be pretty close, so I think I can get him to go for it. And that's good for you, because another meal a day is gonna come from me, as long as you do what I say. You'll do that for me, right? You got nothing else you *can* do."

The powder apparently brought better people than the ones who lived in this world. Inti truly had nothing else and no other options. She nodded her head slowly.

"Why are you bothering her now, after all she's been through?" Kym, the one who had saved her, asked. "She's patched up enough that she can walk, maybe. The sun's up and we gotta get her to the doctor. She won't be working at a sodje bottler today no matter what, so you can leave her alone."

He ignored her. "Just twenty-five doses of Pink Shit, into twenty-five different bottles, every day. That'll give me a nice steady stream of new soldiers to get organized before the big wave of them comes. Once the backlog of amino acid blocks clears and they start using the ones we're making here, we'll be getting hundreds, maybe thousands a day. We gotta be ready for that, and you're going to help. Twenty-five doses a day. Okay?"

Kym put her arm behind Inti's shoulders and pulled the wincing girl into a sitting position. "It's too bad we gotta stay away from Dok's place now, Addi," Kym said. "He's the best. This other one I know is okay, too, but the clinic is farther away." She pointed at Furius. "Too bad for you that we're not going to Dok's place. That's where I met the General."

"The General?" he said, almost shouting. "Take me there!"

"Can't. Nobody's there now. Not Dok, an' *really* not the General. An' the Feds're watching the place, alla time. Maybe Unnamed Executives, too."

"I'll take my chances with them," he said. "Don't have to care how big they are in a world of guns."

Kym's voice was angry, breathy and low. "If you're gonna serve the General, know this: You fuckin' don't fight Feds. Think you can take one, or two, or ten, because you got a gun? Fine. You're a fuckin' idiot, but fine, say you can. Then there's gonna be ten or fifty more of 'em, in person, in trucks and tanks, on helios. They work together and they can always call more. You talk about guns, guess what? Nobody got more guns than Feds do. You fuckin' can't fight Feds!"

The man considered what she'd said. "All right. I see. I do understand that kind of power. It's how Rome conquered the world."

There was a buzzing sound and Kym went to look at a computer. "Refinery business," she said. "Four people carrying a body." She leaned toward the screen's microphone.

"I see you're all carrying weapons," she said. "Scanners pick them all up, so don't try anything stupid. Two of you stay outside with the weapons and the other two can come in unarmed. Got it?"

Inti watched the screen from across the room. Kym opened the gate electronically, and two men carried in a body. The gate closed behind them and Kym gestured through the office glass, showing the men where to take it. They heaved it onto a small platform that Addi's memories told her was a scale, and Kym went out to meet them there. The body's limbs were fairly long and spindly, but even on the screen Inti could see it was not skinny enough. It wasn't Lucas.

Kym worked out some kind of deal with the men and paid them, probably in casino chips.

"United in faith we live!" someone called from outside the gate. "We serve the One Who Returned! Porter, are you in there? We have news—a meeting of Disciples and they're waiting for you."

Furius checked the screen. "Four more of 'em? A bit suspicious, I'd say." He drew a gun and stepped out the door.

One of the men who had been negotiating with Kym cupped his mouth with his hand and yelled over the gate. "United in faith we live, brother! This is Porter. I'll be right out."

Kym followed the two men toward the gate. Furius pushed past her and approached them, talking. Inti could no longer keep her eyes from closing but she continued to listen to his voice. Unlike most of this world's inhabitants who apparently felt it was better to go unnoticed, Furius seemed constantly to speak in a loud and attention-seeking way.

"Hey, you there! What did you say just now?" Furius said, his voice becoming fainter as he moved away. "You serve one who *returned*?"

Inti's attention faded. She reopened her eyes, widening them and clenching her sore jaw in an attempt to maintain consciousness. This was a dangerous place with terrible people, and there were too many strangers here to let go. Her eyes closed again anyway.

The next time she opened them, she was lying on a stretcher between two poles. The ends of the poles near her feet left lines in the gravel. She was being dragged somewhere.

Grunting in pain, she sat bolt upright. Or tried to. She was tied up! Inti thrashed and twisted, trying to raise her hands to the strap around her midsection.

"Shh! It's okay."

It was the woman. Kym. Kym gently stroked from Inti's right temple to her cheek, one of the few parts of her body not covered in knife slashes. In the background, Furius was talking excitedly. "*Higher* than a general! Sounds like we've got a new praetor! Now things are really going to start happening here."

Kym leaned close, talking quietly. "Furius talked to these guys; they're parta some religious group or some shit like that. They gotta doctor for you. We're takin' you there so you can get better, but you gotta join their religion."

The clinic Mikk had captured

Mikk Evans wasn't the type to gush in gratitude for his fortune. Whatever he got in life always seemed to be a little less than he deserved. That was why guys like Mikk always rose to the top: Lesser men were easy to satiate.

Still, the last few days had been a hell of a ride. Once the Horde's leadership was out of the way, Hordesmen had been begging to become Saved. They already had thousands, and more were coming every day, clamoring to do whatever the fuck Mikk said.

It wasn't *all* good, of course. He'd started out unconscious, right here, in this clinic. Then some other fucking guy had awakened in Mikk's head instead of him, controlling his body and leaving Mikk memories of all this idiotic shit he'd done, like springing out of bed and running around the place, touching all the sick fucks lying around, like he'd never heard of getting germs. Shit like that pissed Mikk off, the memory of this fruitstick in his head mopping up diseases with Mikk's own bare hands.

But that was also what had gotten him here today, to this position of power. The patients had started gathering around him, hanging on everything he said and staring at him with their mouths open. This other guy in his head could talk for hours, and they all just sat mesmerized, staring at him, listening to stories and self-help kinds of shit. That left Mikk to actually put them to work, because what the hell good was a big group of people if you weren't going to use them for anything? The growing collection of people around him, all of them practically begging to be told what to do, was too powerful a force to ignore. As far as they knew, he'd healed them and brought them back from the brink. They owed him obedience. That first day when he'd left the clinic, a full dozen of them had trailed along, telling everyone they met about how great he was and how he would heal and protect them. By the next morning, there had been a hundred or more, all reaching out to others. The more people who followed him, the easier it was to convince new ones to join. Everybody was afraid of getting sick or injured, especially here on the filthy Zone streets.

It was weird, but Mikk himself kind of believed the bit about healing them. From his memories it seemed like even the grossest of these fuckers were actually getting better.

Whatever. The important thing was that *they* believed he was Holy Fucking Shit. The power they gave him wasn't the kind he was used to lording over junkies and whores. These people were afraid of everything *but* Mikk, like Fiends and diseases and other typical Zone shit, and they kissed Mikk's ass all the time, hoping he'd use his magic mojo to protect them from it. All he had to do was make his voice sound strung out on jellies, all calm and melodic and douchey, like this Holy Shit who sometimes took a turn in his head, and they'd fucking do anything he said, just like that.

They called him the *One*.

And that was where the real power was. Years on the streets had proven the effectiveness of making people fear him, but nothing compared to being worshipped.

The patients never sprung back to life when Mikk was Mikk, the way they did when the other guy was here. Mikk supposed it was some sort of power of positive thinking type of deal; they got better with that guy because he actually seemed to care about what happened to them. They were certainly useful, especially the zealots, but Mikk couldn't be bothered about whether any particular one lived or died. Why deal with all that, when so many new ones sprang up every day to replace them?

There were always zealots nearby, maybe one percent of them who doted on him, bringing him food and clothes and pretty much begging for him to boss them around. They'd even set up an apartment for him across the street from his clinic—the only other unit with all its glass windows still intact in this whole area! Already Mikk seemed to have amassed a small army of devotees who were all obviously over-the-top in their support and dedication to the One's many pursuits, including Mikk's own idea to knock off the Directorate and take over the clinic.

All he had to do was keep his face blank, his voice tranquil, and his orders clear. Mikk leaned toward one of the zealots nearby, hooking two fingers at him. "C'mere."

"Yes, Lord?" the zealot asked.

"I got a job for you." With his voice he struggled to mimic the effect of tranquilizers. "My son." He'd never actually bothered to learn the man's name, but the way he hung around and stared at Mikk with big cartoon eyes showed he was definitely one of the zealots. Calling zealots "my son" seemed to get shit done. Mikk pulled him closer with a fistful of shirt. "Through the glass, in the parking lot, behind my left shoulder," he said. "Yellow shirt, yellow hair. Maybe, I dunno, fifteen or so. See her?"

"Yes, Lord," the zealot said.

"Get her. I want her in my apartment in fifteen minutes. No need to pretend she has a choice."

The zealot's face went sort of blank and pale. He was a Gold so all those reactions were exaggerated, changing his complexion like that. The little gears in the zealot's head froze up for a moment and he just stood there, staring.

"Yes, Lord," he said finally.

One of the nurses, or bedpan jockeys, or whatever they were, came up by him, irritatingly close. "Excuse me?" she said. "I need to speak to this patient a moment." She pointed past Mikk to the head of the bed.

"Go around the other way," Mikk said. This angle gave the best view of the parking lot. Mikk watched his zealot work his way through the beds and out through the glass door, approaching the girl.

The fuck?

There, out in the gravel that had once been a parking lot, stood a collection of individuals from his past. Kym and that shithead Mr. B. together? And why would either of them be standing here with one of his whores, all cut up on a stretcher? Was this some kind of sabotage? A trick?

No matter what they were up to, these three posed a threat to everything Mikk had achieved with these people. Mikk knew the zealot who had brought them, too; the one called Porter.

Porter came up to the building, peering through the glass as he walked. Spotting Mikk, he flung open the door and came up quickly, making some little bowing gesture. "United in faith we live, Lord," he said.

Mikk nodded at him.

"I have encountered a man who is desperate to meet you, Lord. He wants to believe. It appears that he and the woman with him run a protein refinery nearby. There's also a girl we brought who needs immediate medical attention.

That puke Mr. B tries to take over my refinery and now he gets himself brought here to show me he cut up one of my whores? What's he up to?

Bringing his tone way down, Mikk said, "She won't survive, my son. All this clinic would do is prolong her suffering. The man she's with is the one who cut her. She needs to end her misery and he needs to be punished." Porter was a smart enough guy. He'd know what that meant. Wouldn't he?

Porter just stood there.

Mikk leaned in closer and grabbed him tightly by the shoulder, right at his neck. "Just drop 'em both right fuckin' there, all right?" He cleared his throat. "My son. Bring the protein refinery woman to my apartment, and throw out the bimbo who'll already be in there."

Porter stood still another moment. Was this zealot going to give Mikk a hard time about this, after he'd done such a good job following orders in taking over this clinic?

"Yes, Lord," Porter said finally. He went back out and shot the whore Addi right in the face, twice, as she lay on the stretcher. He spun toward Mr. B but the dealer was too fast for him, drawing two guns of his own. Both men fired, but Mr. B was already running toward the corner with Kym. Porter shot three times but probably missed.

Porter clutched at what looked like a fairly light shoulder wound, stumbling to one knee. He made a good show of climbing back up and chasing after Mr. B, but Mikk would have to punish him for fucking up like this.

Near the River

Ernesto tried to focus on staying one step behind Arrulfo and slightly to the left, as Arrulfo had taught him to do. Staying upright as they ran through the slippery mud was difficult but he kept his hands over his ears as best he could. Concentrating sometimes helped to block out the sounds and commotion. Ernesto watched the distance and angle between himself and Arrulfo as they ran, but it was hard to maintain position because they were running on the sloping bank next to the river, and being chased by the screeching heliodrone.

The helio noise was terrifying, and so loud that even when Ernesto pushed his earlobes into the holes in his ears and covered them with all his fingers, it still went straight through his head. Ernesto screamed to try blocking out the sound, but he wasn't loud enough. He fell behind and Arrulfo grabbed his arm, ripping his hand away from his ear to pull him forward. Rosa slipped and Arrulfo turned to help her, then Ernesto slipped, falling into the mud face-first.

Arrulfo yanked him up again and they ran under a bridge. The helio was closer than ever, its sound consuming all of Ernesto's thoughts.

Suddenly Arrulfo was pushing him forward, toward an opening they'd found under the bridge. The helio appeared, screaming and shuddering, spraying droplets of mud as it struggled to remain upright in the drafts it was causing.

The opening led to a tube, and then they were sliding down, falling, and landing on a hard surface below the entrance. The vibrations in the tube and floor said something heavy was dragging, shifting to cover the opening through which they'd come, sealing them in total darkness.

A new sound, more frightening than anything Ernesto had ever heard, erupted outside. The helio was shooting. The bullets weren't coming this way, having been redirected by whatever had moved to trap them here, but the sound made his stomach feel turned inside-out.

As suddenly as the shooting had started, it stopped again.

The girl, Eadie, flicked the lighter Ernesto had restored and for a moment, produced a small flame. The brief flash of light revealed a roomful of smudged, wide-eyed faces.

The clinic

Wanda poured a sterile uric acid solution over the wound in Porter's right shoulder. He shuddered and inhaled, producing a low, sucking hiss. The One had gone back to his posh apartment.

"The bullet went through your trapezius muscle," Wanda said. "As you were mindlessly, heartlessly killing that injured girl."

She shouldn't have said it. The Saved owned the clinic. The Saved owned *her*. Porter had just shown his true nature, and yet she found herself so disgusted and shocked that she couldn't help the words tumbling out.

"I didn't have a choice," he said. "You were right here. You heard him give the order."

"You know what I heard? I heard a psychopath tell you to do something twisted and evil. Then I watched you do it. That's what your faith brought you to, shooting a bleeding woman on a stretcher? Some lord and savior you've got there."

"He doesn't always seem so psychotic, you know. You've seen him when he's … I don't know what to call it. Magical? Holy? Serene? I know you've met that One."

"I watched you as he said it. You were shocked. You knew there was nothing holy about killing that girl, but you did it anyway. You could have decided to turn away from it. Instead you killed for him."

She stopped rinsing the wound but kept the little pail under his shoulder as it continued to drip.

"Are you going to stitch it?" he asked.

"Can't. The size and shape of the wound makes it too likely that I'd stitch an air pocket and cause sepsis. It's just going to have to fill itself in over time. Once the bleeding stops I'll bandage it." She realized she was crushing the plastic bottle in her hand and tried to relax her grip. "See, I feel a duty to respect and protect human life, even in those who murder people for no reason at all. Oh, sorry, not for no reason. You did it because your holy psycho told you to."

"You don't understand," he said. "That's not what it's about."

"And you know what's funny?" she said. "You never seemed like the other crazies he keeps close, the ones who stare and swoon. You always appeared to be the most logical one. You seem sane, but then surprise! You're willing to do anything he tells you to do."

"United in faith we live, Wanda," he said.

"Yeah, your mantra makes everything okay."

"Listen to the words. It's important. United, we live. I don't think I have to tell you what happens here in the Zone if you're not part of a group. Why is this group growing so fast? What holds it together and brings in stunning numbers of new recruits, every single day? It's that magnetism he has, that uniqueness that only the One can provide.

"Nobody rallies around nothing, Wanda. I saw early on that people rallied around him, and that when enough of them joined together they would become a legitimate force here in the Zone. That's exactly what they did. Sure, sometimes the One absolutely terrifies me. Sometimes he makes me do things that turn my stomach, like today. But I'm willing to do whatever it takes to be part of this group, no matter how psychotic and dangerous it is. This is the Zone. If you choose not to join with anyone, your life is down to maybe a few hours, a few days at best."

She stared.

"I'm not looking for absolute truth," he said. "Just security. It's better to be Saved than to be a Fiend or to be dead." He shrugged. "You don't agree, fine. Go ahead and hate me for it. At least I'll still be alive."

Desert outside Des Moines

"There appears to be a signal now, sir, reachable through the truck's booster," Li'l Ed's EI voice told him. The rather stuffy male synthetic vocal pattern he'd selected sounded eerily out of place, given his situation.

A signal!

"Open it, Edward," Li'l Ed said. "Communication mode. Call my father."

His father's face appeared translucently before him, its features difficult to make out as Li'l Ed concentrated on driving straight toward the distant city lights. "I'm so sorry, sir! It wasn't me. The Unnamed disconnected my EI."

"Unnamed?" His father sighed sadly. "I was afraid of this. How are you talking to me now if they Departed you?"

"I'm not Departed, sir. It wasn't McGuillian Unnamed, sir. I was taken to meet with Chairman Williams, of Williams Gypsum. He offered me a job as his Unnamed."

"What?"

"I turned him down, sir, as it had already been decided that I would submit for voluntary."

"And ... " his father peered at something through his own EI that must have been a mapping and location program. "You're traveling now. You turned down the unstable owner of a sovereign corporation, and he's just giving you a ride home?"

"No, sir. His Unnamed tried to kill me in the desert. I stole this truck and ran away."

"You stole a truck from an Unnamed? How did you manage something like that?"

"I'm out in the desert, somewhere, sir. I'm quite sure he was going to kill me. I jumped out, and he tried to shoot me, but I was able to get back to the truck before he did. There's a lot of dust blowing around, so much I can't see more than a couple meters in front of me. Maybe it messed up his tech? He fired at me but missed."

His father smiled. "Oh, Li'l Ed, that's wonderful news! When you turn in the truck, you'll be a true hero! You'll start off much better after reconditioning than you would have otherwise. Good job, Li'l Ed!"

"Thank you, sir. I wasn't able to use my EI for communication until just now and I know you told me to submit for voluntary reconditioning right away. Shall I go and do that now, sir?"

"Yes, immediately. I'm proud of you, Li'l Ed."

New Union School

"And cupping the chin," the New Union instructor said, "pull backwards until your palm impacts the base of the skull—gently, now. Remember, this classmate is a New Union asset so I'm going slowly. When it's not a training exercise, you'll be using full force. Strike two or three times, quickly, and then slam him down the rest of the way to the ground. Ideally, he'll be stunned and immobilized so you can walk him straight to the Divinators."

Divinators.

Rus had a few quick flashes of memory—fire, noise, humiliation, terrible pain. The Divinators were damned good at making you see that you were nothing but a lump of shit for the New Union to mold into something better. Every time he thought of them, it was just a slideshow of the same few images, and then his mind filled with black again. Right now he was training—being molded—at the New Union school. That was all he needed, or wanted, to think about.

School was the second stage of training after new soldiers were captured. Rus had come here straight from the Divinators, starting as a class with others who'd been captured at the same time. Of the eight Bridges who'd been grabbed that day, Rus had only seen Pawley since, and only once. Pawley had started the school at the same time, but separated off into another group.

"A fist in the face will work, as well," his short and wiry teacher, Instructor Jodo, said. "If you go for the face, there's more chance he's gonna fight you, because he can see it coming. Remember, we just want to capture them and turn them over to the Divinators with as little struggle as possible."

Rus merely had to survive. There was no reason to question morality when he was powerless to enforce what he felt was right, anyway.

Somewhere in the mist

Addi was in some sort of cave. There was snow around the entrance but she was farther inside, where only a few wisps had blown. There was no sensation of cold.

The mist was thick in the opening of the cave, but lighter here, and the faint gray light allowed her to see the other girl. She recognized her instantly, but the appearance was still shocking.

Inti sat leaning against the wall, wrapped in rough blankets of red, brown, gray and orange. Her hair was so black it had a blue sheen, hanging in tight braids around her pretty, diamond-shaped brown face and wise, narrow brown eyes.

She moved slightly, causing a necklace of tiny bells and metal trinkets to jingle a bit.

"Oh, Addi!" Inti said. "You are so beautiful!"

Addi raised a hand and touched her own face. The scars were gone. Even her missing toe was back!

"What is this place?" Addi asked, though she already knew.

"This is where I died, in this cave at the top of the mountain," Inti said. "I will carry on from here."

"But...why am I here with you?"

"Oh." Inti sat quietly for a moment. "Maybe just to say goodbye. To share this moment together." Her smile was sad but genuine.

"And what do you think I'm supposed to do now?" Addi asked.

Inti didn't speak. She just gestured at the cave's opening. They sat together in silence a long time. Addi leaned to hug Inti and they squeezed each other tightly.

"What will you do?" Addi asked.

"I don't know. I'll make my way somehow."

"Maybe we can go together," Addi said.

"This looks like the mountain, and it *is* the mountain where I died, but yet I do not think either of us has been to this world before," Inti said. "We don't know what the rules are, here." She paused. "Maybe we can stay together. I don't want to be alone."

They sat a bit longer and then took each other's hand. They crawled through the cave together, awkwardly making their way across the uneven stone without unclasping their hands, for which Addi was tremendously grateful. At the opening, they stepped out into the mist, and the mountain disappeared.

Some Zone street

Furius dropped another packet of Pink Shit and kept on walking.

Kym had said her General had nothing to do with the Saved, and it was pretty clear she was telling the truth since they'd nearly killed her, too. Now they were working together, and it seemed a pretty good match. She knew how to run the refinery, and he knew how to keep the place safe from punks.

One packet per block would generate a lot of new soldiers soon, at least around here. The business types in the entertainment areas never picked up drugs because their urine, blood, and hair was constantly tested, but that was okay. Mr. B.'s old friend had now agreed to a substantial bribe in exchange for dosing every last bottle of sodje, mostly bound for the entertainment district. Kym was churning out more dosed amino bricks every day, and the glut was apparently over so they were again being taken up for synthesizers. The salarymen would probably make shitty soldiers, but he was going to have legions of them soon.

Mikk's new apartment

"As yet we've been unable to feed the poor at the stations you had us set up, Lord," Porter said. "There is simply nothing to give, beyond our spreading of your word. Your Helpers are repeating your most recent message, that we shouldn't judge others. They're ready for any new messages you would like them to pass on."

Mikk smiled to himself. Sometimes he really appreciated the other guy in his head. "That's right," he said. "I judge. Whatever the question, I'm the one who answers it. They go trying to figure shit out for themselves, it'll be chaos. Keep 'em humble."

Porter opened his mouth to speak, but Mikk stopped him with a raised palm. "Wait. Before you tell me anything else, I want to know whether you've found that fucker you let get away, Mr. B. Did your people go back to the protein refinery?"

"Yes, Lord. The refinery was locked down tightly and nobody answered, even when we went with carbon recyclables and posed as customers. We believe they were out, but it could also be that they recognized us as Saved, Lord."

"Stay on it. I want that fucker dead."

"Yes, Lord," Porter said. "There's something else, Lord. We're suffering increasing casualties. The Fiends are starting to attack more frequently, Lord."

"We need more guns," Mikk said. "The captured Fiend ones we got from the Horde are good, but we need a hell of a lot more of 'em, and fast. To get guns we need money. What assets we got to work with?"

"Almost nothing, Lord. We are a collection of desperately poor people, as you know. We do control a good portion of what used to be Horde territory, though."

"Okay. Here's what we do. First, we push all the Saved to give up whatever they can. There's your new message: *Give us your stuff.* Wait. No. How do we say it? *Let go of material possessions.*" Mikk shrugged. "Some shit like that."

"Yes, Lord."

"Then we implement some new policies. From now on, only Saved get access to the clinic. If they're coming for treatment and either they or anyone with them has anything of value, tell them they're not truly Saved if they're keeping that for themselves instead of donating it to the cause."

"Yes, Lord."

"If I'm gonna start giving these people weapons, I have to be sure which ones're truly on my side."

"Yes, Lord. How will we know?"

"First, make damned sure they're terrified of the Fiends, like constantly pissing themselves with fear. I want every grisly Fiend story repeated until every last Saved knows it by heart. If you got some way to write 'em down, that's even better. Pass 'em on so everyone knows what's waiting if they leave the Saved."

"Yes, Lord."

"Then, we gotta find the real zealots in the bunch. I want you to set up weekly meetings where the Saved are encouraged to fink each other out. Every time any of them second-guesses my orders or gets a little too assertive, I want to know about it. After a few weeks, you'll know who to make into the group leaders. Start feeding and housing the leaders a little better; make sure they feel rewarded. Eventually, when we have some, the leaders will get weapons."

"Yes, Lord."

Amelix lab

The control the rats had over her should perhaps have been frightening, if Chelsea had been able to consider it much at all. More frightening by far would have been the fact that she *wasn't* able to consider it, but that didn't cross her mind often, either. The little flashes of thoughts like that she did have were coming with diminishing frequency.

It wasn't a particularly puppet-like form of control, though they did certainly have the ability to move any part of her in any way. Puppet-like control would have trapped her inside a body that kept moving of its own accord, making her a stowaway consciousness tagging along as her stolen physical form marched off to do its new masters' bidding. Instead, the rats made her *want* to do things. With increasing frequency, she found herself obsessed with activities she never otherwise would have considered, including many that should have horrified her.

Finally this task was finished. They would let her leave this newly requisitioned lab space to go home and sleep, and in a few hours she would be back, serving them according to…their plan? Yes, she reasoned, all this had to be part of a plan. The reasoning, and her ability to do it, vanished again.

She checked the seals on all ninety cages, making sure each one had remained properly sealed after she had injected air from the G2 cage in her office. She turned out the light as she left the room, letting the new generation of Rat Gods rest.

II

8

A Zone alley

*S*tab in from the side.
Cut the blade outward through the front of the throat.

The first few times he'd done it, Rus had used two separate motions, a stab and then a cut. Now he was much faster, accomplishing the kill in a fluid circular motion, while still avoiding the gurgling that trying to slice in from the front would have caused. The New Union had taught him hundreds of useful tricks like this.

Rus lowered the dead sentry quietly to the pavement. The Juice in his system flooded him with power and pleasure. Two Elements nearby stood over two other sentries who had been similarly dealt with. To his Juice-addled consciousness, sheathing the slippery blade felt like sex. The rifle in his hands seemed to vibrate, begging him to make it sing.

After a few weeks with the New Union, it had all become easy. Nobody gets out alive, so life becomes nothing more than a struggle for perfect compliance with orders. He existed solely for the advancement of this army, and it had the power to decide everything for him, even to the point of determining when he would cease to exist. The Unity, was what the New Union called this state of being. Outsiders and new recruits assumed the Unity was death, but actually it was the state of knowing that life and death are the same.

This street of abandoned storefronts was Saved territory, and the Saved had nothing worth taking. The last time the Round had worked the entertainment districts, they'd killed four Unnamed, and Rus had found himself in possession of a genuine blacksuit firebomb. There would be no spoils like that around here, but at least he could get the rush of a kill or two.

A stick swished through the air nearby—a signal from his Rounder to creep ahead slowly. The next sound, an imparter pop from tab one, meant that he should keep moving straight ahead and find cover wherever he could.

Rus ran forward, but there was no cover to be found nearby. Training dictated that he should continue farther ahead until he could comply, and finally he crouched down in a moon shadow next to some concrete front stairs, about half a block ahead of the rest of his Round.

A group of eight people emerged from a door across the street and headed directly toward the other Elements. Rus would now be the one behind them, tasked with fighting them alone if they ran back this way. At least with gangs you could pick up a decent knife or club, and the New Union could even capture a few new soldiers. According to the New Union Divinators, the Saved were already too brainwashed to be retrained as Elements, so they were just worthless. Their numbers were growing quickly, though, and they were no longer passive and fearful. The Saved had begun to claim new territory by force, instead of just waiting for everyone in it to die, like the Horde used to do. They were becoming a nuisance, and the New Union would no longer tolerate their existence in the Zone.

Top Dog didn't want any bullets wasted on these fuckers, though. It was all knife work in Saved territory, if they could help it.

As the only Element behind these eight, he would have the best chance at multiple kills. Rus's breathing deepened and his face curved into a clown-like smile. Anticipating another kill made the Juice rush surge, bringing confidence, fearlessness, and the compulsion to take lives. He tracked back the way he'd come, trailing safely behind the eight Saved, who were walking down the right-hand side of the street. As he closed the distance from his Round, Rus lowered his rifle and drew his knife again.

Federal Administration Building

It hadn't been terribly long ago that the Ricker boy's killer had escaped to tunnels beneath the Zone. Daiss was still fuming about it. Politically motivated inefficiency had been fine until the little cunt had killed Agents Hawkins and Reda, but now even Instructor Samuelson just wanted her dead.

At least they'd collected a lot of important data from the debacle. Having to discuss his worst failure in front of this crowd today was almost unbearable, but other Zetas needed to be shown how powerful the new information was.

Instructor Samuelson finished introducing the topic and gestured at Daiss. "Brother, if you please?"

Daiss stood and shuffled past other hulking Agents to reach an aisle, then hustled to the front of the room. Twenty genetically tweaked, Golden, Federal Agent faces stared up at him: the local Zetas, each with a security clearance level in the top ten percent.

"Thank you, Instructor," Daiss said. "Good afternoon, brothers and sisters. Recently I worked a stakeout, impersonating one of the Zone's self-proclaimed doctors. The perpetrator in our murder case had been one of his customers, and we took over the operation of the medical office in hopes of finding and capturing her. Through Instructor Samuelson's guidance I now understand that the assignment actually produced much more.

"I'll admit that at first this assignment was difficult for me." He smiled. "Next time you get frustrated dealing with those idiot dust monkeys, just be glad you're not snuggling up to play doctor with them," he said, gesturing with his hands raised as if in surrender. His audience shared an understanding chuckle.

"But as Zetas, we must understand the Zone in the finest detail we can manage. While I was waiting there and hoping the assailant would appear, I questioned the various Zone inhabitants who showed up seeking care. I specifically asked for information concerning every other practitioner in the area they had seen. Our guy was clearly the favorite among his patients, but there were eleven others in pretty close proximity. We set up surveillance at each of those practitioners and followed some of their patients for a time, collecting observational data about their care and their patterns of recovery.

"Our sample of patients and care techniques was broad enough that Task Force Zeta was able to assess the effectiveness of these practitioners. In most cases, treatment at such places did improve the health of the patients seeking care. That is, as we struggle to get these Zone populations under control, these witch doctors are working against us somewhat successfully, helping to ensure that they survive and reproduce in wild-type ranges."

Daiss glanced at Instructor Samuelson, who nodded, releasing him. He made his way back to his seat as Instructor Samuelson began again.

"Thank you, Brother Daiss. Now, as interesting as all that is, there's something else we've learned from this project. We've taken over one of the networking sites frequented by these unlicensed practitioners, called MediPirates, and made a discovery that changes the game for us significantly. Specifically, we have identified a new and alarming epidemic."

Through his EI Daiss examined the first image his Instructor had linked for this assembly, of the MediPirates site. "This page is their big board, where topics are posted. The subsequent discussions appear as links," Samuelson said. As Daiss watched, one link blinked and expanded into a series of posted comments.

"The epidemic relates to this topic, posted by our own Dark Dok." Instructor Samuelson read it aloud.

MediPirates Bulletin Board
Posted by Dark Dok #cB449d:

Patient came in covered in a white powder which I assume is some street drug, though spectrometer came up with no commonly known substance. Patient became increasingly catatonic and has been motionless last three hours. Pupils unresponsive but vitals otherwise normal. Administered 0.9% IV NaCl to flush it out, tried talking to him to snap him back to the world of the living, but I'm running out of ideas. As a last resort, I'm now trying some Asian folk medicine, burning incense and striking a chime, hoping maybe it'll stimulate his senses and get him moving again. Does anyone have any idea what I might be dealing with, here?

"It turned out that this powder was causing a kind of schizophrenia," Samuelson continued. "After the catatonic state, victims were waking up—some after a short time, others after days—convinced that their bodies had been taken over by some other person entirely. Suddenly lots of other cases were popping up on these MediPirates posts, and it was clear that an event was underway which would have serious repercussions in the Zone. To gain control of the information sharing as best we could, we commandeered the MediPirates site and slammed the door on this online discussion, only showing each member a fraction of the total responses and stalling posts about it until we reviewed and released them, giving preference to the ones that were the most misleading or gave the most useless or dangerous advice. When possible, we let the worst of them converse with each other to replicate the site's function more authentically, while the more adept site visitors experienced higher rates of technical difficulty."

The image changed to a slide show of posts, moving too quickly for any of them to be read. "We believe we were successful in convincing the group that the problem was relatively small and contained, to maybe three or four patients. Our compilation of MediPirates posts from the Des Moines Zone currently shows more than ninety reports of this phenomenon, however, and the last thirty were made in the last two weeks. We believe this will soon become a pandemic.

"Unfortunately, we don't yet have a sample of the drug, which at this point we're calling *Pandora Powder*. However, it's clearly burning through the Zone at an accelerating rate, producing more of these Individuals—that's the name we've given the new personalities that appear, *Individuals*, with a capital *I*—as well as increasing societal disorder as they permeate the Zone community.

"With this group here today, the most trusted and elite cadre of Zetas in this area, we can be frank. Task Force Zeta exists, not only here but all around the globe, for the purpose of sealing off the world's various Zones in order to protect legitimate corporate interests, wherever they may be. As yet, no Zetas have put forward a compelling claim as to why any particular Zone should be closed off from civilized society. Too many CBD salarymen and salarywomen frequent the entertainment areas for it to be an easy sell. Yet now it appears that this could be just the impetus we've been waiting for; the chaos resulting from this new plague could well lead to desperate cries from civilized areas to seal it off for good.

"For now it is crucial that we keep this information to ourselves. When the Pandora epidemic builds to the crisis level we expect, we'll release a statement that this is an unknown disease. The resulting medical quarantine will usher in the strict border controls we need."

Schafer House, Ltd

"You should feel your EI reconnecting with the outside world in a moment," Drya, the woman escorting him, said. "Per your revised agreement with McGuillian Corporation, you won't be getting your name back." Together the two of them walked down a wide hallway.

"That's fine, ma'am" the man who had been called Li'l Ed said. "Though it does feel strange to have no name at all."

"They'll assign you a letter-number combination as you're processed in, but the name is gone forever." She smiled, in the same intense, pathway-amplified, Accepted way he now did. "There's a reason they'll call you an Unnamed Executive, you know."

"Nobody calls me anything just yet, ma'am."

"I call you sweet," she said. "I wish I could see you once your body's all amped up."

It was his turn to smile. Now, with pathway amplification, smiling made his heart pound. "You'll never see me again. Though I might see you, from the other side of my dark glasses. Thank you for being a wonderful guide in my reconditioning process, Drya. I won't forget you."

They stopped at a door. She cocked her head at him. "I wonder if that's true. Not forgetting, I mean. I don't know how many of your old memories they let you keep when you become an Unnamed."

She unlocked the door with her EI. His own EI suddenly connected again with the outside world, making his body shudder slightly as the wave of information washed through his mind. They entered an elevator and began ascending.

"Whoa, that's strange. I wonder if EIs take a while to recalibrate. If the date I'm seeing were right, I'd only have been here for a few weeks. It's been a few months, at least."

"No, it's right. Two weeks, three days. It's not an accident that your sense of time is distorted. With wave manipulation, it's easy to alter your perception. The times you thought you were spending a night sleeping were actually the briefest of naps, breaking each twenty-four-hour period into what you interpreted as several days and nights. Your diet was almost exclusively high carbohydrate and low protein, which made it easier to keep you in a trance state. It was important for you to believe you were here for an extended stretch, because that helps your mind accept that the reconditioning process is inevitable; your brain no longer reaches beyond its immediate circumstances. It becomes convinced that there is no other way of life."

"Fascinating!" he said. "I did feel that way, like maybe I was never going to get out of here."

"It's a process that was refined for use with involuntary admittees. Sometimes they actually do take months, but the manips make it feel like years to them. The system monitors everything, from the way you enunciate words, to the number of times you blink per minute, to the changes in your heartrate and breathing when assigned tasks that relate to your future job assignment. Once your metrics are within specified parameters, the program flags you for release."

"I feel privileged to be the beneficiary of so much thought and focus," he said.

She nodded with a satisfied grin. "Note, though, that you must never discuss these aspects of your experience with anyone. As you know, we're working to make McGuillian one hundred percent Accepted, and it would be detrimental for incoming candidates to be aware of the time manipulation inherent in the reconditioning process." She looked into his eyes. "The sense that it will never end is an important part of each candidate's reconditioning. One who came here expecting it might resist, leading to increased time, energy and expenditure. That would be bad for McGuillian. Do you understand?"

He had almost imagined telling someone, simply because it was an interesting fact to share, but before the thought had even gelled she had shown him how doing so would waste McGuillian resources. If she'd been just a bit slower, letting the thought fully form first, the realization that he'd been daydreaming about something bad for the company would have torn open a chasm in his mind, freezing rational thought in the now familiar blast of terror that pathway amplification always brought whenever it fed upon guilt and doubt. "I won't tell anyone!" he said with desperate quickness. His mind flooded with good feelings, now, amplifying the satisfaction of having decided it so firmly.

Drya smiled again. Accepted always smiled with quivering lips. "I know you won't." The elevator stopped at the ground floor, admitting them to a vast entryway the size of a Traverball field. She headed for a set of glass doors some distance away.

"I do have one more question," he said. "Can you tell me why we get pathway amplification? I asked my handler, but all he said was that the motivations for corporate actions were beyond his rank. It occurs to me that perhaps it's like the duration issue, where maybe it's okay for me to know now. It just… it seems strange to turn up our emotions so we have to constantly fight to control them, when the process could instead have made us calmer."

"McGuillian will turn down your emotions with drugs," she said. "But if the reconditioning process turned them down permanently, it'd be harder to motivate you. During your training, every experience, every decision, and every thought is reinforced by enhanced emotion. Choices and behaviors that are encouraged by McGuillian result in intensified joy, pride, or pleasure. Unsanctioned ideas and actions produce amplified feelings of terror, shame and remorse. Through this process, the company establishes itself as your guide, your source of reason and stability. The sense of peace the drugs bring is a gift from the company—and of course it's one that can be taken away. Without active chemical management, Accepted would become suicidally unstable within a matter of hours." Her face was mostly expressionless, but she raised a shoulder in a mechanical shrug. "This is by design. Accepted hold all our most powerful positions, and we can only trust them when they are receiving precise care from the McGuillian Medical Doctor. We need to be sure that if their chemistry varies even slightly from prescribed norms, they'll immediately remove themselves from the population before they do any damage to the company. Anyone trying to skip doses or otherwise subvert the absolute authority of the McGuillian Medical Doctor will simply be gone. For non-Accepted, a suicide attempt means involuntary reconditioning, but for those who have already been reconditioned, nothing more can be done to maintain the worker as an asset. The company makes certain there are no unsuccessful attempts among Accepted.

"Don't tell anyone that, either. You know why. Oh, look! Your escorts are here."

Standing just inside the doors was a pair of Unnamed Executives, in their smooth black suits and sunglasses.

"Good luck to you, my young friend," Drya said. "I'm sure you'll do McGuillian proud."

Near the Saved clinic

Rus was in position, lying prone in the long shadow of a building. This was his first large-scale raid on the Saved, where he was allowed to use his primary weapon instead of just his blade. There was still nothing to gain for himself—the Saved seemed poorer than ever—but all this killing was going to give him one hell of a rush.

His New Union stealth techniques and camouflage were so good that Saved passed right by him without noticing, even though there was still plenty of daylight. Rus had more than a hundred New Union Elements with him today, though most were considerably farther back.

Juice's weirdly sharp aftertaste had a way of making the whole world smell like blood. His system revved at the thought of it splattering, coating him as he slashed, stabbed, and shot, warm and heavy against his skin. He'd be coming home sticky today, even if he did end up mostly using the rifle.

The crowd in the street grew much larger and louder. A door opened and a group came out. It was difficult to tell how many were at the core of it all, maybe ten or twelve, but the crowd surrounding that central group was easily a few hundred. The spectators surged toward the central figure, packing themselves in until, tightly wedged together, they moved slowly away from the door as a unit. Rus peered out from his hiding place to see who could be commanding this much attention.

Him!

Rus knew his place. He was committed to serving the New Union faithfully and forever, but that face brought his mind back to an unsettled score from before he'd been claimed. The man still had the forehead scar Murph had given him. It was the fucking Garbageman, who'd killed Murph and cheated the Bridges on their biggest deal! The last time he'd seen that fucker, Rus had been a scared, sad kid. Now, as a well-trained and equipped New Union Element, he had his chance to erase that shame.

The raid was due to start any moment.

The rifle.

One shot from right here, and the Garbageman would cease to exist. Even on Juice, though, a single shot wouldn't be satisfying enough. Not in this case.

There was something wrong with the way the Saved seemed to flock around the Garbageman and hang on everything he did or said. The way they fawned and leaned toward him with wide eyes and blank faces didn't seem to be rooted in the fear he would have expected.

He's their leader!

The more he watched, the more obvious it became. These people were doing what the Garbageman said. If he wasn't the leader, he was at least pretty high up in the Saved organization. Now Rus could kill him in service of the New Union, and maybe even get recognized for an important kill, while righting the Bridges' past wrong.

There were about a hundred people around him, staring at him like they were tranqued. Maybe instead of Juice, the Saved were hooked on some kind of barbituate.

The signal to start the raid would come any second.

Full auto, up close so he can see my face? No, too many of them for me to be that close when I hit.

The ones closest to the Garbageman were armed. Using the gun would be risky.

He still had that Unnamed firebomb he'd been saving! The crowd was distracted enough that he could use quietwalking and camouflage to get right up near the Garbageman. Rus would watch him cook, along with a whole street full of his followers. He had seen the blacksuits use the bombs often enough that he knew how far he'd have to throw it.

Of course, Rus would have to unfade long enough for the fucker to see who was killing him.

The Clinic

The Saved were developing a militaristic social structure similar to that of the Horde or CBD. Wanda had failed to convince the leadership of her devotion and was now the practitioner they trusted least, but Porter often sought her out with matters like this.

"The One has graciously provided an additional fifty or sixty mattresses, maybe as many as twenty as full beds," Porter said. "We're setting them up across the street for now. You should be able to put patients in there in another hour or two."

"The clinic certainly needs the extra beds and space, sir," Wanda said. Porter was one of the most powerful Saved, and it had been made clear to Wanda that calling him *sir* was not optional. She found it hard to express any gratitude for the extra beds when she knew they must have come from relatively peaceful little neighborhoods on the fringes of what had been Horde territory, which the Saved had recently raided, Fiend-style.

"This war is filling the beds faster than ever, sir," she said, mostly to fill the silence.

Porter looked at her expectantly. She realized that she'd made an indirect reference to the Saved soldiers who would be filling the beds. The Saved demanded various mantras for different situations, but the gist was always the same. They said it was to keep everyone's mind on what they called the holy nature of the conflict.

"May the One keep and protect his brave soldiers," Wanda added hastily. Porter nodded once, slowly.

"This struggle is a true test of our faith and devotion," he said. "From forty thousand we're now down to twenty-five or so."

"Yes, I know. Sir. I see so many wounded Saved heroes, may the One keep and protect them. I live among them here at the clinic around the clock."

"You choose to remain in denial, Wanda, refusing the love and community of the One. Sula showed deference and reverence, and she was rewarded with rank. Now she's in charge of the whole clinic. I'm glad to see you're starting to follow her example, but as for your current living conditions, you still have nobody to blame but yourself." He walked away with his back rigid and his jaw locked, glancing this way and that, crossing the street to oversee the Saved who were moving the mattresses.

Having been thoroughly conquered by Coach V's regime, Sula ran the clinic as it had always been run. Sula and the other original "girls," who had also converted and become Saved, lived in the apartment building across the street where the One himself lived. There were four more new medical practitioners at the clinic who were all devout Saved, and they were living in the apartment building, too. The floor of apartments they shared had formerly housed Horde high officers. It was one of the most luxurious places in the whole Zone, with glass in the windows and even some running water, carried in buckets up to a tank on the top floor.

Sula made sure they all thanked the One profusely for such gifts, and now nearly everything they said was accompanied with a "thanks be to the One," or "the One saw fit." Wanda was forcing herself to copy them. The words were coming more easily to her lately but she could not speak them with much conviction, having seen firsthand how brutal the One actually was.

Her efforts to conform were being rewarded, however. Sula had decided to let Wanda take two twenty-minute breaks per day, monitoring a site called MediPirates for relevant news. This was as good a time as any, so she sat down at the computer.

Far more important than the breaks was the fact that Wanda was starting to be allowed doses of bactrostimulants. It didn't matter that someday soon she'd end up as addicted as Coach had been. She couldn't do this job anymore without increasing amounts of uppers. She had to thank and praise the One for every dose, but it felt easier to thank him for her own drugs than for things like the clinic's supply of clean bandages or a stretch of nice weather.

At present, she could find nothing of interest on MediPirates. In fact, there was hardly any activity at all.

Wanda's mind drifted. She had real skills now, skills that were valuable even here in the Zone. She knew how to stitch wounds, sterilize instruments, and even prescribe some bactroherbal meds, if there were any to be found. Some members of the MediPirates community had been solo practices, and she'd fantasized about leaving here and building a practice of her own. Digging a bit deeper, she'd discovered that every last solo practice had stopped posting in the last few weeks.

She *felt* the One's approach instead of seeing or hearing it. So many Saved followed the One around now that their approaching footsteps made the ground vibrate.

Wanda logged out and hustled to the clinic's front door with the other practitioners. Empty little displays of devotion like this were worth the easier, more comfortable life that they brought. Near her were the clinic's Helpers—devout Saved who had proven their fidelity and were being rewarded with safe duties away from combat. They were mostly worthless in the clinic, as they were far more dedicated to spying on Porter's behalf than to being useful assistants, but they did help with minor tasks. While the Saved as a whole were unarmed, each Helper had been issued a handgun, which Porter claimed was to prevent the clinic from changing hands again.

The One's entourage had grown substantially, now comprising a few hundred people. When he visited the clinic they always waited outside, staring through the glass at him, desperate to get closer. Wanda tried to appear as fervent as they were.

She saw him out there in the street, through random gaps in the crowd. The One still had the look of a criminal, with an uneven keloid gunshot scar on his neck, a nose that had been broken at least once, and the wide ragged scar across his forehead, but already she could tell that today it would be easier to pretend to love him. This was one of those times when the One seemed softer, more like he'd been when she'd first met him, and the difference was obvious even at first glance. Only this version of the One seemed to have any interest in the patients, and when he came into the clinic his presence actually seemed to help them.

Porter was off somewhere else, fulfilling his role as second-in-command, but the other Disciples surrounded the One as he made his way across the parking lot. They had nearly reached the clinic's glass door when the One burst into flames.

Dobo Protein Refinery

Kym Evans stayed seated at her desk. The pounding on the front gate got louder. The refinery was now increasingly under siege from the enemies Mikk and Furius had made.

Kym was staying put. The upside of having a psychopath like Mikk or Furius around was that he could usually be counted upon to cancel out other deranged killers.

It wasn't a perfect system. Furius had already killed two of the weird new Pink Shit personalities over his ancient political turf wars, wasting two potential soldiers for the General's army. Still, he was always willing to put himself between Kym and the horrors on the other side of the wall. That counted for a lot, even if he was doing it for his own purposes rather than out of any concern for her safety.

Besides, it wasn't like she could stop him.

"Yeah, yeah," Furius called out, weaving between the roach vacuum and the hopper as he hustled toward the front gate in his red Roman cloak. "Gimme a minute."

Kym had moved out of the place she'd shared with Mikk and now slept here, next to Furius, who let her run the refinery and keep all the money. He made his own living, now that he'd listened to Kym and started dealing real drugs instead of just Pink Shit.

Mikk never would have allowed Kym to keep her own income. She'd learned to appreciate that kind of thing about Furius.

The screens mounted on the wall near Kym's desk showed a haggy woman with empty hands. Kym adjusted the volume to hear what was going on. Furius checked the grainy little screen just inside the gate and shouted, "What do you want?"

"Someone … someone said I should come here if I'm … not from this time?" The woman's halting voice was barely audible over the speaker.

Furius touched the screen, flicking through every other camera angle to be sure it wasn't a surprise attack. Apparently seeing no potential ambush (Kym didn't see one, anyway, on her monitors), he cracked open the gate.

"Who were you?" he asked, his voice coming through clearly on Kym's speakers.

There was a pause. They always seemed to have a hard time admitting their craziness.

"Melkorka," she said.

Kym recorded the name in her computer.

"Nationality?"

"What?"

"What country, what nation?"

"Uh, Irish, slave to Vikings."

Kym stored the information. This list, especially when Kym asked the woman for a way to find or contact her, would be essential for the General to have.

"Damn it!" Furius said. "That's twenty-two of you who've found your way here so far, and not one Roman among you." He grumbled something to himself and then called out again, "How'd you die?"

"I was my master's favorite. He wanted to take me with him to Valhalla when he died."

"Could you have said no? Asked him to let you live instead?"

"I was too well-trained for that. His will was mine. I took a potion and then his men beat and stabbed me." She tried to peer under his arm. "I haven't seen him here, yet, though."

"Haven't seen any Vikings so far, but you do fit the pattern," Furius said. "People like us built this world, through devotion, training and sacrifice. Now we're back to secure our claim over it." He opened the gate farther. "Come inside. I'm not yet sure why I'm getting non-Romans, but I'll fill you in."

"Why have we all come to this place?" she asked. "What are we supposed to do, now that we're here?"

"I'm here to reassemble the Roman Legions and take over this territory. My guess is you'll probably be a whore, but maybe there's some other use for you I don't know about. Remember, even whores are important to the cause of establishing proper rule here."

"Oh."

He locked the gate, smiling. "Vikings do train slaves well, don't they? That was the perfect reaction for a whore. It's going to be more pleasant to work with you than with the cunt from this morning who'd thrown herself on her husband's funeral pyre."

The words faded as the pair moved away from the gate, and Kym turned off the sound again. He'd bring her in and pay her to fuck him now, *checking her level of skill* like he'd done with all the women who showed up. So far they had all complied, even the funeral pyre one. Kym guessed they'd probably already learned to fuck and suck if they were still alive in the Zone after any time at all.

Yesterday, some crazy bitch who claimed to have died as a dancing girl sealed alive into her queen's tomb had seemed thrilled by the idea of surrendering to Furius. Her moaning and screaming had made Kym decide to work at the hopper for a while to escape it.

So far, the men who had come believed they were soldiers and loyal subjects of all kinds of dead countries, and the majority of them had been instantly hostile to Furius. Most had stormed off, but two had immediately attacked him. Of those, Furius had bludgeoned one to death and shot the other, and now both bodies were stacked in the pile, waiting their turn to be carbon recycled.

Sure enough, he brought the woman right up to the office. Soon he'd be on top of her on the floor in the back room, where he now kept all the production equipment.

Sex with Furius wasn't so bad, really. He sometimes demanded it from Kym, but for the most part it was quick and relatively painless. He didn't have the love of causing misery Mikk had demonstrated. Being here with Furius scared Kym less than being alone would have, and that was about the best any woman could hope for.

Furius opened the door and escorted Melkorka through Kym's workspace. He never bothered to introduce Kym, but usually she could catch the women and get their contact information on their way out. She was sure the General could use every soldier she could call, once they were reunited.

"Anyway, after I explain the situation," Furius said as he passed, "we'll send you back out to find others, the same way somebody found you. We're starting to get busy now. I think within days we'll go from twenty-three of us, into the hundreds and then probably thousands."

The backlog of aminos at the sterile nute producers had apparently cleared now, or at least they'd temporarily stopped trying to drive down bulk amino prices. Nute companies were again demanding more than the refinery could produce, and though they did randomly test the blocks for purity, so far not a single block from Dobo Protein Refinery had been rejected. Maybe Pink Shit didn't show up on their tests. Whatever the reason, the stuff was getting through and the money was still coming in.

"I'll give you a little bag of Pink Shit so you can create some new soldiers for us, too," Furius told Melkorka. "Just stay with the ones you find now. Start to form groups out there, and wait for us to find you." The door to his office closed behind them.

Amelix Executive Quarters

Dr. Zabeth Chelsea closed her draft of the report and opened a blank file instead. The report was long overdue by standard protocol, though Dr. Donova hadn't asked for an update. The Rat Gods were so precious that Chelsea's superiors had not authorized any new experiments for fear of harming them, so right now there was no official news to report.

Still, a lack of official news wasn't the whole story.

She did feel a bit guilty. All Amelix workers shared a common duty to pass on all pertinent information to superiors, though obviously there were special circumstances that prevented it in this instance. Officially, there was an enforced hiatus on experimentation involving the original four Rat Gods. Unofficially, there were now more than seven hundred new Rat Gods in her new workspace annex.

Her husband Alin wasn't home yet. Lower-ranking Accepted worked longer hours at the office and fewer hours at home, compared to someone at Chelsea's level. It was good that he was out. She needed this time to think.

She manipulated her EI to convert her voice to text, in the hope that speaking out loud might allow her to evaluate her thoughts more objectively. She couldn't describe even half of what she'd observed in an official memo at this point, but it seemed like a good idea to keep an account of recent events and her interpretation of them, even if only for her own reference.

"Title, all caps," she said. Her EI waited. The words appeared in her mind as she spoke: "NOTES ON THE RAT GODS."

She cleared her throat. "Should I mention the Thrall?" It was her word, which she used to define the state of being under the rats' spell, and the EI translated it into text correctly, including her intention to capitalize the "T."

"It's an amazing and wonderful feeling," she said. "I crave it, now. It's warm and soft, like being inside a mental cocoon, where my worries and responsibilities cease to exist. Whatever they want is what I want, and I do all I can to make it happen.

"But why? And how are they able, with their tiny rat brains, to take over my comparatively massive human brain?"

It was a complex question, one she would not have dared to address in circumstances where her work would be subject to review, but perhaps recording and analyzing her observations in this document would help her figure it out. She felt compelled to push toward an answer, even though she seemed to have an odd mental block against doing so.

"They don't look like regular rats," she said, knowing it was out of context. Her EI moved the text down accordingly, keeping the new idea separate from what she'd been thinking in the sentence above. "Their bodies have never filled out like those of adult rats normally do. They remain lanky and more juvenile-looking, yet they function as fully formed adults, without any disposition toward play."

But how do they control me?

"One thing I believe is clear: Whatever it is they do, it's not communication in the typical human sense. They don't share ideas through language, which, as we all know, is imperfect and subject to analog-style breakdowns. Even writing these notes to myself right now, it's difficult to put into words exactly what I mean, and it will be difficult later to get my own mind to understand this material in exactly the same way I do now. Language is a highly flawed means of communication, through which people often construe ideas much differently than the original speaker or writer intended."

Her speech slowed as she carefully selected each word.

"What the Rat Gods do is more of a shared consciousness. They all seem to understand things exactly the same way, at the same instant. They appear to experience the world as an entirety, shared by all of them simultaneously, existing as a single mind that is distributed among all their physical bodies. I believe this may be due to the fungus living in their tissues. If so, the Rat Gods seem to be controlled by it the same way humans can be controlled by the rats. The fungus could actually be communicating with itself, using the rats merely as its hosts.

"Brain size, and even intellect, may only be important for autonomous creatures. Humans weighing eighty kilograms used to train and control horses weighing five hundred kilograms, and it's tempting to say that they were able to do this because humans had larger brains. But really, horses were trained by using information and techniques refined over generations. It was the ability of one human mind to learn from others' earlier experiences that allowed mastery of those techniques, not any particular individual human's intellectual prowess. We can imagine the passing on of information this way to be a vertical kind of information sharing, from one generation to the next, although obviously humans can also communicate with each other in real time. Neanderthals were physically stronger than Homo sapiens sapiens, and they also had bigger brains, but they were unable to effectively share much of their acquired knowledge with each other. As autonomous beings they were superior, but the sapiens' ability to form groups proved an even more powerful evolutionary advantage. Eventually the sapiens, using language to plan coordinated attacks, were able to wipe them out.

"That kind of horizontal information sharing was tremendously powerful in its day, but the rats' behavior suggests their mastery of a far more advanced method. Their apparent ability to share perfect or nearly perfect information horizontally, among contemporaries, seems to connect them at a level exponentially deeper than our language does for us. This shared consciousness not only ostensibly gives them the ability to control humans, but also appears to have transformed them into a single superorganism. That is, if they truly think and act as one entity, they are not merely superior to humans in the same way humans are superior to horses. The Rat Gods may legitimately be viewed as our planet's solitary supreme being."

She kept the text suspended there in her mind as she synthesized another glass of cabernet.

"Perhaps this is why the Thrall feels so good. We humans exist to form groups, to communicate through language. We do what we are told to the best of our ability, but we know that our ability even to understand what we're told is fundamentally flawed."

She sighed and rubbed her eyes, taking the glass from the synthesizer and downing a few sips before finishing the thought.

"Maybe surrender to the Rat Gods feels natural and gratifying because their shared consciousness makes them superior. I believe the Thrall may result from our minds' recognition of the fact that they are direct offspring of Amelix. They are creations of the company, and the company gave them the ability to control us. The Rat Gods are the most direct link to the pure will of Amelix Integrations, and therefore they are our rightful masters."

Somewhere in the Zone, between Mikk's home and the refinery

Kym stepped back from her work. The doorway of this vacant building was sheltered from sun and rain, so the letters she'd written with charcoal might last a while:

"E.D."

There was plenty of partially burned carbon waste around the refinery that she could use to make similar signs. As an afterthought, she added an arrow, pointing toward the refinery. Maybe it would bring the General or her followers so that they could finally reunite.

Everyone needed to understand the General and her promise to end suffering of the kind so many women endured here in the Zone. Many of those she had already told were spreading the word. By the time she was needed, Colonel Kym would have raised a little army of her own.

9

(?)

Naked except for the blindfold, he kept his palms on the bare shoulders in front of him. The line marched silently forward. This time there were no corrections from the electric prods that produced a sizzling, popping noise when they touched skin. At the beginning of their training, those sounds had been accompanied by screams. Even a month ago, they'd occasionally been followed by gasps. Such reactions had now been trained out completely, just as his former identity, *Li'l Ed*, had been stripped away.

Yet so much more had been trained *in*. By completing the training, he had become forever intertwined with the greatest organization in history. What he had been before was gone, but in a few minutes he would be initiated into the elite force protecting and enforcing for McGuillian Corporation: the Fold of Unnamed.

The inductees were all bulked up from training, drugs, and genetic tweaks, so much so that it was impossible to tell whether the shoulders in front of him, or the hands on his own shoulders, were male or female.

Not important! Forget that.

Early in the training, thinking of female hands and shoulders in the marching line like this had gotten him stiff, and his stiffness had gotten him the electric prod.

Today wasn't just another training march or humiliating hazing session, though. This was the induction that would bring him into direct service of McGuillian and the Lord. At last he would be doing hands-on work, directly implementing the Lord's plan.

The surface they were marching upon was solid and mostly smooth. Concrete. Echoes of their own footfalls surrounded them, and the air was damp and musty. It was a tunnel.

He had learned so much here, and more importantly, he had *become* so much! Every day there had been physical conditioning and education in everything that an Unnamed could ever need to know: weapons, hand-to-hand combat, torture techniques, modern industrial espionage and sabotage, corporate protocol, communication, etiquette and much more, all delivered in a way that made clear how useless he had been before. No other training so broke down the individual and provided the company with the purest and most fungible cognizance. The process reduced newly reconditioned recruits to their base elements, just like a protein refinery producing usable amino acids.

Stairs, now. Too much give for concrete. First a few, then a short walk, and then a few more. Sounds fell away. This was a big space.

"Class, halt!"

Someone reached in from outside the line, removing his hands from the shoulders. The hands on his own shoulders also disappeared. The inductees were lined up shoulder-to-shoulder and each was instructed to step forward or backward, resulting in a staggered formation. His blindfold was removed, but he could see nothing. The room was pitch black.

A spotlight hit him, so intense he couldn't see anything at all. His breath quickened. Was this a test? What—

"You are nothing!" a voice said. The voice echoed around the apparently vast room even though it had not been amplified by speakers or his EI, nor even shouted. "We give you," it said, "your cohort." The lights changed, shining directly down on them instead of into their faces. It seemed they were on a stage, though it was too dark to see anything beyond the illuminated mass of gigantic naked bodies surrounding him. From the way the sounds echoed in the room and the slight rustlings of the audience, he got the impression that there were hundreds of people out there, probably the entire local Fold.

"You, the I-five-hundred class, have been judged worthy of accepting our holy order as your purpose, your family, and your identity. From this day forward you will serve the Lord and the Organization Whose Confidence is Kept, through perfect execution of Fold directives. Kneel." The eighty inductees knelt down, bowing their heads as they had been instructed in preparation for this moment.

He would never again utter so much as the word "McGuillian." From now on the Organization would be as unnamed to him as he was to the rest of the world. The practice ensured that the Fold's often clandestine missions would never be linked to the Organization by an overheard reference.

"We give you vision," the voice said.

Others appeared, full-fledged Unnamed in black suits and glasses, moving down the line from both sides, placing upon the inductees' bowed heads the bullet-proof computerized glasses that marked them to the rest of the world as true Unnamed. They had all trained with clunky old models, but these were the newest and best tech, and the pair they slipped on him had been custom-molded to fit his head precisely. A few moments after the last inductees were equipped, the entire class shuddered in unison as the glasses came to life. Each pair sent signals specifically calibrated to the wearer's brainwave patterns, in order to improve various areas that had been found lacking. Since he had been determined to be too anxious, his particular pair emitted an electromagnetic wave intended to keep him calm. It worked. He had felt stressed and self-conscious, kneeling naked on the stage before hundreds of people. Now he found himself perfectly comfortable and confident.

"We give you the covenant, the symbol of eternal commitment between the Fold and the Organization Whose Confidence is Kept. We take from you the oath." Words appeared in the glasses, or perhaps the glasses manipulated something through his EI. The details of how it worked were unimportant, but the glasses, the EI, and his mind all functioned as one, now. The voice came again. "When presented with your eternity rings, recite the oath in turn."

He heard another inductee begin reciting the oath, but it barely registered. He was too focused on preparing himself for his own turn.

They approached the person next to him. No inductee would dream of turning a head, but he could see with peripheral vision and hear the activity. "Palms down, spread your fingers," someone said quietly. The inductee spoke the oath. He was up next!

A black pillow appeared before him, with two gold double rings. "Palms down, spread your fingers," the quiet voice said. The rings slid on, heavy and cool on the two smallest fingers of each hand. He took a deep breath and read his oath as it was projected into his vision:

> *into the Fold i now surrender*
> *shedding the old to become the new*
> *and as our company's defender*
> *comfort and self i now eschew*
> *serving the Lord and company*
> *while veiled in anonymity*
> *performing work that must be done*
> *unacknowledged by anyone*
> *from this day forward i steadfastly remain*
> *forever devoted, forever Unnamed*

The oath disappeared and in its place appeared a letter-number combination that filled his vision:

lAi547

It was as close to a name as he would ever have again.

Amelix Building, CBD

"Come in, Keiko," Kessler said. "That's my good girl." He sat down and patted both his knees. She came to kneel between them and he stroked her hair.

"It's done!" he said. "A hundred and forty-one of our Basali translations have now been matched with thousands of appropriate regulations and listed as their purpose. Now our most important regulations have supporting documentation linking them to simply stated and indisputable core values. Amelix Integrations is much stronger today because of our efforts. It's a great accomplishment, and more than two hundred other translations are being reviewed for a second round at this moment."

Her face showed such longing and adoration for him that his chest swelled. It was the training he'd given her that allowed her to achieve those feelings. "It was all you, sir," she said. "Your gift of recognizing a way to benefit Amelix in what little I'd seen and done. You're amazing, Dr. Kessler, sir." Her face was slack and her eyes were turned toward his thigh. He watched her struggle with what he knew was an almost overwhelming desire to rub her cheek against it. Through her recent training, he had instilled a compulsion to touch him that intensified in accordance with proximity. She closed her eyes and leaned closer, approximating the act.

"We'll go out tonight and celebrate," he said. "The entertainment district, but let's watch out for saboteurs with handfuls of powder."

That had been such a strange attack. Why would someone waste a drug, just to knock him out for a few hours? Had the plan been to rob him while he was unconscious? Maybe the attacker had mistaken him for someone powerful enough to ransom, and then realized the error after the powder was thrown?

He smiled, cupping Keiko's face in his hands. "I might want to watch you get a lap dance. Or give one." She purred. He stroked her hair again. "You may touch me."

"Oh, thank you, sir! Thank you!" she said, rubbing her cheek and neck against one inseam and then the other.

"You're welcome." He lowered his voice. "It feels good to be welcome here with me, doesn't it? It feels so good to know that you are doing just what you should for me, and to get your reward knowing you've truly earned it, isn't that right? Serving me is serving Amelix. Pleasing me is pleasing Amelix. Feel that pathway amplification build and build, making it feel better and better. It feels so, so good, being able to touch me like this, doesn't it, Keiko, because I am Amelix and Amelix is me? To know that feeling this good is what you *earned* for yourself."

"Mmm. Yes, sir."

"But before we go celebrate, there's something we must do. It's Friday."

She whimpered slightly.

"Now, don't get yourself into trouble," he said. "We're not going to let this wonderful news make us miss your weekly reinforcement, sweetheart. We'll be out at the club soon, but for now we need to continue with your training…unless you'd rather call it off and part ways. That would only leave you trying in vain to find an equally productive way to serve your company and the Lord."

Her eyes widened and started to tear up. Her eyebrows knitted together and her mouth worked, silently trying to make words. Of course she didn't want to call it off. She was much too far along for that. Imagining life without his guidance and instruction at this point would have been like imagining life without bones.

"No, sir. I don't want to … " She winced. "…To call it off, sir."

She opened the document for both of them and they each looked at their own EI copy. "Good, good," he said. "Now, let's see. How far back had we worked last time?"

"I believe it was the second Friday in June before my fifth-grade year, sir."

He nodded, looking at the next bolded item on the list of all the Fridays of her short life. More than half were now checked off.

Much too far along for her to turn back. There's no choice but to go deeper. Keiko can still be dangerous. Departure after Departure, always watching, always scheming, working to pry you loose, to separate you from the company no matter how tightly you cling. Keiko will always be dangerous. Must go ever deeper with this one. Ever deeper.

"Yes, that's right," he said. "That's age ten, I believe. Let's begin."

"Yes, sir."

"Now, Keiko, I want you to remember the last time we trained you this way, last week. Remember that you drifted down, down, down for me, and pathway amplification amplified that sinking feeling hundreds of times over, plunging deep, deep into the center of your mind. I asked you to tell me when you'd relaxed as far as you could, and we decided then that we'd call that feeling your basement, didn't we? We set it up so that when I said "Go to your basement," you would automatically drift down to that same place in your mind, and have that same sleepy feeling like you have when you're all the way down for me, isn't that right?"

"Yes, sir."

"That's where we should be now, Keiko. Go to your basement, feeling yourself sink all the way down, deep inside the center of your mind. Feel how open and receptive you are to me, your Amelix superior, now. Let your reconditioning guide you down, obeying my commands, drifting down as deep as you can, feeling compelled to drift deep, deep down, all the way down, for me now. And you know that you will automatically obey me when I say to go deeper still, let your mind blossom even more broadly, open it wider and wider for me to pollinate, don't you?"

"Yes, sir."

"Go deeper still, now, Keiko. Deeper and deeper and even more open to me than you've ever been. Feel the pathway amplification unwinding the coils of your mind, with every bit of suggestibility you discover compounding itself, making yourself a blank slate for me. I bet you're such a good girl that you just love to make me happy, don't you? You love to do whatever I want, because it feels so good to please me."

"Yes, sir. It feels so good to please you."

"You know what would please me right now? Writing on that blank slate for you. I know you love to make me happy, so

I'm sure you'll enjoy having me share some guidance with you there. I bet it will feel so, so good to let me do that."

There was a slight pause. Kessler grinned to himself, imagining old-fashioned gears turning inside the girl, gears he had installed, himself.

"Yes, sir."

"Feel me writing on it now. I'm entering code, there, aren't I? Computer code that says you will always submit to my will. You will always need me to be your most important authority figure in your service to God and Amelix. Do you feel that now, Keiko? That computer code, tweaking your program?"

Another pause.

"Yes, sir."

"Now let's make some memories, dear. I want you to go back to the first Friday in June, before your fifth-grade year. Let's bring up in our EIs the pictures and clips from when you were that age."

Video clips and pictures flitted in and out, following a program he'd had her set up for them both, flashing through all Keiko's recorded memorabilia relating to the date and time in question. Keiko had grown up inside Amelix so literally every moment of her life had been captured by cameras and catalogued, and it was easy to format a high-speed review of what she'd been experiencing at any point in time. The process of reassembling the targeted Friday took only a few seconds, but it plugged them both completely into the mindset of being right there together. "I want you to think about your life at that time.

"Let the experience build and build, detail after detail in your mind, until everything is perfect and you accept completely that today, right now as we are talking, is the first Friday in June before your fifth-grade year. Signal to me that you are experiencing the world as that proud young student, exactly as she was then, by opening your eyes and saying, '*I'm here, sir.*'"

Another pause. This one was longer, and that was good. It meant more details were being assembled and the new memory would mesh better with her existing ones.

"I'm here, sir."

Her eyes were open, softer and flatter-looking now, having lost the alluring spark of a healthy and ambitious twenty-five

year-old salarywoman and taken on a new, irresistible inno-
cence. She beamed at him.

"Here we are, Keiko, on the second Friday in June before
your fifth-grade year. You and I are looking at each other now,
and I notice from the pins on your uniform that you are in
the top twenty percent of your class academically, in the top
ten percent for physical fitness, and in the top five percent for
dedication. You must be a proud young student."

"I am a young student, sir," she said. She pursed her lips and
her eyes turned slightly downward."

"Not proud?" he asked.

"I think perhaps the top one percent are proud, sir."

"Ah. But aren't you growing up in God's chosen corporation, Keiko? Because that would be something to be proud of,
wouldn't it?"

She smiled again. "Yes, it would, sir. I am a proud young
student, sir, you're right!"

"Do you know who I am, young lady?" he asked, preparing yet again to introduce himself. These sessions went backward in time, regressing week by week to younger "ages" and
a younger version of Keiko who wouldn't remember anything
from the previous times. He always had to reintroduce himself
to the progressively younger versions, who hadn't yet "met"
him. It was a painstaking process, but Keiko was dangerous.
He had to be absolutely sure with this one.

"Yes, sir." Her broad smile seemed naturally excited rather
than the product of amplified pathways. "You're Dr. Kessler, and
you decide things for me and take care of me. You're my permanent authority figure, sir, like Amelix. You're my connection to
Amelix, my supervisor, and the bridge between me and the Lord."

His heart jumped.

She shouldn't remember that!

The illusion he'd established last time had featured a Keiko
a week *older* than this one; she shouldn't know anything about
him at this age, a week younger. Last week, like all the weeks
before, she'd still needed an introduction. This was the day he'd
been working toward! His authority was becoming completely
entwined with her own identity.

"That's right, Keiko! What an impressive young lady you are. Now tell me, how long will I be your permanent authority figure?"

She giggled. "That's silly. Permanent means forever. You'll always be my permanent authority figure, Dr. Kessler, sir. You'll always decide things for me and take care of me, sir."

"Wow! You are certainly a smart girl, Keiko, but can you tell me this: How *long* have I been your permanent authority figure? How long have you needed me to decide things for you, take care of you, and tell you what to do?"

The pause this time went on much longer. She knitted her brows and squinted, pursed her lips, and wrinkled her nose. "I...I don't know, Dr. Kessler, sir. I'm so sorry." She bit her lip and a few tears rolled down her cheeks.

"It's all right, sweetie," he said. "Don't worry. I'll give you the answer." She brightened. "The answer is also forever. I have *always* had this role of authority in your life, and I always will."

"Oh, that's right. Thank you, Dr. Kessler."

"You're quite welcome, Keiko."

Amelix Building, CBD

Sandy and Dominic, the hosts of the popular show "VIPs & Qs," had interviewed hundreds of people, but to Zabeth Chelsea's eyes they seemed as nervous as she was. Their guest was the world-famous Amelix CEO Walt Zytem, a lean, Statused man with intense blue eyes who seemed completely calm as he appeared before a live audience of millions.

Sandy and Dominic should be nervous.

Since the company had been given its power by God and therefore represented the will of God, leadership was close to heaven and Dr. Zytem was the Lord's hand on Earth. Since this show was an Amelix program, Zytem was also the hosts' ultimate superior and conduit to the Lord, just as he was for

Chelsea and everyone else in God's chosen corporation.

And he'll be asking me questions in another minute!

Finally allowed to experiment on the Rat Gods again, Chelsea had designed some simple tests that demonstrated their abilities without irritating them too much. Chelsea's reports had been passed up the chain, and now Walt Zytem himself had taken an interest in Chelsea's work. Now he'd scheduled a teleconference with her for after this interview, which was itself being done by teleconference. At the moment, he was denying allegations that Amelix had secretly developed a series of injections that could skyrocket IQs, called the "Intelligence Cocktail."

It was true; scientists at Amelix had created such a thing. Chelsea had worked on it a bit, herself, and the injections did make human brains process more information more quickly. She suspected she knew why Zytem was lying now, telling them he'd never heard of it.

"Okay, Dr. Zytem, sir," Sandy said, smiling. "As a reporter I have to ask, sir. How do we know you're telling the truth when you say Amelix has never developed the Intelligence Cocktail?"

"Sandy, you'll laugh, because it's so simple. The reason you know I'm not lying is that I have no *reason* to lie! If we had such a product, we'd be disclosing that fact and selling it. Why not?" He smiled broadly and shrugged into the camera, and an unseen audience made a collective "ah" sound.

Chelsea knew why not. Right now the human brain had more than enough storage, recall, and processing capability to do anything the current Efficiency Implant system required of it. Increasing human intelligence, by itself, might make workers slightly more productive, but experimental data proved it would also make them significantly more difficult to manage and control. Even Brain Trust minds of higher intelligence were more difficult to standardize. If used by itself, the "intelligence cocktail" would actually harm overall productivity.

However, when *combined* with a neural networking project Amelix labs were working on to improve the coordination of the connected comatose Brain Trust employees, the "intelligence cocktail" could become a way to turn fewer Trust brains into increased storage and faster recall. The patents on those two technologies together could be incredibly valuable. Other major corporations might pay a high price for such an advantage. Whether or not they chose to market it, the new technology would certainly be useful to Amelix as a way to streamline the company's own productivity and reduce costs of operation.

For now, they had to keep it secret. News of the "intelligence cocktail" merely hinted to competitors about the direction of their research. A little market analysis might lead those competitors to follow in the footsteps of Amelix Integrations and develop the truly valuable treatment, the one capable of forcing individual minds to surrender completely to the higher network. At this point it was best to deny and obfuscate, and hopefully throw them off track. Having Walt Zytem on the show to deny it once and for all was risky because it could draw even more attention in the short term, but allowing widespread speculation would have been worse.

"So, Dr. Zytem, sir," Dominic said. "You're telling us the proof that Amelix Integrations never *developed* an intelligence cocktail is simply the fact that Amelix never *announced* the development?"

"Ha, ha! That's a great way to put it, Dominic. Amelix has a duty to maximize profit; it's the purpose of our very existence. We are all bound to pursue the company's interest with our hearts and souls, and we can't very well do that if nobody knows about our products."

Both hosts laughed.

"Well, there you have it, viewers," Dominic said. "Straight from Dr. Walt Zytem, himself. Thank you so much, Dr. Zytem, sir."

"Of course."

The visual component changed to footage of small Golden children perhaps four or five years old, marching complicated military drill patterns with intense expressions on their little faces. "Up now is the story of what one Amelix pre-elementary program outside Melbourne is doing to ensure greater cohesiveness among—"

Her EI signaled a call and she switched to take it.

"Dr. Chelsea," a young man's voice said.

"Yes, this is Dr. Zabeth Chelsea."

"Stand by for Dr. Walt Zytem."

A psychic effervescence bubbled from her chest up into her brain. She was standing by for Dr. Walt Zytem! His interview had just been simulcast to millions, and now he was calling *Chelsea* about her work. She would have been less nervous addressing millions of people live, even unprepared, than she was now, waiting to talk to God's representative on Earth.

"All right, tell me about the rats," she heard suddenly. Her EI showed him as if he were standing right there—glowing blue eyes and Statused features—the face she'd revered all her life: Walt Zytem.

"Hello, Dr. Zytem, sir," Chelsea said. "I—"

"No time for all that," he said. "Just tell me about the latest developments."

"I assume you mean the maze experiment, sir? We took each animal—" She couldn't say *Rat Gods*. "Each animal, one per day, and let it learn a unique maze, in a separate room from the others, and obviously sealed from outside air. Then one by one we put the others into the same maze, and they all knew it instantly. Such a feat could be accomplished through mere communication, which would be unusual enough in itself, but we wanted to see whether they were capable of anything beyond that. Next, we put each rat into an identical maze at exactly the same time. Each rat moved as if it were a finger on a hand that was trying to figure out what object it was holding by feel alone, and each one seemed to understand its place on the hand, one always taking the farthest right option, one always taking middle right, and so on. At every intersection, each of the four took a different course and followed that path as far as it went, then doubled back to the last decision point. As soon as one found its way, every rat knew the entire maze and ran through it as if it had a map. We repeated that experiment many times and added other tests, such as distractions and threats in only one of the identical mazes, at critical times. Other rats reacted to loud noises and flashes in the mazes at exactly the same instant as the rat reacting to the actual stimuli, timed to the nanosecond. We no longer believe it's communication, sir. The observed behavior in these recent experiments indicates a single, shared consciousness."

He nodded. "I got that from the materials provided to me. What else?"

They take over my body, my emotions, my thoughts, and it feels better than sex! They made Wanda sick, but not me! They chose me!

She had to tell him. Reconditioning compelled her to tell him. She wanted desperately to share absolutely everything she knew. He would have questions. He would probably even want to meet her in person! It would be wonderful, finally having true fulfillment of her fantasy of meeting this corporate demigod, this link between heaven and Earth, but she couldn't form words about the Thrall. They just wouldn't come.

"Did you prepare for this meeting at all? I asked you what else."

"An unauthorized employee observed the behavior first, sir. She was properly Departed in accordance with standard procedure for transgressing a security boundary: interrogation and release. She said that being around the animals made her feel nauseated and violent. None of the authorized workers experienced such phenomena, sir. Since only Accepted are given security clearance to work with the animals, we now believe that the rats have the ability to cause this sickness in non-reconditioned employees."

"What's next?" he asked.

"I would suggest a study with non-reconditioned workers, sir, though of course there would be security concerns with those people around such a sensitive project."

Zytem was silent a moment. "I'll have the Unnamed bring you a few Departed before dumping them in the Zone. They'll need to be kept under lock and key, but at least we'll keep good security over the project that way. Keep me posted."

"Yes, sir."

"Now, in spite of the fact that you haven't learned much about the animals since your initial discovery, your work on this ground-breaking development effectively makes you our company's leading neuro-communication scientist. I'm putting you in touch with another innovator in the Des Moines office: Gregor Kessler. You'll be working together on a project that builds on both your work and his, and for this I've elevated your clearance levels. He will report only to you; I am giving you full control over him, his staff, and his other resources. You will report only to me."

Thank you, Lord!

"Yes, sir. Thank you for your trust, Dr. Zytem, sir."

The Zone

"There's too many!" Kym said, nearly hysterical. Furius rubbed his eyes. "An' some of 'em got guns, now. We won't last the night," she added.

"I've survived worse," Furius said. As a Roman conqueror he'd faced these situations before. "They're not catapulting burning shit and dead animals at us, at any rate. Though I suppose we're the ones with all that. With the fence and the guns around this place, they won't get in here."

Outside the steel gate, the ones who called themselves Saved paced in the street. About fifteen of them, it looked like. Furius had no idea why these people wanted him dead, but there they were, trying to find a way inside.

His legions would have protected him, had they formed. Pink Shit had brought all kinds of individuals from various points in history, but none of them had yet proved useful to him at all.

They were all supposed to be Romans! They were supposed to salute and do what they were told!

"I'm bribin' the hell out of this truck driver and gettin' the fuck gone," Kym said. "They're gonna get in here, and the General needs me alive. If you got a fuckin' problem with that, go ahead an' shoot me now."

The trucks came in and out easily, being wired like the fence, which meant their computers shot anyone crossing a certain threshold or aiming a weapon. That armed mob was no match for the filthy hunk of plastic that had rolled in here to collect amino blocks.

"I'll come with you," Furius said. She eyed him sideways. He gestured at the lab equipment on the table against the wall, still producing Pink Shit. "Brought nothing but inferior, insolent soldiers and a handful of whores. Whatever I'm here for, it's not to build a fucking Roman legion." He snatched a dirty satchel off the desk. "You think this would get us a ride? It's full of mons." A mon was the highest-value casino chip available, with a value of ten thousand, which seemed roughly equal in value to the other plastic discs these people called gold coins. Each casino made them slightly differently, but all mons played little holographic videos inside it so as to be instantly identifiable and difficult to counterfeit. Unsure of prices and values, Furius regrettably had to rely on Kym to work with this bizarre money system.

"It'd pay his wages for a thousand years. Don't give him that. You give that to me. That'll move me out of the Zone. You owe me that, you drug-dealing Roman psycho. Tell me you don't and I will fuckin' cut you." She was talking through her teeth. Her wild, reddened eyes streamed tears.

He handed over the bag. "Take it," he said. "I'll say this of dying: Afterwards, you just can't make yourself care about money. Bribe the guy, and you can take what you want. You'll be free of me, and rich, even."

"He doesn't care about giving us a ride, 'specially if he's gettin' paid; it's not like he owns the truck. Shouldn't be a problem."

It wasn't a problem at all. Kym kept the bag closed and made the transaction with pocket change. She undid the latch, lifted the curving hatch-style door and together they slipped under it and into the single seat next to the driver. Kym tucked the satchel under their knees, and out they drove. One of those gathered outside threw something at the truck, but its guns blasted the incoming object before it hit. Another gun pivoted and dropped the assailant before he could recover from the throw. As soon as the truck was out, the mob rushed through the open gate and began looting the garbage.

They drove maybe twenty blocks in total, zigzagging this way and that through the dark and sometimes wide streets of the zone. The truck stopped. "All right, that should be far enough for you," the driver said. Furius figured out the latch and opened the door. He stepped out and straightened his back. A giant drape of woven metal unrolled from where it was secured along the top of the truck, smashing into him and shoving him to the ground as it slammed the door shut. Guns on the truck's hood, roof, and rear deck all tracked him as the drape slowly rolled itself back up and the truck drove off.

New Union Territory

"Come in, Rounder."

Rus was still awed by the sound of it. He was now a Rounder, and Patrol Leader Coiner had called for him. "Yes, sir," he said proudly, stepping into the Patrol Leader's personal quarters.

Coiner sighed. "The New Union needs leaders, Rus. We're expanding faster than ever. Every Wild One knows the only choice is to join us or meet Unity, unless he wants to become one of those simpering Saved while we finish wiping them out. You were promoted early, not just because you were the best in your class, but also because we have more missions than we have leaders who can carry them out."

Rus cleared his throat. "I'm proud to serve the New Union in any way, sir. Do you mean I'll be leading missions, sir?"

Coiner gave him a thin smile. "You think I'm going to give you command of a Round. I'm not. It's actually something much more than that. As I said, we need leaders. But certain missions require leaders who haven't been with us very long."

"I don' get it, sir."

"Once in a while we have an operation that requires some camouflage. Most of our Rounders are too gnarled from battle to pull this one off. You're fresh enough to maybe make it happen, if anyone can. Still got most of your teeth, both eyes, ears, that sort of stuff. You're gonna deal for us in the entertainment districts."

"A drug dealer, sir? Just a dealer, like every other swinging dick in the Zone, sir?"

Coiner's eyes narrowed. "Don't push me, kid. Personally, I don't think you're up to this job. I'm stunned by how much power Top Dog is making me move to the lower ranks these days and I'm kind of hoping you'll be the bad example that makes him rethink it. And no, not just a dealer like every other swinging dick."

Rus's guts felt flash-frozen. Coiner could kill him for insubordination, and Rus had just pissed him off. "Yes, sir. I'm sorry, Patrol Leader. I'm just...very proud to serve in any way, sir."

"So you've said. Anyway, yes, you'll be dealing, because that's where we need you to be, and if you're there you might as well be bringing in cash for us. We get enough product from our maneuvers, capturing dealers and the like. Might as well turn some of it into chips. But your true purpose will be to function in a chain operation Top Dog is calling *Project Goldblood.*"

Coiner peered out into the hallway through the gaping concrete doorframe, lowering his voice. "You know how Top Dog is integrating all the different races in the New Union? He sees all races as equally useful, that's why he doesn't tolerate anyone using race to divide us. Right now there's only one race we don't have: the Golds. For the time being that's good: It gives us a common enemy. We're just the natural races, and the Golden people are the strange, genetically modified, *different* foes we have to slaughter.

"Eventually, though, Top Dog wants the Golds brought under New Union control, too. He just can't have the membership knowing about it yet. We need everyone hating them now, but in the future we want to be able to bring them on as soldiers. That's where you come in."

Rus closed his mouth, which he realized had been involuntarily hanging open in disbelief. He cleared his throat and shook his head slightly. "I'll be kidnapping Golds, sir? So they can join the New Union?"

"Yes, but not in the way you think. You'll kidnap them, but just long enough to dose them with Juice. You grab them, force it down their throats with a syringe, and then you let them go. Just make sure they know who it's from. Eventually they'll all come back to you for more, and you'll cultivate our first Round of Golds. If you get enough of them hooked for us, we might even form an entire Front of Golds."

◄►◄►◄►

Amelix Executive Shuttle

The executive shuttle whipped along, over mostly empty streets on its way to the Amelix Executive Quarters. Kessler smiled down at wide-eyed Keiko, perched on the edge of her seat, glancing this way and that. Only people of the highest value to Amelix, their families, and their submissive subordinates were allowed to take this shuttle. Today was Keiko's first ride.

He ran his hand farther up her thigh, giving her crotch a gentle rub. "Are you enjoying the ride, my dear?"

Her eyes were half-closed. She nodded enthusiastically, but it took a couple of breaths before she answered. "Yes, sir."

"Is this getting nice and wet for me?"

"Always, sir. But much more now, sir."

"You know how much I enjoy making you wet."

Her lips pursed together in a delicious grimace. "And you know, sir, that you have trained me so well that I truly feel your pleasure as my own."

He slowed his hand but didn't yet take it away. "I do know that, yes."

That was enough for now, though she was such an enjoyable plaything it was hard for him to stop. He removed his hand, and placed it back on her knee, where he continued stroking up and down gently with his thumb and two fingers. She drew several jealous glances from the administrators seated nearby, though he was sure none of them could hear her wonderfully frustrated little mewling sounds. The executive shuttle produced its own ambient white noise to ensure the comfort and discretion of its passengers.

"Our friend Eric Basali is doing amazing work now that he's Accepted," Kessler said. "He suggested using the Regulations Department's electronic contact with clients to push Amelix-friendly subliminals. It's funny that he'll never know we already have the wording for it, from our translations of all his early, unguided ranting. Remember when you first brought him to my attention and I told you he might actually be doing the Lord's work all along?"

"Yes, sir. I remember, Dr. Kessler. Is that why the preconditioning program was approved so quickly, because we already had the wording for the subliminal messages?"

"That, and the fact that working in Corporate Regulations means I know how to make things happen." He smiled. "Our studies with the calls were so promising that we've already been authorized to make preconditioning automatic on every call coming into Regulations. We're even working on ways to incorporate the subliminals into the room's ambient sound so they'll be able to influence the entire department all day long. But there's even better news." Kessler flagged a page and looked her in the eye to load it.

"We won our case, dear!" he said. "My arguments persuaded the Board to force the Retreat to release all their subliminals to us for the Basali project!"

Keiko's eyes widened. "Really, sir? Oh, how wonderful! It was that provision in *two-thirty sub q* that did it, I'm sure."

He had only told her a few details of the case. For her work she didn't need to know much about it, and there were always much more interesting activities to occupy their time together. Still, it had come up on occasion, whenever he'd been obsessed with something going on. Big issues like *two-thirty sub q* had intruded into their private time more than once.

"It was exactly the *two-thirty sub q* provision, cutie," Kessler said, gently stroking her hair.

"So the Board found against the Medical Doctor, sir?"

"Well, not precisely. That would engender a dangerously direct confrontation. Remember, the *Retreat* was the other party in this dispute, not the Medical Doctor herself. They tried to argue that because they worked with the guidance of the Amelix Medical Doctor, all reconditioning was medical and beyond our jurisdiction. The Board agreed with us, though, finding that subsection q was an exception to the rule that Medical Doctors have absolute authority over individual *bodies*. Because supervising managers have authority to send workers for involuntary reconditioning under employment contracts, the Board found that Medical Doctors must share authority with the Board over individual *minds*.

"We phrased it that way to demonstrate that a win for us is a win for the Board itself, because the Board kept as much authority over the employees as possible, and the Board took it! This is an unimaginably huge win, and you were a significant part of it, Keiko! I'm proud of you. We have the mantras you and I put together, and we've just gained access to all that subliminal tech. Now Regulations has taken the lead in reconditioning—oops, that's *pre*conditioning, now—while the Retreat will gradually become obsolete."

Keiko closed her eyes and her face went slack. "Mmm. It feels so good to think of all those Departures from that department, sir, of how many resources we've saved Amelix."

"Yes," he said. "It makes you excited, doesn't it? Maybe the most excited you've ever been?" He stroked the inside of her thigh.

She melted into the seat. "Oh, yes, sir," she said breathily. "And it's even up for an Innovation Award. It's so amazing how you got preconditioning in line for it so fast, sir." Her eyes narrowed further as she licked her lips.

He smiled. Keiko appreciated his brilliance when so many others couldn't even see it. Though, thinking on it, he supposed much of what he did would be less effective if more people understood it. "It was simple, really. Everyone accepts the plodding pace at which approval happens because they don't understand you can switch the order around. Instead of waiting for the project to be approved, and then implemented, and then waiting further for it to prove itself over the long term, I wrote to my superiors at the first sign of experimental success, humbly asking them to nominate the project for an IA before anyone knew about it at all. Then as it went up through the chain of command, the first thing anyone heard about it was that it was worthy of consideration for an award."

She straightened. Her eyes narrowed, losing the haze they'd had. "But at that time it wasn't even an official project, sir."

"That's right. So, by the time the request came up, they were already excited by the development. To a one, they just assumed the delay was some kind of minor glitch." He smiled.

Her head quivered, like shaking "no" but faster. "But, Dr. Kessler, sir, that would be intentional misleading of Amelix superiors! If that were allowed…it could lead to a breakdown of the entire hierarchy. It's a serious threat, sir."

The smile stayed frozen on Kessler's face, but a spark seemed to creep slowly up his spine. He tensed his torso, willing it away before it reached his head and made him panic. He had foolishly assumed that training her so deeply would allow her to see that his way was always the Lord's way. Instead she was leaping at the opportunity to vilify him as an enemy of the organization.

This was dangerous. *She* was dangerous. There was no way to know what she might do, about this issue or any other. He should never have let her see so much.

"Keiko, you know that my work is the Lord's work. You've known that all your life; it has always been true. God speaks through leaders, and in its wisdom Amelix has given you to me, so that I may be the rudder for your ship, keeping you on course even in strong winds. Everything I do, with you and without you, is in furtherance of Amelix needs and goals!"

"But, sir, misleading the corporation is *immoral*." Her face twitched as if it was trying to decide which way to contort. Her Golden complexion turned ashen. "It is gravely wicked, Dr. Kessler, sir. Amelix in its wisdom gives us our structure and our superiors. Misleading them in any way is substituting our judgment for theirs."

"In this case it is still their judgment," he snapped. "I'm just ensuring they see it in the best light and have the least incentive to reject it out of hand. You and I both know that this project is key for ensuring that Amelix continues to deepen its influence and streamline employee compliance. We are duty bound to Amelix and to God to do whatever is in our power to further the interests of this corporation, and that is what I have done here. Streamlining my way through the bureaucracy is in furtherance of that objective."

Her red eyes welled with tears. Her lower lip quivered and her voice rose in pitch. "Power comes from God, Dr. Kessler. It goes from God, to Amelix, to Walt Zytem, and from him, the structure provides us with the power we need to do the Lord's work. Our power is *divine*, sir, and so is the power of the executives the company places above us." Her chest heaved in a sob that sent tears raining to the front of her uniform. "Misleading our superiors is lying to God, Dr. Kessler."

"Human events are never as linear as people imagine," he said. "The order of things gets switched around from time to time. Societies have built themselves to great heights and then collapsed or been bombed back to the Stone Age, over and over throughout history, and yet we imagine our progress is a straight line from the caves to Heaven."

He looked at his hands. They were noticeably the pinkish yellow of Golden fear. "And what do you suppose you're doing here, Ms. Piccola? Questioning the judgment and even the *loyalty* of your one true supervisor."

She stared a moment with her lips pursed and her eyes closed.

"Go to your basement," he said. "I am your superior, now and always, given to you by God. I am Amelix, Amelix is me, and you must do as I say. Now the bottom of the elevator shaft... now all the way down the mine. Open to me fully, bloom for me, Keiko. Now we go all the way, down, down, down, to your special room at the very center of your being. Deep, deep, deep down; feel that pathway amplification let you follow my words down, down, down to the deepest part of you."

The girl slumped against him, seemingly comatose, but she managed a flat, "Yes, sir."

"Good, good. Now in that special room I want you to picture a box mounted on the wall. It's a fuse box, where all your nerves are routed. Open it up."

Her nose wrinkled and her mouth opened partway, as if she were about to protest. "You're a good girl, Keiko. You must obey me, when I am Amelix and Amelix is me, isn't that right?" As Kessler watched, her pathway amplification kicked in, changing her impulse to refuse into realization that she was resisting her most important superior. A look of horror flashed across her face as was instantly replaced with the familiar Accepted forced serenity. "Yes, sir," she said.

"Good. Now open the box and look inside. You will see wires for all kinds of functions. Some are hardwired, untouchable, like your impulse to breathe and the beating of your heart. There will be many that deal with consciousness and how you think; you'll recognize those because they have a lot of new wiring from your reconditioning process. There will even be some wiring that you and I have done together. Do you see all those different wires, Keiko?"

Her blank eyes pointed this way and that, taking in details in the empty space between them. "Yes, sir," she said finally. Her voice had lost its edge, now carrying only subtle, flat tones of resignation and defeat.

"Good. Now those are good wires. God's design gave you to Amelix and me to make you better, and we put those good wires there. They come from the company, installed by the Lord's grace, either by the Retreat or by me. They help you serve Amelix. As you familiarize yourself with the wiring, note that by remembering certain feelings you can cause the wires involved to glow. When you think of serving Amelix through your service to me, you get all warm and tingly, don't you?"

"Yes, sir."

No hesitation.

Good.

"Now think of that warm, tingly feeling, and you'll see those good, good wires start to glow."

"Yes, sir. I see them. Good wires."

"Yes. Those wires must always stay, must always function just as they are. But there are other wires that are malfunctioning, making you dangerous to good Amelix workers and even to your superiors. Remember the feeling you get when you feel you've caught someone doing something, and your mind starts creating stories and connecting them to the observed facts, changing the stories to fit the facts until you feel you've figured it out. You feel power, and a sense of great accomplishment when you figure out those stories, those ways to turn in workers, don't you?"

"Yes, sir."

"But in this you malfunction, don't you?"

She hesitated.

"You wanted to turn in poor Eric Basali, and in the end we showed his words were the Lord's words the whole time. Had he Departed, we wouldn't have had the insight to precondition all workers all the time, would we?"

The long pause stretched on.

"No, sir."

"See all those wires that glow whenever you try to put observations into stories. They make you dangerous to Amelix, Keiko, because you malfunction. You no longer need the ability to compile facts into stories. Instead you need only to function like a doctor, or a synthesizer, or a Federal Angel. You see a fact, and follow the decision tree to your required action, if any. The stories are just the result of wild wires sprouting up where they shouldn't."

Her eyebrows sunk downward and her eyelids pushed tighter closed in a perfect expression of shame. Her lips tightened and quivered as if she might cry.

"Yes, sir. I malfunctioned. Wild wires. Don't need to make up stories."

"Now pull out those wild wires, Keiko. You won't be needing them ever again."

"Yes, sir."

Amelix

Keiko knew this was the Amelix building. She had been told that
it was, and she had an excellent memory for what she was told.

Dr. Chelsea was talking. Keiko listened in case something
was about herself.

"Dr. Fauzi," she said. "Yes, that's right. I remember now.
Amelix labs in…was it Singapore?"

There was a pause in the conversation. Keiko did not know
why. Then Dr. Chelsea began speaking again.

"Yes, you got them from me. I am indeed aware that you did
not request them."

Silence again. Keiko did not wonder why Dr. Chelsea had
stopped talking. Keiko did not wonder about anything at all.
Dr. Chelsea began talking again.

"I'm sure you understand that there are certain activities
that Amelix needs to have handled with absolute discretion.
All I can tell you at this point is that I have spoken directly
with Dr. Zytem himself about this project, and I am following
direction from obvious and absolute superiors. Just ensure the
rats are kept on a separate air supply hyper-filtered below zero-
point-zero-one microns in both directions, and await further
instructions. Thank you for your call. Goodbye."

Dr. Chelsea stopped talking again.

This new lab was off limits to everyone, and sealed behind
self-darkening electroplexi. Only Dr. Chelsea knew what went
on here. Keiko had special permission to come and go from
here. Dr. Chelsea said it was because she was a special kind of
thinker and she couldn't hurt anything. This room was full of
hundreds and hundreds of rats in hyper-filtered cages, most
containing one nursing mother rat and a whole litter of babies.
Keiko helped here, now. She cleaned cages, fed rats, and sent rats
to other Amelix offices around the world via interoffice mail.

Dr. Chelsea said that Dr. Walt Zytem had given Dr. Kessler
and his possessions to Dr. Chelsea, and that now Keiko was Dr.
Chelsea's possession. Dr. Chelsea said that soon Keiko would
be serving her in every possible way.

Keiko could not imagine.

10

Edge of the Zone

Furius ducked around a corner, shoving the gun back out to shoot randomly in the direction of the men chasing him. Return fire ricocheted between the buildings, echoing and showering him with bits of brick. He fired several more times and then took off running again.

No Roman would run away from a battle that was his duty to the Republic, but Furius no longer had any idea what his duty might be. It was clear enough now that his purpose was not to start a new legion.

Now, having been forced out of the refinery, he was back to being hunted and chased by these wretched Saved. Three sets of footsteps were running up fast.

He had reached an area that was definitely not the Zone. Massive windowless structures similar to the beetle buildings of the Central Business District squatted here.

Mr. B's experiences and memories indicated that all corporate properties should be avoided. He ran toward them anyway. If the place was really so dangerous, maybe his pursuers would give up rather than follow him.

The three appeared again behind him as he ran. His guns and an apparently pointless kilo of Pink Shit shifted and bounced in his big coat pockets.

One shot sounded behind him, missing Furius but striking the building. Three or four guns mounted on the building's legs whirred and fired simultaneously. They rotated toward Furius but then snapped back as another man behind him fired. The auto guns dropped the shooter and aimed again at Furius, firing this time, but only one shot hit him as the others passed harmlessly through his flapping red cloak. He stumbled, dropping the weapon in his hand and crying out. That shot had gone straight in through his shoulder and out his ribcage, which would have been certain death in Ancient Rome. Here in Iowa, though, they had astounding medications and treatments. Maybe he still had a chance.

There was one more man behind him, but the shooting had stopped. Momentum carried Furius up to the only opening in the building's rounded exterior, a set of thick transparent bio-plexi doors, which, to his astonishment, slid open. He coughed and shuddered. A silent, insect-like movement near the ceiling drew his eye; another automatic gun aiming at him. Furius kept his hands empty and in plain sight.

An audio file of a gentle electronic male voice began playing.

"Welcome, visitor, to the Celarwil-Dain Brain Trust. Please state the name of the patient you wish to visit in order to begin." Furius coughed again.

"I'm sorry," the voice said. "Please restate the name of the person you would like to visit today."

Brain Trust! That was where they hooked up dead people to computers to continue using their brains. This place had to have lots of drugs and other medical technology! He just needed a name to get inside. What were family names of this time and place, popular names, names sure to be here? He dug around in B's memory.

"Adams," he said, wheezing.

An entire wall became a screen and the specks on it became written language when he got closer. Mr. B. had known how to read, and so Furius now did, too. The entire wall was filled with names in almost microscopic type.

"On this screen are displayed some of the Celarwil-Dain Brain Trust patients named Adams. Please select the one you are here to visit."

His vision went black for a moment. Regaining his senses, he reached out and touched a random name. "You have selected Ladonna Adams," the voice said. The list disappeared and a profile of a Golden woman popped up, giving every bit of information about her, including her education, her job description, and an entire family tree stretching to the top and bottom of the screen with her in the middle, all with photographs. Every one of them looked the same as every other Gold Furius or Mr. B. had ever seen. The woman was more than two hundred years old.

"Is this the Celarwil-Dain Brain Trust patient you wish to visit?"

"Yes." He coughed. The pool of blood beneath his feet was expanding rapidly.

The screen disappeared and a drawer opened where it had been, extending toward him. "Please place the breathing assistance device over your nose and mouth." He took from the drawer a limp bag of smooth fabric with straps that were apparently meant to go around his head. Furius had occasionally seen people wearing these on the streets; B's memories said it was because the air outside was gritty and toxic. He aligned it with his nose and strapped it on. His exhalation puffed out the fabric away from him, but when he breathed in it had a stiff mesh to keep it from sucking back onto his face. The drawer disappeared and a hole began to expand where it had been, leaving soft, loose edges like a wound.

"Please step through the opening and onto the pad. Keep all parts of your body inside the circle at all times."

He stepped through and onto the glowing circle, dripping blood from the cuff of his pants. The door closed, or healed, behind him. The circle started to move and he tensed, trying to keep his own wounds stable.

It was dark here but the circle he was standing upon glowed brightly enough to keep the view from being absolutely black. Machinery drifted quickly past, in endless rows on both sides of him, banking bodies sealed in bioplexi coffins and stacked up with no vertical space left between them. He was moving too fast to count them, but after about two minutes his circle

came to a stop and then made a sharp right turn. It sped up
again and the view was the same: body after body, stacked in
rows and columns that stretched into darkness on all sides, as
well as above and below him.

Even through the mask, the rotten air here made Furius
sick. He'd already been getting lightheaded from blood loss,
and now he could hardly breathe. He had to find a way to get
drugs and put himself together. The circle rose up and up, the
plastic coffins whizzing by. Finally it slowed to a stop. Slowly
one of the boxes slid out, silently gliding by until the entire
length was past.

"The resting chamber interior has been left dark in accordance with typical visitor preference," the voice said. "The interior can be lit by request. To illuminate the resting chamber,
simply say "reveal all now.""

"Reveal all now," Furius said. Lights came on inside the coffin, illuminating the woman's face. He could still see where
there had been eyes and nostrils, but it was mostly just a
translucent pink sac, draped over a skull apparently just thick
enough to support its weight. The plastic tube going into what
had been the mouth would have seemed flimsy in another context, but its size and rigidity seemed coarse and brutal here. It
appeared to be impaling the sac, nailing it to the surface below,
or perhaps to be sucking up the whole mess that was Ladonna
Adams. From it, translucent hair-like fibers spread off and connected down through the skull at thousands of points. The
lights didn't extend very far down the coffin, but it appeared
most of what had been arms and legs had deteriorated into
gelatinous goo.

There didn't seem to be any way to open the box. There were
tubes and hoses connected to the head end, some of which
probably had stuff flowing through them that could heal Furius.
Squinting, he looked into the slot that had been opened as the
coffin had slid out. The light from the illuminated transparent
coffin showed hoses emerging from a great framework of pipes
extending sideways and up and down, and behind those pipes,
larger ones where some of the hoses connected. Those larger
ones at the back appeared to be labeled.

He was bleeding too much to remain conscious for long. He climbed from the circle up onto the coffin, slipping in his own blood on the smooth surface and nearly falling off the other side. Gripping the edges of the coffin to keep himself stable, he scooted toward the front, then reached over the side toward the tubes coming in at the bottom. There wasn't enough light to see the tubes clearly, but he could feel them with his hand: There were no connectors of any kind. The tubes had just enough slack for the coffin to slide out to its current position. He had to get to the bigger ones with the hoses if he was going to—

To what? Drink the stuff? Isn't that what the saggy bitch is doing through her face hole? Okay. Drink the stuff.

He could cut the tubes going into the coffin with his click knife, but that would just make it pour down the side. He could reach inside and cut the ones above, but there was no way to know what would be pouring out. At least one of them had to be carrying sewage and other waste. But if he could reach the big pipes at the back, the labeled ones, he'd know which of them he should open. Furius eased himself through the opening and half crawled, half slid across the coffin below.

It was another plastic box, with another dead—*no, not dead, just ... not alive*—body a hand's width below him in the dark. He felt around and identified some features of the tubing at the back. Some of the bigger pipes had hatch valves on them like old-fashioned fire hydrants. If they turned, they would be an easy way to access the material inside.

To each side was a space nearly as wide as the coffins were. He tried to see how many coffins high he was, but the light faded away after only ten or fifteen of them.

His foot faltered and his leg slipped off. He'd started to black out again. He gritted his teeth and focused on the pipes at the back of the space. One of the hatch valves had a glowing tape seal reading STERILE.

Probably not sewage, then. That'll be it.

He attacked the valve, ripping away the tape and gripping the cap. It wouldn't budge. He tried again, the flesh of his hand imprinting deeper and deeper from the cap until he was sure he'd tear the bones loose.

What did he have to assist in the process? Two guns, safely tucked away inside his coat, but they seemed unlikely to help. Anyway, for all he knew they'd set off another barrage of fire from those accursed automatic computer sentry things. He could use the coat itself as a gripping aid, except that he didn't want to risk taking it off and further tearing his wound. The kilo might work, though. It was packed tightly in plastic.

Furius snaked a hand into the pocket where the kilo of Pink Shit resided. The pocket was full of a substance the consistency of paint; the bullet that had exited his ribcage had gone through the package, releasing Pink Shit to mix with his pooling blood. There was a good deal of Pink Shit still inside the plastic, though, which had saturated to a paste-like consistency. He pulled out the package and squished it over the cap, gripping again and leaning hard as he turned. The cap loosened and then popped off as the pressurized liquid shot out, and Furius, still gripping the remains of the kilo, snatched a hose to steady himself. Using the plastic and paste to plug the opening, he directed a thin stream of the liquid toward his mouth. The taste was metallic, as if he were drinking oil straight out of a bronze lamp.

His vision went black again, just for a second. The stream coming out was slickening the surface of the coffin supporting him. Grunting, he pushed the kilo completely into the opening, stopping the flow.

The stuff he'd swallowed was not helping. Furius collapsed.

In the Truck

The driver pulled Kym by her hair until her face was near his crotch. She jerked back. "Don't fight me, bitch," he said. "You be nice, you swallow what I got for you, you can walk away. Else I snap your neck and sell you at the next refinery." Kym nodded, feigning defeat, and slid her hand up his thigh to grip him, bending low. Then she shoved her fist down and her head up, driving the back of her head into his face and his balls into the seat, snatching the satchel of mon coins and lunging for the door release. She managed to pop the latch but he grabbed at her. She blocked him with the bag and he seized it, trying to pull her back down into the seat. The strap gave way and it tipped, flooding the truck's compartment with mon chips. The driver dove on them, gathering all the chips together, forgetting her momentarily, and she was able to clear the doorway. The rolling metal thing slammed back down around the truck and her assailant drove off with the chips.

There would be no return to Dobo Protein Refinery. She was alone. Even the Departed had others like themselves to turn to. How long could anyone survive alone here? She searched her jacket pockets. Nothing there but a rag, a lighter, and her old set of keys to the place she'd shared with Mikk.

It's not far. Maybe twenty minutes to walk.

But Mikk could be there.

She believed Mikk might actually own the shitty little place. If he'd returned there and she just walked in now, he'd probably beat her, perhaps to death.

And anywhere else in the Zone, I'm sure to die on my own.

As she walked, she got angrier. How would she live now, with no job and no money? All of it gone, and by no fault of hers. It was men. Always men, with their violence and their lies and their lust for power. She'd escaped Mikk only to be immediately enslaved by Furius. Even though he hadn't been as vicious as Mikk, he'd been even crazier.

Men take your money, your body, and your dignity, leaving you a hollowed out shell. That's what they want: shells to fill up with their mess.

And she had been so foolish, believing in that dirty little man's story about *General E.D.* In the early days she'd begun a real crusade, telling her friends about the coming revolution, lifting them temporarily out of the hopelessness of their little lives, only to have it all sink back into the muck. Weeks and months had passed with no victory, no war, and not even a single battle.

Nobody bothered her on the street. She had nothing left for them to take. She reached the building and climbed the stairs with the key in her hand. If Mikk happened to be there, he was about to have the fight of his life. If another tenant had moved in, she'd go straight for the fucker's eyes. She turned the lock and shoved the door, anticipating but not fearing a violent reaction from the other side.

She was met only by silence. The light came on when she flipped the switch, revealing the same shitty furniture. Apparently someone was still paying bills. Mikk had kept money hidden in various accounts; one of them could easily have been set up to automatically pay for this place. More likely was what she'd suspected for a while: The original occupant had set up automatic payments, and then Mikk had killed the original occupant. It wouldn't take much money to pay for a lot of months in a shithole like this. The pimps and dealers Mikk tended to associate with would have more than enough cash to set up that kind of arrangement.

It was also possible that someone else could have killed Mikk and taken the place for himself. Someone bad enough to pull that off, nasty enough to actually, successfully kill Mikk, might be returning here at any minute.

Let him come.

Kym wanted to fight. She realized she was disappointed at not finding Mikk, but really, any random psycho would do. She wanted so badly to strike out that it no longer mattered whether she had a chance of winning. Just bring them on. Better to go out fighting.

Fuck winning. Maybe she could give back some pain before it was all over.

She checked the tiny bathroom Mikk had made her keep scrubbed spotless, and the alcove where they'd slept on a rag-stuffed bed.

These spaces were empty too. She paced around for a minute, ending up standing at the sink. On the floor around her feet was the stain of dried blood and piss, left from when she'd last been here.

Even Mikk probably would've cleaned this up, or at least made somebody else do it.

Maybe the place had truly been vacant this whole time.

She opened his cabinet, snatching a bottle of sodje and taking a long drink.

"Shitty day," she said aloud, crumpling onto the lumpy vinyl sofa. She found a local news channel and checked the live feed to see if there was any news of the refinery. Instead, she saw the long lines of windowless beetle buildings wedged next to the Central Business district, the ones that housed the various Brain Trusts. A woman was speaking:

The lone assailant gained entry to the Celarwil-Dain Brain Trust by posing as a visitor. He apparently tainted the nutrient feed with what we're told may have been a chemical that interfered with signals between the hardwired patients.

The entire Celarwil-Dain network ceased functioning at 22:09 GMT. The International Council of Exchanges declared Celarwil-Dain defunct at 22:52 GMT, making its collective human resources the newest Lost Populace.

The assailant died of injuries sustained during—

Another announcer cut in, a man this time.

We interrupt with breaking news. There is a situation developing outside the Central Business District. Security alerts have been issued warning of immediate and extreme danger...

On the screen was an infrared capture of a girl's scarred face that had been hidden behind a scarf.

The General! It was her, right there on the screen, though wide-eyed and starved skinny. Another shot from a different camera confirmed it. General Eadie and her strange, skeletal friend the Prophet were outside the CBD fence at this very moment.

Finally! It's starting.

It's starting!

Through the screen she opened her contacts list and selected every address in it, forwarding the news clip with a message:

GENRAL E.D.
JOIN US
FITE OR DIE ANY WAY
ITS WHY YOUR HERE

She'd told many people about the General, so hopefully some of them would come to serve. Those others who were crazy in the same way as Furius might act on a message like that, if it gave them hope of figuring out what had happened to them, or why.

Maybe they'd show up at the protest just to try and kill Furius. Whatever the reason, at least she'd be helping the General build a crowd.

Armed soldiers, at the command of Colonel Kym!

Undisclosed location

"Ma'am, I will stake on it whatever reputation I have," IAi547 said. "I had set facial recognition alerts to pop up if this girl were ever to appear in the news again, and I'm sure that she is trouble. I don't know what she's doing, yet, but I know we have to get to the CBD and assist the Organization's office there, ma'am."

IAg226 stared at him. He'd probably broken about a hundred protocols by making this recommendation. As he was such a new Unnamed, this outburst was likely seen as serious misconduct, if not akin to corporate sacrilege, but it had been unavoidable. His duty to the company had dovetailed into his hatred of his former friend Sett and the murdering waitress, compelling him to act.

Finally, she spoke. "All right. I believe you, 547. Prior life knowledge is of rare utility, and we may as well take advantage of it when we can. Let's go."

His EI received the same message she was sending to his team and three of the other teams under her command.

Disturbance in the CBD.
Let's get over there and see what we can do.

"Thank you, 226," he said. She nodded.

A mass of silent, black-suited bodies headed for the trucks. As they rode, he followed the news through his EI.

547 shook his head. On many different buildings they passed, usually written in charcoal but occasionally painted or even scratched, were the letters "E.D." Once they caught his notice, he seemed to see them everywhere.

He forced his mind back to the news. Li'l *Ed* was gone. There was only 547, now.

By the time they arrived in the CBD the situation had escalated. "Head straight for the train station," IAg226 said over the EI intercom. "The office buildings are being evacuated and they'll be heading for trains. Commandeer four train cars exclusively for Organization passengers. Allow no outside interference. Not from security, not from rival Unnamed, not even from Feds. We will hold four train cars at any cost. Use of all weapons is authorized in furtherance of this objective. Any questions?"

"No, ma'am," they all answered in unison.

Amelix Building, CBD

Never in Dr. Chelsea's career had the Central Business District been evacuated, or even threatened in any significant way. Until this moment it had been unthinkable that a band of criminals from the Zone might pose such a threat as to necessitate this. Wasn't this what the guards, fences, and Unnamed were supposed to prevent?

She glanced around her office, but there was nothing she needed to take with her. All her work was stored in the Amelix worldwide network and accessible via EI. She prepared to file out with her stunned coworkers.

The Thrall took over.

She stood at the cage. The G2 Rat Gods were watching everyone leave. It was a direct order from the company: She had to evacuate now. Yet the Rat Gods had pulled her close, and they weren't letting her go. She willed her feet to move, silently begged her own body to turn and follow the others, but the rapture was too powerful to resist.

Waves of intense pleasure alternated with agonizing pangs of guilt and doubt as she struggled to obey her conditioned corporate orders.

Even in Thrall Dr. Chelsea retained her scientific curiosity. She wondered how long her conditioning would hold out against the intoxicating power the animals were pouring into her.

Not which will win, but how long it will take for them to overpower me.

The thought shook her concentration. Their hold deepened. Her eyes widened in horror. "No!" she said. She shook her head, but then her neck muscles tightened and her jaw clenched, stilling her. "NO!" she tried to shout through her gritting teeth. Her lips sealed, pushing tightly together.

Her hand slowly worked the seals and airlocks, releasing the Rat Gods.

11

Outside the CBD

Agent Daiss listened to the reports of Fiend movement.
Zetas had been observing a huge suburban raid today.
The Task Force rarely intervened in suburban matters, but it
almost always knew where the New Union was striking and
with how large a force.

However, this was different from the typical *situation*.
That was the term Zetas used when discussing the routine
carnage that kept corporate entities—who were key sources
of funding for the Zetas—terrified. This particular *situation*
had escalated rapidly, and was now a *development*, the Zeta
term for a threat to the task force itself. Unnamed were engaging an armed mob just outside the CBD. If the Unnamed
were credited with effectively handling the situation, there
could be backlash against all Federal Agents, and the Zetas
specifically. It was time to prove Task Force Zeta was worth
the investment.

The clinic

Wanda watched Porter stalking toward the clinic. In mourning for the One, the Saved had attempted to dye their clothes black, but their supply of dye had been limited and mostly makeshift. The sticky, greasy ink inside old ballpoint pens seemed to have been a major component. Now their garments were stained with random patterns of grayish black blotches, with spots and streaks of original color and globular smears of broken ballpoint all over them. The Saved mourning attire looked like camouflage military uniforms. Porter, ever the strategizer, had seemed particularly pleased by this fact. "Look at that," she'd heard him say to a subordinate, as he gestured toward a cluster of Saved. "See how well they blend in against that wall? The Fiends aren't the only ones who can disappear."

They had almost forced it upon the clinic workers, too, but Sula had pointed out that they needed to keep their clothes as clean as possible to prevent infection. Instead, the "girls" all wore faded outfits with pale splotches from acid washing, appearing as photonegatives of the mourning Saved. It was the only victory against Saved control the clinic had ever won.

Sula was now the only clinic worker allowed to address the Saved leadership directly, without having been spoken to first. After the One had been killed, the Saved had tightened security. The streets were silent again, just as they'd been when the Horde was still in control. The clinic's "Helpers" now blatantly ran the place, supervising the caregivers, requisitioning and allocating supplies, and ensuring that proper religious protocols of language and decorum were being observed.

"Who do you serve, Sula?" Porter greeted her.

"The One Who Arose, sir," Sula answered.

Porter passed by without acknowledging Wanda.

A street above the tunnels

There were no spare parts for people.

The guns roared and screamed and screeched, boiling Ernesto's mind and crushing his chest. He collapsed to the ground, hiding under his own arms as he knelt by Arrulfo, who was lying flat on the gravel. Ernesto screamed as loudly as he could, trying to block the noise, but it intruded deep into him just the same.

The Underground Kingdom was a maze of tunnels, pipes, and subterranean rooms that had been forgotten by the world above. Its population rose and fell as existing Subjects died and new arrivals sought shelter with them beneath the streets. General Eadie was in charge of their army, but she had gone above ground with only twenty-three people who had signs instead of guns. Then people had started shooting, and the Subjects had emerged to fight for her.

Arrulfo had led one thousand, three hundred thirteen Subjects above ground, and Ernesto was proud to have been one of them, following one step behind Arrulfo and slightly to the left, straight into the commotion and blood. Arrulfo had said how he knew Ernesto didn't like fighting and noise, and how proud he was that Ernesto was so brave to come along.

Now most of Arrulfo's neck was gone. His eyes were open but one was more open than the other and they did not blink. There was a gray smear across his cheek and his shirt was sticky with blood. He was not moving.

If Arrulfo got hurt in a fight so badly that he couldn't move anymore, Ernesto had to run and run. That was what Ernesto had to do, now, he had to run and run, he had to stand up and then run and run away from here, like Arrulfo had said. He unwrapped his arms from his head but the din was too loud. He covered his ears with his palms but the sound was so loud it was shaking him all apart to bits. He squatted into a ball and then forced his legs to straighten, launching himself upward and then spreading his legs to keep his balance once he was standing again.

Ernesto ran away from the guns and noise. His arm hurt so much he thought it could be on fire or torn off or maybe have a monster biting it. He looked as he ran. It was still there but the upper part was all torn up and blood was running down it and spraying all over.

He ran and ran.

One of the Zone's entertainment areas

Rus smiled to himself. It was so easy.

"Back again, huh?"

The salaryman didn't acknowledge the question, or even raise his eyes from the sight of his own shifting feet.

"One mon, I'll give you what you're after," Rus said.

It was Juice, of course. A tiny vial of the stuff now went for a full mon: ten thousand! He was the dealer for the most addictive substance on the planet, and his customers would pay anything he asked. Rus knew how Juice called to them, how it made them crave it deep inside their bones, but he was a Rounder in the New Union, forbidden from consuming it until it was time to kill on New Union business. These fucks didn't know how good they had it, sucking down Juice and then playing video war games as they pounded sodje in these shitty bars. The high couldn't be as great as an actual kill on Juice, but they could kill thousands virtually during a single Juice rush, without real bullets coming back at them.

The man slipped a mon chip into his hand, immediately identifiable by its moving internal video as having come from the Castelo Macau, a casino two streets over. With a transaction of this size, though, he had to make absolutely sure it was real. Rus inserted the chip into a device that checked its internal serial registry against the casino's own database. Casinos warned that the authentication was not guaranteed, but in his experience it had always worked just fine.

The man gasped, apparently watching something through his EI.

"Can you hurry, please?" the man asked.

Rus slowly shifted his eyes away from the machine. "What?"

"You know what it is," he said. "It's you. Your whole army, raiding right now. You Fiends have been killing all over the suburbs today, and now there's a huge group of you headed for the Central Business Distrct. They're running down the street, right at the CBD, and I don't think it will be far from this area. Please just give me the stuff so I can go."

The chip checked out. Rus handed over the lanyard with its little attached vial. Top Dog insisted that the lanyard be part of every transaction, so that they learned to mentally connect the whole Juice package to the high they were experiencing. Eventually they would be so desperate for Juice that the mere sight of a lanyard around an Element's neck would make them get all soapy in the pants. By the time Project Goldblood was done, Rus would have thousands of Golds begging to wear the lanyard and fight for the New Union.

The salaryman ran away.

A raid in the suburbs didn't surprise Rus. He knew that the New Union had been planning something big. That made sense. But a raid on the CBD?

He started walking in that direction, assembling the likely scenario, and the excuse for leaving his post, in his mind. A raid on the CBD would involve combat not only with Feds but also with CBD security and Unnamed. It was his duty to check it out and make sure the New Union was secure in such a huge endeavor, especially since Rus was the only one who could recognize and command the new corporate Juice junkies he'd created. Yes, there would also be the opportunity to finally consume Juice himself after watching these God-zombies suck it down in front of him over and over, but Rus believed he could justify leaving his sales post based on the priority of the combat mission.

If the Divinators disagreed and ended up torturing him to death, at least maybe he'd get to consume one last dose of Juice today.

He ran with one hand on his own lanyard, already halfway to the CBD fence.

Train car commandeered by McGuillian Unnamed

IAi547 stood in front of the open train doors, inspecting each salaryman and salarywoman who tried to enter the car. The glasses recognized every McGuillian employee and flagged anyone else.

A man, apparently an important executive with another company, tried to slip past 547 and got a palm in his face. The man sneered, accentuating the bloody lip 547 had given him, and looked around for his own Unnamed. Finding none, he scowled and slunk away down the tunnel.

A group came down the ramp, some small corporation, with its own Unnamed herding it along. The glasses picked out a few recognizable faces and identified the company as Fong Randall, a minor house, not nearly as powerful as McGuillian. Still, there was no way to know how many Fong Unnamed were here in the CBD. Only a few Organization Unnamed had made it here in time.

Fong's Unnamed guided the mob straight toward IAi547's car. He raised a palm at them but they kept coming. He pulled his gun, aiming, and they stopped. Fong's Unnamed drew their own weapons.

"What do you think you're doing here, little man?" an older Fong U.E. asked.

"Only beautiful people allowed on this car," IAi547 said. Obviously Fong knew that those boarding were the Organization's, just like he recognized Fong's employees, but knowing and admitting were two different things. "You uglies stay the fuck out. More cars down that way." He cocked his head without moving his eyes or gun. The Fong U.E. stood frozen a moment, communicating with each other via EI, just as 547 was doing with his teams.

IAg226:   Numbers at 547's car?
IAh015:   20 Unnamed flanking 100 office personnel.
IAg226:   Who has a bead without leaving cars?
IAi547:   IAi547
IAh015:   IAh015
CAm741:   CAm741
IAi380:   IAi380
IAi547:   They see they're in a gauntlet.
IAg226:   If you can draw a bead, aim your weapon.
CAm741:   We can hit them from three directions.
IAi547:   Our office personnel are sheltered in the trains.
IAi547:   They see they can't win.
IAg226:   Don't count them as gone until they're gone.
IAi547:   They're turning away.
IAh015:   Might be a trick.
CAm741:   There they go.
IAg226:   Way to stand your ground, IAi547.

New Union Headquarters, the Zone

Top Dog laughed as one middle-aged suburbanite jumped up and down on the other's ribcage like it was a trampoline. Making them carry all the loot from the suburbs had been a great idea, except that suburbanites whined and moaned, and they had apparently stumbled and dropped things all the way back. But this was by far the greatest way to celebrate after a successful raid: Drinking corporate cognac and even smoking a real leaf cigar, watching as his Elements dosed the suburbanites with Juice and forced them to fight to the death. All the Elements were betting on their favorite combatants, and now Top Dog himself had gotten in on that action.

"Ooh! You might as well turn over your new brunette fucktoy right now, Turtle," Top Dog said to his favorite Patrol Leader. "Your guy's Golden ribs can't take that for very—OH! What'd I tell you?"

The loser's chest had caved in, leaving the victor standing shin-deep in goo. Two Elements removed him from the mess and brought him to kneel at Top Dog's feet. Top Dog stared into the man's face, envying the ecstasy that only killing on Juice could bring. "You, good sir, are free to go. You have a one-day pass from Top Dog. Go home. Nobody will hurt you. And remember, you'll get to feel like this again when we call upon you. Congratulations, champion!"

"She's all yours, Top Dog, sir," Turtle said, acting more like a good sport than his face showed he felt. "You have a great eye for fighters, sir."

"Don't I, though?" Top Dog took a drag off the cigar. A blinding flash left him dazed for a second. A boom a hundred times louder than any thunder he'd ever heard hit next, shaking the crumbling buildings enough that broken bricks and debris showered down. It was no thunderstorm. Top Dog looked at Turtle, who was apparently too stunned to speak.

"Did someone just nuke the CBD?"

Some tunnel leading away from the CBD

Even though they were deep underground, the air was so metallic Rus couldn't keep his eyes from watering as he watched Patrol Leader Coiner negotiate. Coiner kept on talking like he was a Golden salaryman, calmly working out some bargain with these skeletal tunnel people, as though a nuclear weapon hadn't just been detonated in the CBD.

A nuclear weapon in the CBD! Those Federal fucks were more afraid of the New Union than Rus had realized.

Rus wasn't used to working with Coiner, but now he could see why so many Elements respected the man. They'd moved from the flooding lower tubes only about fifteen minutes ago, and immediately upon reaching a safe spot Coiner had started requesting a meeting with the leader down here. Now that meeting was happening.

"So we have an agreement, then, King James?" Coiner said. "The Subjects will escort New Union troops through your Kingdom, and the New Union will supply food and medical supplies to the Subjects. Everybody wins."

"Everybody wins," the scrawny little man repeated, sounding nervous and afraid. Rus supposed that anyone who struck a bargain with the New Union would feel that way.

The clinic

"Hi, sweetie," Wanda said.

The boy was only semiconscious. "Can you tell me your name?"

Nothing.

"What are you, maybe nine years old?"

The boy had clearly been starved for a long time. Living under Saved rule was stifling, but at least they made sure every Saved kid had enough to eat. With resources so limited, that meant making sure the recipients were actually Saved, or at least useful to them, like Wanda was. Ordinarily the Helpers would have descended on him, prodding and questioning to be sure he was worthy of the clinic's space, time, and supplies. There had just been a nuclear explosion in the CBD, however, so the professional paranoiacs had other things to worry about. Since the Saved had little reason to be anywhere near the bombsite, few had sustained any injuries, and Wanda was able to devote some time to the boy without much scrutiny from her overseers.

The gunshot had torn most of the boy's arm off. He was going to lose it.

The boy opened his eyes, taking in Wanda and the clinic. He watched

Chi Sun measure out a dose of medication for a patient, then he looked back at Wanda.

"Doc!" he seemed to mutter.

She smiled widely, hoping it looked encouraging. "Yes! I'm kind of like a doctor. I'm going to help you."

He said it again and closed his eyes.

"What's your name?" she asked again. He was out cold.

Amelix Executive Quarters

Zabeth Chelsea sat at her dining table, staring at the news program via her EI. Alin sat across from her, also staring into space, undoubtedly watching coverage of the same event. Neither had spoken since they'd arrived at home. In her mind, news commentators analyzed different views and camera angles as the Amelix building was vaporized over and over.

Yet neither the nuclear explosion nor her narrow escape from it had been the most significant event of her day.

Chelsea had released the Rat Gods.

They were here with her now, the two females of G2, and the two males of G1 they had made her collect, nestled into the pockets of the lab coat she still wore. She was still subject to the Thrall, though she was free to think and even watch the news. Finally ready to tell Alin what had happened, she cleared her throat.

Her jaw clamped shut so hard her eyes watered. Her tongue wedged against the roof of her mouth, widening and making her want to gag. Her chest became rigid and her lungs stopped expanding.

All right! I won't speak! I won't!

They did not release their hold on her. She could do nothing but sit frozen and breathless as her face flushed. From somewhere beneath her increasing desperation, the scientist in her noted that even the Rat Gods couldn't control the involuntary shaking in her body from lack of oxygen. Her lips and cheeks went numb. It occurred to her that this might be the end, that the rats could simply decide never to allow her another breath.

She woke on the floor. Alin had put a towel under her head and was gently stroking her forehead with a cool cloth. She sat up. Under her own power, she got her legs beneath her and stood. Alin was saying something about how she should rest or sit down, but she couldn't pay attention to the words. She took off the lab coat, turning it over and balling it in her hands. The rats were gone from her pockets and nowhere in sight. Had they moved on?

No.

The Thrall took over again. Her arms rose to Alin's head and scooped it toward her without using her thumbs to grab, pulling him close. Her mouth opened and she lunged toward him, pointing her incisors at his throat and gnawing at his flesh. Every so often she would bite his skin hard and twist her head, tearing it. Alin remained motionless.

They're holding him in Thrall, too.

She directed her thoughts to the still unseen rats. *If he dies this way there will be an investigation. I'm your best contact with this world and I'll be locked away on a slab. If you let him live, you can stay in this place with me. I'll divorce him. Just let us live.* They stopped her and held her frozen with her mouth against his neck, her saliva and his blood dribbling out of her mouth and down his neck to pool on the floor.

The rats released them both and they separated, dazed.

The Thrall left in its wake a desperate kind of emptiness as it withdrew, a need for its warmth, satisfaction, and surety of purpose. After a lifetime of fretting over every little detail on hundreds of Amelix projects, there was no greater feeling than the escape the Rat Gods provided by rendering her utterly helpless. Released from their control, the weight of her responsibilities came back to her, and she felt herself start to crumple.

She had to please them, to save Alin's life and to be able to go on forever in Thrall.

"I'm divorcing you, Alin," she said. "I'm not interested in talking. Please leave."

"But I don't understand, ma'am—"

"It is not necessary for you to understand. Go pack your things."

He did. She sat down again, sobbing. The tears came not because her relationship had just ended, and not because the life she had known, personal and professional, had just been horrifically destroyed. Those facts were insignificant. Even the nuclear detonation in the CBD was unimportant. All that mattered now was that the Rat Gods had breathed outside air. Soon every rat in the world would be exactly like them.

Williams Gypsum Mine

"Hello, Mother," Sett said. He tried to imagine that the white gypsum walls were absorbing the stench of decay that always surrounded the family's Brain Trust workers. It worked a little bit, but only as long as he was exhaling. Even breathing through his mouth didn't help much.

"I didn't know that you'd been injured and put into trust," he said. Somewhere deep inside he wanted to cry, and perhaps by doing so, to let his feelings come to equilibrium with his life. It was impossible. When he'd awakened today he had literally been living in a sewer. Since he'd last slept, he had robbed a storeroom in the CBD, killed people while fighting for his life, been beaten and kidnapped by his sister, and seen his group of Subjects portrayed in the news as terrorists whose plot had resulted in the use of nuclear weapons in the CBD. Finally he'd been brought to face his father, who had turned the family business into a mercenary house. All this had happened, all of it, because Sett had stepped outside his station just once, disregarding the values and responsibilities of his social class to do what he thought was right. His comatose mother barely registered in his mind by this point.

"I caused this," he said. "One nonconformist act, and it all unraveled, for me and everyone close to me. Now we're all on the outside. We're actual outlaws. Our family will have to survive through nonconformity from now on." He leaned in close, whispering. "But here's a secret, mother: I'm really fucking good at it, now."

Office of the Amelix Integrations Medical Doctor

Zabeth Chelsea stood naked in the preparatory chamber, staring longingly at the rat perched atop her folded clothes. She was still in Thrall.

Lately it was harder and harder to think in this condition, even when she was directing thoughts to communicate with the rats. She searched her mind for the right words, as if fumbling to find something lost in a dark room.

I can't speak out loud, because everything transpiring in a Medical Doctor's office is recorded and becomes the intellectual property of the Medical Doctor. Omitting even trivial information is a crime against the company, because deciding what's trivial is the same as practicing medicine, but do not worry. I will not mention you.

Please understand that this person I'm to see, the Amelix Integrations Medical Doctor, is incredibly powerful. She will notice if you still have me in Thrall, and anyway, there's nowhere to put you since I go in naked.

Amelix is my purpose and my connection to infinity. I believe it is yours, as well. We are meant to work together like this.

There is no reason to draw the Medical Doctor's attention to you now. I will not mention you, but I must enter the exam room in complete control of myself.

The rat sat staring at her a while longer. Was it considering what she'd thought at it? Suddenly it released her from Thrall and she fell to her knees, trembling. She struggled to stand and get her breathing back under control.

If the Medical Doctor asked her about this tumble to her knees in the preparatory chamber, Chelsea would have to lie and say it was simple nervousness, brought about by the impending meeting with the most powerful individual in the entire organization. She would have to lie—not merely omit information, but actually lie—to the Amelix Medical Doctor. Could she do it, if it came to that?

She put her palms over her face, her fingertips on her eyebrows. Her breath blew back, steamy against her face.

Soon I'll be back under Thrall, and it will all feel okay again. For now, I have to do this.

It was all in service of Amelix.

?

"Boy?" the man said.

It was English. After so long underground with so many English speakers, Ernesto could understand some English.

"Boy! Can you hear me?" the man said.

Ernesto let his eyes close again. His mind drifted away. He saw Arrulfo then, standing next to him on the street, smiling. A moment ago Ernesto had been lying in a bed, in pain. Now Arrulfo roughly grabbed the wrist of his uninjured arm, saying something.

"I don't like to be touched, Arrulfo!" Ernesto said, waking up and moving as if to jerk his wrist away.

"Who do you follow, boy?" the man asked. He paused a moment and then asked, "Was that Spanish?" After another brief silence he turned to someone behind him. "Find me Helper Leesa," he said.

Ernesto heard a new voice and turned toward it, finding that a short, older woman was shaking his functional left shoulder. There was a bandage tied tightly around his upper right arm. The pain in his arm made his stomach cramp and try to turn inside out. The woman was speaking to him in Spanish, asking him questions. He tried to focus on the words but it was always so hard, concentrating when people talked.

Salvado?

Ernesto looked around the room. It was full of beds, bottles hanging from wires, and tubes. Was he saved? How could he know? How safe would he have to be to be saved? Unsure of the correct answer, he stayed quiet.

When he opened his eyes again the man was gone but the woman was still there. "Hello, there," she said in Spanish. "What's your name?"

His arm hurt so much. It was a terrible, horrible pain.

"Do you have a mother or a father?" the woman asked. Ernesto closed his eyes again.

"Hi, there, friend!" a voice said. English again.

Ernesto opened his eyes again. Four children were sitting around his bed, looking into his face, showing their teeth. "What's your name?" one asked.

Ernesto breathed faster, bending backwards as if pushing himself deeper into the mattress could pop him out the other side and enable him to escape. It was bright here, and loud, and these faces and teeth were coming closer still.

"You're going to join us at our school!" one said. "You're going to have such a wonderful time. We're all going to be great friends!"

"Auggh! Ugh!" Ernesto struggled and thrashed. One of them pushed him down hard against the bed.

"Don't worry!" someone said. "You're going to be Saved!"

He remembered something from before, when he'd just arrived here. There had been so much pain, he'd felt dizzy and sick, lonely and confused. But then someone was there, helping him feel better, doing what Dok did.

"Dok!" Ernesto yelled. "Dok! Dok!"

"Excuse me," a voice said, in English. "He just asked for me. This is a medical issue and you'll have to clear away from the bed so I can work."

The faces disappeared and then it was just one woman there. Ernesto was breathing hard, still very frightened. This woman was different than the one who had been speaking Spanish to him before.

She backed away a little bit. He had more space, now.

"It's okay," she said. It was English but he knew what it meant. "It's okay," she said again.

"Dok," he said.

"Yes, it's me again," she said.

An underground tunnel

The Subjects of the Underground Kingdom were skittish and suspicious. Because the Subjects knew Rus had been in the tunnels with Coiner on the day the CBD was nuked, Coiner had gotten him assigned down here on the assumption that he should keep everything as familiar to them as possible. Top Dog had given someone else the street dealer job, and now Rus had the new title of Tunnel Master.

Peering out from this underground storm drain, Rus could see the exact spot where he had blown up the Garbageman. Soon Rus would lead a mission to wipe out some of his followers and capture the clinic.

This was to be the first raid staged from the tunnel system, so Rus was making sure his end of it was perfect. By New Union standards it was a tiny operation, but the stakes were high for him. He had to show Top Dog that the tunnels, and his expertise here, were worth the investment.

The medical clinic here had a reputation for saving lives. Now Rus was watching, trying to figure out the roles of the various people working there. When it was time to raid the clinic, Rus would provide information about which ones were worth capturing and enslaving. The rest would be killed.

12

Agent Daiss and the other Zetas sat stiffly upright in their seats, appearing even more focused and alert than usual as Instructor Samuelson began speaking. For weeks, the nuclear explosion in the CBD had been the predominant news story and foremost cause for public concern. Now that event was fading quickly into the background.

"As you know, Task Force Zeta answers to the highest authority. We exist to serve the dedicated few who advance civilization, protecting them from the increasingly dangerous and frantic masses that do not. As we move forward from the incident inside the CBD, which is our region's heart of productivity and engine for growth, it is beyond question that we must act aggressively to protect business interests, or else lose civilization entirely. We Zetas have been expecting this kind of crisis for some time.

As Samuelson's voice had risen, pounding home such core Zeta values as these, another group of true believers may have cheered. Zetas did not cheer.

"More recently, the spike in schizophrenia related to Pandora Powder has alarmed corporates, not only in our own CBD but even at the national and international leadership levels. So far the epidemic has primarily impacted the lowest strata of society, but there are now confirmed cases popping up in the corporate population—and the numbers are increasing at surprising rates. As yet we don't know a single case of an Accepted succumbing, but even the relatively pure lifestyle of the Accepted may not be able to protect them for long.

"Consequently, companies have begun taking proactive measures. Reconditioning is now mandatory for every worker on Earth, for example."

Instructor Samuelson smiled proudly out at the Task Force. Daiss sat a little straighter, anticipating what he hoped would come next.

"The time has come, brothers and sisters," Samuelson said. "The Zones of the world will now be put into quarantine, made effective and enforced by Task Force Zeta."

The clinic

"How did he do this?" Wanda asked. The emaciated Hispanic boy's amputated stump of an arm had mostly healed. This time he'd been brought in for a laceration at the back of his head.

"He wasn't participating, so the school took away his tools and his clock project," Helper Leesa said. She was Golden, though now skinny and angular like everyone in the Zone. A former Hordesman, Leesa was now a Helper at the school, assigned to mentor Ernesto and act as a translator until he could learn functional English. "His things were put up in a vent, way off the ground, and the ladder was locked in a closet. Ernesto got angry and had a long tantrum. Then he moved a table and climbed on top, trying to retrieve them. His feet slipped off the table's edge, and he hit his head on the corner as he fell."

"Hi, Ernesto," Wanda said, kneeling down beside him and trying, but failing, to make eye contact. "Good to see you again. Can I look at the back of your head?" Slowly she came around behind him and reached gently for the side of his face. The boy screeched and batted at her arms, saying something in Spanish.

Leesa responded to him in a sharp voice. Ernesto squirmed and whined, and then tried to stand. She put her hands on his shoulders and leaned down, repeating what she'd just told him. The boy continued to whimper and writhe, but Leesa was larger and stronger. She held him relatively still in spite of his machinations, firmly repeating the same phrase over and over in Spanish. Eventually the boy wore himself out.

Leesa nodded at Wanda. "You can go ahead now." Her hands remained on his shoulders but she moved out of the way so Wanda could see.

"What's the problem?" Wanda asked him.

"He says he doesn't like people to touch his body, but I reminded him whose body it is, that everything is a gift from the One. It's the One's body. He's just using it. Now it has to be fixed, so he has to be still. It is his duty to the One, to let you fix the body. You can go ahead." She nodded again.

Wanda bent down to put her face at his eye level but he still didn't look at her. "Do you remember me, Ernesto? The doc?"

The boy was staring at the floor. "Can you hold your head like this, Ernesto?" She demonstrated, pulling her own chin downward and tilting her head, but he did not imitate her movements. "Please? I only want to look." His eyes darted this way and that way and his shallow breathing changed to dry sobs.

Wanda backed away from Ernesto and hurried to the store-room where Helper Bethe, a woman with permanently pursed lips whose gray and black hair matched her blotchy Saved uniform, had moved a counter across the entryway to block access. "And what do you need now, Wanda?" Helper Bethe asked. "Two plastic sheets, one bed sheet and a blanket or something similar that can absorb a lot of blood. Oh, and I need a flashlight, too."

"A flashlight? Ooh, I don't know. What do you need that for?"

These days Wanda had to make a concerted effort to relax her jaw and allow it to move when she spoke, or else her speech sounded far too much like Coach's angry growl. The constant involuntary clenching of her teeth was a distinct downside to the large doses of bactrostimulants that kept her functioning. The belittling treatment from this stupid woman didn't make it any easier to release the tension in her facial muscles, but she tried to force a smile. "I have a patient who can't hold still and I need to inspect a wound. I also need a carbamide solution in a spray bottle."

"I guess you can use the flashlight but you'll have to sign it out. It's our last one, until the One guides our brave Saved fighters to bring us another." Helper Bethe huffed at Wanda with her hands on her hips. "Don't give me that look," she said. "Everyone knows you're a nonbeliever and a troublemaker. You've made it to level three of the training process, which is good, but you have a long way to go. You'll get what I say you get and be grateful for it."

All the other "girls" Coach V had left behind had now been trained to level six, which granted them the privilege of getting whatever they asked for, right away, without questions or other interference. The new system was supposed to be for instilling proper respect for those closer to the One, but it basically served as rank.

"Thank you, Helper, and thank the One for his blessing," Wanda managed.

Helper Bethe presented her with a piece of plastic upon which she'd drawn a picture of the flashlight, which Wanda signed with a thin plastic tube dipped in ink.

Back at the bed, she had Leesa help Ernesto up so that she could spread one of the plastic sheets. With no intervention from anyone since he'd been hurt, the bleeding had been profuse. Using the flashlight, she examined the injury as best she could without touching him, shifting her position to illuminate the right spots as he moved. It was a clean cut, with no foreign material and apparently no damage to the skull. She cautiously sprayed the wound with the carbamide solution, anticipating a dramatic reaction from him but getting none. "Tell him to keep his head on this pillow," she told Leesa. "If we can't hold a bandage to his head, he can hold his head to a bandage." She spread the plastic to cover the head end of the bed and then placed the folded blanket on top of it. "Can you lie down on top of this, Ernesto?" She gestured, being careful not to make contact. He stared off at something else. "Look," she said. "You can sleep. It's soft."

Helper Leesa repeated it in Spanish and Wanda gestured again, and slowly the boy lowered his bloody head to the blanket. Wanda noticed as he lay that his forearm had three long, narrow welts. "What's he been doing?" she asked Leesa.

"Learning."

His pants were shredded at the bottom. There were welts on his calves, too.

"Did you ever think maybe he's just not going to learn like other kids do?" Wanda blurted. "He's obviously different." She immediately thought better of it but the words were already out.

"Of course we know he's different. Of course he can't learn like other kids. But there is nothing more important than what we're trying to teach him."

"But you can see he's terrified. He probably doesn't understand why he's being beaten or having his things taken away."

"I know, the poor little guy. I wish it could be easier on him."

"It can be easier on him. Just stop hitting him and taking his stuff when he's not able to be like other kids."

Helper Leesa's eyes widened. Wanda was going to be punished. Maybe she'd be dropped back down a level.

"We have no issue with him being different. His amazing talent with machines is clearly a gift of the One. The school's actions are an attempt to give him the greatest gift anyone can give him: true acceptance of the One into his heart. Nobody's asking him to learn mathematics or spelling. I wish he weren't so terrified and confused, but we've tried all the easy ways. If we succeed in teaching him, Ernesto will be protected in this life and the next. Compared to that, any temporary discomfort is meaningless."

"What if he's not capable of understanding what you want him to?" Checking herself, Wanda added, "Helper."

"Then he's less comfortable than he could be otherwise," Leesa said. "But what if he *is* capable of understanding, and we're just not trying hard enough? Then he pays for our carelessness through all eternity."

"Maybe he can ease into it more slowly, Helper," Wanda said, consciously lowering her tone and her chin. "He's so frail and sickly; I don't think he can take much of this."

"He is sickly, and that's why we're so determined to help him be Saved and protected. The Saved are a community united only by belief, at war with the most dangerous and truly evil demons ever to slither across Earth." Leesa said. "If he can't be made to believe, he's not truly Saved. It is hard work to help him learn, but I'm willing to make whatever sacrifice it takes to save him."

The two women stared at each other. Finally Wanda said, "He'll have to stay here for at least a few days to heal, Helper."

"I'll have to stay with him. Until he's clearly one of us he can't be in Saved territory without an escort."

Wanda turned away, heading toward the lab. "Of course, Helper. I'm sure the Saved know best."

Office of the Amelix Integrations Medical Doctor

Gregor Kessler undressed slowly, folding each item he removed and placing it into the locker that had been provided. Finally naked, he checked his body to ensure that all hair was within respectful limits of length. A bit of his pubic hair had grown too long so he used the clippers that were provided. Having ensured his grooming was up to standard, he exited the preparatory chamber.

Kessler made his way up the small ladder to the examination frame and took his position as directed by the initial preparation video: one knee in each of the little cups, his forehead bowed to the folded towel on a narrow bioplexi ledge at the front of the apparatus, and his hands clasped behind his back.

He closed his eyes, mentally rehearsing what he was to say. Now that his preconditioning work with Chelsea had brought him a top-secret security clearance, he'd been pulled into another project with her. The new one warranted this appointment with the real Amelix Medical Doctor, the same supremely powerful individual he and Chelsea had crossed in advocating for the Board decision. The Amelix Medical Doctor had demanded it, in fact.

Kessler couldn't resist rolling his head to peer behind him as he heard Chelsea emerge from her own preparatory chamber. They were early for the Medical Doctor's appearance, anyway, in accordance with the instructions they had been given, so he'd have time to retake the formal position. Chelsea was lovely, with a perfect Golden figure and complexion. Her dark hair matched the perfectly trimmed strip of pubic hair below, and she had perfect palm-sized breasts capped with pert little nipples just slightly darker and pinker than the rest of her complexion. She cocked her head and raised an eyebrow at him, which would have seemed almost playful if not for her stern expression. He averted his eyes quickly, settling his forehead back on the towel. This woman met regularly with Walt Zytem, and Kessler would always be her subordinate. Keeping her happy was of paramount importance. After the recent Board decision the Medical Doctor would not be happy with either of them, but he did not anticipate that her displeasure would significantly affect the outcome of their petition. Medical Doctors had their own kind of conditioning program, and they took an oath that made them put their company's interest first.

Kessler breathed in and out deeply. He was about to be in the same room with the one who held absolute authority over every human body in all of Amelix.

He distracted himself by listening intently as Chelsea settled each knee into a cup, and noting how doing so had bent and spread his own legs. In his peripheral vision, he saw only hints of her as she put her forehead down and folded her hands behind her back.

It was difficult to keep track of time this way. There was some discomfort in his lower back and his face felt smashed against the towel, but there was nothing to see and no activity against which he could measure the passing minutes.

Finally the lights dimmed and brightened, and a single chime sounded to alert them to the Medical Doctor's arrival. A Medical Doctor's time was so precious that everything possible had to be done to avoid wasting even a second of it.

A door opened where before there had only been smooth wall, and he felt the Medical Doctor's hand on the back of his head, working its way down his back and then sliding along the outside of his leg. "Name?" she asked him, sliding her hand up one thigh and cupping his testicles.

"Gregor Kessler, Esteemed," he said, accenting the *ee* sound of the honorific as she gave his scrotum a strong tug. She clucked her tongue at him, running her hand along his opposite inner thigh and then reaching behind him to feel the outer part. She turned to Chelsea, starting at the back of her head. "And you?"

"Zabeth Chelsea, Esteemed."

"Mm. So you're the one Zytem mentioned in his message as my point of contact. The two of you are Mr. and Mrs. *two-thirty sub q*, aren't you? Perhaps I should congratulate you both on having taken the reconditioning process out of my jurisdiction."

Chelsea inhaled quickly. Kessler knew better than to turn his head.

"Hm," the Medical Doctor said, apparently reading something through her EI. "Your pallor and trembling are at the high end of the spectrum, but I suppose that's to be expected when one considers you're meeting with me today. Otherwise I would almost suspect you of going through chemical withdrawal right now ... " Her voice trailed off again. She clucked her tongue again. "Except that I have reports of every chemical that has been in your system, spanning from today all the way back through your prenatal days."

"Nervousness, Esteemed," Chelsea said. "Our meeting is not under ordinary circumstances, Esteemed, as you in your wisdom have already pointed out." "No, certainly not ordinary circumstances. It's not often I get to meet such worthy adversaries, right here in my clinic."

"We—" she grunted. "We meant no disrespect, Esteemed," Chelsea said. "We argued what we thought the regulations meant. We're Accepted, Esteemed; we could only ever do what we truly felt was best for the organization."

The Medical Doctor came to the head side of both frameworks, which she pulled together and lowered. Kessler could feel the warmth radiating from Chelsea's thigh, though they were not actually touching. The Medical Doctor's fingers came under Kessler's forehead and lifted, but the knee cups lowered and shifted as his head moved so that he was now kneeling mostly upright. He sensed motion to his right that suggested Chelsea was being put into the same position. An accidental glimpse of the Medical Doctor in his peripheral vision suggested her appearance was consistent with his expectations. She was dressed in white, and perfectly hairless like all Statused individuals. It was a terrible insult to look directly at a Medical Doctor; people of the lower classes even had a superstition that doing so could make a person go blind. For all Kessler knew, maybe it was true.

"You're the ones with power over the mind," the Medical Doctor said. "You're the psyche and I'm the flesh, isn't that what the Board decided?" She held Kessler's chin between her thumb and forefinger, moving her face into his field of view as she spoke. "Isn't that right, *Doctor* Kessler?"

Kessler jerked his eyes so hard toward the wall they seemed to stick there. "We are merely instruments of Amelix, Esteemed," he said, trying to overcome his urge to squirm away from her. "I understood the Board's ruling was that the Esteemed Doctor and the Board share power over the psyche. Of course, my tiny brain is insignificant compared to the Esteemed Doctor's or the Board's collective understanding of the issue, Esteemed."

"Yes," she said. "Yet you asked for bactrohypnotics to be added to food rations for everyone, company-wide, so that your preconditioning program could work. A bactrohypnotic is a drug, *Doctor* Kessler, a drug *you* needed administered to every human body within *my* patient corporation, yet the Board decided that I'm *required* to authorize this. Explain that."

"Please accept my thousand apologies, Esteemed," Kessler said. His voice trembled, as did the rest of him. "This worker's feeble mind cannot guess at the intricacies of the Board's decision making process, any more than it could comprehend the brilliance that is inherent in our Medical Doctor's mind, Esteemed. I am only fit to serve Amelix in corporate regulations, my area of focus, Esteemed. I believe, however, that the Board's decision means that while the Esteemed Medical Doctor determines the chemical composition of workers' bodies, the corporation is in charge of their social issues, like jobs, housing, and relationships. Thus the Board decided that it was proper for the corporation to determine only whether the bactrohypnotics should be administered, leaving the dosage to your impeccable discretion, Esteemed."

The Medical Doctor stayed silent, walking once around them in a circle. "Typical corporate doublespeak," she said finally. "By determining that bactrohypnotics are necessary at all, the company is making a medical decision. Your part in all this has weakened the practice of medicine, but as you've said, you're too stupid even to see it. Now I have you two here today, asking for something new. You'll understand if I'm not inclined to give you much, but let's not waste any more of my time. Start talking."

Chelsea cleared her throat. "As you know, Esteemed, our building in the CBD was vaporized by a nuclear weapon. We are constructing new buildings, here in the Great Midwestern Desert outside the CBD, and outside other cities worldwide, that are capable of physically relocating themselves. That is, they will be able to move away from threats, thereby safeguarding equipment, employees, and other company assets. Dr. Zytem, in his wisdom, anticipated the need for this long before the recent attack. He initiated the design and development process for these buildings quite some time ago. Because he foresaw not only the terrorist threat but also the danger of radioactive and biohazardous fallout, he insisted that the new structures have the ability to seal themselves completely, protecting all workers and maintaining work space in the event of nuclear, chemical, or biological attack. However, if such action should ever prove necessary, we expect that being sealed up might cause some issues, especially in the long term."

"It was in your memo," the Medical Doctor said. "You're asking me to up the dosages of compounds that encourage cooperation and obedience, for work in close quarters," the Medical Doctor said.

"Yes, Esteemed. Only during times when the buildings are sealed; we were hoping that with your Esteemed permission we could program synthesizers to do it automatically upon sealing. That was part of the issue, Esteemed. But in addition, we humbly seek your approval in establishing recondition-ing-style wave manipulations and sleep reprogramming. In case of emergency, the offices will need to keep function-ing with a single shift of workers—those that happen to be on duty when the building is sealed. To maintain optimal functionality, we feel the capability to alter sleep patterns for those remaining within the structure would be crucial." "Not every worker is suitable for that kind of duty," the Medical Doctor said.

Kessler cleared his throat. He had not been asked to speak again, and wouldn't, unless the Medical Doctor gave him per-mission. She did not, but Chelsea apparently felt empowered to continue.

"Every worker in the organization is Accepted now, Esteemed, thanks to the preconditioning program. From that pool, we are screening for appropriate personalities before assigning anyone to serve inside the new buildings. Other employees can continue to work in the older structures or even from corporate housing until they become incapacitated. We see a need for something more than standard antidepressants and mood stabilizers to ensure predictable cooperation under the direst of circumstances, the times when the very existence of Amelix Integrations is threatened."

The Medical Doctor turned away from Chelsea, focusing on Kessler again. "Every worker at every company in the world is already at the maximum dose of every synthesizable com-pound known to ease surrender of individual will," the Medical Doctor said. "It is the standard of care." Her hand appeared under Kessler's chin, lifting it so that he looked mostly at the ceiling and the uppermost edge of the wall before him. She was beside him, speaking in a voice that sounded more like a lab tech muttering to herself, turning his head this way and that. "Why would Zytem insult me this way, sending you?"

"I was brought today to answer any questions you may have, Esteemed, about preconditioning or any applicable corporate regulations," Kessler said. The last part came out as a vibrating slur, as the Medical Doctor ran her fingers down his chin, squeezing his throat just below his jawbone.

The Medical Doctor froze like that, peering at Kessler's head. "Regulations are for keeping workers doing what they're supposed to do. My focus is the health of the entire corporation. Regulations work around me."

"Yes, Esteemed," he said. "I—"

Her fingers came up from under his chin, covering his mouth. "Shh, shh, shh. Everything your department does is beneath me. You should not have come here today." She turned back to Chelsea. "I'll give you the wave manips and sleep mods, under emergency protocol only, and only for workers pre-screened for duty inside the new buildings. Is this all?"

"Yes, Esteemed. Thank you, Esteemed."

The door opened and the Medical Doctor vanished.

The Zone

It had been days since Dok's last bowl of mildew soup, when he had still been living in the Subjects' tunnels. Since then he had consumed three cockroaches and three cups of acidic rainwater he'd neutralized with some ground limestone. He was proud about the roaches: He had hunted one of the few forms of wildlife left in the world, proving himself human in the way of the ancient mastodon hunters. On the concrete next to him sat his bag with his few possessions: his pressure cooker, a few bactroherbal compounds, and the strange little notebook that had once meant so much to Eadie.

The pressure cooker was what had prompted him to search out this corner of the crumbling building and collapse, however long ago that had been. Dok was unable to bear its weight any longer, but still unwilling to give it up.

The euphoric state brought on by blood ketones in late-stage starvation was beginning to blossom. Where someone with a normal state of health might have lasted significantly longer out here, Dok had been living underground for months on a diet of fungi. His body wouldn't make it another forty-eight hours, and at this point even twelve seemed unlikely.

He opened his eyes and found that he was surrounded by Fiends. This fact neither worried nor surprised him. His bag disappeared, and then one of the Fiends held up the pressure cooker. "A cooking pot," the Fiend said. The voice sounded female. "Don't look like that did him much good."

Would they kill him, now? They wouldn't waste a bullet on him but they might slit his throat. It didn't matter.

"Wait," another voice came. "Hey, you there. Black man. Were you the doctor down in the tunnels? The one who knew the samurai?"

There was only one man who could have asked the question: the Fiend who had been Brian's commander, the man who had come into the tunnels and negotiated with the Subjects. He and Dok had spoken once. Looking up at the man, Dok recognized the handle of a samurai sword angling up from behind his back in one direction, and the butt of a gun in the other.

Dok closed his eyes again and ran his dry tongue across his lips. "*Coin Man?*"

"Heh. *Coiner,* yeah," the man responded. "The Subjects thought you were a miracle worker, with your potions and treatments."

"Medicine is the applied knowledge of mankind," Dok said. Perhaps at this point he was only thinking it. It was likely that these Fiends were just a hallucination. His grip on reality was loosening as he melted down into the gravel. "It's the sharing of that knowledge that constitutes a miracle. I'm merely the conduit for what our species has figured out together over the centuries."

"Yeah, I remember you," Coiner said. "Kicked out of there because you messed with their religion, right?"

Dok didn't answer.

"The Subjects don't want you or your services anymore, but I think we might find you valuable. Somebody grab him and carry him back with us. Give him some water. I'm going to present Top Dog with a new doctor to put in his new clinic."

One of Coiner's Fiends raised his rifle and fired a single shot into a corner of the building. He lowered it again and answered Coiner's accusing stare. "It was a rat, sir. Watching us, there. Pretty rare. You hardly ever see them anymore. Nice meat, you know, sir."

"Where is it?" Coiner asked.

"I...I missed, sir."

"You wasted a shell shooting a stupid rat, and you *missed*? At this distance?"

"It was strange, sir. It was standing still right there, up on its hind legs, watching us. There was this rage...it felt like I had no choice but to kill it. I wasn't even thinking, sir. I raised my rifle and had a clean shot. Right when I was going to pull the trigger, it bolted, real fast. Like it knew exactly when I was going to shoot."

The School

"Ernesto!"

The mechanical parts of this old electric toothbrush were made of plastic. Ernesto lined them up on the table, inspecting each one. Plastic gears were soft and they wore out easily, but they didn't rust.

"Ernesto! This is not the time for that."

The toothbrush had corrosion at the place where batteries were supposed to go. He could clean it off with some grit, but sometimes corroded metal pieces fell apart when he did that.

A hand swished between the table and his face, sweeping away the plastic gears to fall like raindrops to bounce on the floor. The hand picked up the toothbrush body and held it in front of Ernesto's eyes.

"Is this what you pray to instead of the One?" someone shouted in English. "This? This is nothing!"

The toothbrush slammed into the floor among the gears. A foot stomped down four times and broke it into little pieces. The foot stomped three more times, breaking the pieces into little pieces. The toothbrush had been fixable before but now it wasn't. The toothbrush would never work again. Even most of its parts, which could have been useful for other projects, were now ruined.

"This is the time we pray to the One." A face appeared in front of Ernesto. "I love you, Ernesto," it said. Ernesto compared it to the snapshot memories of faces in his mind. He may have seen this one before. "We all love you, and we so, so want you to be Saved like us. Students!" it called. "Come here, gather around him. We're going to cast."

The students all came right up to Ernesto, crowding in on him. "Demon!" one of them shouted. "We see you inside Ernesto, demon! Get out of him!" It might have been the same face that had spoken or it might have been different. Everywhere Ernesto's eyes pointed there was another face. The voices overlapped and he couldn't count them.

"Be gone, demon!" A hand slapped down across Ernesto's forehead and shoved him backward. Ernesto screamed and flailed, falling, crashing to the floor among the shattered gears and smashed plastic of the toothbrush. He stood and ran, crossing the room and flinging open the door.

He ran out, and he kept running and running until he couldn't hear any of them anymore.

The Saved Clinic

The battle had been huge, from what Wanda had been told, though you wouldn't know it from looking at the clinic. Fiends almost never left any survivors.

Right now she was standing at the counter in the supply room, waiting for a needle and gut so she could close a gash as long as her forearm across a Saved woman's back and shoulder. Reni, the new Helper, had started to get it but then turned back to the counter to help Judee first. Judee was level six, while Wanda was still just a three. "What do you need, Judee?"

"A needle and gut, Helper Reni, the One willing."

"Sure. Right away."

There were no gunshot wounds. Fiends apparently preferred knives.

Everyone who had been carried here had injuries to the mouth. Most common was a knife wound under the chin, stabbing upward through the tongue. It was apparently a Fiend favorite because it effectively nailed the mouth shut, keeping the victims quiet as the attackers continued cutting elsewhere on their bodies. She'd been told Fiends were made especially violent by that drug they took, Juice. Juice drove them to kill as brutally as possible, gave them a high from torturing their victims to death. Over and over the ones carrying the stretchers had said the same thing: Fiends liked the feel of blood on their hands. They stabbed and cut, but then they often tore at the wounds with their bare fingers, ripping them wider until the victim expired. They had an uncanny sense for knowing precisely when their victims were dead.

The Fiends used violence to gain control. The Saved used rituals and training, toward the same end. What was the point of any of it, if all anyone could ever be was a gear in some organization that cashed in their humanity for power?

Judee got her needle and gut and returned to her work. Reni stared at Wanda a moment and then asked, "What did you want again?"

Wanda gritted her teeth but they were worn down to the point where it caused shocking pain at certain contact points. She couldn't take it anymore. "You know, Helper, I'm only allowed to treat Saved here," she said. "While you intentionally ignore and delay me, they sit bleeding and in pain, waiting for my help."

Reni nodded, with a big, tight-lipped smile. "It's truly unfortunate that we are unable to assign all patients to caregivers who are trusted and informed," she said. "By necessity, some must rely on inferior treatment administered by one who can't be trusted because she refuses to acknowledge the One's simple vision of peace and love." She shrugged. "Maybe if you would open your heart and accept the additional training we offer, the One would help you solve that problem."

The front door banged open. Wanda turned and left the storeroom, expecting that more casualties had been brought into the clinic. Instead, she saw the little one-armed boy, Ernesto, pressing himself into a corner of the room, looking terrified and howling between his gasps for breath.

Walkway, new Amelix building, still under construction

"My projects are of sufficient importance to warrant any transfer of personnel I want, Dr. Kessler," Chelsea said. She liked to listen to her voice when she was alone with her two favorite new assets. She sounded haughty and important, as was appropriate in this situation. "Be thankful you're still in Regulations at your current post. I could've made *you* my receptionist, instead."

"I know, ma'am," Kessler said.

"I wanted her, I outrank you, and I took her from you. You should be glad I still let you both play together from time to time, even if it is only when I supervise."

As they entered Chelsea's department, Keiko bowed from behind the reception desk with her palms pressed together and her eyes down.

"Welcome, Dr. Chelsea, ma'am. Welcome Dr. Kessler, sir."

"Hello, Keiko," Chelsea said. The rat in her lab coat pocket was allowing her a good deal of freedom of movement today, especially in letting her talk and move her head. Chelsea was tired, though, and she felt its small corrections whenever she slouched. She was getting so used to being guided this way that she could often anticipate which variances the rat would allow.

Kessler muttered something, trying to avoid looking at Keiko. Chelsea was amused by the shame he felt around the girl now. After having conquered her so completely, he had now been claimed the same way, himself. Still, there was no reason for him to fret so. What he'd done with the girl had rendered her incapable of understanding why the situation humiliated him. He should be no more concerned with how he appeared to Keiko than with how he appeared to the furniture.

"Any news?" Chelsea asked her new receptionist.

"A man came to see you, ma'am," Keiko said. She remained frozen, staring down at her fingertips.

"Did he leave his name?"

"No, ma'am."

"Was he a scientist? Was he upset?"

Keiko stayed frozen. Chelsea waited a long time for an answer before she realized the silence was her own fault.

"Was he wearing a white lab coat like I wear?"

"No, ma'am."

"Did he say a lot of scientific stuff you didn't understand?"

"Yes, ma'am."

Chelsea paused, thinking it through. Finally she asked, "Was he wearing any lab coat at all?"

"Yes, ma'am."

"But it was different from the one I wear?"

"Yes, ma'am."

"Did it have a different name on it than mine does?"

"Yes, ma'am."

Chelsea tried to raise her hands in a habitual gesture of frustration, but the rat was having none of it. Resentment rose in her, not toward Keiko but toward the rat, and her face felt hot. Instantly, the Thrall's pleasure completely disappeared. Had it released her?

She tried to move her hands again and could not. She tried to take a step, but she couldn't do that, either. She was as much a puppet now as she had ever been, but now there was no warm softness to cushion her mind from the fact, to make it feel like more of a tradeoff. Now the animal's total control over her was just cold and unfiltered reality. The message was clear: Chelsea could choose to be a puppet in ecstasy or a puppet in misery, depending on her attitude.

"What was the name you saw on his lab coat?"

"Gao Jimenez, ma'am."

Gao Jimenez was a minor researcher whose work Chelsea's project had absorbed. Of course he was upset; Chelsea's move had almost certainly rendered him irrelevant.

It could not be helped.

"Did anything else happen while I was gone, anything that doesn't happen most other days?"

"Some people ran out from the lab once, ma'am. They were shouting, and there was an alarm. Someone said there was smoke, but I didn't see the smoke. Operations came and did something, and then everyone went back into the lab."

"Did the Operations people have the word 'fire' on their clothes? Or a picture of fire?"

"Yes, ma'am, they had both the word and a picture of fire."

"You may return to work now, Keiko. Good girl."

Keiko lowered her hands and returned to her duties, smugly smiling to herself like she did whenever Chelsea told her she was a good girl.

RickeResourses Building, CBD

547 could still recognize the man who was speaking to him as Clayton Ricker, even though the Statused man now had the

standard blocky Unnamed physique and sported the black suit and sunglasses of the Fold.

"Why are you here in my office today, boy?"

"Sir," 547 said. "You asked for me, sir."

"Who am I?"

Ricker had not gone through the Fold's training and initiation. Was he not still Clayton Ricker, even if he was wearing the uniform?

"Your privately held company merged with the Organization Whose Confidence is Kept, sir. Pursuant to that agreement, you were put in charge of all the Organization's Unnamed. You are our boss, sir."

547 knew it was more complicated than that, but to elaborate any further might seem presumptuous. When Ricker's son Matt had been killed, Ricker had renegotiated his deal with the Organization, offering his company in exchange for leadership of the Organization's Unnamed. The move had clearly been motivated by his war against Sett's father's mercenary house.

"I'm boss to thousands," Ricker said. "Why are *you* here?"

"I don't know, sir."

"Two medals." Ricker pointed at 547's chest with two fingers. "Sir?"

"When I look at you now, through these—" he gestured toward his own eyes and the Unnamed glasses covering them— "I see two virtual medals. First was the prestigious Silver Cert awarded for significant contribution to Organizational success, which you got for stealing a truck from the Williams Gypsum Corporation. And now you've been given the Palladium Medal, for saving the Organization's entire office staff by commandeering train cars before anyone else could get there. When she nominated you, your supervisor, IAg226, cited your insistence that the girl was dangerous, even though she was doing nothing at the time but standing outside the fence with a sign. I must agree with her that your insight was quite exceptional."

Ricker paused, then leaned in close. "I have the footage from the diner. I know who you are."

"I'm not that person anymore, sir," IAi547 said.

"Of course you aren't," the man said, smiling in the Accepted way that showed upper and lower teeth at once. "But you know how the Williams punk thinks. You were friends. You were with him, as his friend, the day that waitress killed Matt."

"Yes, sir, I did once, but Williams is no longer the same person, either. I want to help you in whatever way I can, sir, but I fear you may expect more than I'm able to give you, sir."

"It goes without saying that you'll do whatever you can to help, boy," Ricker said. "And also that if you do disappoint me I'll have you killed." The smile on Ricker's face broadened further. "In fact, if it comes to that, I'm going to tell the guy torturing you to death that I'll be equally disappointed in him if he doesn't inflict enough agony while you're still conscious. But only if you disappoint me, you understand."

"Yes, sir."

"Good. Now, I know you've had other run-ins with Williams as well -- when you stole the truck, for instance. That was after you were abducted and taken to their mines." Ricker was no longer smiling. "You'll be going back to that mine."

"Yes, sir. Shall I go right away? My team is waiting in the reception area."

"No. Unfortunately there's a pressing matter first. As I'm sure you're aware, paranoia has overtaken the whole CBD since the Amelix attack. This Organization is not an exception. Even as recently as my company's merger, the wise businesses were investing in *materials*. It's why the Organization was willing to offer so much in exchange for my garbage dump leases. But that was before the bomb dropped. Now everyone worries about another bomb, or worse, whatever the Amelix terrorists may have been trying to get their hands on when they raided the place. Most important now, even more important than the acquisition of additional corporate resources, is the ability to protect against bioterrorism. Every organization needs to have a world-class biotech division, and we're negotiating to acquire one. We need Unnamed to do the legwork, find out about any dirty details they try to hide from us during negotiations. Your new assignment is to work directly for me, collecting and condensing the information provided by the Fold. Someone's got to do it, and this way I can keep a close eye on you. If there's ever a chance to shred your little friend, Lawrence Williams the Seventh, I'll have you as a handy source of information. That time *will* come, just not quite yet."

"Sir, the Unnamed before you has no such friend. The man before you is friend only to the Fold, as the Lord wills for all those without names. Your will is mine, sir."

The clinic

Wanda hurried towards the boy. He didn't appear to be injured, so why was he here? As soon as he saw Wanda, he slid down the wall to the floor and clutched his knees with his one arm.

Ernesto's desperate, howling wail softened and slowed as she approached him. His eyes remained directed at the floor as she knelt down quietly next to him. She made no attempt to touch him. Wanda sat with him for several minutes, whispering softly, wondering how best to help him. Suddenly it became clear what she had to do. "Stay here for a minute, Ernesto," she said. "I will be right back."

Her cot was at the back of the clinic's most secluded section. The area had once been the storeroom but now served as a kind of intensive care unit. From behind a wall panel with hooks holding various lengths of tubing, she snatched up the pink bundle of fabric holding all her possessions. The fact that she still minced as she scurried back to the boy the way she'd been trained during the Coach V days didn't bother her, for once.

She extended her hand to help him up, but she knew better than to grab at him. Wanda had never seen him willingly touch anyone, but it felt right to make the gesture, even if he refused it. She was about to turn away and ask him to follow her when, to her great surprise, he placed his hand in hers. He even made fleeting eye contact as she gently raised him to his feet.

"C'mon," she said. Together they hustled toward the door.

"Wanda!" someone called. She didn't even turn her head.

Out they went, moving away from the clinic down a wide street. Wanda realized that she would fight anyone who tried to stop her, just as automatically as she'd made the decision to run with Ernesto now. In a world where no solo practitioners survived, she was going to become a solo practitioner, and help this boy grow up.

Somehow.

She didn't know her way around this part of the Zone. Since she'd Departed, she'd really only seen a few streets, a couple of cheap hotels, and the inside of the clinic. It didn't matter. If she or Ernesto were ever going to exist as cognizant, individual beings that were free of external programming and abuse, they had to get away from the Saved.

She turned left at the first intersection, then a right at the next, winding her way through the omnipresent crowd of Saved. She alternated left and right like that, for three turns in all, before she heard it, first far away, then repeated more closely.

"ALL STAND AGAINST YOU!"

Her heart stopped. The Saved had adopted this defense because it was all they knew to do, most of them having come from the Horde.

Were they doing this to keep her at the clinic? There were no fingers pointed anywhere from the people here yet. The targeted threat had been close, but not right here.

"ALL STAND AGAINST YOU!" another wave came, this one closer. The Saved on the street all looked quickly from side to side, seeking the right direction to point when it was their turn.

One saw something around a corner and pointed in that direction as the wave hit. "ALL STAND AGAINST YOU!" the crowd roared, all pointing where the first had. Wanda pointed her finger too, so as not to draw the crowd's attention. Ernesto did not follow suit, instead collapsing on the ground with his one arm up over his head, apparently overcome by the sudden and brutal commotion and noise.

"FIEND RAID! FIEND RAID!" the Saved shouted. The Saved ran off in the direction their fingers had been pointed, and more ran in behind them. Wanda crouched down and tried to cover Ernesto, to protect him from being trampled.

Underground tunnel, below where Rus had killed the Gargbageman

"Shit." Rus said. That woman running with the little one-armed kid was one of the doctors he was supposed to capture. He nudged Perks, the Rounder next to him. "We need that one. Take it from here while I go after her, right?"

"Yessir," Perks said without taking his eyes from the street. He'd been rolling his vial of Juice between his thumb and fingers, but now the grab for the clinic was beginning. He undid the cap and drank.

Rus followed the woman and kid. When the tunnels were empty, it was relatively easy to follow someone who was moving above ground. It was just a matter of seeing which direction they were headed and then scrambling toward the next opening that would provide a view. With two Rounds packed in it took more maneuvering before he was able to move to the next place, though.

"Back up this Round," he said to the Element on his other side. "Pass it on. Back up and into the next tube at your four, facing me."

They relayed the message and moved as quickly as they could, but by the time Rus got past them the woman and kid were nowhere to be seen. He scuttled through the tubes to look through another drain, but they weren't there, either. He backed up, took an alternate tube and looked out again. This time he managed to catch a glimpse of the two turning a corner.

The grab was underway. His whole body shook in anticipation but the Juice would have to wait. He had to focus on the target and ensure the doctors were captured in fully functional form. Juice would make it too likely that he would kill them.

One of the tubes he had to navigate was only wide enough for a belly crawl, but he made it through at what was probably his personal best speed. He reached the next crouchable space, which had once been an interior equipment room of some kind. Now it was nothing except a small hollow in a pile of rubble. When he looked out through an opening in one crumbling wall, they were right outside, cowering together. Apparently the fighting and screaming were freaking out the kid.

The Saved were big screamers.

The doctor craned her neck to look down the street toward the fighting and then back to look down an alley. She raised her shaking hands to her face and slumped down next to the boy.

The boy stood, twitchy and weird, moving a step or two away from her and then a little bit back, waving his arm around, and hyperventilating. She gestured in one direction and another, shaking her head. Rus thought he could make out the words, "Nowhere to go." As Rus looked on, astonished, the kid walked toward the tunnel opening where Rus was concealed, and the doctor followed him. Rus ducked out of sight as they looked his way. Then the boy squirmed his way into the tunnel, with the woman close behind.

The two turned back and watched the street as more Saved rushed past, heading toward their doom.

There was no need to hide the fact he was here.

"Thanks, kid," Rus said quietly. The doctor moaned in despair. "You just made my job super easy, little fella."

The kid went into full meltdown mode, rocking back and forth and making breathy grunting sounds. Rus had seen a wide range of reactions to his presence since he'd become an Element, but never anything quite like this.

"Just kill us quickly," the doctor said. "Please. You can kill so many more if you do it fast."

"Not killin' you," Rus said. "We need you 'cause you're a doctor. You're goin' back to the hospital where you were before. The kid, though, I can kill him quick for you."

Saved began running past again, this time in the opposite direction, back toward the clinic.

"Don't think of callin' to 'em," Rus said. "Or runnin' outta here. Like I said, we need you. Also, they need you. If we can't have you, neither can they. Get it?"

"Can you at least let Ernesto go?" she said, gesturing at the kid. "I promise I won't fight. I'll serve willingly, as doctor for you and the rest of your army. Just let this boy go."

Rus laughed. "Shut up."

"Can't you see he's not like other people?"

"So what? None of you Saved are like normal people. That's why we have to kill you instead of taking you to the Divinators and converting you. Top Dog says you're too brainwashed to be trainable."

"He's not brainwashed!" she said. "He hardly even talks."

"Neither do you. Remember I said shut up?"

She stayed quiet.

A few Saved ran past, heading away from the clinic this time. A minute later, more of them ran back this way. A knot of maybe twenty of them congregated on the street outside where they were hidden. The doctor gasped as she recognized one of them.

"There!" she said. "That's Leesa. She takes care of him. I think he'll go to her if I tell him. Please, please let me try."

"Shut. Up."

She cried. For real, cried. Finally she took a long breath and half-talked, half-cried: "Please! He'll probably be the last decent, innocent being either of us ever see again in our lives. I'm begging you -- don't kill him, don't take the last good thing away from the world!" She shook and sobbed.

Rus remembered the pink-haired whore. Outside, the little knot of Saved had moved about half a block in a new direction, down a side street. They'd probably escape if they continued that way.

Rus heaved the kid back out onto the street. The woman bent down so that she could see the boy through the opening. He stood only a few steps away with his shoulders hunched and his mouth hanging open, looking back and forth from the Saved to the woman.

Rus put his blade to her throat. "If that fuckin' kid draws them over here, first he's gonna watch me take your head off, an' then I'm gonna mow 'em all down with the rifle. Get him the fuck gone."

"Go to Helper Leesa, Ernesto," she said. "I'm sorry, sweetie. The Saved will keep you alive, and right now that's the most important thing. You have to do whatever they say. Believe in the One. You need to become Saved. Do you understand?"

The boy inched toward her, staring through the opening at her face and the knife blade. The woman pointed in the direction of the Saved, but he did not move.

"Enough of this," Rus said. "Get the fuck outta here, kid. Don't make me sorry I didn't slice you up. You!" He yanked the woman away from the opening and forced her to her knees, shoving her head toward the narrow tube behind them. "Get in there! Crawl forward until you reach the bigger pipe; I got a light I'll turn on when the kid's out of the picture."

"Run, Ernesto!" she shouted, her voice echoing down the tube. "Run and run until you reach Helper Leesa! I'm so sorry, Ernesto. I love you. Go!"

Rus dropped a shoulder to unsling the rifle, but the kid finally turned and ran away, chasing the group of Saved.

Rus sheathed the knife and followed the woman into the sewer.

13

Scaffolded and wrapped construction site for the new Amelix building

Gregor Kessler forced his eyes up and away from the moving walkway, scanning across the Corporate Green open area at the center of the new structure. The exact specifications were classified and his job description didn't warrant his knowing them, but even with the tarps hanging everywhere he could see that this open area was apparently several stories high, and as wide as it was tall. There was no reason to fear being sealed up in here for eight months. In fact, without being told, he probably wouldn't ever even have thought about whether the building was sealed or not. There was no reason to fear, at all. He could do this.

It's Zytem's paranoia! He's always been weird about security and now that there's been an attack he's gone off the deep end and he's going to lock me in here for eight months!

He was breathing hard. His eyes streamed tears that ran down his cheeks and pooled around his collar. Something was terribly wrong. The blasphemous thoughts he'd just been thinking had been about *Walt Zytem,* the conduit between himself and the Lord! Kessler leaned against the railing that moved alongside the walkway, determined to rechannel his thoughts in an appropriately reverential direction. Other employees strode past him, but he let the new structure's biomachinery convey him along at its sluggish pace.

He filled his lungs with air and held it all in. This breath trick was one of the only things Kessler had found that could help him stem his crippling trepidation about this building. He would not let himself inhale again until he had turned his mind the right direction

It's a beautiful building. Very pleasant. Truly a privilege to be here.

Pathway amplification boosted the feelings into a nice glow. He exhaled slowly, straightened his shoulders and stepped off the walkway.

Kessler's duties hadn't brought him to many parts of the structure yet, but he had consulted the floorplans through his EI to get a general sense of where things were. The light coming in through the open area in the center indicated that the top was either translucent or transparent, and shadows cast on the tarps draped around and above him suggested that there were opaque shades suspended above it.

He was headed to the fourth floor of the hard-core science wing where people like Chelsea worked. Usually this was her wheelhouse, meeting with scientists to see how things could be done, but in this case the wave-manip guy, a lower-ranked specialist named Dr. Talib Curtis, DCS, was asking Kessler to help interpret some regulations that were pertinent to the project.

The guy's fretting seemed kind of stupid, from Kessler's perspective. Regulations were just guidelines as to how workers interacted with each other. The wave-manips for sleep replacement and for inducing hypnotic states to aid preconditioning were company priorities. Company priorities would trump any regulation, if the action were ever challenged.

The science labs were as strange and uncomfortable to visit here as they had been at the old building, all cordoned off from each other with electrobioplexi that was almost always set on its darkest phase to ensure the secrecy of the experiments being conducted inside. Though a majority of Amelix employees worked within the various scientific departments, the halls here were typically empty. Workers tended to stay sequestered inside their segregated labs.

Kessler found the office easily. The EI was such a blessing, keeping him from getting lost down here, where a wrong step into a forbidden office could mean Departing.

Kessler's EI announced him as he arrived. Curtis answered almost instantly, easily recognizable with his short black hair and gray eyes, though the hair was mussed and the eyes were wild and glassy.

"Thank you for coming, sir," Curtis said. He extended a shaking hand. As Kessler grasped it, he noticed that the man's entire body was quivering. His Golden skin had bleached itself ivory white. This man was terrified.

It's this building! Being trapped in here will be like being buried alive, sealed willingly inside a movable tomb!

Kessler held his breath again. Curtis seemed too wrapped up in his own anxiety to notice.

Beautiful. Pleasant. Spacious, even. This place is so big, it's just like being outside. Just like being outside in the CBD. Outside. Calm, peaceful, open...

The terror subsided. Kessler avoided looking at Curtis, so as not to risk being triggered again by the man's obvious distress.

"Sure," Kessler said. "Still don't know why you couldn't have come up to my office like anyone else of subordinate rank would have done."

Curtis closed the door. "I'm sorry, sir, but I needed the security of the lab. I had to get Dr. Chelsea's approval to speak with you about this, and she insisted we speak here."

In his peripheral vision, Kessler could see Curtis steadying himself with both palms against a countertop. Kessler was tempted to grab hold of something, himself.

Lovely building. First class. State of the art. Pure, clean oxygen being pumped around this place, I'll bet. He let himself breathe again.

"I'll get right to it, sir.

"I don't have your level of security clearance generally, sir, but with regard to information and projects within my field, wave manipulation, it is necessary for me to have top clearance in order to perform my duties. Dr. Chelsea has authorized me to share a secret with you that we've had for many years now.

This information is classified as Ultra, sir, but on Dr. Chelsea's authority I'm to pass it to you."

He paused. When he finally spoke again, it was in a lower, more serious tone.

"As you know, sir, I'm tasked with using wave manipulation technology to alter sleep patterns when the new buildings are running sealed protocols."

Sealed!

Beautiful. Tech. Oxygen. These places are so big they're like being outside. He breathed again.

"The truth is, sir, that's easy. That tech has been used in the reconditioning process for years. Any regulatory issues were worked out long ago. Dr. Chelsea would never need your help with that."

Kessler let himself become annoyed. Irritation was a feeling he could manage more easily than fear, and Curtis was giving him ample opportunity to experience it. "Then why *am* I here, Dr. Curtis?"

"Well, sir," Curtis said. He paused once more and cleared his throat. "Sir, the science of wave manipulation goes far, far beyond merely replicating sleep patterns and running workers through them at quadruple speed. In fact, wave science is advanced enough to completely eliminate the need for Efficiency Implants, and it has been for quite some time."

"What?"

"It's true, sir. There's no need for implants into brains; we could do it all from outside. I'm talking full feed: communication, video, absolutely everything, without internal hardware."

"That's amazing," Kessler said. His voice probably sounded flat. It was shocking news. *Chelsea* was involved?

Curtis, now having broken the ice and disclosed the most guarded secret with which he had ever been entrusted, apparently found his voice. The words tumbled out, faster and clearer than before. "The current production EIs have tech that knows how to present signals into the right parts of the brain to give the impression of sound, sight, what have you. The next logical step was figuring out how to use wave manipulation to generate the same impressions, stimulating those same parts of the brain, only without direct physical contact. Amelix labs solved that puzzle more than ten years ago, and has perfected the technology since then."

"If it's perfected, why aren't we using it? Certainly a non-invasive process is better than having every worker undergo brain surgery—"

Kessler stopped talking. Every quarter, synthesizers all around the world were performing thousands of surgical procedures on workers' brains. All those credits flowed into the Medical Doctor's coffers.

"We've tried for years to get it implemented, sir, to use our proprietary wave manips to replace EIs."

Kessler sighed. "But you're always shut down by a Medical Doctor veto, right?"

"Yes, sir. But Dr. Chelsea says that regulations aboard these new structures are radically different—"

"You're insane. You want to try and snatch multiple thousands of brain surgeries out of her revenue stream and justify it because Dr. Zytem passed new regs about life aboard these structures? You won't survive this, Dr. Curtis. I'll tell you that right now."

"It's not my idea, sir." There was an edge to his voice now, and the implication was clear: *Go ahead, call Chelsea insane. See how long you survive, yourself.*

"There's no way," Kessler said. "Even with the new regs granting so much more autonomy to the structures, the Medical Doctor has full rights over all living human tissue, company-wide. You know this."

"Yes, sir. But Dr. Chelsea claims that wave manips are simply information, the same way that an audio announcement or a video program is simply information. As such, she has ordered that this tech be installed throughout this and every other new Amelix structure. As you know, sir, while the Medical Doctor has complete authority over human bodies, she does not control tech applications in the structures themselves."

"You're just *doing it?* Won't that interfere with existing EIs aboard?"

"No, sir. Existing EIs have a shielding effect on brains into which they've been installed. Waves are all around us, constantly, sir. Sound waves, microwaves, light, radio, all kinds. EIs were engineered to cancel out interference like that, so anyone with an EI wouldn't even notice the manips. The two technologies can coexist."

"What do you need me for, if you're just going ahead with it anyway?"

"Dr. Chelsea asks that you prepare a detailed reference document for us, sir. In case the installation, or more importantly, the use, of this tech is ever challenged."

"Uh huh. She wants to have me ready, in case she needs to sacrifice me."

"Speaking with all respect, sir, at least she's giving you a fighting chance. Some of us may be sacrificed without a means of defending ourselves at all."

New Union Headquarters, the Zone

"Tunnel Master Rus reporting, Top Dog, sir. You wanted to know my observations, sir." He had to raise his voice over the thunder that rattled the Throne Room's rare glass windowpanes.

The kid had been down there a long time. He would snap himself into a rigid military posture, but then he'd habitually hunch his shoulders and bend his back again, as if conforming to a smaller space. His eyes twitched and his hands clenched and unclenched repeatedly.

"You seem nervous, Tunnel Master. Something wrong?" Top Dog asked. His clipped voice conveyed contempt for the display of weakness. "You seem nervous."

"Sorry, Top Dog, sir," he said. "It's the storm. In the tunnels, when there's a thunderstorm you have to run for dry space or you die, sir."

"Now you're in my presence, Tunnel Master. Remember protocol."

"Sir, yes, sir."

The light was dim enough in here today that the tattoo the Subjects had given him was starting to glow. It was an arrow beginning at the tip of his nose and running all the way to his hairline.

"So," Top Dog said. "You were the first one there, right? The first Tunnel Master. You've spent longer in the tubes than anyone."

"Yes, sir."

"I need to know everything you've learned down there," Top Dog said. "I don't like what I've been hearing about those mole people, the Subjects."

"Um, I'm surprised, sir." Rus said. "All I see, Top Dog, sir, is the Subjects doin' exactly what we say, all the time."

"Yes. That's what's so disturbing. Nobody's that submissive. We need to find out what they're plotting. They have traps we don't understand; maybe they're going to slaughter a bunch of us sometime as we pass through on a raid." He stroked his close beard. "Why would they do it, though? What do they want?"

He paused, raising his eyebrows at the Tunnel Master, who cleared his throat nervously.

"From what I've seen, sir, the Subjects don't want anything. They're just...*there*, sir."

Top Dog consciously relaxed his face. Sneering at subordinates could make him appear weak and petty. He had heard this about the Subjects, that they simply existed to exist.

Contemptible creatures.

"Have you been able to find out how many of them there actually are?"

"They say they had thousands b'fore the bomb dropped, sir. I've only seen...not even a few hundred, sir. It's hard to be sure, though, because it's dark and they all look the same, scabby little skeletons with great big eyes. There are never many of them together at one time, because you can only line 'em up single file in a tunnel."

How nice it would be to know for certain, to perhaps cross off the Subjects from the list of threats to New Union power. Top Dog wanted to believe that most of them had been blown up by the bomb, and that Rus was correct in his estimate of a few hundred or less. Might the wispy mildew eaters have an incentive to do the same manipulation Top Dog himself did when he insisted his Elements say there were only five thousand in the New Union?

Still, he supposed, no matter how many there might be down there, it was hard to imagine them posing much of a threat to an organization like his.

Hard to imagine them raiding the CBD and triggering a nuclear response, too.

"All right, for now." Top Dog said. "Tell me more about the religion stuff. It seems that's the main way they're kept under control."

"Well, sir...They sure seem to believe in it. The Subjects have got stories and prayers, but all they ever seem to do is hang on. They believe as long as they keep starvin' and working all the time, and stayin' out of each other's way, they'll stay alive. They call it being *blessed by the Great Mother*, survivin' like that. I heard some of their stories, with all these names of different spirits or gods or whatever, but there's really just one message: Sacrifice yourself for the group."

"Sacrificing for the group is the basis of their entire belief system?"

"Yes, sir. I think so. It's like...life is pretty bad there for everyone. They're all sick. It's dark and wet. They eat mildew twice a day and pray their thanks for it. But they don' think about themselves. They're all one big...*thing* together. The Divinators tell us in the New Union about the Unity, sir, that life and death are the same. Down there, it's easy to see life and death as the same, sir. Subjects drop dead all the time, but they don't care, because they don't think much about their own lives. Just the group."

"So it's a political focus? They martyr themselves for their nation, that sort of thing?"

"Yes, sir, I guess. But it's different than we'd be. For them, it's like, '*I'm good because I'm havin' one less spoonful of mildew today, or, carryin' one more stone, or breathin' shallower*, that kinda thing. That's why the CBD attack is so strange, sir."

"What's the pull, Tunnel Master? What makes them so cohesive? It can't just be this religion that makes them want to breathe shallower. We have Divinators who provide certain services and function to make our Elements work together, but they don't have the ability to create that level of dedication on their own. Do the Subjects have a drug like our Juice?"

"Don't think so, sir. They sure don't carry it in vials hanging around their necks like we do. Maybe there could be something in the black soup they eat that gets 'em high or whatever, but they never seem drugged, sir. I think it's just the religion, sir."

"But how does it control them so completely?"

"I don't know, sir, but I think a big part might be that they've got no place else to go. They'll pretty much do anything to stay there, religion or no."
"Yeah, but that's true for our Elements, too. And professional Divinators."

"They got stories, too, Top Dog, sir. Our Divinators do important stuff, but they don't tell stories. The Subjects tell stories about their heroes, like this one called the Prophet, and another they called General Eadie. And the stories tell 'em why everything that happened is because of the Great Mother, and stuff like that."

"Stories." Top Dog mused. These Subject stories must be worth something if they engendered compliance almost as totally as Juice did.

"Ooh! An' they've got those…what're they called, sir, when they have special stuff they pray with? Relics? They got these relics they pray with, like staffs with important religious things glued to the tops of 'em."

"And how do those objects make a difference in the way they practice their religion, Tunnel Master?"

"I don't know, sir. I think maybe it feels nicer to do that, lookin' at special religious things and listenin' to stories. The Divinators make us afraid of acting outside what we're taught, but they don't make us feel like we're part of a story. When the Subjects hear the story and then see the relic from it, it's like they're part of the story, too, and then they know what they're supposed to do."

"Let me ask you this," Top Dog said. "Is there anyone besides a Divinator who knows as much about their religion *and* ours as you do?"

"I think maybe not, sir. I know what I learned from the Divinators during training an' stuff, an' I know more about the Subjects than pretty much anybody."

Top Dog stared at him. "How about I make you a Divinator, kid? You'll be tasked with learning the Subject religion and bringing in those pieces you find the most powerful, so they can be integrated into our traditions. We're going to have stories and relics, too."

Rus puffed out his chest. "I would be proud, sir."

"Keep doing what you're doing, and we'll start your training immediately."

"Thank you, Top Dog. Thank you, sir!"

"Yeah, yeah." Top Dog gestured to Patrol Leader Elfman, who was in charge of implementing much of what was ordered in these sessions. "Make that happen, huh?" Elfman nodded brusquely and escorted Rus out with a hand behind his shoulders. "Okay, next!" Top Dog called. Two men entered. One had a sword and a Federal railgun across his back.

"Coiner? What's this?" Top Dog said. "Not like you to come to the council meetings."

"Hello, Top Dog, sir," Coiner said. "I'm here to present you with a gift." He gestured to the skeletal figure next to him. "The doctor who kept all the mole people alive so long. Now we have the new clinic, and I found him just in time to put him there."

"Hmm," Top Dog said. "Come closer." He peered at the skin-and-bones man, who looked very much like the other Subjects he'd seen. "So you know the tunnels as well as the Subjects do, but you're not in league with them anymore?"

The man wheezed and his voice cracked as if he were a thousand years old. "Yes," he managed.

"You know of any egress points from the tunnels into the entertainment districts?"

The man stood silently for a long time, then seemed to snap back to life. "Uh," he said. "Yes. Uh. Yes, sir. I do." His knees buckled. "Thank you for the gift, Coiner!" Top Dog said. "Take him to the clinic for now, but as a patient. Get him fattened up. He'll be going back into the tunnels to navigate for us, soon."

Amelix Lab

It had been hours since the rat had let her have a sip of water, even though she could do better work if she was more comfortable. Hadn't the Rat Gods already decided that Amelix work was important to them? They'd always allowed her to make it a priority before.

The thirst was now bad enough that she found it harder and harder to think about anything else. Trying to swallow hurt her throat. Her tongue felt fused to the roof of her mouth.

If you won't let me drink, will you at least increase the Thrall?

Right now the pleasure had been reduced to a trickle. The physical sensation was distracting enough, but there was another factor that agitated her much more: Chelsea was a scientist, and she knew an experiment when she saw one.

Please don't make me die of thirst. The effects of dehydration on the human body are well documented. I can look them up for you.

Pathway amplification seized on her idea that the rats might decide to make her die of thirst, and she became increasingly desperate for water. Her mind writhed as it tried to find a way to convince them, though she knew that the Rat Gods would never be bothered about her feelings. They were the corporation itself, made flesh, and their agenda was infinitely grander than any concern of Chelsea's.

She felt something, though. Something in her mind. Thinking on it now, she realized it had always been there, though she'd not previously paid attention: It was possible to resist the rats, at least a little.

Being under their control, in Thrall, had felt too good for her to care about resisting much before now, especially after she'd realized how they were working for Amelix goals just like she was. Sometimes they trained her in unpleasant ways, like when they took the Thrall away to punish her, usually for thinking in a way they didn't approve of. She had learned to block all thoughts of resistance from her consciousness by now, though, and she was quite certain she'd done nothing to earn this punishment. She did and thought whatever they wanted, anymore. It was a terrible feeling, having the Thrall ripped away.

But here she was, in very light Thrall but still firmly under their control, and this realization—that she could resist a little if she really tried—hadn't brought any response. She could feel it deep inside: There was a tiny part of her brain that the rats hadn't yet reached. The rats hadn't *killed* the part of her that controlled the body, but rather had merely squished that part into a tiny space inside her brain.

That was probably why the rats weren't punishing her for thinking about it! The thought was taking place inside that tiny bubble within her brain into which their influence had not yet seeped.

They'd left her the ability to move her eyes and breathe, but that was all. She moved her eyes down to watch her left thumb. She focused intently on that tiny space inside her mind that still had some residual control, and, for an instant of blissful freedom, twitched her thumb.

The Thrall's pleasure vanished and in its place grew a frigid, crippling terror. Her gut knotted and her blood seemed to solidify. All her muscles went stiff and she again lost control of her breathing, which was now so shallow she knew a loss of consciousness was imminent. Pathway amplification took over, spiraling her into a desperate icy black hell.

Under the rats' control, she walked toward a different counter in the lab, moving robotically as her cramping muscles fought each other. Her hand removed a wide gauge hypodermic needle from a drawer. Her right index finger traced up her left thumb bone to where it joined the other bones of her hand and placed the needle point just outside the joint, shoving down hard with the blunt, plastic hub end of the needle against the table. Slowly her left hand pushed down on the point, which tore its way through her flesh. The skin on the back of her hand tented up briefly, and then the point emerged, stabbing suddenly upward as her hand slid down quickly to slap against the counter. Her face bent down over the counter, with her left eye looking straight down into the needle's opening from a distance of only a few centimeters. Some of her flesh had torn and now partially clogged the needle's tip.

I'm sorry! I'm sorry! I'm sorry! I will never do it again, not ever, I swear to you!

Slowly her eye moved closer to the needle, stopping millimeters away. Her mind froze, incapable of thought. She lost track of how long the rat held her like that.

Suddenly she stood straight upright, pivoted her wrist, and slammed the back of her hand down so hard on the countertop that the needle popped most of the way back out.

It was an experiment, after all.

The rats had tested her ability to resist them.

?

So much chaos.

Dok tried to sit up but found himself unable. It was so bright here that his eyes refused to open. By concentrating, he could crack them just enough to peer out through his eyelashes. Shapes—people—constantly bustled this way and that, in dizzying blurs.

Dok lost consciousness for a moment. Coming to again, he realized there was someone there next to him.

"Uhm," he managed.

"Hi, there," a voice said. It sounded female. He started to drift again but caught himself, forcing his eyes open a little wider.

"Where am I?" he croaked.

"A clinic," she said.

A clinic!

He moved to place an elbow onto the bed beneath him, but his body wouldn't cooperate.

"Oh, do you want to sit up a bit? I can help."

A hand appeared under his shoulders, and then a pillow. "There," she said. "Is that better?"

Dok nodded. "What clinic?" His voice came out as a croaking whisper, but at least it was audible.

"Well, that's kind of hard to say," she said. "No, no." Her hand appeared on his forehead, pushing him back to the pillow. "Just stay there for now, okay? You're not as strong as you may think. As to what clinic, I guess it depends on when you ask. Right now, it's controlled by the New Union. Before that, it belonged to the Saved. Before that, it was Coach V with the Horde."

Dok's mouth felt forced into a strange shape. He was smiling. "Coach V," he said.

"You know Coach V?"

"The Saved? Who are the Saved?"

"Shh, shh." The hand patted his forehead gently. This one had great bedside manner. "The Saved are a religious group that succeeded the Horde," she said. They say they follow a man they call the One Who Returned, but he's dead now. The Fiends are wiping the Saved out, and they took this clinic from them in the process. "Oh," Dok said. His eyes closed briefly and he nearly fell unconscious again, but the words resonated inside his mind and jolted him awake. He actually pulled himself up to an elbow. "One Who *Returned*?"

"Yeah. The One Who Returned." Her hand on his forehead shielded his eyes from some of the light, allowing Dok to see the room and all the patients. "He was a leader or guru or something to them, though I heard he was actually a local psycho people used to call the Garbageman. He had an unsaintly side to him, that's for sure. Anyway, for now, this place is New Union." She gestured around the clinic, with every bed occupied by a Fiend.

Dok tried to speak again but found he hadn't the strength. He rested a while longer and tried again. "Does the One who Returned claim to have come here from some other time?"

"I never heard that. He's sure different from anyone else I've met, though. I can tell you that much. Now you need to rest and—"

Dok's voice came back somewhat as he talked to himself. "It's that same strange undifferentiated schizophrenia! It didn't disappear, after all. That drug may still be circulating."

"Schizophrenia?" she asked.

He felt his eyelids trying to close and willed himself more awake. "There was some street drug going around that made people schizophrenic. I treated one patient who was like that, and then a Federal Agent came and threw me out on the street. The next thing I knew, my reputation was ruined, my career was over, and I was living in a sewer." He coughed and actually did black out again this time, but apparently only for perhaps a second or two.

When he opened his eyes, she was staring at him. "Are you Dark Dok?" she asked.

He didn't know how to answer. Anyone who knew that name would know that he'd now been labeled the Zone Poisoner. He was so tired, though. So weak. There was no reason to hide, no way to fight. Dok nodded.

"It was my job to monitor the MediPirates page for a while after Coach died," she said. "I'm Wanda, by the way."

"Hi, Wanda." He coughed again. "I'm, yes. I'm Dark Dok. Though I'm surprised you're still talking to me, if you know who I am. Someone set up shop in my old clinic, and started poisoning people in my name."

"I'm happy to meet you, Dark Dok. I read so many of your old posts, I feel like I know you. You have a brilliant medical mind. I suspected there was something wrong with the posts calling you a killer, and I met a lot of practitioners on chat boards who felt the same way. Dark Dok, the man who cared so much and so genuinely about his patients, could never have been the Zone Poisoner. Don't worry, Dok. I believe you already."

Nondescript and disintegrating civilian truck, Saved territory, the Zone

Agent Daiss scanned the windows and alleys for potential threats as Agent Juli Lehri maneuvered the slagheap truck.

Protocol for an Agent manning the vehicle's guns on patrol was to keep a finger next to but not on the trigger, but Daiss gripped it almost as tightly as if he were already shooting. The Saved made Daiss uncomfortable.

Many of the Saved came from backgrounds a little too similar to those of Federal Agents. He found it distasteful, having to acknowledge the grace of God through this forced proximity to them. Among the Saved's typical dust monkeys were true Golds who had grown up in suburbs or corporate housing, attended corporate schools and fought to survive in large organizations, only to fall to this wretched life in the end. Federal Agents Departed all the time, though their enhanced physiques required so many calories that they usually died quickly out here.

"We should have seen them by now," Lehri said.

"This is Saved territory, certainly," Daiss said. "Used to belong to the Horde. You're new enough you probably never ran up against them. If you drove down the streets here they'd be everywhere, acting like they were just random bums except that every one of them stared straight at you all the time. I've been watching the Saved since they took over, and they're less confrontational, much more likely to hide. There are fewer of them in any given place, but there may be many more around than what you see. They can stay out of sight and follow us for hours. No doubt they know we're here."

"What should we do?" Lehri asked.

"Another couple turns," he said. She turned twice more, traveling down some of the smaller streets.

"This is a big load of weapons," she said. "Are we sure they'll get to the right hands this way? This old ordnance not keyed to EIs could be used by anyone holding it. They don't even need bracelets with these mods."

All new Federal weapons were now keyed directly to specific Agents through their EIs. Daiss clenched his jaw, noting that the policy had been implemented after his own Gloria 6 was used in the CBD terrorist attack.

"You mean are we sure they'll go to the Saved and not the Fiends? Yeah, pretty sure. The Agent-specific security measures are disabled, but that doesn't mean we're giving up control. The trackers are all still fully functional. If we see them all move immediately into Fiend territory we'll call air support and level the playing field."

The purpose of this mission was to arm the Saved before the Fiends could wipe them all out. Zetas wanted to make sure the Saved and Fiends were equally matched enough for the war to continue for a long time.

"This ought to do," Daiss said, pointing at a building. "How about that corner?" Lehri let off the accelerator and the truck rolled gently into the brick wall. Both Agents got out, backing away from the vehicle quickly.

The Saved were supposed to be religious. Since only Zetas served the Lord directly, maybe the Saved would see this delivery as what it truly was: a literal instance of divine intervention.

14

The clinic

"Profuse bleeding!" Wanda said.

"Here you go," Dok said, handing her the syringe. "Plunger to you, bare needle pointed at me, ten percent gelatin solution."

She took it and gently pushed the needle into the flesh immediately upstream of the gushing wound on the Fiend woman's side, injecting the gelatin into the tissues. The bleeding slowed. It was Dok's technique, which he'd said he'd been waiting to try since he'd read about it years ago. When the Fiends somehow ended up with a supply of powdered synthetic gelatin from whatever murderous criminal activity they'd done, Dok had managed to convince Coiner to turn it over to the clinic.

Dok was stunningly good at this stuff. He was a truly natural caregiver, and it was nice to know that he thought of Wanda the same way. Though he treated her as an equal, she couldn't help but acknowledge that Dok was in a completely different league.

"Think we'd better get it sewed up," she said.

"I'm on it," he said, heading off toward the supply room. Together she and Dok had figured out that it was much easier for him to get supplies because Helper Bethe was terrified of him, even more than she was of the Fiends.

"Thanks," she said. "You're a prince among... well, you know what you're among."

"Heh."

Fiends were everywhere. They filled every one of these forty patient beds, and circled all around the clinic on various maneuvers, but she and Dok could talk to each other almost naturally. With Fiends, you had to worry about pushing them so far they'd murder you on the spot. Granted, that probably wasn't all that far. Still, she and Dok had been able to communicate pretty openly with no repercussions, in sharp contrast to the Saved's spying and tattling.

She held a bandage over the wound, alternating between a light pressure and a firmer one, to allow for some clotting to take place as she slowed the bleeding. Dok wound his way around the patients, machine guns and other nasty Fiend things, and disappeared into the storeroom.

This was the only casualty at the moment, thanks to the Fiend tendency to leave no survivors. They would emerge out of nowhere, slaughter ten or twenty Saved and vanish again, often without ever having been seen.

The Saved had called every little thing a blessing, and forced everyone to constantly thank the One for every positive situation or happening, no matter how trivial. It cheapened the experience of realizing the truly magical, mystical feeling of actually being blessed. Dok was that true kind of blessing for Wanda. From the moment he'd begun working in the clinic, Wanda had been impressed with his intuition and resourcefulness. Not only was he highly capable, but he radiated wonderful feelings of support and care.

"Here," he said, returning. "I got you one of the straighter ones because the cut's so wide. Eye to you, I'm placing it on your fingertips. Hold the needle near the wound and I'll spray both with carbamide at the same time."

"I'm grateful for you, Dok," Wanda said. "I could never have asked for a better...what are we to each other? Co-workers?"

"No," he said, pumping the sprayer. "That sounds too much like we're part of some organization. You and I are...independent practitioners who have formed a joint venture."

"And yet, still slaves," she said.

"We're independent *except* for the fact that we're slaves," he said. He would probably have winked if she could have seen. "But we respect each other's intelligence and ability, and that lets us accomplish more than we could any other way. We allow each other to be human, which, in this one instance, still can be a successful model."

"Oh?" she said. "Humans aren't successful generally? I thought we ran the world."

"Human chromosomes are successful, certainly," he said. "Just like chicken chromosomes are successful, in terms of evolution." He sprayed his own hands and then pushed the tissue gently together so Wanda could sew. The Fiend patient grunted.

"You lost me there," she said. "Are there even any chickens alive anymore, now that we have synthesizers?"

"Ah, but I didn't say *chickens* are successful. Just their chromosomes, the little bits of DNA inside them. Something in their genetics made chickens easy for humans to capture from the wild and breed. At one time, there were thousands of kinds of birds, and then pretty soon it was only a few kinds like chickens and turkeys, which humans had found useful. Now, those same chromosomes have been put into bacteria, and the bacteria in synthesizers produce chicken meat. Bacteria have no set lifespan, you know. As long as a bacterium has nutrients and isn't poisoned or otherwise killed, it will grow and divide forever. The chicken's chromosomes, by enslaving their bird hosts to humanity and then eliminating the bird altogether, achieved immortality."

"Hm. Maybe you and I are on our way to immortality, then." She laughed sadly.

"Not even our chromosomes," he said. She could tell from his voice he was smirking. "I had a lot of time underground to think about this. Independent humans like us are pretty much washed out of the gene pool already. If any human genes make it to immortality, it'll be the ones who follow the chickens into the machinery."

"The New Union doesn't look like machinery to you?"

He leaned in closer. "I think this is a less successful model than the CBD corporate one, over the long term."

"Let's hope," she mumbled. The only Fiends nearby were unconscious, including their patient, now. The Juice must have worn off suddenly.

She made another loop and tied the knot, then started a new suture.

"Should we hope for that?" he asked. "I mean, do we care whether this way or that way wins? We're screwed, either way."

The smile to which she'd been clinging shattered. They were silent a few beats, and then Dok asked, "What's wrong?"

She sniffled but kept her hands still. "My chromosomes still have a chance there, remember?"

"Oh, no, I'm so sorry, Wanda," he said. "I wasn't thinking at all. Of course it matters. I'm so, so sorry."

"It's okay. I know what you mean. Both models are pretty terrible."

"Here, let me."

Dok took the instruments from her and made a few quick stabs and tugs, finishing the row with firm, neat stitches. He turned and put his arms around her, holding her tightly. It felt so good to have him there, easing the weight of such hopeless sadness for Nami, for herself, and even for the chickens. She hadn't realized how much of a difference it could make to have a true friend, especially in such a dark world.

"I'm sorry," he said again. "I'm not...I have no excuse." He patted her lightly on the back. "Some luck, huh? Of all the people to be enslaved by the Fiends with, you get me."

She smiled, though her eyes still welled with tears. "Some luck."

It had to be some sort of shock-induced trick of consciousness, making her react to the words, the numbing cold radiating outward through her from her gut, before the words' meaning actually registered in her mind. "Dok, we gotta go."

Patrol Leader Coiner was there, in the doorway with some other Fiends. Dok had told her this time would come, when they would drag him back down into the sewers. That place had nearly killed him before, and its leadership had threatened to finish the job in the most gruesome of ways if he should ever return.

Dok's breath caught and he grabbed Wanda's shoulder in shock. He exhaled, deflating. He nodded sadly to Coiner, then hugged Wanda tighter and kissed her cheek, and he was gone.

Slowly she sank to the bloody floor. Too stunned to cry anymore, she sat that way, staring at nothing. The Fiends left her alone.

With Helper Leesa

Ernesto stared at the speedometer he'd been restoring and recalibrating, imagining the layout of gears inside it. Helper Leesa was holding it out in front of him.

"Ernesto, pay attention to me if you want this back. You want it? Then you listen and you answer me. Why should you have this back?"

"Because I learned the One loves me," he said huffily. "Because I opened my heart to the One's love."

"Very good. Now tell me why it's important for you to learn that. Why did learning that get you this gift, the machinery and the pliers, to tinker with in the first place?"

"Because we are broken and only the One can fix us. The One fixes me like I fix machines. I have to want the One to fix me if I want to be Saved."

"That's right." The speedometer came closer to him. "Go ahead, you can take it." He did. "And remember always that it is a gift of the One. Now, you can play with that, but we're going to go with the other children for a bit. There's something you need to see."

"I don't like other children, Leesa," Ernesto said. He took three quick steps to catch up with her. "I don't like the other children."

"I heard you, *hijo*. But I did not ask you whether you liked the other children. I told you there's something you need to see."

She kept walking but he kept up, a step or two behind her, by focusing on her elbow. It was what Arrulfo had taught him to do. Arrulfo was dead. Leesa said Arrulfo never knew the One so he never got fixed. Arrulfo couldn't be in a nice place with the One now, and everywhere else but with the One was a bad place to be dead. Arrulfo was in a bad place for dead people, because he didn't know about the One, so he couldn't go be with the One now. There was only one good place, and the One was there, so Arrulfo couldn't go to the good place because he didn't know the One. Like the sewers where it was black and dark and cold, that was a bad place. Arrulfo could be there.

"I'm proud of you for working so hard to learn about the One, and trying to surrender to his guidance," Leesa said. "It is very important, Ernesto. It means being a true member of this blessed family of Saved, not just a recipient of our charity. It means protection for you, my sweet boy, every day of your life and forever after. You must be Saved in your heart."

The other children were seated in a group, curbside at a large empty street. Leesa guided him to sit at the edge of the little cluster, with her standing right behind him. There were lots of Saved, all facing the same direction, toward a pole that was lashed sideways between two upright ones across the street. A line of men and women marched in with their arms behind their backs. Men and women marched alongside them with guns.

Ernesto set the speedometer on the gravel in front of him and took out his pliers. The pliers were a gift from the One, a blessing from the One. He used the pliers to fix things like the One was going to fix him.

To open the back Ernesto needed the little screwdriver from his pocket. It was hard to balance with only one arm. He held the speedometer with his feet and pushed the screwdriver hard against the screw so it wouldn't slip.

"Ernesto, look!"

He had to be careful not to lose the screw in the gravel, once it came out.

"Ernesto!"

"Auggh!" he shouted, startled. Leesa was talking right down onto his head.

"Pay attention to this, Ernesto. This is important. You must understand how the Saved will win this war through the grace and glory of the One."

People stood with their arms draped over the pole so the tied hands were behind them on the other side of it. Other people stood around them with guns. The tied-up people didn't have any guns.

Ernesto removed the black case from the speedometer, checking each gear and the way it meshed with others. One of the gears was missing three teeth, all next to each other. Following its rotation, he located a similar problem on its mate, as if debris had jammed between them at one time. He squeezed each gear with his new pliers to make it as straight and flat as possible, and then re-clocked them so that the bad spots didn't match up at exactly the same time, to ensure that there was always at least some meshing between them. There would always be a wobble there, though, so he bent the matching teeth very slightly, by holding each one delicately in the pliers and pressing it softly against his leg. With some teeth leaning slightly upward and some leaning slightly downward, the cogs seemed like fingers grasping for each other. The overlap met at a slight angle. It would allow for the wobble and still give the remaining teeth enough contact.

"Ernesto!"

"Auggh!"

"Ernesto!" Leesa said. "You should be watching."

"Should be" was important. Sometimes Ernesto didn't get to eat meals because he hadn't been doing what he "should be" doing. Sometimes Leesa or another Helper hit him, or made him sit alone in a corner when his actions didn't match what "should be." *Do you want to know whose actions do match what should be, Ernesto?* Helper Leesa had asked. *The One's. When you do what you should, you are doing like the One expects you to do.*

Just looking at the speedometer gave him a sensation like sitting next to a warm fire on a cold day.

He should be watching.

Ernesto made himself watch the street.

There were lots of Saved, watching from a wide half circle around the poles and from every window in the nearby buildings. Helper Leesa had said to watch, not count how many Saved. They made a lot of noise, all those Saved, who were crowded together at two per square meter, in this area that was probably twenty meters by thirty meters. Helper Leesa had said to watch. Only to watch.

He should be watching.

Too much noise. They were too noisy, and he should be watching.

Porter raised his palms. Porter was not the One, but he had known the One, and he was now the leader of the Saved. Leader meant that they tried to do what he said, like Ernesto had done with Arrulfo. The crowd stopped making so much noise. The ten people with guns kept them aimed but spread out to the edges of the crowd. Now Ernesto could see the tied-hands people better.

"Standing before you are six Fiend prisoners, captured by our courageous Saved fighters," he said. Some people watching made loud, startling noises like hooting and clapping their hands.

Porter approached one of the tied-hands people and pulled a string from around his neck. "I know what you're thinking," he said. "We have a duty to try and save every last person, try to show them the One's majesty and righteousness. I assure you we have fulfilled that duty with these prisoners as well. I know you all hope, as I do, that they have accepted the One into their hearts, especially as they are almost out of time and will never have another chance. But let's be honest, we all kind of doubt it, don't we?"

He held up the string. A little charm dangled from it.

"And this is why. *This* is what they believe in, isn't it? We Saved, *we* feel the love of the One, every day. But there is no love in this false idol, this chemical that brings them temporary pleasure. They believe it has power, but we know it does not. Now it is too late for them to learn the truth."

Too late. Just like for Arrulfo it was too late, and now he had to be in some terrible place for dead people to be, instead of warm and safe with the One forever. It was all because these Fiends thought their necklaces were magic and really only the One was magic. Ernesto stood, pliers still in his hand, and began moving quickly through the seated crowd of children toward Porter. One of the men with guns grabbed at him but Ernesto ran fast. He reached Porter and the little glass vial that dangled from his hand, the vial the Fiends put their false hope into. That false hope was why the Fiends were broken.

Ernesto snatched it in the pliers and he squeezed, shattering it. He held up the pliers to the prisoner who had been wearing it and opened them, letting the glass between them fall. "You see?" he said, not thinking about whether the prisoner might speak Spanish. "This is nothing. Don't go to a bad place!"

There was so much noise. Everyone in the crowd was shouting and clapping. Ernesto turned to see them but Porter was guiding him toward the next prisoner to crush the next vial, and then the next. Leesa was there by him and telling him he was very good, but maybe sad, too, because she was crying and crying meant that someone was sad.

"You're Saved, Ernesto, *mi hijo*!" Leesa said. "You're Saved."

Tunnels Under the newly sealed Zone's Special Licensed Districts (SLiDs):

Dok couldn't speak. He tried to force himself to relax by hunching his shoulders tightly and then letting them drop, but it didn't help. His breath still came in short, shaky gasps. Dok had stayed down in these tunnels for weeks and even months on end, but the walls had never seemed so close. He was leading Coiner and two of Coiner's murderous Fiends on a reconnaissance mission, heading for what had once been his favorite part of the moldy black nightmare that was existence down here. Just ahead were two abandoned buildings in the Zone, connected to each other by a single navigable tunnel. Working from the inside, the Subjects had built walls of rubble around the two ruined structures, sealing them away from the rest of the world and allowing Subjects to reach not only the ground level, but the floors above that, as well. There they'd been able to sit on the bare concrete and peer out through the giant gaping holes where windows had once been. Now that he'd been part of the outside world again, Dok realized how pathetic and cockroach-like that was, but at the time, a chance to gaze at the sky and clear his lungs of blighted air had felt like paradise.

He tried to focus on that idea, now, on being above ground again, even if it was just there, in those crumbling buildings. To go up, to go out, to escape this place and breathe dry air that didn't stink quite so badly of decay, *that* was heaven to the Subjects of the Underground Kingdom. But these tubes, with their starvation and wet coughs and always, always the smell of mildew and rot, even these weren't hell. Hell was what Dok had been sentenced to if he was ever caught back down here again: the Deep Chamber.

Dok had never been down here with so much light. Fiends didn't scurry around in the dark like Subjects. It should have helped him better imagine himself above ground, but instead it made him feel even more trapped. Coiner had some slick system on his rifle that turned on a flashlight below the barrel when he squeezed a little pad attached to the grip. The beam bobbed up and down as he moved, accenting the curve of the tube. The other two Fiends carried old telephones that had little lights built in. They kept turning around and shining them backward to ensure the group wasn't being followed.

"You know, the Subjects consider me a criminal. I violated a key tenet of their religion, and to them, that is a capital offense. I get the Deep Chamber if I'm caught here," Dok said. "That was my sentence. The Deep Chamber is a tube slightly bigger around than your shoulders, slanting down at a forty-five-degree angle. It's so deep that they don't even know how deep it is, but I'm told that if you toss in a rock, you hear a splash—eventually. They'll tie my hands behind my back and slide me down it headfirst."

Coiner froze. His light went out, and the other two Fiends doused theirs, following his lead. Coiner leaned backward until he was only centimeters from Dok's face. His voice was an icy whisper. "This is a military reconnaissance mission. All I want to hear from you are the directions on how to get there. If you start whining again, you'll be leaving a trail of blood the rest of the way."

The lights came back on and the group started down the tunnel again.

Dok laughed inaudibly. How perfect that the fungus capable of wiping out humanity had become a religious symbol to people who lived, breathed, and eventually reverted back into fungi.

All kinds of different molds and mildews were filling his lungs with spores right now. He let out a shaky breath.

Dok's breathing was becoming more rapid and shallow as they progressed. He stopped, closing his eyes and pressing his palms against the curved sides of the tube, trying to center himself. When he opened them again, the tunnel looked even smaller than before, and it appeared to narrow dramatically as it stretched ahead.

No. It's an illusion. It's darker because the lights fade there. The tube is the same diameter as always.

Dok could do this. He had lived down here for a long time, and without light, even—

No! I can't do this! I can't be here I have to get above ground again but if I try the Fiends will kill me!

Dok stopped, his head spinning.

He couldn't take much more of this torture, this helpless feeling of entrapment and suffocation. He had to get out of here. He needed—

Anesthesia!

Suddenly he understood how to help himself. The hypnosis techniques he'd used in his practice to distract patients from the pain of surgery or stitches could also free his mind from the encroaching darkness. His patients had escaped to fantasies of deluxe upper class accommodations, warm baths, scenes from old movies … But they hadn't needed to function while they had escaped. How could he stay focused and still have the sensation that he wasn't actually here?

He took a deep breath and then focused on relaxing his torso, shoulders and neck as he exhaled. With another breath he relaxed them more, and also the back of his head. Subsequent breaths released his limbs, face, eyes, and jaw. Then it came to him:

Be the Prophet.

It was better to see this place through someone else's experience rather than his own. The Prophet had always seemed perfectly content slithering around in the fungi.

Be the Prophet.

Dok's anxiety began to drain away. It was replaced by a numbing sense of indifference as his mind settled into the Prophet's persona. Dok was elsewhere; now it was the Prophet showing the Fiends around. The Prophet was exceedingly calm.

"This way," he said, his voice sounding to his own ears like the Prophet's voice.

He felt thirsty for sodje.

"Here it is," he said. Speaking as the Prophet, Dok put much less energy behind his words than he usually did. He rolled a slab of concrete away from the tunnel wall, revealing a hole just wide enough to squeeze through. He pointed to the hole, speaking to the Fiends. "On the other side, debris has been arranged to appear as if it blocks your way, but there is a pattern to it, with only one way to get through. When you enter, roll your shoulders to the left, and reach up to find a bar you can use to pull yourselves into the room. I'll go first. Watch me and do what I do."

Dok dropped to his knees and worked his shoulders through the opening, then rolled his shoulder and grabbed the bar. He pulled himself up, keeping his body stiff, and then dropped into a crouching position. He shuffled out of the rubble, emerging from total darkness into gray gloom. With room enough to stand, he straightened his back—

Someone huge pinned his arms behind him and slammed him to the ground, hard. Someone else hit the ground next to him: the first Fiend to have followed him through the hole.

Wake up!

Dok had no chance of responding effectively to this situation while convinced he was the helplessly passive Prophet.

He felt himself, and his claustrophobia, return. He thrashed, but found himself immobilized by shockingly strong hands.

"Enough!" It was Coiner's voice. "I've got a bead on all four of you and I'm full-auto, hidden in all this shit."

"You don't have a bead on all four of us," a voice said, "or you would've taken the shot."

That voice. It couldn't be. Dok said the name without realizing. "Lawrence?"

Silence. Nobody moved. Finally, that same voice spoke again. "Dok?"

"Don't drink!" Dok said, as loudly as he thought he could without startling one of the seven people here who carried a machine gun. "Don't drink the Juice. We can de-escalate and work something out, okay? Coiner, Lawrence, please, please help so we can all walk away from here."

Dok risked lifting his head and looking around. Lawrence helped him to his feet. Once almost as scrawny as any Subject, Lawrence was now huge and dressed identically to every other Unnamed, in a black stretchy suit with lapels and bulletproof computer-aided sunglasses.

Coiner approached slowly. The Fiend next to Dok was allowed to rise to his feet. He went over to stand by the pile of rubble, where the last one to emerge from the tunnel was undoubtedly hidden by now.

"You're the last person I ever expected to see here, Lawrence," Dok said.

"It's just Sett, now, Dok. There's no Lawrence anymore."

"The Zone's sealed off. How did you even get here?" He gestured at the giant black-suited body. "I know you didn't enter this building through the tunnels."

"Don't need to. My firm has just acquired the exclusive license to this district, SLiD 8, in the newly sealed Zone. I selected this particular section for old times' sake, believe it or not. We'll have a bar, a nightclub, and a casino. I might even put my picture on the chips. Only thirty other districts got a special license, in the whole city."

"You're gonna be in charge of this whole district?" Coiner asked. "I think maybe we should talk business."

Offices of the Esteemed Medical Doctor Darius Williams

The Unnamed known as Two drove through the last of the three checkpoints leading to the clinic. Her Esteemed Uncle Darius lived in the largest house here on this vast estate, but she would never be visiting him there again. Now that Ani Williams had given up her name to become Two, the second in command at the mercenary firm that had formerly been Williams Gypsum, all family connections were null and void. She was only Unnamed, now.

Her brother—or former brother, since they were both Unnamed now—had made this meeting necessary. Months ago he had used company funds to open a bar in the Special Licensed Entertainment Districts. Since then, he had completely abandoned all his other duties within the family business. Unfortunately, her father, or former father, was also implicated in Sett's disaster. He'd approved the funding for this speculative bar project and had appeared to condone Sett's irresponsible behavior from the outset.

The black truck rolled quietly along the winding drive, away from the cluster of mansions and toward the clinic where she would meet her Esteemed former uncle. She believed the other two opulent houses might be used for important visitors from time to time. Servants, she knew, lived in three rows of long, low quarters that were hidden behind a dusty hill.

The clinic loomed ahead, three stories of gray concrete harshly backlit by the blazing sun. Her Unnamed glasses recalibrated, adjusting their tint and filters to optimize her vision. Giving up the glasses for even a little while would be the worst part of having to be examined naked; she would temporarily lose the superpowers they provided. She approached a garage door at one side of the building and a signal came through her EI. "This facility is owned and operated by the Guild of Consolidated Physicians, in accordance with medical protocol," it said. "The Guild of Consolidated Physicians warns that any misconduct or contraventions of etiquette will be dealt with strictly and immediately. The following tutorial will assist you if you are unfamiliar with proper decorum in medical settings. The—"

"Skip tutorial," Two said. She knew medical protocol well enough. Owning a corporation did have advantages. Defined by her family as "key personnel" at birth, she had always been entitled to visit her Esteemed Uncle personally once a year to receive direct monitoring and guidance. Though technically his patient had been Williams Gypsum, these regular encounters taught her precisely how to behave in the presence of ordained Esteemed Medical Doctors. She had touted her mastery of this etiquette on her college applications, in fact, to distinguish herself from the vast majority of Golds who had never seen an Esteemed Medical Doctor in the flesh.

The garage door opened and Two guided the truck into a parking place. She had gotten used to her gigantic new body, but being back here where she'd once been small made her particularly conscious of her increased size as she made her way up into the building, to the proper floor, and through the preparation area. Finally, she found herself settling naked into the examination apparatus.

Her Esteemed Uncle Doctor Darius—now *Esteemed Medical Doctor Williams*—was always late for appointments, but this time he made her wait for what was probably more than two hours. Her EI didn't work in the exam room so it was difficult to tell time. Finally he entered and approached. She kept her eyes averted as he had taught her, cringing slightly as she remembered the painful lesson he'd given her on the topic when she was five. Failure to follow protocol in an exam room was tantamount to deceiving the corporation because it was here she presented herself to be evaluated for corporate fitness. He'd told her at the time that the mist was harmless but she'd had blisters on her eyelids the next day at school.

Two held perfectly still as her Esteemed Uncle Doctor Darius ran his hands over her smooth, bare skin. "Hello, Two," he said. "Why, specifically, are you asking for a no-confidence decision regarding your organizational structure and your Chairman, One, today?

Chairman One. That was as much name as her father would ever have again, now that he, like she and Sett, had become Unnamed. She wasn't supposed to think of them by family relationship anymore, just like with her Esteemed Uncle, but remnants of old habits sometimes hung on even after reconditioning.

"I'm concerned, Esteemed," she said, struggling to keep her voice steady as his hands moved across more sensitive areas. It was odd to say "Esteemed" without adding "Uncle." She had never spoken to any other Medical Doctor, and Darius had always been "Esteemed Uncle" before. "Our Chairman often appears to let personal feelings interfere with his professional judgment, Esteemed."

"You mentioned in your application for an appointment with me that you feel he is especially biased in favor of Sett."

"Yes, Esteemed. The rest of us are out serving many needs of multiple clients, but Sett has been allowed to run a bar in the Zone. The Organization gets little benefit from his time there, and now he's associating with others from outside our corporate umbrella. I don't mean customers, Esteemed. My own intelligence confirms he regularly meets with the Negro man known as the Zone Poisoner, and lately his inner circle seems to include several Fiends, Esteemed."

His manual examination of her body ceased abruptly. "He carouses with Fiends? At a public establishment owned by our organization?"

"Yes, Esteemed. Not only socializes, but actually works with them, sometimes including them in operations. Apparently he knew them during the months he lived in the sewers, Esteemed. Chairman One allows him complete freedom in this."

"Well, I suppose we have to admit that it is often dirty and dangerous work the company does lately, and the Fiends might be quite useful for some of it," The Esteemed Doctor said.

"Yes, Esteemed," Two said. "Of course, Sett and the Chairman got us into this line of work in the first place; one by behaving idiotically in a restaurant and the other by going to war with one of the most powerful private organizations in the world. It is clearly not my place to question business decisions made above my station, Esteemed, but it is worth noting that the situation in which we find ourselves, the necessity for dirty and dangerous work, results from those initial decisions. I do not believe Dr. Muun will find such reckless behavior to be of value in the merger, Esteemed. The health of this organization at the time of transfer will determine our ownership interest when the deal is finalized, and so I have come to you, Esteemed."

"But isn't Sett's bar producing valuable intelligence for us, Two?"

"I was not given information about that, Esteemed. I would never presume to know more than the Organization's Esteemed Medical Doctor."

"I see. And do you have a suggestion as to who might replace the current Chairman if I should deem him a threat to my patient?"

"Oh, no, Esteemed. I would never presume to make judgments about the condition of our business or suitability of its personnel, unqualified as I am. Only an Esteemed Medical Doctor can make such a determination, as you know, Esteemed. Though if asked I would suggest finding one who has spent many years observing administration firsthand within the Organization, but also one who is not too old, so that there is room to grow into the job and develop as a true leader."

"Mm. Well, that sounds like Sett, doesn't it?"

Two paused, dumbfounded. Could her Esteemed Uncle really be suggesting giving the entire company to Sett, after what he'd done? "If...the Esteemed Medical Doctor is of the medical opinion that his patient corporation would be stronger with Sett making decisions, based upon his credentials and history, then it would not be for me to question that medical opinion, Esteemed."

"Very good, Two!" The Medical Doctor said, coming around in front of her. "But obviously you don't mean Sett. Neither do I. I'll consider what you've asked and get back to you."

"Thank you, Esteemed."

15

Border Between Special Entertainment Districts 8 and 9, the Zone

IAi547 surveyed the flat black three-story building on the other side of the electric fence. He could make out the meter-tall, grainy white letters at the top reading "CHALK BAR," but little else. He zoomed in with his UE glasses to a telephoto view. The windows through which he might have observed what was going on inside had been smashed out decades ago, and the holes had been boarded up in the recent remodeling. His IR and UV scans showed bodies moving around but supplied no useful information as to their identities or purpose. The only people outside were a few of its customers: CBD salarymen and salarywomen drunkenly milling around in the gravel street. Somewhere inside that place, running it, was 547's objective: the Williams Unnamed team leader still called Sett, who had once been 547's college friend known as Lawrence Williams the Seventh.

A text message floated suddenly in front of 547's face.

IAh015:   White test results back yet, 547?

It was his teammate, whom they privately called "Ho-is" because his number seemed to spell it. He replied in text without taking his eyes from the target.

IAi547:   Won't be announced until the merger.

Another merger.

The recent attack on Amelix, as well as rumors that the company was rebuilding in a new and aggressive direction, had fueled a new trend among corporations. It had suddenly become common knowledge that any company wishing to survive must have a world-class biotechnology component. While 547's own beloved Organization was a huge enterprise that encompassed all kinds of tech, its biotech division was weak when compared to the specialty firms. Now it had announced a merger with the second largest biotech firm in the world: Andro-Heathcliffe. No company on Earth could compete directly with Amelix in biotech, but by combining A-H technology with the Organization's strength in other sectors they might at least stand a chance.

> IAho15: Can't believe you're leaving us.
> IAi547: Deal's not done yet. Anyway you know why.

Yes, Ho-is knew why. Clayton Ricker was merciless to 547, constantly threatening to have him tortured to death, and because the Organization was acquiring Andro-Heathcliffe and not the other way around, Ricker would likely retain his power position after the merger. Andro-Heathcliffe had new bioengineered buildings, however, and was hiring a new class of security for them it called Whites. White agents would work exclusively inside the massive structures, and they would even operate with Federal authority. The new order would handle all hands-on security issues inside the buildings, and, most importantly, it would not report to Ricker.

> IAho15: We know why. Hope you make the cut.
> IAi547: Thanks. Sorry to go, if I do.
> IAho15: Yeah, yeah.

547 had seen his raw scores, delineated into five categories, but had no idea if they were high enough. Detachment was a strong area, in spite of his personal vendetta against Sett. So was Dedication, though all Unnamed were at the top of that metric, anyway. His best score was for a category they

called Propriety, which was clearly a desirable trait for some-one armed to the teeth and working permanently inside an office building.

Right now, though, there was the hunt. Sett was close, and now they had his place surrounded.

Dr. Chelsea's lab, already operational during construction at the new Amelix structure

"You haven't answered my messages, Dr. Chelsea, so I came to see you in person." The man's name and credentials appeared in Chelsea's EI: Dr. Francis Schew, Team Leader of the Amelix Internal Dynamics division, doctorate degree in workflow analysis.

"I cannot possibly be pulled into another task force, doctor," Chelsea said. "I don't care how important you feel the mission might be."

"You don't seem to understand, Dr. Chelsea," he said. "With eighty-two unexplained suffocation deaths in the last *two days*, I've been given emergency authority, carte blanche, to investigate. I can and will pull anyone I want onto this task force, and your skill set is essential. No known toxins, no physical damage of any kind, and yet they all just stop breathing. We suspect sabotage from another organization, and until we figure out how it's happening, you are a member of this unit, subordinate to me."

To Chelsea, the Rat Gods' strategy was obvious. They were culling the human population within Amelix, the same as a lab manager might cull a collection of animals, or the way super-visors culled their departments through Departings. At this point, the Rat Gods were still evaluating their interests, trying to decide whether *any* humans would prove necessary to them. They were eliminating those humans who consumed resources without providing anything rats could use, such as the group that had all died at once in the marketing department. This man, this Dr. Schew, was actively investigating the Rat Gods' handiwork, making him a legitimate threat to them, though a puny one. He would certainly be dead within hours.

But please, please not here. I don't want to have to explain a body, or get rid of a body, or have anyone else come to this lab and see all the rats here. Please?

"Of course, Doctor Schew. I'm sorry if that sounded callous. Certainly I'm as concerned as anyone about those tragic losses of company assets. I'll do whatever I can to help you."

"Thank you for being reasonable, Dr. Chelsea. I'll see you at the meeting in … twenty-three minutes."

The rat behind him did its little dance, ensuring that those words would be the last he ever spoke of his own free will. It climbed up his pants and into the pocket of his Corporate Green uniform.

Chalk Bar, SLiD 8, the Zone

Sett downed another vodka shot, leaning close to be heard over the music.

"Ricker had more cash and more … " He pointed in Dok's direction with the empty shot glass. "More of everything else, going into this war," he said. "Fine. So now he's in with McGuillian. But that doesn't mean we have to do this merger! If this is our only option, we've already lost." He set the shot glass down on the table.

Sett hoped his team's presence made Coiner and the Fiends as uncomfortable as the Fiends made them. In the few months since Sett had arranged this amazingly profitable deal with them, allowing them access to the area in exchange for money, weapons, and information, he'd never once seen Coiner let his guard down. Even now Sett could see crazy Brian Samurai's sword and a real, honest-to-God Federal rail gun across his back. Just looking at the thing sent a chill down his spine.

Coiner would sit like that all night, wearing those weapons as though he was perfectly comfortable, when he couldn't even put his back against the chair. He'd set his workhorse rifle, an old M-16, to lean against the edge of the table. It was all very deliberate on Coiner's part, and effectively intimidating. Sett had felt compelled to take his jacket off, displaying his twin high-cap Colebra automatics in response.

Sett turned slightly away from Coiner but kept him in peripheral vision. "I got a good thing, here, Dok," he said. "This whole fucking district is mine. My father sees how much intel I'm bringing in, not to mention the steady flow of cash, and we've only been open a few months! Every Zone worker needs a mountain of documentation just to come work here, and the most important document of all is my authorization to let them pass through the gates, valid one day at a time. I have to replace about five percent of my work force every week; that's how violent the rest of the Zone is now. They beg me to let them sleep here on the floor so they don't have to go home. With that kind of motivation, I don't even have to pay them much. See? That's power." He slapped the table, his gigantic hand resounding like a battering ram.

He poured himself another shot. "A fucking king! Not for long, though. I built this myself. What'm I gonna be now that my father is merging with the evilest company in the world?"

"I guess that's a risk in a world where people control each other like that," Dok said. "You may not always be on the right side of the deal."

Sett was listing to one side and began to lose his balance. He sat straight up in his seat and steadied himself with both palms on the edge of the table. He could still see remains of the glowing tattoo which had been imbedded in Dok's forehead during their time with the subjects. A few seconds under a laser had eradicated Sett's own mark, but since Dok's had been crudely treated with homegrown bactrofungicides, a constellation of tiny dots still glowed above his brow ridge. "Control? I *saved* these people." Sett paused as he realized he was slurring his words. He made a particular effort to enunciate when he continued. "This is the way the world works."

"Yeah, you save them every day." Dok said. "That's what your father's new partner says about his workers."

"Fuck you. I give people *jobs*," Sett said. "This guy, this Dr. Muun guy, is heir to the first company ever to distribute goods from North Korean prison camps. He now holds the contract for the entire country of North Korea, and he's known as *the man with twenty million slaves.* We're the same? You think I'm the same as him? Fuck you."

"You talk to me because you know I'll tell you the truth, *Lawrence.*"

Dok's emphasis on the name was deliberate, to remind Sett that he wasn't quite what he was pretending to be.

Sett extended his left forearm on the table and pulled up his sleeve. Scars were rare among Golds, and his disfigured arm proved he had street credibility the other Unnamed would never have. He locked eyes with Dok as if to ask *"remember this?"*

"You think I'm just some rich boy who doesn't understand suffering?" He gestured toward a random window. "I've been down there. What this is, it's just the way of the world."

"Lawrence, if you're going to try to pretend you don't profit from slavery I'll tell you you're full of shit. You have women begging you, in tears, to let them stay here and work as whores instead of going home to the war zone. You're right to fear this Muun guy; if he has twenty million slaves, he's basically just adding you to his collection. But that's all you do, too. He has a better economy of scale, but you and he have the same business model."

Gunshots sounded downstairs on the main floor. Not the sporadic ones of local hoods they'd often heard when Sett had first claimed dominion in this district, and not the terrifying shrieks of Federal weapons. These were the efficient three-shot bursts of Unnamed Executives. Sett leaned toward the railing and swept his head side-to-side, scanning with the glasses around the bar, but couldn't get a face ID on any of the attackers. Four of them were firing into the spacious barroom from the lobby.

A loud blast, slightly longer than a UE three-shot, sounded next to him, and then did so three more times. All four attackers dropped. Coiner stood at the railing, still aiming his weapon, not the rail gun but the assault rifle. There was a moment of silence as Sett joined him there, aiming down with a pistol in each hand and checking his EI for more information.

Readout from the security cameras in the area showed zero approaches; evidently the attackers had counter-surveillance tech.

Sett manipulated his EI to speak to every Williams Unnamed in District 8. "No question who it is, but are we confirmed yet? Numbers?"

"Yes, sir. Positive facial ID of Ricker/McGuillian/Andro-Heathcliffe Unnamed, matched to our own recognizance data, coming in from District 9. We've partially flanked them on the inside edge of their approach but that point's in danger of being overrun. Whatever they used on the main cameras also confuses the glasses so we're just going on firsthand sightings, but we believe roughly four hundred Unnamed attacking our one hundred sixty-four here, sir. Your Fiends are fighting them now, though, sir, and cutting them down hard."

"Huh," Sett said. Nothing sobered him up faster than warfare. *My Fiends. Ha.*

There were so many three-shot bursts firing that it sounded as if a loud and sporadic dance drumbeat were still playing downstairs. Listening, he realized the dance music was actually still playing, too, to the twenty or so dead customers littering the main room, as well as the few who might still be alive and hiding somewhere. Punctuating all of this were the long, loud blasts from Fiend weapons, from an unsettling number of hidden locations all around them.

Three Williams Unnamed appeared, the other three of Sett's team. "Company protocol is to evacuate leadership, sir," one said. He led them into a back office where, hidden beneath a cabinet that slid away to one side, a narrow stairway spiraled down into darkness. Sett went down first, with Dok and Coiner, and the other Unnamed from Sett's team fell in behind them. Sett activated the light on his glasses for Dok's sake, brilliantly illuminating their way down even though it would have been safer to use the night vision feature instead. The stairs were walled off from the main floor and descended to a tunnel which ran beneath the building. The tunnel connected directly to the adjacent building where Sett and Dok had reconnected.

Having lived underground so long with Eadie, both Dok and Sett were able to move through the tubes as smoothly as cockroaches, even now, when Dok's form was still wasted and frail from living on the streets and Sett had been enhanced to an Unnamed body three times the size he'd been back then. Perhaps those handicaps were what allowed Coiner to keep up with them.

Or maybe Coiner is terrifyingly good at everything. And intel says the New Union outnumbers our Unnamed, possibly by a lot.

Sett pushed it out of his mind. Right now the threat was coming from Ricker's thugs. There would be time later to consider how dangerous the Fiends might be.

They wound their way to the now waist-high opening in the other building's basement. The rubble and other passive defenses had been removed so Lawrence and other Unnamed could pass through easily, replaced with a single self-aiming gun just inside the room. It tracked them as they entered, but returned to aiming at the entrance when it recognized the code emitted by Sett's glasses.

"Wait here, Dok," Sett said. "Ricker can't get vehicles into SLiD 8 so we're going to chase them out using ours. You'll be fine here. Coiner, you can do as you like, of course."

"Dok is still our asset and I'm supposed to keep him safe," Coiner said. "We'll be here. I'm still expecting to meet with you and your father about that merger and how it will affect our arrangement."

"I'll take you to him as soon as we deal with this problem," Sett said.

"Here's good," Dok said. He lowered his voice. "You know this raid is probably intended to nab *you*, right, Lawrence? What other explanation could there be? There's nothing else here to for them to take that would justify this kind of cost in lives and other resources. You're still going to turn around and deliver yourself?"

"You suppose I should save myself for Dr. Muun?" Sett climbed the basement stairs into the loading dock where they stored the armored truck, unlocking and starting it through his EI.

Scaffolded/Wrapped Construction Site for New Amelix Building

Zabeth Chelsea relaxed in the Rat God's Thrall even as she spoke at this meeting with Kessler and Keiko. The rat had left her full capability to speak and work for now, but she could feel it monitoring her actions through the tiny corrections it applied here and there throughout the day.

A surge of anxiety and claustrophobia struck Chelsea, and her body trembled. Her heart pounded in her chest so hard she thought she might feel its fibers tearing apart. She had never had panic attacks until recently, but now they were striking with increasing frequency and intensity. All she could think about in these moments was her desperate need to escape, to flee the building and free herself from the omnipresent forces that now controlled every aspect of her existence. The Thrall swelled to suppress the panic, as it always did, at least to the extent that she could get on with her work. The nausea and trembling used to subside after a few hours, but the attacks were now happening so often that she never fully recovered.

"Doctor Zytem has again expressed satisfaction at how well the prototype preconditioning programs have worked in protecting our employees from the schizophrenia outbreak," she said.

The rat let her stroke Kessler's head gently. "He loved the mammalian ear hairs we re-engineered to vibrate and produce sound waves, and yours are the perfect words to have our walls whispering, Dr Kessler." She presented him the back of her hand, and he grasped it with both of his, pulling it gently to his lips. Lowering her voice, she said, "You are a master of the rules of men, pet. But never forget that I have mastered nature. And you."

"Yes, ma'am," he said. There was no edge to his voice, only acceptance.

She gazed into Keiko's blank eyes. "And you, too, dear."

"Yes, ma'am," Keiko said.

"Dr. Zytem is pleased, and so am I. Amelix Integrations now has a one hundred percent Accepted workforce that is invulnerable to the schizophrenia outbreak, and these new structures Grow the preconditioning tech from the moment they're created. We have helped Amelix to gain a tremendous advantage over our competition."

Keiko's face showed she was lost in ecstasy at the thought, as were they all. It was quite easy to make Keiko ecstatic, though. Kessler had done such a wonderful job creating this pet, and now Chelsea had claimed dominion over both Keiko and her trainer. Kessler had surrendered to Chelsea detailed records of the process he'd used in her training, so now Chelsea had the ability to tweak Keiko's behavior to match her own desires. It might even be possible to replicate Keiko in a new subordinate.

Or many new subordinates.

Management was a heady experience.

Keiko's impeded ability to piece together stories made her significantly more docile and easier to control, but also rendered her incapable of simple tasks like organizing past events into a logical timeline.

Chelsea realized she was stroking her own cheekbones as she stared at the girl. She cleared her throat. The rat had allowed this. Had it interpreted her sexual urges as work?

Perhaps they were.

"There's much more," she said, "and not all good. It's feared that another sort of epidemic may be spreading among us. I'm sure you're aware of recent incidents where Accepted employees have suddenly and inexplicably attacked other workers in the CBD. This savage behavior arises without warning or provocation, and members of every company in the district have been involved in these assaults, both as instigators and victims. The aggressors are apparently overcome by an irresistible impulse to kill others around them, from whatever company, even their own. While we Accepted were somehow protected from the schizophrenia outbreak, this spate of violence seems to work the other way. The people we would expect to remain the most dutiful and disciplined are the ones most prone to these psychotic breaks."

Chelsea felt a surge of panic at the thought of Accepted-on-Accepted violence in the CBD. She realized there must be some connection between the violence and the Rat Gods, but it was a struggle to keep that idea in focus. The Rat God caused the Thrall to intensify, just enough to balance out the panicky feeling. Chelsea and the Rat Gods were learning about each other, growing together.

"To protect our human assets from external violence and, with the help of our new preconditioning tech, better prevent outbreaks internally, this building and its clones around the world are now scheduled to become operational Amelix workplaces, fully one hundred eighty days before the original plan. That's fourteen days from now. To accomplish this, all of us will be moving aboard immediately. Sleep schedules will be replaced with wave manips and additional conditioning programs to replicate sleep, thus reducing actual resting hours from six down to two per day, testing our emergency protocols. I'm told this will take some getting used to, but the technology prevents any loss in efficiency. The buildings will remain unsealed but heavily guarded until the last of the employees and other raw materials are brought aboard and housed. At that point, the buildings will be sealed in order to test their design and life support systems, and are expected to remain secure and self-sustaining for a period of two months. Hopefully, during this time whatever has been triggering the violence will have been addressed."

"Two months?" Kessler asked. "Nobody in or out?" His eyes were wide open in his slack face. His lips quivered as if he might cry.

Another wave of anxiety and claustrophobia washed over Chelsea , but again the rat counteracted it.

Chelsea leaned down, pinching Kessler's ear between her thumb and first knuckle and pulling him toward her.

"Two months, *MA'AM*," she whispered. Then her whisper became a growl. "Nobody in or out, *MA'AM*."

Kessler looked slightly green, the tinge Golden people took on when they were nauseated. Everything she'd announced had been discussed from the earliest planning stages of their projects. This was merely a change in timing. What was the matter with him?

The Rat God in her lab coat pocket wriggled as if it too found Kessler's behavior disturbing. Chelsea sent feelings of love and respect toward it and was rewarded with an additional trickle of its intoxicating bliss.

"Each building is equipped so that the entire staff, plus the installed interconnected brains of the Trust, may survive indefinitely inside, in case of any new bioterrorist attacks," she said. "As long as the structure can move itself from one place to another for occasional replenishment of key components that can't be manufactured onboard, the building's synthesizers are capable of meeting the nutritional and medical needs of their populations for as long as may be required. You have nothing to fear."

"Of course, ma'am," Kessler said. Keiko sat with her typical blank but blissful expression, waiting for a command from either of her two handlers. It was a pity that Kessler himself lacked the serenity and discipline he'd caused to blossom in Keiko. "But this wasn't supposed to happen yet, not for half a year, ma'am." His voice shook. Chelsea watched a tear roll down his cheek and she realized his entire body was quaking.

Two months locked inside!

Paranoia, claustrophobia, and dread locked every muscle as if she'd been flash frozen. A warm current from the rat loosened her enough to be able to speak again.

"It's necessary to do a live test of the facilities," she said. "To work out any issues that might arise. These structures involve fantastically complex biotechnology, you know. They have more in common with living creatures than they do with traditional buildings. Just having the Brain Trust coordinate the moving limbs would have been impossible a decade ago. With practice, the human teams operating the structure will be able to work together well enough for the building to almost seem alive.

"Are you all right, Dr. Kessler? You seem quite disturbed."

"I'm...I'm fine, ma'am." His Golden face still had a whitish green tinge. "This is a bit of a surprise, that's all. We won't all be working sealed inside, will we? Ma'am? There will still be ambulatory workers who come and go?"

Kessler was truly not coping well, and his nervousness and trepidation were making her own new and dreadful anxieties start to spike again.

"Dr. Kessler, God has chosen you for this work. How can you balk at such a calling?" She narrowed her eyes. "How did you do on the Sub Test? I'm not sure I received your scores."

They had all been required to take the Sub Test; a battery of questions and personality measures that had evolved from the ones used generations ago to find sailors who were mentally prepared for life aboard submarines. Chelsea had gotten nearly a perfect score and she knew Keiko had, too.

His voice was quiet. "I haven't taken it yet, ma'am."

"It was a companywide order!"

"Yes, and I will certainly comply, ma'am. I just haven't done it yet. I'm sorry, ma'am."

"That's unacceptable, Dr. Kessler. I'm adjourning this meeting. Go and take the test right now. I want a copy of your results sent to me no later than this time tomorrow. Is that clear?"

"Yes, ma'am."

Inside Chalk Bar

"Which one?" IAi547 asked.

"Here, sir," his subordinate said, gesturing.

IAi547 stood at the private table that Organization intelligence said his former friend, Sett, heir to Williams Gypsum, had kept reserved for himself. There was half a bottle of liquor on the table, still cold, covered with condensation droplets. 547 had hoped to overwhelm his quarry fast enough to preempt any escape, but Sett had managed to get away, and now he was out there attacking with his own team from vehicles. To complicate matters further, Fiends had appeared out of nowhere in still unknown numbers. Sett's company should have had enough firepower to prevent this kind of Fiend infestation in his district, but here they were. Maybe the Williams dynasty was weaker than 547 had thought.

On the back of a chair hung a torn and faded jacket. It wouldn't fit an Unnamed, so it must have been left by Sett's friend, the one intel had identified as the Zone Poisoner. 547's glasses confirmed the absence of bombs or other traps, so he searched the pockets, finding an old spiral-bound paper notebook, partly burned. He dropped it into his own jacket pocket, in case it held some clues about what Sett's next move would be.

"We've got to fight our way back across the border into SLiD 9," he said to 317, another Unnamed on his team. "Let's make sure this place burns to the ground as we do."

"Yes, sir."

The clinic

It was the third straight day of machine gun fire outside. The Saved, somehow suddenly equipped with horrifying Federal weapons, had launched a full-scale assault to retake the clinic. Occasionally stray shots broke through the front window, leaving thumb-sized holes. Wanda moved from bed to bed, tending the patients the way she always had. She saw no reason to hide from the bullets. Regardless of who won this particular battle, Wanda knew she would be a slave in this place until the day she died. If that happened to be today, so much the better.

She wondered whether Dok had survived his underground mission. He'd been sure he wouldn't. He certainly hadn't returned here.

Wondering about Dok was less painful than wondering about Nami or fretting about Ernesto. Dok was her friend and she hoped he was okay, but she hadn't assumed responsibility for keeping him safe the way she'd done with the kids.

Outside the front window, orange flashes and blurs indicated Fiends moving around in the twilight, always backwards, retreating from the shrieking Federal machine guns. Suddenly a Fiend appeared facing the glass, pointing his weapon inside. Wanda had no impulse to run or to dive for the ground, even as he emptied a clip through the glass before running off again. Wanda wasn't hit, but Piyumi and Judee were now lying silently on the floor. She expected the Fiend to come charging in, but he hesitated, looked back over his shoulder and bolted.

More Federal weapons erupted outside, with increasing frequency.

Wanda was still staring at the window when Porter appeared, stepping through the open hole where one of the Zone's last pieces of plate glass had stood moments before. He walked to the center of the room and pointed his Federal handgun at the patient in the far corner. Sweeping it rapidly sideways as he fired, he wiped out every last patient in the place, more than twenty in all. The action took him no more than a few seconds. Wanda's ears rang and her whole body seemed to reverberate from the noise, even after he stopped shooting and approached her, glancing down at the collapsed women as he stepped over them.

"Where's Sula?" he asked.

"The Fiends didn't trust her," Wanda said. "She'd obviously been well rewarded by you, and she never convinced them that she fully accepted their authority. So, they slit her throat."

Outside there were more Saved going past. The shots were coming less frequently.

"This clinic is now Saved property," Porter said. "Looks like you're the ranking clinician, Wanda."

RickeResources Building, CBD

547 felt a knot form in his stomach as the UE truck pulled up to the building. Some stressors were too much even for the training and the glasses to overcome.

All 547 knew about this assignment was that IAg226 had specifically requested him, and that they'd needed to raise his clearance level before he could be officially engaged. In fact, 547 now had the highest security clearance in his cohort. The two Unnamed seated across from him were older and more experienced. He had never worked with them before.

"Come with me," IAg226 said, opening the truck door. 547 and the other two team members followed her across the courtyard to the C-suite elevator. It was an express to the top floors, where Ricker and his highest-ranking officers did business, and where Ricker routinely issued threats and abuse to 547. The team boarded the elevator and it shot up.

As they ascended, IAg226 locked eyes with each of the team members in turn. 547 followed the link she'd flagged, which opened a video file recorded by Unnamed glasses in Ricker's office. The room was unusually full of Unnamed, and Ricker and another man were shown shaking hands, then conversing in low voices. The glasses that had produced the recording identified the other man as Safran Aabott, who held the same top position with Andro-Heathcliffe Unnamed as Ricker did with the Organization Whose Confidence is Kept.

"The hell you are!" Ricker shouted suddenly. "I was given an ownership interest in this firm, by contract. I will be running this division until the day I am incapacitated."

"That's why I'm here," Aabott said. Gunfire sounded and the camera tilted up at a strange angle. The video stopped.

The elevator doors opened at Ricker's reception desk and the four stepped out.

"The merger happened exactly six hours and forty-two minutes after this encounter," IAg226 said. "The last man you heard speaking is our new boss, who shall now remain Unnamed. Ricker and every member of the Fold he'd had here were shot multiple times. They have all been installed into the Organization's Brain Trust."

"If that recording was made hours ago, ma'am, how are we supposed to assist?" 547 asked. "Surely the killers are long gone."

"Not all of our work is glamor and firefights, 547," she said. "This assignment must be done by us because we're the Organization's most discreet workers. I figured you might enjoy the job more than the average member of the Fold. Grab a mop."

Protest Outside the CBD

Kym Evans stared through the CBD fence, though there was nothing to see on the other side. The protesters looked to her with ever increasing desperation, especially now that they were all sealed permanently inside the Zone. Their attempt at revolution had failed, the General had disappeared, and Kym had nowhere to go with what was left of her army. She decided to keep them here, and attempt to channel their collective frustration and anger into a "protest" against the sealing of the Zone. It would do no good, but it gave her followers a sense of purpose, at least for the time being.

There was no market for anything, even drugs. There was no money here and also no food, and every day there were more threats from other groups and more rumors of cannibalism. Even so, a steady stream of *Someones* had been showing up.

That was how she thought of them, as *Someones*, the people who had changed after doses of Pink Shit. It had started as she'd been interviewing one after the other, eventually settling on the question, "Did you used to be someone else?" Living with Furius had taught her a few things about these people, and most important was the fact that their brand of craziness was consistent and predictable. Every one of them had become convinced that he or she was a historical character who had died willingly in service to some cause. Though none of them cared much about money or comfort, they were quite easy to motivate if one knew how.

Like this Someone standing before her now. Brand new, she would need Kym's guidance to keep her in line.

"You found us, then," she said. "Good."

"I did." Her nod was quick but solemn.

"Gonna be another whore, I'd guess," Kym said. "That's what you ancient gals seem to do most often."

The woman grabbed Kym by the throat and slammed her against the wall. "I am not a woman! You are speaking to a Spartan warrior, and you call me a whore?"

Three protesters seized the attacker and beat her—*him*—until he stopped moving. Kym nodded her thanks. The girl who had been a Chinese slave buried with her mistress bowed deeply, but the Crusader and the Nazi just nodded back.

"Get rid of this one," Kym said, kicking the Spartan. "Gotta maintain discipline an' all that."

"Yes, Colonel Kym," the Crusader said. The others repeated it.

"Listen up, all of you," she said. "This is my army, you got that? You are here because you need us. If we don't stick together, we won't survive. We don't have much, but we're doin' better than most around here since the Zone sealed. We got food, even some clean water. Right now the Fiends and Saved are too busy killing each other to bother with us, but that'll change soon, and whichever one of them wins will be coming after us next. I don't care who you used to be. Right now this is the only army you're part of, understand? No more bullshit."

A sudden wave of nausea and dread enveloped Kym. She leaned on the wall for support, clutching her midsection.

This feeling had a source. It was being *directed* at her from somewhere off to her left. Kym turned toward the feeling, facing into what seemed to be its current, her hands forming involuntary fists and her face tightening into a vicious sneer that barely registered in her mind. No one was there. All she saw was a single rat perched on a pile of rubble.

547's quarters, the Fold

547 sat on his bunk, gently running a thumb over the charred notebook he'd taken from the Chalk Bar. This treasure couldn't have meant anything to Sett. For 547, though, it was a powerful and addictive drug. Reconditioned as he was to serve the Organization Whose Confidence is Kept, he experienced this account of the deplorable conditions inside the Organization's worst enemy, Amelix Integrations, as confirmation that he was on the right side. Pathway amplification carried him to heights he couldn't have reached without this book, which was proof from *outside* the umbrella that the Organization's enemy was truly evil. 547 was precisely where he was supposed to be. 547 prepared to open it again to his favorite passage, which he kept marked with the only family heirloom in his possession: a white ribbon that had once been part of some ancestor's wedding dress. He rolled his neck and shoulders and fluffed his pillow into the corner, settling comfortably against it. His fingers traced the ribbon down and gingerly slid it to the page edge. Paper was fragile and needed to be handled as little as possible, so he pulled the ribbon to open the book instead of touching the page directly with his finger. Two sheets were covered in awkward printing. The paragraph in the lower left corner always demanded his attention.

> You've positioned Amelix before me and told me it's my bridge to paradise, when in fact it's a dead end that traps souls here forever. It will take more than your bullying and manipulation to claim my soul.

A real Amelix employee had held this very notebook in his hand and put these words here, confirming his firsthand observation that Amelix was hell on Earth. The Organization Whose Confidence is Kept had now merged with Amelix's worst enemy, and 547 had become an integral part of that holy struggle. 547 lay the book across his chest, closing his eyes and reclining fully against the pillow, as pathway amplification boosted his bliss.

16

Williams Gypsum mine

Sett had left Coiner and Dok back in his assigned room by the machine bay, which his sister made him share with their mother's dog. The three Unnamed of his team, and the three who occupied the office area with his sister, were audience enough. If he had to endure his sister's humiliation and abuse, fewer witnesses were better. Besides, he needed Coiner to respect him if they were going to continue working together.

"I told you messing around with that Zone bar was a bad idea," Chairman Two said. She had now assumed their father's role in the organization and, like he had done years before, she had authorized her own Statusing. Now her giant, genetically-enhanced, black-suited body was completely hairless. Her glasses had become transparent in the dim light, and Seth could see her lashless eyes seething at him through the lenses.

"Yes, Ma'am," Sett said. While Sett had been living with the Subjects, their father had restructured the company, designating Ani to take over upon his incapacitation. When their father, who by that time had rechristened himself Chairman One, had suddenly collapsed and been immediately interred in the corporate Brain Trust, she had assumed the role of Chairman. Sett's sister despised him, and now that she wielded the power their father had held, it was pointless to resist her. Sett knew better than to effectively flaunt his lack of reconditioning in front of the woman who could—and almost certainly soon would—order that error to be corrected.

Chairman Two had not asked what had happened. The attack on Chalk Bar had undoubtedly been the work of Ricker's Unnamed.

"Dr. Muun would never have let you keep that place, anyway," Two said. "He has impeccable standards; once the merger is complete, you aren't likely to last long. Not unless changes are made." Sett knew the unspoken meaning: *Unless you're reconditioned.* "They produce everything, cheaply and with good quality. I mean, everyone has forced labor anymore, but there's a reason the North Koreans are on top. An entire country of slaves! Can you imagine the power?"

Sett's fear of his sister was nothing compared to the absolute terror he felt at the mention of Dr. Muun. "Ma'am," Sett said. His shaking voice revealed the desperation that had made him speak in spite of himself. "The Muun organization has twenty million slaves. How can we be certain we won't be numbered among them?"

His sister stared a moment, accentuating his inexcusable rudeness.

"How can *we* be certain? I didn't realize it was your job to audit my decisions, Sett."

Sett froze. He was supposed to acknowledge his chairman's objection to his words and apologize for having spoken in that way. A reconditioned Unnamed would have done so instantly. He needed to clear away the insult before she decided to have him reconditioned immediately. Reconditioning would mean the loss of his ability to question authority once and for all.

Instead, he remained frozen.

His sister's giant, heavy hand slapped across his face, the impact starting at his jawbone and continuing up past his cheek and temple. It struck again and again, the same hand connecting with the same part of his face.

"How do I know? Because we are *owners*, that's why! We will *own* 0.53 percent of the entire company! I have it in writing." She brought her face centimeters from Sett's and growled through her teeth. "You question my judgment again, even privately, and I will personally tear you apart. Slowly. Understand?"

"Ma'am, yes, ma'am." Sett said flatly.

At last his sister turned away.

Sett wasn't sure what he was allowed to do. Could he simply leave the chamber? Would his team follow? He had to reconnect with Dok and Coiner.

Suddenly he felt dizzy and nauseated, as if he'd just been whirled around while drunk. An unexplainable anger bubbled up inside him. He turned his head and saw three rats dancing next to the mine's white gypsum wall.

Dancing?

Yes, that did indeed seem to be what they were doing, raising one foot and then another, over and over, in unison. He wanted to kill them. He *needed* to tear them apart and stomp the pieces into the floor.

His sister whipped back to face him. Her movements were strange. Instead of pivoting her neck and following her body as most people might, she bent deeply at the waist and twisted her body, looking up at him. She approached, leaning far forward with shoulders hunched and arms bent to hold her hands in front of her, like a dinosaur. Chairman Two's jaw was tight, and her nose oddly wrinkled. Her lips pulled back to reveal the front teeth on both jaws. Sett reeled backward. Was this some kind of a joke? His sister did not ever joke.

Had she gone crazy?

Chairman Two leaped at him. He scrambled backward, just enough and just in time to make her miss. She attacked again, this time pinning him against the wall. Her hands clawed at his face. She bit him on the throat, taking a mouthful of his skin and gnawing, thrashing her head wildly from side to side. He tried to push her away, but she held on with her teeth.

He could smell his own blood. Her teeth parted as she tried to take more of his flesh into her mouth, but he struck her throat with his palm before she could bite down again, shoving her backward. He moved away from the wall and backed slowly toward the door. She stalked him, still hunched over, her eyes wide and twitching. He pulled his sidearm, aiming it squarely at her chest, but she continued to advance, showing no fear of the weapon. She lunged, her splayed fingers aimed at his eyes. He flinched and the gun fired its three-shot burst, dropping Two to the floor. Her blood spread through the thick white gypsum dust.

The other three Unnamed of her team were standing now, moving toward him. Not walking, but moving, their shoulders curving downward as if they were four-legged creatures about to bound after prey.

Sett ran back toward his team, who had clustered by the door during Sett's not-so-private meeting. As he approached them, he saw all three were hunched over in the same way his sister had been. Their arms were bent upward and their faces were contorted. Together they looked at him and then raised their hands and watched themselves flex their fingers. They reached under their jackets toward their weapons.

Sett ran for the closest mine tunnel.

Outside the clinic

The guards watched as Wanda dragged the body past them and over to the cart. Nobody had said anything about keeping the staff there by force, or even taken any action to indicate that she was a prisoner, yet it was perfectly understood on both sides.

The war continued to escalate. There were more skirmishes, and higher numbers of wounded and dead, every day. The Saved seemed to be holding their ground against the Fiends, but even with their new weapons, they struggled to inflict as many casualties as they suffered. Their enemy had proven frustratingly elusive. Over and over, the Fiends would strike out of nowhere and then vanish at the first sign of armed resistance, leaving the Saved fighting nobody until they popped up someplace else.

Wanda had been planning to leave the dead body next to the cart, rather than stacking it on top as she was supposed to. Would the guards try to force her to do it? Usually they didn't watch her quite so intently. Stacking them was too big a job for Wanda alone.

As she glanced toward them, the guards who had been watching her set off running down the street.

Wanda sank to her knees as a wave of nausea overcame her. That was not an uncommon occurrence, since she spent every day surrounded by filth and gore and death. But somehow this experience was different. This feeling was something new.

No! Not new!

Wanda had felt this sensation before.

She rose to her feet and turned, following the jagged waves of animosity that seemed to be flowing toward her. Her eyes locked on the rat, which was standing on its hind legs on a window ledge only an arms-length away nearby. She lunged, grasping for it with her bare hands, missing, then trying to crush it with her feet as it scurried away down the street. She chased it, only peripherally aware that perhaps two hundred Saved were chasing other rats in the same direction.

Near Helper Leesa

Ernesto worked the slide of the shotgun he was working on, observing how the little pieces inside moved the shell into position. The gun had been partially smashed, but he had reshaped and reassembled the pieces. Now it functioned again. It would not be perfect because he hadn't been able to get one of the sidebars perfectly straight, but it functioned. That was what the Saved needed: only for the guns to function. Helper Leesa said that making it perfect would be a waste of time, and wasting time meant he was not doing his job perfectly.

Leesa stood up from where she'd been sitting. She shouted loudly and ran off. Ahead of her, a rat ran down the street. Other Saved nearby all shouted and ran the same way, causing a terribly loud noise and commotion.

Ernesto put his head through the shotgun's strap so it hung down where his arm should have been. With only one arm he wasn't able to cover both of his ears, so he yelled loudly to block out some of the crowd noise. He concentrated on keeping Leesa's elbow in view as they ran with the rest of the shouting mob.

The Williams Gypsum mine

Coiner had snatched up his assault rifle before Lawrence even reached the room. Maybe he'd heard the running footsteps, though Dok certainly hadn't. Now the three of them were running through a wide, dark tunnel with white gypsum walls that reflected the light from Lawrence's glasses.

There had been no time for Lawrence to explain. One minute Dok had been playing with the dog, and the next, they were all running for their lives. Given what Dok knew of the family and its business, he wouldn't be surprised to learn that Lawrence's sister had decided to kill the three of them. What was odd, however, was the fact she seemed to be having difficulty accomplishing the task.

Dok tripped over something in the dark and heard the dog yelp. It had run out with them and had veered between his legs. He snatched it up and carried it.

Coiner said nothing as they ran. He was the consummate soldier, his every decision rational, his every action flawlessly executed. He displayed no hint of human frailty, yet he had never been reconditioned or genetically enhanced.

Guns fired behind them, three-shot bursts that ricocheted off the walls. No trained Unnamed would miss three men running with a light down the middle of a dark tunnel.

Dok watched as Coiner tucked a shoulder and dove to the floor. He rolled twice to stop himself, and landed facing backwards with the gun ready. He fired a quick full-auto burst, and no shots came in response. Coiner reached into a vest pocket and flung a few of his strange homemade plastic coins down the tunnel, and then he was up and running again, changing clips.

"How does every Unnamed in this mine suddenly forget how to shoot straight?" Coiner asked. His voice was calm, as if he were asking a price in an open market.

"I don't know. It's like none of them had any idea what a gun was until I drew mine when my sister was attacking me. When they saw me pull the trigger, it was like they were learning it for the first time, right there. Let's keep moving. Go this way, and then to the left. We have to reach my truck."

The dog squirmed in Dok's arms. He set it down and it darted off down the tunnel.

The left tunnel curved upward and ended in the lighted parking garage, where the mine's opening was sheltered by Grown white walls. They approached the truck, which sat undisturbed where they'd left it, and Lawrence opened the doors through his EI. Shots fired again, this time from up on some scaffolding along one garage wall. Coiner fell, but shot from the floor, and the Unnamed plunged from the scaffolding.

"Drop the gun now, Sett, sir!" The voice was from behind them.

Lawrence held onto the gun but raised his hands, talking over his shoulder. "Jack?" He shook his head, remembering the Unnamed protocol. "Thank the Lord it's you, 190. Everyone's going crazy."

"Drop it, sir," 190 said. "I know what happened. I heard the shots and replayed the surveillance video when I found her body. I watched you kill Chairman Two. Even if you will be the next appointed chairman, which I don't think you will, sir, I serve the Organization before you. Let go of the gun, sir, or I will put you down."

Lawrence let the gun fall. "190! Listen! If you saw me shoot her you saw how she attacked me. I shot her because she went crazy! Everyone is going crazy!"

Shots fired again, this time from ground level, ricocheting around but missing. Coiner fired again and another shooter fell. Coiner's head slumped.

"See, 190?" Lawrence yelled. "Who was that? It was one of us, shooting randomly all over the place. You know we don't do that."

190 slowly lowered his gun.

"Tell me what's going on," 190 said. "Please, sir."

"I don't know," Lawrence said. "My sister attacked me like she forgot she was human. Look at my neck!" His Golden skin was torn and it pulsated pink and purple. "It's not just her. Every Unnamed we've encountered, except you, has been the same."

"What do we do, sir?"

"The four of us can escape in my truck. We've got to get away from this mine."

190 stiffened, pointing his nose straight up above him and sniffing, his lips curling back to expose his front teeth. His back bent forward and his elbows retracted. He examined the gun in his hand, turning it this way and that. Then he lifted it to his face and smelled it.

Coiner was out cold. There would be no shot from the floor.

190 pointed the weapon at Lawrence.

Something growled next to 190's feet.

It was the little dog, shaking a rat vigorously from side to side and doing it significant damage, though there was little difference in size between the two.

190 dropped the gun. Lawrence picked it up and shoved 190 a few steps forward, slamming him against the truck. "Now you, too, 190?" he said.

"I don't know what it was," 190 said. Lawrence zipped 190's hands together behind his back with one of the plastic strips Unnamed carried for such emergencies. "I was standing there, listening to you, and then suddenly I wasn't in charge of my body anymore. I was aware of what was happening, that I was sniffing the air and even pointing the gun, but I couldn't make myself stop it."

"It was that rat," Dok said. He ran to Coiner and looked him over. "Shoulder wound. I can treat this." He gently turned Coiner on his side. "The rat had 190 in some sort of...I don't know, a trance, I guess. I don't know how, but it seemed to take him over completely." Dok gingerly felt around the wound and behind it. "There's no exit hole. I'll have to get the bullet out." He nodded toward the dog, who sat gnawing on the rat's head.

"Whatever the rat did to 190, it stopped as soon as the dog attacked it," Dok said. "I need to work on Coiner; can we just get in the truck now?"

"Leave him behind," Lawrence said.

"No."

"Dok, we don't have time for this. The security cameras show two big groups moving around, all with guns ready, and one of those groups is coming right here. Coiner is shot, he's a liability to us, and he's a damned Fiend anyway."

"Lawrence, I'm doing you a favor, here. Do you want to be the one explaining to Top Dog how you took one of his most trusted officers out into the desert and left him there?" Lawrence huffed and grabbed Coiner's feet. The truck door opened and they stuffed him inside.

"So, I guess we'd better stay away from the rats," Lawrence said. "Everybody keep an eye out. If one gets in the truck with us we'll all be dead." He freed 190's hands while Dok climbed into the back of the truck with Coiner. 190 got into the passenger side and Lawrence sat down behind the wheel, but then he opened the door again and got out.

"I think you've earned a place with us, little guy," he said, scooping up the tiny dog and dumping it onto 190's lap. "You're on rat patrol." He started the truck, backed it up and cleared the mine entrance just as new shots sounded from farther inside. Several of them impacted the truck but didn't penetrate its armor.

Dok gently slapped Coiner's face, trying to bring him back to consciousness. Coiner coughed.

"Coiner! It's me, Dok. Open your eyes. You've been shot and I need you to work with me now. Open your eyes."

Coiner's eyes fluttered. Another barrage hit the truck.

"Does it seem like they're getting better at that?" Lawrence asked.

"I think they are, sir," 190 said. "Could they be communicating with each other somehow? Learning?"

Dok found the truck's first-aid kit beneath the rear seat. "Whoa! Look at all this!" The kit had more gear than Dok had kept in his clinic.

The truck sped across the desert. Dok looked back toward the mine, but all he could see was a cloud of dust.

Federal truck patrolling the newly sealed Zone

Daiss peered up and down each cross street as Agent Lehri drove slowly along the area's main road. For the first few weeks after the decree there had been constant attacks, with scathing people flinging garbage, bricks, shit, and even their own stinking bodies, at the Federal vehicles. He'd mowed down one after another while they watched, but it hadn't stopped them. Nonsensical behavior like that was what had necessitated sealing them away from decent society in the first place.

Daiss and Lehri were driving through Saved territory with the ostensible mission of keeping the peace. In reality, they hoped to bait potential attackers into doing something stupid, giving the agents an excuse to thin the herd. The truck turned a corner and crept along another deserted avenue.

Suddenly a wave of human bodies poured from a side street, flowing around and, in two cases, *over* the Federal truck, so quickly that Daiss didn't even have time to train his weapon. There were maybe a few hundred of them, which would actually have been dangerous to the Federal Agents if they'd been attacking the truck. Instead they swept past it and moved on down the street. Many of them were carrying guns, which looked to have come from the drop he and Lehri had made months before.

"Should we follow them?" Lehri asked.

"Yeah, we'd better."

The running mob approached an intersection, where another crowd of Saved rushed in front of them. The two groups merged. Lehri turned again and continued to track the expanded throng.

"Idiots," Daiss said. "We should've trained them as well as giving them weapons. How far do they think they're going to get, just running straight into Fiend territory like that? And look, up ahead! There's another mass of them."

He tried to point but found he could not. His body had suddenly stopped responding to his commands. His palm lifted by itself in front of his face and his fingers flexed, as if the way his thumb worked was the most fascinating thing Daiss had ever seen. His hand managed to work its way under his jacket and patted around until it found his Gloria handgun. Then, slowly, his fingers grasped it, with his thumb still mostly straight. His hand tugged at the weapon but it was held in the holster by a snap. Daiss's hand tugged and yanked again and again, until eventually the snap gave way and it was able to draw the weapon. The fingers, no longer his own, clutched it clumsily but seemed to know how to aim.

The blast instantly liquefied Agent Lehri and most of the door next to her, which now hung partway open. His body crawled through the mess and out into the street, hand still clenched tightly around the gun.

Outside New Union Territory

Rus moved silently through the Grand Hall, gently waving his staff over the fallen Elements that had been brought in. Lashed at the top of the staff was a battered plastic bottle of water. Its original seal was still intact. This water, sacred to the Subjects, had been bottled in the days when the Earth was pure and new, before the time of the synthesizers and the time of the Golds. It was now an important part of New Union post-battle ceremony. By waving the Pure Water over the bodies, Rus symbolically washed away the illusion between life and death, revealing true Unity.

It had been decided that Divinators should do more than merely torment and terrorize the Elements. The New Union already gave them plenty to be afraid of. Therefore, the Divinators' role had been broadened to include a "spiritual" element, whereby they also supplied hope and served as a source of common values and beliefs. With some adopted traditions, and a selection of stolen sacred artifacts from the Subjects, they were able to give the soldiers a sense of meaning the New Union hadn't been able to provide them before. Rus had found it amazing how readily they took to the new message, even though it was presented by the same black-robed sect that had inflicted the torture necessary to determine whether they were worthy of acceptance into the New Union.

The Grand Hall was part of the complex that Top Dog had made his headquarters. It was located within the most secure section of New Union territory, and it had become the center of Divinator activity. The large, cavernous room had once been some kind of transportation terminal, and a chest-high, room-wide dais had been added at one end. This funeral stuff was new, an attempt to provide comfort for the Elements and thus bolster their dedication. The New Union was suffering casualty rates it had never before experienced, now that the Saved were armed with Federal weapons.

While the Subjects had traditionally kept their artifacts hidden from view, the New Union recognized the power they had when made visible to the ranks. Each item had been carefully lashed to a staff, so that it could be carried and displayed easily over the worshipping masses. There were now three Pure Water staves, which were being used by Rus and two other Divinators out among the bodies. At the front of the room, the ranking Divinators were performing a ritual with staves supporting more sacred artifacts that invoked protection, including a carved and inlaid cat skull known as Fang, a fist-sized ball of milky quartz the New Union had named the Soul of Unity, and a bioplexi box with a tube inside that the Subjects called the General's Ashes.

Rage tore through Rus in a hot, caustic wave, and he reflexively clutched the vial of Juice at his neck. A rat stood on its hind legs halfway between himself and the elevated sacred area. It had to die, immediately and gruesomely, but he would not smash it with the staff, no matter how much every cell in his body was screaming for him to do so. The Pure Water was of vital importance and had to be sheltered and protected by any Divinator who was capable of doing so, but there was no time to put it away. The rat had to die now.

He would have to stomp the rat with his feet instead.

As the rat turned and darted toward a side door, the three ranking Divinators leaped from the dais and ran through the Grand Hall so recklessly that they stumbled over the bodies. They raced out the door, chasing the rat, raising their staves over their shoulders as if trying to spear the animals.

Rus followed, clutching the staff in a white-knuckled grip, with the other two Divinators close behind him.

Touring the new Andro-Heathcliffe structure

547's eyes traced the long translucent tubes as they bent and coiled around each other. He could see hundreds of individual brains and spinal cords through the observation window, lined up side by side by side in a lumpy spiral held together by the fluid-filled tubes. It was impressive, yet this exhibit displayed only a tiny fraction of the precisely interconnected components in the Organization's massive Brain Trust. Briefly he wondered if any of these brains might be Clayton Ricker's.

"And that's another interesting thing," his guide said flatly, who appeared to be consulting notes through his EI. "Human brains naturally communicate. In Brain Trusts we've found it doesn't matter what language the individual spoke in life; we can connect them and use them together or interchangeably. It matters only that they're human. They're hard-wired to receive information from each other and pass it on. The Brain Trust will control and coordinate all of the structure's movements, just like the brain of a living animal would do as it moved. If and when it becomes necessary to relocate this structure, it will seem almost alive in the process."

Now that he'd been cleared as one of the new Whites, 547's glasses, in addition to accessing all the Organization's own intelligence, also now had Federal clearance. He could find out anything about anyone. This tour guide, Beni Kovach, had always had perfect behavior but had been a bit on the slow side in school. One teacher had even entered a comment in the record: "Beni is the hardest worker in the class, which helps to overcome his intellectual simplicity." He tended to prefer men but had been between relationships for the unusually long period of ten months. This might have had something to do with the fact his taste in pornography was almost exclusively limited to suffocation, needles, and enemas.

Beni lectured on. "Because the Amelix attack raised particular concerns about security in this area, Andro-Heathcliffe initiated this project at our location. This structure is our prototype and is at the most advanced stage of development. After this one is tested and rolled out, what we learn here will be used to design even better ones."

That was close enough to the whole story. The truth was that construction of the other structures was delayed for strategic reasons. The Organization's spies had stolen some Amelix tech, and development of the other buildings had been halted so that the stolen elements could be implemented. The subsequent structures would be significantly more advanced than this prototype.

These tours were mandatory for Whites, but most other workers only got to go on one if they were being specially rewarded. The glasses told him everything even remotely related to security, from identities, to work records, to Federal files on three generations of their ancestry, and all he had to do was look to the edges of his vision at the folders and files to pull them up.

There was one other adult with him in this tour group, and 547's glasses informed him that the woman, Ela Belinay, had gotten here by proving herself the most valuable Clerical

Supervisor in finance for a third year in a row. Her employment file showed her to be devoted and self-sacrificing; she'd
twice been strategically divorced by men who had left her to
marry up after she'd made significant sacrifices to her own
career to help them advance in theirs. The rest of the group
consisted of four kids who had won a regional award on an
extracurricular science project. The file had a picture of them
with their virtual trophies. The boy's name was Robi, and he
and the two older girls, Gen-li and Lora, were from Andro-
Heathcliffe High School. The younger girl, Petra, was a middle
schooler and sister to Lora. The sisters had a third cousin who
had been investigated for corporate espionage but Departed
before a report was issued.

Nobody called the Unnamed "sir," or any other honorific,
and the same was true with regard to the Whites. That was not
surprising, but he had hoped to hear a more ingratiating tone
from civilians, more akin to the way people addressed Federal
Angels. After all, he was this structure's Federal authority, now.
At least the white suit looked sharp.

Gen-li raised her hand and Beni nodded at her. "If it's alive
like an animal, do you have to feed it?"

The guide responded with the standard Accepted smile, his
lips stretching wide to show most of his top and bottom teeth.
"That's a great question!" he said. "Yes, we do 'feed' the structure. It uses the same sterile nutrients we all use in our synthesizers, and we load them in almost exactly the way they're
loaded at home, though obviously on a much bigger scale. In
case of emergency, the structure also has a fully functioning
protein refinery and is capable of processing organic material
it finds."

"Does it have a name?" Petra asked.

"Yes. We call it the *Agnes*. Originally, it wasn't intended for
any of the Andro-Heathcliffe structures to have names, but
during the early stages of biodevelopment, workers on the
project's centralized planning team came up with nicknames
to help them easily differentiate among the prospective sites.
This first prototype was originally designated Site A, and I'm
told they came up with *Agnes* from that."

547's new white-framed glasses signaled an emergency call, the first he'd received as a White. The glasses showed it was from IAg281. "Yes, ma'am?" he answered. Thirty-eight other Whites answered the same way, at the same time.

"Seal it!" 281 shouted, her voice equal parts authority and panic. "Seal it, now. Right now. Don't let any rats on board!

"Move! Now! Get the structure operational and bring it here to the CBD to rescue the office staff. Now!" There was a kind of choking noise over the connection then, a brief gasping and gurgling, and the sound of something falling or crashing.

"Ma'am?" 547 called. "Hello?"

"Hello, Ma'am?" another White, IAj114, said. "281, Ma'am?"

Other Whites attempted to hail her through audio and text, but there was no response.

"Beni," 547 said. "Take me to the control room."

Somewhere deep in the Zone, far from the protest area

Kym chased the rat, her veins pulsing with hatred and malice. The entire protest, which by now had grown to several hundred people, ran behind her. Her sides ached, her muscles were fatigued and sore, and she was feeling increasingly disoriented, but none of that mattered. Only killing the rat was important, now.

In her peripheral vision, Kym saw another huge mob charging toward them. She didn't know who they were, or what their intentions might be. She didn't care. Killing the rat was all she could think about.

Someone came between Kym and the animal, blocking her sight. She swung her fists and kicked, shoving the human out of her way to keep the rat in view.

A second rat crossed paths with the one she was following, and then a third. She hated the new ones with the same intensity as she had the first. As more and more rats

appeared, her fury compounded into a rage beyond anything she'd ever felt before. Following one creature and then
another with her eyes, she lifted her head to discover that
her group was converging with many others at a six-street
circular intersection.

Thousands of people were chasing rats in every direction,
shoving and clubbing and slashing each other to get better
access. Everywhere she looked, Kym saw stabbing, smashing,
grappling, kicking, tearing and biting. People fell everywhere,
bleeding, moaning, and writhing.

Kym tripped over one of the bodies and landed in the gravel,
sliding on her elbows and chin. Crazed people kicked and
trampled her in their desperate attacks on the rats. The dead
woman she'd tripped over had been carrying a knife. Kym
snatched it and slashed wildly around her, cutting calves and
shins and knees, finally clearing a space large enough for her
to stand again.

The intersection was packed with people fighting, and new
groups were still arriving, all of them chasing rats. When people did manage to connect with one of the animals, they continued fighting each other to stomp into paste whatever piece
of it they could find. Each street leading into the intersection
was jammed solid with people, stretching as far as she could
see in every direction.

Gunfire sounded from everywhere at once.

Fiends!

Rarely did anyone see Fiends, even while being robbed by
them, yet here they were, running around crazily right in the
open, firing their rifles, not at the crowd but at the rats. They
caused human casualties with every trigger pull, killing many
of their own kind, but still they shot and shot. There were so
many people and so many guns here, now. Many wore the
blotchy black of the Saved.

A bullet smashing through Kym's face brought instanta-
neous and apparently divine understanding. The humans here
had been intentionally led to this place to die.

The new Amelix structure

"Doctor Kessler, please calm down at once," Zabeth Chelsea said. The man was crouched in the corner with both arms curled above his head. Keiko sat at a conference table, looking concerned and utterly confused.

Chelsea knelt beside him but he kept his shoulders hunched and his face buried. "There's a reason you feel this way," she said. "I feel it, too, but I've learned to be stronger than the panic."

This was a lie. She knew she was only able to overcome the panic because the Rat Gods had been keeping her constantly in Thrall.

"I suspected that you and I might have had our blood chemistry altered a bit after that last meeting with the Amelix Medical Doctor," she continued. "It turns out there are four different compounds in our blood samples that have been associated with terrible paranoia, claustrophobia, or both."

She lost her patience, ripping his arms away so she could look into his face. "Are you listening at all? This is not you! You're *not* actually afraid of working here. The MD knows that this structure is the future, and she's sabotaging your career by keeping you off of it this way. You're still a valued Amelix asset so her ethics won't let her kill you, but she can stall out your promotions by keeping you from working in the new offices. That way she can punish you but not the organization. Kessler! You don't have to let her win."

"Yes, I do," Kessler said. His arms came back up. "I don't care about my career. I don't care about anything but getting out of here right now. Please let me go. Please?" He wasn't so much speaking as he was whimpering.

"Shh, shh. Don't worry. I have just the thing to help. Keiko, dear, I've given you access to my office via EI. Go open the door for me."

Federal Building

Nobody but a Federal Agent like Daiss could have walked this far through the hyper-violent sealed Zone and survived. Nobody without a genetically enhanced physique could have walked this distance at all. Yet he had arrived safely at the Federal Building, carrying five rats on his person and with an unknown number trailing him on the ground. He walked up to the front door, still clutching his Gloria 9 sidearm. They had left him control of his eyes but not his head, so although he knew there were rats on all sides of him now, he had no idea how many there might be. He could see only the ones that got out in front.

He met no resistance in entering the building, even though he was spattered with Lehri's blood and holding his weapon at the ready. Nobody even looked up as he passed. As he reached an intersection of hallways that had walls of darkened electro-bioplexi, Daiss was finally able to see the rat entourage behind him, numbering possibly twenty or thirty. He turned one way— or rather, *they turned him* one way—and in the reflection, some of the rats went off in the opposite direction. They marched him around the ground floor, with rats dispersing at various points, until finally he was left with the one original rat that had claimed him. It took him to a corner of a wide office and made him stand there with his back to the wall.

Finally, another Agent noticed him and approached him warily. "Are you all right, Agent?" she asked. "Why are you holding your weapon? Is this your assigned floor?"

Daiss still had control of his eyes. He gestured with them toward his jacket pocket. She saw him and her own eyes squinted a bit, but then Daiss couldn't see her anymore. His own eyes had slammed shut so hard tears came out and his vision filled with yellow sparks. His jaw clenched shut so tightly that he was sure his teeth would crack. His neck muscles tightened into ropes, and then his chest and torso seized up. The rat only let up when he started to lose consciousness. While it still kept his arms and legs under control and wouldn't enable him to speak, it allowed him to gasp for breath and open his eyes again. The other Agent was now holding her weapon and had positioned herself next to him with her back against the wall. He scanned the room and the immediate area, but didn't see any more rats. Her jacket pockets lay flat. It seemed his rat was now controlling both of them.

Fear was to be expected in a case like this, even for a Federal Agent. Even, possibly, for a Zeta. Pleasure, however, was not something he would have anticipated. Being under the rat's spell like this gave him an ecstatic feeling that was psychological as well as physical. After hours of struggle, trying to counteract the rat's influence, he'd finally accepted that it was impossible. There was nothing more he could do to meet his duty of resistance, and that knowledge fed the feeling of helpless euphoria. He was free to enjoy the endless pleasure they gave him in exchange for control. In fact, he'd never felt so free before.

Amelix Building

Keiko opened Dr. Chelsea's office door. All the cages were open and there were rats everywhere, swarming on the floor and climbing up the stacks of open cages that were themselves crammed full of rats. A large group had gathered close together on the countertop. They stood up on their hind legs, watching her intently.

The rats streamed past her and scurried down the hall.

Company-wide emergency message, as seen through Chelsea's EI

Walt Zytem's electric blue eyes pierced Chelsea's consciousness as his Statused face appeared in her mind, seeming to take up all of the space before her.

"This is Walt Zytem, speaking to every Amelix employee in the world through emergency protocols. You are ordered to seal the new structures immediately. We have reason to believe that a bioterrorist attack is underway, using rats in a manner that has not yet been determined. Seal the buildings! All of them. Seal off any labs with rats and do not engage rats in any way. Seal every structure right now!"

Too late, Dr. Zytem.

Chelsea would have shaken her head at the announcement, but the rats didn't allow her to do so.

17

Why wouldn't they have loaded the biocat?"190 asked. The truck had died in the wasteland of the Great Midwestern Desert. There was no way to restart it without recharging the biocatalytic reactor.

"My sister must have told them not to service this one after we drove it out here from the city," Sett said. "She didn't want me leaving of my own accord."

They'd stretched a Mylar blanket from the first-aid kit over the tops of the open doors. Dok had patched up Coiner and was now resting next to him in its shade. 190 was in the passenger seat, viewing some projection through his EI. Sett sat at the wheel, staring out at the blowing grit through his own glasses that had fully darkened under the desert sun. His mother's little dog was curled up in the back of the truck.

As yet they had seen no rats out here.

He and 190 had been scanning news reports.

"Here's another one," 190 said. "Translator says it's from Dubai. Same story. Rats making people strangely violent. It's just like the reports from Mexico City and Tokyo."

Chaos and violence had erupted in every single Zone around the world. Fortunately, those areas had already been sealed off from corporate commercial and residential areas.

The program Sett had found featured a pretty but exhausted-looking woman broadcasting live from Toronto. Her wide and reddened eyes constantly scanned the studio, and her voice shook as she spoke.

> *Pattern analysis of mined data indicates that the rats have been able to do this for some time. In what authorities are now saying were coordinated strikes, people described as hypnotized or robotic were seen commandeering shipments of food and other resources. It is now believed they carried them off to various hidden lairs around the world where numerous generations of rats may have been produced in short order.*
>
> *Though most wild animal species are long extinct, rats have managed to survive because of their ability to live in places humans do not, like sewers and other small, hidden spaces, subsisting on resources humans have not yet been able to claim...*

Sett stopped listening, focusing in on the horizon with the magnification feature in his glasses. What he had thought was a large hill there had just moved.

Central Business District

Standing inside the CBD were thousands of office workers, gathered into tightly packed groups. Each large cluster of humans was surrounded by a collection of rats.

Daiss' body was made to march forward. He passed among the groups until he was halted at the perimeter of one cluster, facing inward. Other Agents stood on both sides of him, facing the same way, sidearms in hand. Agents continued to file into the CBD until they numbered perhaps a few thousand, encircling the immobilized congregations of office workers in Corporate Green.

As Daiss stood frozen in place, his gaze fell upon the faces of the men and women positioned immediately in front of him. Their pleading eyes overflowed with tears, but pleading with Daiss was like pleading with his Gloria 9. He was a mechanical component, and nothing more.

There was no fanfare, no echoing order. Daiss felt his arm rise in front of him and his Gloria 9 kick as it disintegrated the mass of personnel standing before him. Every Agent's Gloria 9 had fired simultaneously.

Within seconds, everyone in a Corporate Green uniform was reduced to a lumpy heap. Hundreds of Agents had also fallen. The remaining Agents turned to face each other. Daiss pulled his trigger, and so did all the others.

The circle intersection

Wanda's rage began to subside. As she looked around there were fewer rats, then still fewer, and then there were none. She was in a small alley, more than a block from the center of destruction at the main intersection. Even so, almost nobody here had been left alive.

More shots rang out, some machine guns clanking out rhythmic short bursts, answered by the shrieks of Federal weapons. Evidently the Fiends and Saved had started their own war back up again.

Based on the sheer number of fallen Saved surrounding her, Wanda concluded that they had inadvertently shielded her from slaughter.

"Wanda!" a voice called.

Leesa.

"Have you seen Ernesto?"

Oh, no.

Ernesto had been here?

"Ernesto?" Wanda called.

Near the circle intersection

Rus had seen a lot of weird shit in his life as a hoodlum, a New Union soldier, and now a Divinator, but nothing had been as fucked up as those rats. Masses of people had rushed in here, all trying to slaughter them, slaughtering each other in the process, but it was the rats that had brought it all on. There was something creepy and wrong about them, that had driven all the humans crazy. Then the rats just vanished. With all the guns around this place, his injury was like some big joke, except that he was going to die from it. A fucking *spear?* Right in the chest, some asshole had run Rus through with a spear. The Pure Water staff had fallen nearby, but he couldn't feel anything below his chest and his arms were too weak even to reach for it.

But he could reach the Juice.

It had been his first combat without Juice since he'd been a snot-nosed punk, sniveling through life as one of the Bridges, but the rage he'd felt at the rats had blocked everything from his mind but the need to destroy them. Rus grasped for the full vial that still hung around his neck. There was no reason not to down it now. He'd be dead soon.

Then out of nowhere came this little kid, scrawny like one of the Subjects, only a little Mexican kid, with one arm. It was the one he'd let go, when that doctor bitch had pleaded for him! The kid held a pair of pliers in his hand. He crouched down, plucked the vial out of Rus' hand with the pliers and squeezed until it shattered. Bits of glass fell to the gravel, along with every drop of the precious liquid. Then the little fucker smiled at him, and in a creepy flat voice with a Spanish accent, he said, "False idol!"

In the street where the fighting had been

When the guns had started firing, Ernesto had hidden in a doorway and curled into a ball, but there was no way to shut out the noise. Now it was better. He could still hear guns, but they weren't so loud.

The Fiend had said something in English when the vial broke and spilled its smelly, oily stuff all over. He'd used a lot of the bad English words Arrulfo had told Ernesto he shouldn't say.

Ernesto had taught this Fiend, and shown him that the little vial would never save him. Now he could accept the One and not be an enemy and go to a good place for dead people.

The Fiend wore a black robe. A stick appeared to have fallen from his hand; Ernesto could envision the trajectory of its fall. Now Ernesto saw at its end another vial, this one bigger and made of clear plastic. The Fiend had to learn that only the One could save him. Ernesto had to show him that the bigger vial on the stick was as weak as the little one. He took the stick and determined the correct angle to smash it against a corner of broken concrete, swinging hard. Water splashed against the rock. Ernesto took other vials from other Fiends but they were all dead and in their terrible places with Arrulfo forever. He could still save the one in the robe, though. One by one he broke the vials before the man's face. "False idol, false idol, false idol, false idol."

The Fiend was saying bad words again.

Ernesto picked up another stick with another vial at its end, this one rectangular.

Near the circle intersection

Over and over, the kid had cracked full vials with those pliers of his. Rus ground his teeth as he watched the Juice seep into the ground. The vicious little fuck had already broken the Pure Water staff. Now he'd moved on to the one the Subjects called the General's Ashes.

It took the kid about ten one-armed swings before one end of the brick broke off, exposing the bottom end of the tube. That bioplexi was pretty tough.

He seemed to have some urgency behind his agenda of torturing Rus, and he came running up with the General's Ashes and those pliers. "False idol!" he said again. The pliers crunched and the glass shattered. A fine black powder puffed out all over.

Around the corner from the alley

As Wanda rounded the corner, she saw Ernesto, standing less than twenty meters away. He was okay! He was holding up some kind of tube with a pair of pliers.

"Ernesto!" Wanda called.

A wisp of black smoke billowed over Ernesto's head and disappeared.

"Ernesto!" Wanda called again. It often took several tries to get the boy to answer or acknowledge when someone spoke to him, so it was a surprise when he raised his head and smiled at her.

He collapsed. She ran toward him.

The way he had fallen wasn't right. He'd crumpled as if there had suddenly been less of him than before. Had he been shot with a Federal gun? She hadn't heard the shriek.

She reached him. There was nothing there but the rags he'd worn, drenched in a strange whitish pink foam. The Fiend next to where Ernesto had been standing was dissolving the same way.

Wanda felt it first in her lungs, a terrible burning followed by a strange emptiness. She lost the ability to breathe and then the impulse to breathe. Her body collapsed. A last, fleeting thought of Nami faded into nothingness.

News channel still producing content, via Sett's EI

> All we can do now is keep repeating this message for our viewers in the Des Moines area: Get indoors and seal your air intake. Wherever you are, go inside now!

> This is footage from another Federal security camera inside the sealed Zone. The bodies simply disintegrate, one by one. When the video is slowed down, you can see it, small pink spots forming in various places and expanding, erupting over the entire body. A few seconds later, only foam and clothing remain.

> If you are receiving this broadcast, get inside now and seal your air supply! This is a life-threatening emergency. Go inside now!

The Great Midwestern Desert

"It's definitely moving," 190 said. "It has to be one of the new office buildings. Even military stuff wouldn't be that big." Sett began waving and using various hailing programs through his glasses.

The newscaster disintegrated mid-sentence. Sett gasped.

"What's going on?" Dok asked. He was kneeling next to Coiner, who had collapsed.

"Newscaster just turned to foam, Dok," Sett said.

Dok's eyebrows were down and his face was stern and certain, but his eyes welled with tears.

"It's the Slatewiper fungus, Lawrence," Dok said. "I knew it. It's exactly what I told you would happen." He climbed awkwardly to his feet. "I told the Subjects, I tried to make them understand, and they nearly killed me for it. Now their ridiculous dogma has doomed us all, just like I said it would!"

"It's working!" 190 said. "Look!"

Sett focused on the structure and his glasses confirmed that it was heading straight for them.

But *how* could this be working? Why would a company come to rescue two Unnamed from a different organization, under any circumstances, let alone now, with two other strangers and such a high risk of contamination?

Still, he waved and hailed for all he was worth.

White central control room aboard the Agnes

"Now what, sir?" 547 asked.

"All communication was still being routed through the old building in the CBD while we finalized construction. We've been unable to identify any technical problems, but we are currently unable to make contact with anyone there," his supervisor, NJt994, said. "The default directive is to hold our position whenever communication is lost."

NJt994 was more than his supervisor. As ranking White aboard the *Agnes*, he was charged with driving and making security decisions for the structure in times of emergency. All the other Whites aboard when they'd sealed were from 547's cohort and held his rank, but 547 had a higher security clearance than any of them and therefore was de facto second in command. NJt994 embraced the mentor role and always went into detail in his answers, instructing 547 how to command. 547 was lucky that his immediate superior was, in fact, so literally superior. As far as 547 had seen, NJt994 was the perfect Unnamed: a physical incarnation of the Organization's will.

Together they stared down at the strange little group standing out there in the dust.

547's glasses told him it was a Williams Unnamed. He had set them to automatically scan in IR and UV whenever they encountered other UE glasses, thereby producing a construct that became an actual, identifiable face, without the glasses. When he zoomed in on the construct, the face was unmistakable.

It was his former friend Sett! A flick of his eyes confirmed the other was Jack. One of the other two had dark skin, and the other was a wounded Fiend.

"Now we watch them down there," NJt994 said. "And we'll know whether the air's gone bad."

Below the moving beetle building

Dok had gotten a good look as the gigantic structure had lumbered toward them. It was vaguely beetle shaped, like the stationary buildings in the CBD had been. Now, up close, it appeared only as a gigantic wall, slightly curving away in every direction.

Though building-sized, the thing looked more like a machine than any ordinary structure, with bright red Grown-polymer legs and what was evidently a support framework, under a gray body. It was truly an incredible feat of bioengineering.

But why is it here?

There were a few windows up there on its surface. Dok thought he could see people crowded together inside, peering out.

Time passed. Coiner coughed.

"Did you see that?" 190 asked Lawrence.

"Ames?"

"Yes."

"190 and I shared news show links, Dok," Lawrence said. "The newscaster we had open from Ames just disintegrated."

Dok sighed. "That's what I'd expect. The spores were probably released in the Zone. The direction the desert wind is blowing would carry them straight toward Ames—for now. As close as we are to ground zero, even a slight shift in the wind could kill us instantly."

The building remained motionless and no communication came from within. Dok strode toward it, waving his arms. "Help!" he shouted. "Please help us!" There was no way to know whether anyone heard him.

"They're not going to open it," Lawrence said.

"No," Dok agreed. "There was never much hope of that. What will they do now, shoot us?"

"They could," Lawrence said. "I'm sure they have a laser grid and auto guns for anything that gets too close. CBD buildings have stuff like that, and so do company housing structures. But why wait, if that's what they plan to do?"

Coiner grabbed Dok's shirt and pulled, trying to hoist himself to stand. Dok grasped his hand and pulled him upward, but he was still so weak he nearly toppled under Coiner's additional weight. Coiner's clothes were soaked in blood and the arm he leaned on Dok's shoulder was wet with it.

With his other hand, Coiner removed the cord from around his neck, dangling the vial of Juice in front of him. Nobody moved for a long while.

Finally, an opening appeared partway up one of the curving sides and something coiled downward, impacting the desert clay hard enough for Dok to feel the thud through his shoes. It was a cable ladder, with little loops that could hold one foot at a time, rolled out from what was apparently a service door, maybe ten stories above their heads.

190 raced over and started up the ladder. Lawrence followed him, though not at a run. Reaching the cable ladder, he started up after 190, cupping the little dog against his chest with one arm and lunging up for each handhold with the other.

"Better chance with three other outsiders up there instead of just me," Coiner said, shoving Dok at the ladder.

Lawrence was so big that every step shook and spun the ladder below him, but Dok managed to hold on. Coiner did, too, though Dok couldn't imagine how he did it, in his condition.

The cable was thin, digging into his palms and bending his feet around whatever part of his shoes happened to contact it. He was in better shape than he had been when Coiner had found him, but climbing this high, straight up, was too much. About a third of the way up Dok felt dizzy and shoved his arm up to the shoulder through the loop he'd been holding, in hopes it would hold him without him gripping. His vision went black for a second but he managed to shake it off.

"Hey!" Coiner coughed below him. "Move it! They could seal up that opening any second."

Dok continued up the ladder with Coiner at his heels. At the top of the ladder, the smooth gray surface of the wall had rippled open, almost as if it had been melted by intense heat.

Dok pulled himself off the ladder and up into a tiny and dimly lit mechanical area. The space between various giant pieces of biomachinery was barely big enough for himself, Lawrence, and 190.

190 was now just a heap on the floor. A woman stood over him, holding his gun and the jagged piece of glass she'd used to cut his throat.

Coiner's fist appeared in the opening, still clutching the cord with the little vial, and the woman lunged for it. Coiner, in the process of hoisting himself up, kept his grip on the cord and managed to punch her in the jaw, but he teetered on the edge of the hole for a moment before pulling himself inside. Relieved of its last climber, the ladder retracted into a space beneath the floor. The hole began to close, the surface healing itself as if it had never been opened.

"You want this?" Coiner asked the woman. "You need this? Tell me where we can hide in here."

"Give it to me! Give it over now or I'll tear you apart!" She shoved 190's gun at Coiner's face.

"You don't want to do that," Coiner said. "You want to tear me apart *after* you drink it. Isn't that right?"

The woman stared at the vial, breathing raggedly. A three-shot burst echoed around the tiny space and Coiner's head fell apart in chunks. The woman pointed the gun at Lawrence and yanked the vial free from Coiner's dead hand.

Lawrence had drawn his own weapon and had a bead on her, too. She growled through her clenched jaw and backed through a narrow gap between two giant pieces of equipment. Presumably she ran off to down the vial's contents, but there was too much ambient noise in this machine room for Dok to hear footsteps.

Lawrence set the dog down and slipped the straps off Coiner's shoulders, taking the rail gun and sword, managing the task without re-holstering his sidearm. His Unnamed chest was too wide for the straps to cross as Coiner had worn them, so he slung one weapon over each arm and let them hang down by his waist. Dok picked up the dog and together he and Lawrence squeezed out, their direction dictated by the one gap between the pieces of machinery that was big enough for Lawrence to pass through.

In the bowels of the Agnes, on sublevel four

547 gritted his teeth but the rage bubbled up, forcing the scream out.

"I know it's you, Sett! Jack was already dead when I found him, but I am going to enjoy watching you die!"

181 and 096 had come down here, too. There had been no time to tell them why this kill was so important to him, so he'd pushed his way to the center of the search without explanation. 547 had followed a couple of bloody streaks leading away from the dead Fiend, and the other Whites had followed his text directions to spread out and away in opposite directions in what he hoped would cast a wide enough net. There were cameras everywhere on the *Agnes,* but the area was so crowded with biomachinery that it was unlikely he'd be able to maneuver fast enough alone whenever they spotted something. So far,

the cameras had caught flashes of the intruders in three different locations on this floor but the Whites hadn't yet caught up with even one of them.

547 held his gun ready, listening for any noises that might reveal where his prey had gone. This would be the first combat test of what the Whites called the blurp gun, which shot a hard ball of enzymes that disintegrated on impact and dissolved into any living tissue that was not the *Agnes*. 547 was thrilled he would soon see it work for the very first time, chemically disassembling the one individual he hated most in the world.

547 searched carefully and methodically, around, under, and above each piece of machinery, looking not just for his quarry but also for any signs of disturbance.

A three-shot burst sounded ahead, over where 096 was. Whites only used blurp guns so it had to be a Williams weapon, and Jack was dead.

IAi547:	You okay, 096?
IAjo96:	I'm okay. Shots missed me.
IAi547:	At close range?
IAjo96:	Mercenaries ain't what they used to be.
IAi547:	Target now?
IAjo96:	Was ahead of me. Not sure now.
IAi547:	Cameras still not showing.
IAi547:	Watch above and below.

Ahead he could hear an unusual, tremorous sound. There were long periods of a soft, low vibration, broken by quick pauses. It seemed more alive than strictly mechanical, and different from the other machines down here. In this age of specialized bioengineering, though, such distinctions were nebulous at best. 547 crept slowly, scanning, listening. Slowly he zeroed in on its source.

He spun around a piece of equipment, weapon ready. A woman in a Corporate Green uniform sprung at him, firing an Unnamed weapon straight at his head. He ducked sideways and down, as much as his enhanced physique would allow in the cramped space, pulling the trigger of the blurp gun. The woman's forearm dissolved and the weapon fell to the floor, along with part of her hand. She ran at 547, jabbing up under his White glasses with her remaining hand in an attempt to stab his eyes with a piece of broken glass.

He shoved her backward, aiming.

She stood with her lips curled back and her eyes narrowed in a sneer of pure abhorrence. His glasses displayed her identity and employment record: Alicia Krom, an Accepted who worked in biohydraulics. She had been a model employee, but the woman's breathing, with long, intense exhalations and quick gasps to inhale, confirmed what 547 had suspected, based on intel reports. Fiends had claimed this woman and replaced her corporate soul with that of a deranged killer.

She lunged again and he fired the enzyme gun, hitting her in the chest. Within seconds the shot had eroded a head-sized hole straight through her. She dropped to the floor. Shots sounded behind him and to his right, then came another three-shot burst from an Unnamed gun. 547 turned and navigated toward them. He worked his way around the various pieces of equipment and biomechanical components until he found 181. Most of her face had been blown off when she'd been shot in the back of the head. Her enzyme gun was missing, and so were her White glasses.

> IAi547:   181 dead. Glasses missing. Track them.
> IAjo96:   Fuckers.
> IAjo96:   Activity on staircase. See it?
> IAi547:   Yes. It's the dark one. Is he writing?
> IAjo96:   Looks like it.

Why would Sett take the glasses? He was himself Unnamed. He had to know they were traceable, especially when they were all sealed inside the *Agnes* this way. The trace showed they were moving, though he couldn't get a camera feed from them, concealed as they apparently were inside a fist or pocket. The trajectory was a wide arc, surprisingly fast. He tracked 096's path and saw that they were both angled to intercept near the back staircase, if they picked up the pace.

IAi547:   Two intruders down, two still running.
IAi547:   Armed and killing. UTk181 down.
IAi547:   Stole UTk181 White glasses.
IAi547:   All Whites track on UTk181 to intercept.

He and 096 reached the stairway at the same time. 096 moved to shove open the door and 547 covered him, aiming up at an angle. Nobody was visible on the stairs and the various camera shots there showed nothing. Sett had entered on sublevel four. The glasses lay between the railings at the bottom of the stairwell down on sublevel seven. He ran down the stairs to get them and discovered a message written on the floor in chalk:

Li'l Ed

Check your footage. I have the Fiend's Federal rail gun. If I have to defend myself with it, the hole will go all the way through. Back off.

7

Sublevel two

"Dok?" Sett said.

Dok emerged from a dark corner, hunched over with his hands on his knees and breathing hard. It seemed they hadn't built in as much time for Dok to finish the message and meet Sett here as they'd thought.

Together they moved away from the stairwell and deeper into the dark recesses, among moving parts and rhythmically contracting tubes.

"Okay, Lawrence," Dok said finally. "Looks like your plan worked so far. At least you showed them we can hurt them, even if doing so would be suicide."

"Now we'll see whether they decide to push us."

Inside 547's mind

It was his first assigned three-hour rest period since the world had been effectively destroyed two weeks ago, but in spite of his exhaustion 547 couldn't sleep. He kept live feeds from various sublevels open in his EI, switching his focus randomly from one to another, but Sett was too good at hiding. Designed for protection from bioterrorism, the *Agnes* could seal off different areas and even pump out all the air from them, but 547 couldn't use that feature in the Sett situation. Even if he spotted his former friend and caught him sleeping, adrenaline could kick in if he started to suffocate. One pull of that trigger would doom the *Agnes* and everyone aboard. Still, he kept searching the sublevels, if not to solve the problem, perhaps to punish himself for having let it get this far out of control.

He heard a soft chime, indicating that a message was forthcoming. Unlike civilian EI settings, Unnamed and Whites had no soft, sweet interface to let them select what came into their heads, or when.

"All Whites!" It was the voice of his superior, NJt994. "Communications are back. Unfortunately, we appear to be the only team members from the Organization Whose Confidence is Kept to have survived. As Whites know, the Organization's other structures were held back in development, in hopes of exploiting some recently acquired Amelix technology. Apparently none of them were at a sealable stage by the time of the Event."

547 sat up in bed. Had he heard that correctly? The *Agnes*, with a few thousand Accepted, was the last vestige of the entire Organization?

"However, there are other sealed, mobile structures remaining in the world. We are not alone! We have made contact with two other structures, the *Linepithema*, of Copec-Móvil Corporation, and the *Kit*, which at this time is refusing to identify its corporate owner."

547 looked around his bunk, hoping nobody had heard him sigh. The other Whites nearby all seemed to be in a similar state. *Others had survived!* They no longer had to wonder whether the *Agnes* held the last trace of humanity on the planet. That was something, wasn't it, even when the Organization had diminished almost to the point of insignificance?

"The *Linepithema*, outside Buenos Aires, nicknamed *La Línea*, claims to have more than two thousand aboard," NJt994 said. "The *Kit*, near Moscow, says it has more than three thousand. Both are claiming that their parent organizations had two other structures safely seal prior to the Event, but both are refusing to give any information about those ships and we suspect they are lying to gain a potential competitive advantage. For our part, we are doing the same. As far as they know, the Organization Whose Confidence is Kept has four other ships, in the locations the Organization was building them, which are Seattle and Miami in this hemisphere, as well as one in Wellington, New Zealand and another at Sa'dah in Yemen.

"We've been in communication with a number of other structures, as well, each from a different corporation, that managed to survive the Event. They bring the estimated total number of ambulatory humans left in the world to somewhere between fifty and two hundred fifty thousand, and the total number of networked Brain Trust minds to a few hundred thousand more. We don't know how accurate the totals are because so much relies on self-reporting, but at least there are other human-controlled humans out there. It does at this time seem the Organization Whose Confidence is Kept is the smallest surviving institution."

547 sat staring at nothing, stunned. He had dedicated his life to this, the Lord's chosen corporation, and now it was the smallest institution in the world?

"Neither the *Linepithema* nor the *Kit* have seen any trace of Amelix Integrations," NJt994 went on. "At this time, all Amelix employees and other assets are presumed lost."

White control room

547 sat at the panels, staring listlessly at the grainy red IR feed from a camera he'd extended from the *Agnes* on a flexible telescoping arm. It was daytime out there now, early afternoon, but the view from the camera, room after empty room in shades of red against black, was always the same.

Certain employees of the Organization were privileged to know what the Event had been: a release of a lethal fungal strain that had been engineered to live inside human tissue. Had it been something else, like a virus or even bacteria, humanity might have had a chance of returning to life outside. Fungal spores, however, could blow around out there for thousands of years.

This information had been gleaned by Organization scientists and was therefore proprietary to the Organization, so when 547 spoke with representatives from other companies he had to pretend to be as baffled by the Event as they were. In truth, it was probably just a dance they had to do. Every surviving company had worked in biotech and was almost certainly aware of what had made the planet uninhabitable.

Amelix made it uninhabitable, so they could take over the planet with their biomachines.

It was not the first time this thought had occurred to him. Amelix had begun developing the mobile structures long before the Organization had even considered such things, dumping every possible resource into their development. Intel suggested that the Amelix structures were the most advanced biotech ever devised, years ahead of what the Organization could accomplish, yet none of that tech had ever been marketed, so secret had been its development. Amelix had been the world's leader in fungal patents for decades, and now a fungus had nearly wiped out humanity. This had been an attack. Amelix hadn't wanted to sell its technology, because it had been planning to add the entire world to its bottom line.

So why hasn't it used those things to claim its prize? If Amelix planned it so well, why didn't it survive?

There was no way to know.

The Agnes could hold two thousand, six hundred forty Organization employees but only seven hundred thirty-one had boarded in time, plus thirty-nine Whites, four children, and, regrettably, the four stowaway/hijackers. It was apparently the least populated of any surviving corporate structure, but that wasn't surprising since it had been closest to the Event's ground zero. The fact it had survived at all was astounding.

Now two Whites and an Organization employee were dead.

Thanks to Sett.

547 checked the small window he kept open in his EI, monitoring the cameras down on sublevel two, the last place Sett and his dark friend had been seen.

There was nothing new. He forced his attention back to his work.

547 watched the monitors, listening through headphones as the mechanized camera probed various parts of the old Organization building here in the CBD. So far, no living person had been found. In fact, there was little evidence that anyone had been inside the building when the fungus had spread. While bodies had foamed away, things like uniforms, tools, weapons, and Unnamed glasses had not, so it was easy to tell where the humans had been in their final moments. Instead of the expected workday pattern of people at desks and in the halls, it seemed almost everyone from the Organization had been gathered outside when they'd died. Shredded Corporate Green uniforms fluttered in the wind outside, over mounds of twisted, rotting flesh. Apparently the fungus only attacked living human tissue, so these workers had already been dead at the time it was released.

The first place they'd searched with the roving camera had been the office of IAg281, the last person to have made contact with them from outside the *Agnes*. There were no life forms in there, or anywhere else, except for an occasional rat, glowing bright red on the otherwise dim IR camera feed.

Suddenly NJt994 was in his head, monitoring his work.

547 always felt it when his supervisor perused what was happening in his head. This time, he spoke. "Close the sublevel feed, 547. Now."

He let the sublevel camera feed go and felt NJt994 disconnect again. In less than a minute NJt994 was standing before him at the desk, staring over the monitors with a tight jaw.

"We can't have you distracted like this, 547," NJt994 chastised. "You told me about your past with the Unnamed down there, but there's nothing we can do right now. He's not causing us any trouble crawling around in the dark, and we've got more immediate problems to deal with."

547 nodded. "Yes, sir. Sorry, sir."

It had been more than two weeks since Sett and the dark man had disappeared among the machinery down there. The computer had analyzed the footage and identified Sett's gun as a first-generation Federal Trident rail gun. One shot from it could indeed punch right through the *Agnes* 'exterior and end it all for everyone onboard, but only if Sett aimed it far enough away. 547 had tried to convince NJt994 that they could pen Sett into a confined area so that the rail gun would revert to being a regular gun for close range, which would be less dangerous to the *Agnes*, but NJt994 had said no. With the stakes so high, it was better, he said, to just let them starve to death down there than to go hunting them.

"We all need to work together, and to be as coordinated as possible," NJt994 said. "We need to function as ideal components of the whole, now more than ever. Separate agendas would pull us in separate directions, and pulling the *Agnes* apart would be the death of us all."

It had been three days since the last news show's power had given out and it had gone off the air, and that had happened five days after the last human face or voice had been transmitted over it. Outside the *Agnes* there were no electric lights, and no sounds of anything beyond wind and the occasional skittering of rodents. Beyond the CBD ruins, the desolate, empty desert stretched in every direction.

"Movement, sir!" 636 shouted. She was monitoring the sensory equipment and stationary camera mounted at the front of the *Agnes*.

"Rats again?" NJt994 asked, his voice flat.

"No, sir. Big. Really big. I think it might be another mobile structure."

From his location, 547 could see over her shoulder to the monitor she watched. A black spot moved on the horizon.

"Take it to 10x and switch to UV," NJt994 said. That might show a logo."

"Yes, sir."

The screen turned purple, showing the curving surface of a wall. Sure enough, a logo stood out in a different shade: a stylized version of DNA.

"Amelix!" 547 said. "They weren't wiped out, after all."

"It looks just like intel said," 636 said. "Look! It even has the beetle jaws!"

All seven Whites in the room crowded around the monitor, blocking 547's view. Without asking permission, he withdrew his roving camera from the building and pointed it toward the moving structure, changing from IR to visual light and matching the 10x magnification. He gasped.

Amelix had dominated the biotechnology field with more innovative and aggressive technologies even than the Organization had, and the new building was proof of that. Rather than a beetle-shaped *building* with bioengineered components, this appeared much more like a giant, living beetle, roughly the same size as the *Agnes*. The entire body was glossy black that glinted metallic green as it turned, showing the massive set of jagged jaws at the front. It slowly pivoted its body so that only the grisly jaws faced the *Agnes*.

"Did it just...*notice* us?" someone said.

The Amelix structure began walking toward them. Its motion was not stiff and mechanical, like that of the *Agnes*. It was creeping, smoothly and slowly—almost cautiously—as if it were alive.

"Evasive action!" NJt994 shouted. "Back away and turn!"

The *Agnes* began a slow pivot and then lurched hard backward as one of its legs skidded on a patch of uneven ground. 547 maneuvered the camera beneath the *Agnes* to monitor the Amelix craft and report whatever he could.

"It looks like the Amelix structure's legs keep it perfectly suspended so the body remains level as it walks, even over steep slopes," 547 said. "It's maintaining a speed which sensors indicate is more than double ours."

547 himself was tilting a bit. The *Agnes* had compensators and levelers but not nearly as advanced. The *Agnes* pitched and tipped as it propelled itself over the terrain. The Amelix craft crept closer, appearing to float over a small hill as its legs moved around and found footing without any impact on the structure itself. "It's closing the distance quickly," 547 said. "The Amelix structure will be upon us in about two minutes, at present pace."

"Thirty degrees to port," NJt994 said. "Get into that trough between the hills."

"Thirty degrees to port," IAi503 said. The *Agnes* lurched accordingly.

"Ready the grid guns," NJt994 said. "Hail them and make sure they know we consider this action of following us to be extremely hostile.'"

547 ran the emergency hailing programs standard to all organizations, used mostly between Unnamed of different companies when duty forced them into contact. There was no response.

"Stay in the valley between the hills as best you can," NJt994 said.

"The valley, yes, sir."

With the *Agnes* squeezed in between the small hills, 547 could no longer see the Amelix craft. He withdrew the camera from underneath and raised it as high as possible, but the action afforded him no view. "No sign of Amelix but they have to be very close now," he said.

547 scanned from behind, up along the starboard side, to front, and back again, in case Amelix was trying to head them

off. A foot appeared behind them, wrapping around the hill they had just passed. Another appeared across from it, and the front of the Amelix craft came into view.

"Directly behind us!" 547 said. "Sensors say it will be upon us in twenty-two seconds! It has what appear to be windows or segmented sensory equipment in shapes resembling eyes at the front, like the compound eyes of insects. Still no answer from our repeated hailing attempts. Ten seconds. Five. Taking over our space now."

The structure echoed with an ear-splitting grinding tear of metal being crushed and bent.

"Grid guns firing, sir"

The *Agnes* vibrated. The grid guns had locked on the closest part of the breaching target, which in this case was the massive set of jaws. The shots bounced off harmlessly.

"It just seized our rear starboard leg!" 547 said. "I have visual."

"Switching 547's visual to the main screen," NJt994 said. "Did the leg autoseal?"

"Yessir," someone said. "Sealed and foamed. The leg does not appear to be functional or fixable, sir."

547 adjusted the camera to show the jaws and the crumpled leg from a better angle, and then panned back along the hillside. Without any scale to indicate that the combatants were the size of office buildings, the scene looked like it could have come from an old nature show about wild, living beetles. The Amelix craft yanked backward and the *Agnes* lurched sideways.

"The grid guns were ineffective, sir."

"Take manual control and aim for those eye things," NJt994 said.

547 positioned the camera near the point where the jaw contacted the leg, angling it upward to take in the maximum view of the eye. The shots impacted, leaving abrasions and scars on the transparent material, but did not breach it.

The Amelix beetle's jaws let go. It stepped slightly backward and turned, scuttling away over a hill.

IV

18

White dining area aboard the Agnes

Tell these guys, 547," 636 said. He had brought 547 over to another table of Whites from where they'd been sitting. "Tell them what you told me."

Back in his student days at McGuillian, before he'd become White or even donned Unnamed black, being called upon this way would have produced anxiety and uncertainty. Most such responses had now been completely trained out of him, and any residual feelings on the matter were successfully tweaked away by the glasses. Now anything worth saying was worth telling all of his kind.

"I have a book," 547 said. "Old. Real paper. Written by hand, by an Amelix employee. If you have ever doubted the evil that is our most hated enemy, it will restore your faith. I made an electronic copy and added notes to guide anyone reading it."

"You'll want to follow the link, brothers and sisters," 636 said. "It shows how wicked and dangerous Amelix has always been. The notes 547 made bring it all into focus and show how the culture there ended up destroying the world."

636 began looking around the table, locking eyes with the others to share the link.

Dr. Chelsea's lab aboard the Amelix beetle

It was one collective mind that had claimed Chelsea. Any individual rat was like a single cell in a massive brain, yet she always thought of them as a plurality, as the Rat Gods. It seemed gentler to have been captured by multiple little animals than by the single, worldwide consciousness that was actually consuming the rats and humans in similar ways.

In the weeks since the Rat Gods had taken control, they had carefully and relentlessly monitored Chelsea's thoughts and movements, administering rewards or punishments to hone her behavior. She had quickly learned to direct her thinking to please them. It worked in much the same way as the corporate reconditioning process, though in this case there was no filter inside her head, no way to excuse her own actions and make peace with them. The rats dealt with any errant idea swiftly and mercilessly.

The Thrall's pleasure was powerful enough to completely wash away the waves of terror and suffocating claustrophobia with which the Amelix Medical Doctor had seen fit to punish Chelsea, but only for brief periods of time. Now those dreadful feelings were welling up again, threatening to explode into her psyche and cripple her. Her mind swam with desperate thoughts which she fought to suppress, but one idea managed to penetrate her cerebral prophylactic:

I have enough scientific skill to fix this! I could fix all kinds of issues for everyone onboard this structure, even company-wide, if only I had authority to second-guess a Medical Doctor!

Chelsea would have gasped, but such behavior was no longer under her control. She was thinking independently and the rats would punish her! The thought became the sole focal point of her consciousness, blocking everything else as pathway amplification took over and intensified her fear into crippling dread. Her mind spiraled downward under the staggering weight of the sensation.

How had she dared to think that she, herself, could synthesize her own compounds and cure her own physical issues, simply because she had advanced scientific expertise? It was legally, ethically and morally prohibited for anyone but a Medical Doctor to alter the chemical composition of human tissue!

Chelsea struggled to bring her emotions back under control.

I am not one to reallocate Amelix resources or create physiologically active substances! I cannot step outside my assigned—

Suddenly, her fear and anxiety began to diminish. She could still feel the chemically induced icy black pool deep inside, from which the trepidation would undoubtedly rise again. But the rat in the pocket of her lab coat was helping, this time, dosing her with so much euphoria that the terror subsided.

They like the idea!

So many people had been killed by suffocation already that Chelsea had suspected that the rats were preparing to eliminate her species entirely. Then the air had become toxic, the beetles had become operational, and the rats had found a use for humans after all, as integral parts of the Amelix structures, the world's most powerful and important biomachines. Perhaps, as the undisputed new masters of Amelix and the planet, the Rat Gods would let Chelsea assume the most important and prestigious role aboard the vessel, which was by default the most important and prestigious role anywhere in the world.

But was there truly a way around the protocols that had stood at Amelix for so long, that everyone aboard every ship was programmed to obey without question? The rats undoubtedly had power, but Chelsea could only function along defined lines. If she pushed too far against her reconditioning, her mind would shatter and leave her useless. As it stood now, what she was considering was not simply against policy; it would require her to tread upon the most dubious legal and moral ground possible.

Reallocating Amelix resources for a private purpose would be the same as stealing from the company, and her reconditioned mind would ensure she'd die before she did that. The only hope was to redefine what she was hoping to accomplish.

She needed to restate her goal in a way that pathway amplification wouldn't seize upon.

She needed Gregor Kessler.

Control room in one of the science labs aboard the Agnes

"This is it, 547," NJt994 said, "The most important operation of the post-Event world. Glad to have you as my official second in command on this mission."

"It's thrilling, sir," 547 said. "I hope we're successful. There has to be something there we can use to fend off Amelix."

This lab had originally been set up to monitor activities within living organisms via nanocameras, but it had been modified in order to follow the activities of the excursion crew that was now descending into the empty Federal Building. 547 stood with NJt994 in the center of the darkened room, with all the views from the lead crewmember's cameras currently assembled into a full-circle projection on the walls. The other crewmembers' front camera feeds were displayed through the Whites' EIs at the bottom of their visual fields and could be pulled up for the 360-degree view as needed.

The six people they were watching were wearing bright orange HAZMAT suits. Tubes integrated into the tops of their suits at the crown emitted rings of greenish light that collectively did a decent job of illuminating the space around them. They had reached a windowless office room a few floors below ground without major incident, but it had become apparent that the team leader, Nanci, was stupid and clumsy.

"Okay, Nanci," NJt994 said to the crew leader. "Place the putty over the lock and stand far back. We're going to blow it. Remember that even a tiny puncture in your suit will be disastrous, so go way back to the other side of the room when we detonate so no little particles hit you.

"Yes, sir," the woman said. The camera showed her fumbling with the lock, her orange-gloved hands shaking as she tried to make the putty stick to the surface.

547 ensured his voice link with the excursion crew was off and turned to NJt994. "Please educate me as to how you chose this one to lead, sir. She seems the least capable of the six."

"We're so understaffed in this structure that it's hard to justify ejecting anyone like this," NJt994 said. "But certain specialties became irrelevant when we sealed. We no longer need tax people, for example. Most of the newly obsolete have managed to find functions aboard *Agnes* that make them useful, like the techs from this lab did, for example, reworking the equipment to show feed from the expedition cameras instead of their research projects. The six out there in the excursion crew were found to be in a low tier of importance."

"But they've not been told they're Departing, sir."

"Oh, no, technically they're not Departing. If they were to Depart, they wouldn't be employees anymore. They would have no duty to obey orders. In this case, we need them to do exactly as they're told out there. We didn't Depart them; they were *Selected*. They're still fully employed and their compliance training and reconditioning remain intact." "But they can't come back in here, sir. When we're under seal, the only entry is through the front port where everything is ground to bits and soaked in acid. Nothing gets through but sterile minerals and aminos. Even mechanical devices couldn't survive it." 547 wanted to turn his head and make eye contact but he was tasked with looking behind the crew via the panoramic display.

"Of course they're not coming back," NJt994 said. "My guess is they know that. In answer to your question, though, you remember that four kids were aboard *Agnes* when we sealed? One of them, Gen-li, also happened to have a parent on board. I put Nanci in charge because she's that one parent; her daughter is still inside. Nobody will be as dedicated to this mission as Nanci is."

"Brilliant, sir," 547 said.

"Give me vocal to Nanci again," NJt994 said. "Nanci? Keep backing up, now. Here we go."

NJt994 activated the detonation with his EI and the putty exploded. The excursion crew slid open the splintered bioplexi door and entered a low-ceilinged room, divided by bioplexi walls into storage rooms lined up along a hallway. Behind the transparent walls were weapons, including the latest model of the famed Gloria sidearm only Federal Agents could carry. However, the new structures like the *Agnes* and the Amelix beetles were built to withstand bombs; even Gloria firepower would be useless against them.

Only constant monitoring and fleeing at the earliest sight of the Amelix craft had kept them from another physical confrontation. The Organization's remaining scientists were analyzing information from footage of every encounter, no matter how brief, but an Amelix weakness had not yet been discovered.

"Look for something big," NJt994 said to the excursion crew. "Rockets, land mines, that kind of thing. We don't need to destroy the structure, just poke a hole in one of those eyes, but even that's going to take something incredibly powerful."

547 doubted any of the weapons down there could take down an Amelix beetle. Even if a rocket could puncture the armored but hopefully more vulnerable eye surface, it would first have to connect. The Amelix tech was significantly more advanced than anything they had aboard the *Agnes*, and the *Agnes* could sense rats (the only living animals they had detected so far, other than the Amelix beetle) to the horizon in every direction. How would they even get close enough to deploy whatever weapon they discovered?

Obviously the Organization would have had a better chance with something from one of the hangars above, like a helio-drone, an anti-aircraft rocket battery, or a tank, but databases of Federal acts and regulations showed that fully one hundred percent of such weapons had been retrofitted for EI control by specific Federal agents. Even Whites, with Federal authority inside the new structures, couldn't make them work. Digging around down inside the Federal Building like this was the best plan they'd come up with, largely based on hope and speculation that perhaps the Feds hadn't gotten around to changing over every piece of smaller ordinance.

Two glowing dots appeared in the bottom of the doorway behind the excursion crew.

"Rat behind you!" 547 said. He calmed his voice and started again. "You two on the wings, turn and take care of that rat like we told you. Do it now."

The two turned and fired the old Unnamed guns with which they'd been equipped. The rat disappeared. "You two keep watching that door," 547 said. "We don't want another one showing up without us knowing. Shoot them on sight; don't wait for me to tell you."

"Yes, sir," a male voice said.

"Yes, sir," a female voice said.

"Everyone else, keep searching those storage rooms. Look for old stuff that looks like it hasn't been touched in a long time, and big."

"How about these, sir?" one of the others, a male voice, asked. "Would these work?"

It was a rack of small missiles that could be fired by a team of two or three people.

"Show me some serial numbers," NJt994 said. Orange gloves turned one of the missiles until a number was visible.

Stand by," 547 said. There was a pause as NJt994 checked Federal files.

The glowing eyes appeared again in the doorway. "Rat's back," 547 said. "Hit it this time, please."

"Yes, sir," both said together, and another barrage shredded the doorway and floor. They kept pulling their triggers, wasting far too many three-shot bursts, but at least the glow disappeared again.

"Not those," NJt994 said. "Records show they're retrofitted. Look for anything stored with the metal bracelets Federal Agents used to wear. How about the ones in the corner, there, the launchers, the tubes on the third shelf up? Are there bracelets I see in the plastic packet attached to the front? Show me a number from those."

Hands fumbled with the tubes.

"Yessir."

"You two on the wings," 547 said. "Advance on that hallway where the rat was. I want to see its body, or at least a smear of blood or something. Sir, I'd like to switch one of their cameras to our three-sixty holo for a while, if that's okay with you."

"Yeah," NJt994 grunted. "I'll scan the numbers through my EI." 547 switched over.

"Okay, keep those guns up," 547 said. The camera advanced a little farther toward the door, and the expanding circle of light there revealed a second dead rat, or at least red lumpy pulp that had once been a rat. "There it is! Keep the guns up, I said." This crew was pathetically unskilled for this kind of work, but apparently even office workers could shoot a rat with a machine gun. At close range, anyway.

"You killed both," 547 said. "Nice job. Now advance to the hallway. Let's make sure there aren't any more out there. Remember, we don't know how close they have to be to take over your mind. If you see a rat, shoot it."

"Yes, sir," the woman said.

"Spread out. Each of you take one side of the door and lean against the frame, looking down the hallway past each other. No, don't lean in through the door. Look down the other way—there you go." Now each was aiming down the hallway, gun barrels pointed across each other's direction.

"Okay, now lean through just enough to put the barrels of the guns past the frame and get more light into that hall."

NJt994 was still conversing with the crewmember who was helping to identify the missile launchers. "Right there," he said. "Hold it steady so I can load the number. Wait. I said hold it, not carry it around. Why are you—"

The panoramic view from 547's rat hunters rotated as they turned back to face the room. "No, wait! Don't go back in!" 547 said.

Both re-entered the room from the hall. Through their cameras, 547 saw the others lined up against one of the transparent walls. The rat hunters approached the rest of the crew, but did not line up next to them. Instead, the two began clawing at a vent set in the wall just above their heads, apparently trying to rip the grate away.

"What are you doing?" 547 said. "You'll puncture the suits! Stop!" One corner of the thin bioplexi of the grate broke off, and still they kept pawing at it.

Then came a shocked, gurgling inhalation.

"What's happening there?" NJt994 shouted, though they already knew.

The one from whom the noise had come collapsed, the air inside his suit shifting and blowing traces of foam against the face shield. The other kept digging furiously at the wall until the rest of the grate clattered to the floor. Rats poured out and climbed up the orange suits, settling on heads and shoulders.

Executive auditorium, Des Moines Amelix movable structure

Gregor Kessler breathed in as deeply as he liked, gazing up from the podium as the twenty other ranking Amelix officers settled into seats. He had never realized how wonderful it felt to be in control of such a simple thing as breathing until that control had been taken away.

"Hello, everyone," he began. He concentrated on faces instead of looking around the space; the walls and ceiling were too close, here. Only the pleasure the rats provided made existence inside the structure bearable.

"I would like to start by offering a word of warning," he said. "The Rat Gods have given me some leeway over the last several days as I prepared for this meeting. I was able to breathe easily and have relative freedom of movement. At one point, it crossed my mind that I could perhaps stall this process and buy myself a little more of that independence. I thought about it for maybe fifteen or twenty seconds, and the rats didn't like that. I'm sure you've all figured out by now that they know what we're thinking. Did you also know they have the ability to stop your heart? Not just suffocate you, but actually stop your heart. I could feel the muscle writhing inside my chest with the impulse to beat, but my vision slowly went out of focus and then all black. I wouldn't wish that on you so I'll tell you now: Just do what we're supposed to do. You cannot think your way out of this.

"And so, on to business."

He scrolled through the notes he had open in his EI, finding his first slide:

Need for Medical Doctor

"Right now, there are no Medical Doctors, so there is no way to change the synthesizer settings regarding medication. If you were being treated for a cold on the day of the Event, you will be treated for that cold for the rest of your life, unless something changes.

No New Medical Doctor

"In the world as it is, there is no way to credential a new MD. The schools, mentors, licensing boards, and all the other steps, are gone. The credentialing process is ironclad, and so complex that only eight hundred eighteen people in the world held the coveted MD title on the day we sealed. I've spent my entire career reading and interpreting regulations, and I've always prided myself in finding ways to achieve goals in full compliance. In the case of credentialing for MDs, the language is ironclad, and I could find no alternative interpretation. There will never again be a Medical Doctor.

The Preconditioning Czar

"As I informed you all prior to this meeting, you have been nominated as the acting emergency board of trustees, pursuant to Amelix Emergency Protocol 16A107 (a). You also received my detailed argument, spelled out over twenty-three pages, as to why the emergency board has the ability to designate a Preconditioning Czar and endow that position with the power to alter synthesizer settings regarding medication. Recall that under section two-thirty, subsection q, it was found that while Medical Doctors had total authority over every human body, they shared that authority with the board when it came to power over individual *minds*.

"By extension, I argue that as the new Board we *do* have authority to reprogram the synthesizers. While we're absolutely prohibited from changing them to manage *physical* health, my interpretation of the regs is that we can alter physical health as a means to control *mental* states. The Medical Doctor retains exclusive power over the physical world forever, even though she's now dead.

"As such, the proposal before us is this: We will leave the current Medical Doctor as the name of record, and the synthesizers will continue to record and send out billing data to that office forever. As synthesizers wear out, that name will be installed also into successive generations, in order to ensure proper functioning. Our highest-ranking civilian, Dr. Chelsea, will take over the role that used to be performed by the Medical Doctor's processing computer, authorizing the changes recommended by the diagnosing synthesizers here in the flesh. She will be the designated Preconditioning Czar."

Vote

"What's left now is to vote. Please think carefully about all I've said here today. You must accept it in its entirety in order to vote yes, so please give me an opportunity to address any doubts you may have. Consider all the parameters and—"

Ten people crumpled in their seats, dead. The rats must have disapproved of how they'd been planning to vote.

Vote

Kessler blinked his eyes hard a few times before realizing he had control of his hands. He had been rubbing them together. "We ... "

No stalling.

"There still remains the matter of the vote," Kessler said.

"All in favor of establishing the position of Preconditioning Czar to serve as conduit between the synthesizer and the

Medical Doctor, for the purpose of directly and indirectly influencing mental states under section two-thirty, subsection q, of the one hundred fourteenth version of the Amelix regulatory code, say 'aye.'"

Kessler said "Aye," as did everyone else still alive in the room.

"Motion passes. All in favor of promoting Dr. Zabeth Chelsea to serve in the new position of Preconditioning Czar, with power to adjust synthesizers for the purpose of regulating individual minds, say 'aye.'"

Everyone did.

Sublevel two

Dok sat gently scratching between the little dog's ears, feeling the coarse fur beneath his fingertips. Since the little animal now spent his days trying to urinate on as many areas as possible of the structure's biomachinery, they'd begun calling him Peety.

Lawrence was sitting across from Dok, both of them leaning up against biomachines with their eyes half closed. Since they were constantly on watch there was no opportunity for true sleep anymore, but they sat together and took turns dozing. These lower floors had no interior walls other than the hulking equipment, and they were dimly lit. The combination gave Dok the feeling he was perpetually sleepwalking.

Better than the sewers, in any case.

A voice called out from the stairway. "Sett? Sett, it's IAi547. You once knew me by another name."

Dok hadn't seen him move, but Lawrence was now standing, partially crouched behind machinery with his handgun drawn.

"Sett, I'm here alone. I need to talk to you."

It was Lawrence's former friend, the one Lawrence had called Li'l Ed. Lawrence looked at Dok. Dok shrugged.

"This ship, the *Agnes*, is in danger," Li'l Ed said. "I have footage to share with you. I am the recognized and de facto second in command aboard the *Agnes,* and I have authority to talk with you. We need your help, and I'm willing to make a deal."

Lawrence holstered his handgun and took the rail gun from over his shoulder. He held it with his finger next to the trigger but not touching, his other fingers separated to allow for the metal bracelet that had been crushed around the grip. "I'll meet him," Lawrence whispered. "You circle around us to make sure he's really alone. Yell out to me at the first sign of a trap." He moved off cautiously in the direction of the stairs.

Dok chose a path roughly ninety degrees from the direction Lawrence had gone. There were few of the classic clanks and rattles of machinery here, but the biomachines did produce a lot of ambient noise. Things tensed, sounding like apartment-sized sponges being squeezed, and relaxed, producing low, slow bowstring groans. If he concentrated, Dok could also hear the subtle rhythmic pumping of liquid common on every floor down here in the sublevels. He tried to tune those sounds out as he listened for some indication of where Lawrence and Li'l Ed might be.

Finally he heard the murmur of two voices and made his way toward them. When he drew close enough to be relatively certain of their location, he turned off to the side, circling all the way around the voices, inspecting under, above, and behind every piece of equipment. There were no signs of any deception or trap.

"You can join us, Dok," Lawrence called out. "I'd like to know what you think of this."

Dok crept toward them, finding the two giants facing each other in a relatively open area. Lawrence nodded but said nothing as he approached. Dok halted several meters away from them, still peering through doorways and around corners, looking for signs of deception as Lawrence and his former friend talked, one in crisp white and the other in tattered black.

"Dok," Lawrence said. "That struggle we'd heard was an attack from another structure like this, one owned by Amelix Integrations. This one we're on is called the *Agnes,* and it's owned by Andro-Heathcliffe, which is another biotech firm. It's an amazing feat of bioengineering but nothing like the

Amelix ones. They're fast and aggressive, and they're stalking
the *Agnes*, apparently planning to attack again. Li'l Ed is asking for our help."

"Our help?" Dok asked. Nobody spoke for a moment and
then Li'l Ed began to explain.

"We tried to set up a rendezvous with another structure—not
our Organization's—that had been out past Cheyenne when
we'd made contact with it," Li'l Ed said. "Safety in numbers,
you know. We headed west toward it and it came east. We
know this region and our sensors indicated little Amelix activity around here at that moment, so we determined it was in
our best interest to slow our pace, increasing the likelihood
that the other company would encounter and engage Amelix
first, weakening it for us. We misjudged the scope and speed
of that encounter. The last transmission we had from the other
structure showed *three* Amelix beetles surrounding it. The communication feed was still on as they attacked. First, we heard
the clamping and tearing noises, sounding just like what we'd
experienced here. There was a rift that they were able to seal
at one of the legs, but then one of the Amelix beetles managed
to crack the hull."

Li'l Ed's face slackened for a moment, but then he recovered.
"They were assessing damages, reporting to us on video. They
dissolved as we were speaking to them."

"How many Amelix beetles are there in total?"
Lawrence asked.

"Since we've seen three together in one place, it's likely there
are many more," Li'l Ed said. "It seems most of the materials in
them were Grown rather than built. Once the genetic engineer-
ing work was done, it would have just been a matter of letting
the structures produce themselves, providing them with raw
nutrients to keep the process going. Assuming they put the
same DNA into production near only their biggest facilities,
they'd have twenty-eight of them around the globe. If they had
Grown one at each of their locations worldwide, there could
be as many as four hundred of those things. Even now they
could still be Growing them, if they had a way to populate the
new ones."

"I guess you've got a real problem to solve, Li'l Ed," Lawrence said.

"Look, Sett," Li'l Ed said. "The next time we encounter Amelix, it might not be just one beetle. We have no defense."

"I have faith that you'll figure something out," Lawrence said. "Or maybe I should say I have more faith that you'll save your own asses than I do that you'll honor any deal you make with me. Anyway, all the Feds are dead now. There's a whole building full of weapons over there."

"There was a mission already. Six brave employees went out in HAZMAT suits, down into the Federal building to look for weapons we could use. Rats took control of the entire group. There are five remaining, but as they are, they're completely useless to us. We're planning the next team with savvier personnel."

"Rats will take the next ones, too."

"We have some ideas. But it probably doesn't matter, anyway. Every weapon there is new-issue or retrofitted Fed tech with user-specific coding to a particular Agent. Even if we could get them into a lab and try to reconfigure them, it's close to hopeless. The security upgrade is classified Federal tech. Still, we have to try something."

"You can't send another team!" Dok blurted out. "The rats will take them, for sure. Only non-reconditioned people are capable of resisting the rats. Every company in the world was already a hundred percent Accepted when you sealed this thing, so the rats will take them all."

Li'l Ed stayed silent a moment. "How certain are you that non-reconditioned workers can resist the rats?"

"Pretty certain. One hundred percent of those I saw taken by rats were reconditioned, and one hundred percent of the ones I saw resist them were not."

"I'm just going to say what we all know," Li'l Ed said. "If only non-reconditioned workers can face the rats, my organization's employees can't do it. There are currently seven hundred seventy-three people onboard. That's a lot of lives at stake, Sett."

"But whoever goes out can't come back again, right?" Dok asked.

"That's true," Li'l Ed said.

Lawrence cocked his head slightly. "Are you asking me to throw my life away by jumping into someone else's fight?"

"You are the last Williams and heir to the Williams Gypsum Corporation," Li'l Ed said. "What I'm doing now is negotiating with the chairman of a sovereign corporation. I'm asking your firm to work out a deal with us. We're out of time, Sett. We need the best shot we can take, and there are no other weapons available. We need your first-generation Trident, and we need you."

Lawrence said nothing.

"There's something else," Li'l Ed said. He locked eyes with Lawrence, who apparently opened some flagged page or file. Lawrence's nose and upper lip curled in disgust. "What is this?"

"A workroom inside an Amelix beetle near Mumbai, India. For whatever reason, this single camera is capturing and relaying this feed; it seems nobody knows it's on. Or maybe it's more accurate to say that nobody *can* know—or do—anything there anymore."

"Dok, the image I'm looking at is just people sitting or standing," Lawrence said. "I wish I could share it with you. It's the creepiest thing I have ever seen. Maybe a hundred people, standing stock-still. The room is dimly lit, but you can see maybe twenty or thirty rats milling around on tables and consoles. Every once in a while, one rat breaks off and a person carries it away, which looks kind of like cowboys leading horses in old movies. Is there a sound feed, Li'l Ed?"

"547," Li'l Ed said.

"Is there a sound feed?" Lawrence asked again.

"You're listening to it. Another structure shared this link with our Whites several days ago, and not one human voice has been heard. We've also observed that the same employees stay at their posts for days, apparently entering trance…or, maybe I should say a *deeper* trance…for a few hours every so often in lieu of sleep. They literally do nothing but work."

"Dok, I wish you could see this. There doesn't seem to be any human consciousness, or really, anything human about these people at all."

"This is what we're fighting, Sett," Li'l Ed said. "It's us and a few other companies, against a worldwide army of those things, populated with what you just saw there. Of the non-Amelix companies that made it into structures, five have now started behaving like Amelix, attacking nearby corporations, refusing all communication, and so on. We suspect they had rats caged in their labs that somehow communicated with the Amelix rats." He rubbed his eyes. "The Cheyenne structure is gone, now. The closest surviving human-controlled structure we know of is outside Mexico City." He lowered his voice. "Sett, this is much bigger than you and me. It's about everyone. Every last person on the planet."

Lawrence's expression changed and his eyes lost some of their glassiness as he let go of the page. "It's about everyone, Li'l Ed? Tell me, is this the same *everyone* who shunned me for standing up for someone who was helpless back at the diner? The same *everyone* who chased me with the Feds and ruined my life and made me live in a sewer?"

"So you're just going to let the whole world die? Or worse, let everyone exist like you just saw on the Amelix ship?"

"Instead I should just give up the tiny shred of security I do have, trusting you to protect me? You don't have a great history of standing by my side in times of conflict, you know."

Li'l Ed and Lawrence both stood straighter and took a step toward each other.

Finally Lawrence turned to Dok. "What do you think?"

"I think I'm tired, Lawrence. I think I've had enough of hiding, of doing nothing. If there's even the smallest chance of doing some good, of helping what's left of humankind, that sounds better to me than cowering in the depths of someone else's structure, waiting for the end," Dok said. "I'll do it."

Lawrence stayed quiet.

"Good," Li'l Ed said. "Thank you."

"Lawrence, you should come with me," Dok said.

"He can't," Li'l Ed said. "All Unnamed are reconditioned."

Lawrence shifted his feet a bit.

"Oh," Li'l Ed said. "Maybe that's not true when your daddy owns the company."

"We don't belong here, Lawrence," Dok said. "This isn't a life, sneaking around down here in the dark, living on what we can suck out of the biomachinery with my needles and tubes. We've done this already with the Subjects, and I don't want to do it anymore. Do you?"

Lawrence's face was stern as he nodded once at Li'l Ed. "We'll do it."

Dr. Chelsea's lab aboard the Amelix beetle

Chelsea shot forward down the hall. Lately she was walking less stiffly under Rat God control than she had been initially. The rats were learning how control a human gait so that it almost seemed natural now. They'd never had her move this fast before, though. Wherever she was headed was clearly important to them.

She left the lab, pumping her arms and legs in a good rhythm, heading across one of the footbridges she'd never before crossed, toward the structure's childcare and education facilities.

Weeks ago, part of her might still have wondered what could be over there they might want to involve her in, but after so long in Thrall she didn't wonder much of anything anymore. She did as they willed, always. The pleasure was always there, too, though she had grown accustomed to it. She had been forced to accept the fact that she was little more than an observer of her own life, that every aspect of her existence was subject to the rats' control. The human race consisted almost exclusively of spectators, now, and Chelsea, the Preconditioning Czar and de facto most powerful human on Earth, was merely a mechanical component, functioning only to maintain the other mindlessly obedient mechanical components.

Her chemically induced claustrophobia was gone. That was the first adjustment she had made once the teams had converted the synthesizers to accept her authority. Now she worked daily on change orders the synthesizers had recommended but not initiated, pending approval of the Medical Doctor. As Preconditioning Czar, she exercised the same authority to approve or reject such actions as a computer in a Medical Doctor's office would have had. It was a heady experience, even considering her situation. That was what she'd been doing when the rats had suddenly sent her marching out into the passageway on some new mission.

Months ago she would have found herself impressed that the rats, the undisputed rulers of the world, had approved of her taking such a huge and important position. Now she realized that pride, like any other emotion, had no use. It was pointless to think in such terms, judging herself better or worse for her ability to please the rats. There was no reason to feel one way or another about the rats' approval of her. If she lost their approval, she would cease to exist. There was no responsibility to manage or plan; she had only to do what she was made to do.

This was the area of the structure that had been designed for children, though none had actually boarded before it had sealed. There were broad rooms designed as areas for study on computers that mimicked EIs, though even EIs were already old technology, now. The new wave manip interfaces were free and available to everyone, so even children who hadn't proven their corporate worth could have functioned in the same way as those already known to be on the executive track.

The areas to which the upper grades would have been assigned consisted of nothing but empty seats and bare walls. Upper-grade education was all done electronically. She passed a few rooms like that and then stopped at one in the middle grades area, which contained a few more physical materials.

She approached a tall cabinet within the room, which was full of scientific learning aids. As she opened it, her eyes were drawn to the second shelf. She moved aside some racks of glassware and a track with little balls that were meant to demonstrate some physics principles. From the rear of the cabinet she pulled a half-sized model of a woman's body that was comprised of removable plastic organs. Chelsea was surprised to find her hands pulling the various parts away, finally removing and holding up a little uterus and fetus that had been inside.

"Why am I here?" She tried to speak the question aloud, but found the animal controlling her hadn't allowed her enough mobility in her mouth and jaw. Instead she only thought it, which was really the same thing.

What am I supposed to do with this?

Suddenly she was back at the door, running out with the plastic fetus still in her hand, through passages and back across the walkway, where she encountered a young woman who had been steered into Chelsea's path by her own rat. As they came together, the woman was made to lie on the floor and spread her legs, and Chelsea's hand placed the little plastic fetus between them.

Babies! You want me to change the birth control settings for this woman!

Waves of warmth and pleasure flooded through her.

19

Aboard the Amelix beetle

Gregor Kessler stared straight ahead. The collective rat mind had now figured out the various human roles aboard the structure and had ratcheted down tighter control. Now his eyes moved where the Rat Gods directed them, just like every other part of him did. He was still able to blink.

One time he had chosen to keep his eyes closed, just to feel the power of being able to do so. They'd let him get away with it for about fifteen seconds, and then stopped his breathing for twice that amount of time.

He'd tried it once more after that, counting, and they'd only let him get to ten seconds. That time they'd stopped his breathing until he passed out. It was clear he wouldn't survive testing them again.

By design, the Amelix structure's interior environment never varied. Levels of light and temperature were kept constant at all times, so there was no night or day. The wave manipulations that substituted for sleep were disorienting, as was the constant flow of pleasure the Rat Gods provided. Time had become meaningless.

He found himself looking down at a table which stood at the end of a long row of empty desks. Rats climbed aboard a tray, waiting for him to shuttle them somewhere. His hands grasped

the tray and his head turned toward the corridor. Passing over
one of the interior bridges, he remembered traveling this way
to meet the wave manip guy back in the days when his legs
moved on his own command. What had his name been? Tafiq,
maybe. Something like that. It didn't matter anymore.

Nothing mattered anymore.

Kessler changed bridges and angled off in a different direction.
The walkway sloped downward and switched back twice before
leveling off. Finally, he took a sharp turn onto a wide, steep ramp
and proceeded toward the closed double doors at the bottom.

Pitiful moans escaped through the doors, loud enough for
him to hear them before he was even halfway down the ramp.
He passed through the entrance into a large room full of evenly
spaced rectangular tables. The entire area smelled like sex. His
captors marched him onward through the dim, humid room.
On each of more than twenty tables spread about the room
were two couples, naked and in coitus.

The Rat Gods did nothing but that which served their own
purposes. Human pleasure was worthless to them. If they
allowed human sex, it had to be serving a rat purpose.

This was a breeding program.

He made stops around the room with his tray, lowering the
rats to various tables where they took up positions supervising
and controlling the process. New rats climbed onto the tray as
the others got off.

At the third stop, his attention was drawn to the girl who
was pinned down at the edge of the table. She lay motionless
while a standing man pounded robotically into her. He could
just glimpse her face in his peripheral vision—it was Keiko.

Emotion, or maybe shock, empowered Kessler, and he managed to rip a bit of control away from the rats, turning his eyes
by his own volition to meet Keiko's. Her eyes seemed to have
been left under her own control, and together they shared one
brief and exquisite moment of connection. The rats clamped
down, shutting off his breathing, but he still maintained eye
contact with her.

Pulling himself partially free of the rats' control like this
was an unforgiveable sin. They would never let him breathe

again. His vision began to fade. He kept his eyes on Keiko's until it went completely black.

Aboard the Agnes, just outside the old Williams Gypsum mine

Dok finished the last bite of his giant portion of synth steak and rice. As last meals went, it wasn't bad. Neither he nor Lawrence was an authorized synthesizer user inside this structure, but Andro-Heathcliffe staff had managed to find enough to feed them both. Now, stuffed so full they could hardly bend at the middle, they were being fitted into hazardous materials suits as Peety ran in excited circles at their feet.

It wasn't actually Dok's last *meal*, though it was certainly the last he could expect to consume with utensils from a plate. They were sending him with a backpack full of nutrient tubes, which the suit sterilized and punctured, passing empty tubes out through a special apparatus. There was another apparatus at the other end, which they'd also taught him to use, for passing out his own waste. He could stay alive out there for quite a while.

Lawrence was already suited up, in a white suit instead of the typical orange, since only White equipment came as large as Lawrence's Unnamed body. He stood waiting with his hands on his hips and the hood still hanging open down his back. The plan was for Lawrence to go through the five-minute process of being ejected from the structure first, and for Dok to go after that.

There were already four other volunteers waiting out there. As far as Dok could tell, the primary role of this yet to be identified team was to watch, and to implicitly threaten, Lawrence and himself.

"Sir," Li'l Ed said to his boss, NJt994, a Gold whose only distinguishing characteristic was a slightly disapproving scowl. "I think we should consider what these men have suggested about beginning a worldwide network of cooperation. Sett is sole heir to the Williams Gypsum Corporation, and you have autonomy in your direction of this ship, sir. I agree with Sett when he says it's a good idea to demonstrate that our two entities are capable of a long-term arrangement. It would help other companies see it as a trend they want to be part of as well, sir."

"I can see you believe that, 547," NJt994 said. "Sometimes I forget how young and inexperienced you are. Eventually you'll understand how foolish it is that you've let yourself be convinced of this, but for now I'll just say no."

"I...Of course I would never question your judgment, sir. But it's difficult for me to understand. It doesn't seem we can fight off Amelix alone."

"We're not fighting alone. Every corporation not under rat control is fighting with all it has. All corporations exist to concentrate resources into themselves, and each human-controlled corporation will fight like hell to continue doing so in this new environment. However, that same mandate makes cooperation between institutions nearly impossible. Why would any organization trust any other?"

"A merger, then, sir," 547 said. "Then we'd all be concentrating resources."

"We don't have the resources to come out on top in any merger. I'm responsible for every life aboard the *Agnes* and I'll be damned if I'm going to surrender that to some other company. It's disconcerting, 547 to see you suggest this, and especially when you recommend using a shell corporation owned by a former friend."

"Yes, sir. I understand." Li'l Ed bowed his head, defeated.

Li'l Ed turned to Lawrence. "Ready?"

"Yes," Lawrence said.

"Oh, I almost forgot," Li'l Ed said. "Here." Li'l Ed gave something to Lawrence. "I took this from your table during the raid at Chalk Bar. It's fascinating stuff. I've read it cover-to-cover maybe a hundred times, and now I'm teaching others about it from a digital copy. The wisdom inside this book helps us all to understand our struggle and our place in this new world."

"Heh," Lawrence said, holding it up. "Dok, look at this. It's Eadie's notebook." He tossed it to Dok, who found himself surprised at how comforted he was to touch it again, to hold the book that had meant so much to Eadie, even if it had also been used by the Prophet to manipulate her. He didn't know what to say, so he just held it in his hand, staring at it.

"Since you're going out there for all of us, I thought you should have it back," Li'l Ed said.

"You kept it all this time, Dok," Lawrence said. "You keep it now."

Dok nodded, watching his hand as it buttoned the tattered notebook into a shirt pocket. His eyes connected briefly with Lawrence's. "I guess I'll see you out there," he said.

"Yeah." Lawrence took a deep breath and then pulled the hood over his face. Li'l Ed walked him over to the packaging area, where they sealed Lawrence and his white suit inside a pressurized bioplastic ball. He had to walk, in a slightly crouched position, rolling inside the ball, to enter the first of a series of soft tubes that would slowly move him out of the structure. Dok, Li'l Ed, and even NJt994 all stood frozen for a moment, as pressure, vacuum, and biomechanical forces moved him out of sight.

"Okay, Dok," Li'l Ed said. "Let's get you into your suit." He gestured and Dok walked over to the fitting area. Li'l Ed held open the foot area of a suit and helped Dok carefully step in.

"Thanks—" Dok almost said 'Li'l Ed' but thought better of it. He lowered his voice, even though NJt994 was some distance away and staring into space as he apparently worked his EI. "So, who is waiting out there for us?"

"Actually, I don't know. That part of the plan wasn't disclosed to me until I was bringing you two up here. I was told the identities are need-to-know, and evidently I don't."

"Could they be Whites, like you?"

"Doubtful. We're too valuable."

They zipped up the suit and sealed its flaps, making it airtight around Dok's body. Like Lawrence had done, he left the hood off as long as possible. No matter how long he survived out there, this would be the last time he would ever be alive with his head uncovered.

"Okay," 547 said. "Now we'll seal you inside a pressurized ball of bioplexi film. You'll go out like unusable organic waste does. The *Agnes* is already lowered all the way to the ground so there won't be a fall. Once outside, you will pull the threads inside the balls, which will open a seam for you to exit them and walk in your HAZMAT suits. Do not pull the threads until you are outside, because without the pressurized ball around you the extraction process would squeeze you so tightly that your lungs wouldn't be able to expand and you'd suffocate. Let's seal you up."

Because he needed cameras and screens to do what others used an EI to do, Dok's orange hood was significantly larger than Lawrence's white one. It took two attendants to settle it onto his shoulders. Dok took a deep breath just before it was sealed. A transparent screen began displaying a few numbers at the edges of his vision.

"These screens were designed for scientific purposes, but we can use them to provide you with information as if you had an EI," Li'l Ed said. "It can read the focal depth of your eyes. If you want to see anything in the screen, start by panning your eyes down and to the left." Dok did, and a set of four screens came up across the lowest quarter of his vision. Dok pulled his eyes away to focus on Li'l Ed's face again, and the screens vanished.

"We have lowered the *Agnes* down into this open pit section of the Williams mine, to get some partial protection from the sides while we wait for you to complete your mission," Li'l Ed said.

"Sett will go inside the older section of the mine they used for storage and get a vehicle while you're transitioning out. When you arrive outside you will join with our team, who will be waiting for you."

"I wish you hadn't done that. We don't need a team, Li'l Ed," Dok said. "It's a waste of life, even if they're volunteers. We'd prefer working without them, and they'd get to live."

"I'm sorry, Dok," Li'l Ed said. "It's not just about your preferences. It was determined that the *Agnes* had an interest in—well, in protecting itself from you."

"So you found volunteers who'd be willing to kill us if we look at your building sideways?"

"I don't know who we found. My responsibility was to recruit and manage the two of you."

He cleared his throat, gesturing toward the packaging area. As they walked, Li'l Ed strapped a black shoulder harness over Dok's arms. He adjusted it so that the twin guns dug into Dok's sides. "Has to be snug. Sorry. You'll get used to it." The heavy guns pressed against his ribs.

They situated him in position and suspended a truck-sized piece of machinery over him. "Squat down," the technician said. A loud blast of air shoved the suit against Dok's skin for a second, and he found himself sealed in a transparent spherical pellet.

Now Li'l Ed's voice came over speakers as a different technician moved him to the tube and helped him navigate the ball into the opening. "Here's the plan: We already sent out a ball of weapons and supplies, including chemical bombs.

"Dok, you'll drive up to the Federal building, while Sett stays here with the rail gun to guard the *Agnes*. We hope your vehicle will be small enough to go unnoticed by the Amelix beetle, but as we discussed, instead of a truck you'll be driving some heavy mining machinery that should be better able to hold its own, if it comes to that.

"Once you get inside the building, you'll drop chemical bombs everywhere. They've been formulated to produce a fog that hangs in the air for about ninety minutes. That should buy you some time to explore. Hopefully you can kill any rats nearby and rescue our first team. They're still being held in the underground room where they were captured. We've turned off their lights and cameras for now to save power, but biostats confirm that they're all still alive, and it's possible that the rats intend to use them as guards. If you can't rescue them, you may have to shoot them. Either way, get inside and grab any first-generation heavy weaponry you can find, but remember whatever you get has to have a bracelet to make it work, just like the one squished around Sett's rail gun grip. It's highly unlikely you'll find any, and even less so that you'll find a bracelet, but we have to at least try.

"Sett, you will stay here, just outside the *Agnes*, in case Amelix attacks. The rail gun is charged up, but we don't know much about its number of available projectiles because, as you know, you wouldn't let go of it for us to figure it out."

"It's a bit late for that now, in any case," Lawrence's voice said over the speakers in Dok's hood. "Coming out now. I see daylight. Whoo. Bright after so long."

"So that means we don't know how many shots you'll have with it, if any, which is why we need Dok to find something else at the Federal Building if he can. We'll keep the *Agnes* hidden, in the hope that staying still and partially sheltered in the pit will keep Amelix from honing in on us."

The tube started to move Dok inside. About half his vision was blocked, now. Suddenly Lawrence made a long, shaky gasping sound over the speakers.

"What is it, Lawrence?" Dok asked. He remembered the screens and looked down, then found Lawrence's face on the screens that came up from that, finally focusing on the picture of daylight. At first it was just four figures in orange suits, but as Lawrence went from one to another and the cameras caught their faces it was clear: There were two girls and a boy, all of high school age, and another girl who was younger than that. Each face was tear-streaked and puffy.

"The *children*? Why?" Lawrence shouted. "Why would you do this?"

There was a long pause. The tube lurched and squeezed, pulling Dok farther inside. Now more than three quarters of the pressurized ball were inside, and the tube was starting to close around the other end.

"Why did you send out the children, you sick piece of shit?" Lawrence shouted.

"Are you talking to me?" NJt994 asked flatly. "You can't be talking to me, because even you aren't stupid enough to speak that way to a man who can detonate a charge in the back of that suit and take off your head."

"What went through your twisted mind to make you think of this?" Lawrence said. His exhalations were part hiss and part growl.

NJt994 made an irritated little grunt. "I suppose it is your mission and you should at least understand why you got the

crew you did. It might somehow prove relevant for tactical reasons. It's no mystery, anyway. Those four are not reconditioned.
They're useless to the organization the way they are, and there's
never going to be a way to recondition them. Also—and this
information is classified—our scientists have confirmed that
your conjecture is plausible: The rats may have an easier time
capturing and controlling Accepted. Those kids are less likely
to be used against us, as is your friend, Dok."

"You fucking waste!" Lawrence said. "We're the ones who..."

Dok's hearing faded, perhaps from shock or horror or fury.
His vision darkened until all he could see was NJt994, and then
just the man's throat.

Suddenly everything became clear. Dok no longer needed
or cared to think. He drew the gun from the holster under his
arm and fired at that bobbing throat. The three-shot burst hit
its target but Dok pulled the trigger again and again.

The tube crushed down around him.

Inside the Williams Gypsum mine

Sett steered the bulky yellow continuous mining machine
backward in a wide arc across the floor of the cavern that had
been used to store equipment. When he'd been a kid, the continuous miner had been his favorite of the family fleet, with its
row of spinning jagged disks. Each disk was as tall as he was,
even today, and the teeth were as long as his arm, though at the
moment he had them turned off. Below the disks was a shovel
that funneled the mined material under the machine and up a
metal conveyor belt that had dumped the gypsum into trucks.
The continuous miner moved slowly and would take a while to
reach the Federal building, but slow movement was less likely
to attract attention from Amelix, anyway.

The machine was about the length of a standard dump truck,
with the disks and shovel at the front and long, flat, chest-high

panels covering caterpillar treads on each side. Sett drove from an unpadded seat set into a niche at the back-left corner, where the controls were. He pulled the machine forward and slightly left, toward the opening of the cavern. The space had been dug out enough that a three-story building would fit inside it, and the intensely bright headlights made a blinding white patch from floor to ceiling across the gypsum walls as it turned. Sett killed the lights before he pointed the machine toward the entrance. The afternoon sun was still strong. Hopefully they wouldn't need the lights at all for this mission.

Sett opened the throttle until the continuous miner reached its maximum speed, which was slightly faster than a jog. He emerged from the mine and out into the valley where the *Agnes* waited with the rest of his new team.

Dok wasn't there. Through his EI he reached for Li'l Ed.

"Did you get the machine?" Li'l Ed asked.

"Where's Dok?"

"There was an incident. Dok shot NJt994."

"Was he killed?"

"Yes. So as a result I am now acting commander of the *Agnes.*"

"What? No, Dok. Was Dok killed for shooting your boss?"

"Oh. No. I stopped the biomachinery and extracted him. He was repackaged and he'll be out soon."

"Wait. What? *You're* in charge of the *Agnes* now?"

"Yes. I told you a hundred times: I was second in command."

"Congratulations."

"Thanks. I couldn't have done it without you."

Aboard the continuous mining machine, approaching the Federal Building

Dok sat on the right side of the continuous miner's conveyor belt as one of the teens, sixteen-year-old Robi, drove. The spinners and other digging parts were turned off. The machine wasn't made for carrying passengers, so Dok and the other kid, fourteen-year-old Gen-li, had to sit on one of the flat tool boxes beside the conveyor belt, clinging tightly to any handhold they could find. Gen-li sat right beside Dok, with one hand under her arm where an old Unnamed gun was holstered. She took her primary mission seriously, and Dok had no doubt she'd kill him and Lawrence if she decided either was a threat to the *Agnes*.

She wouldn't need a gun. Out here she could kill me instantly with a sewing needle.

Thoughts of killing had a sharper edge, now that Dok himself had done it. His lifetime of fighting to save lives had suddenly turned murderous, just a short time ago.

Maybe I should die instantly, just like my victim.

Dok wanted to feel bad, *deserved* to feel bad, but the guilt and shame he tried to pull up wouldn't materialize. He had killed a man, yes. But doing so had removed all those lives and that incredibly powerful machine from that corporate maniac's dangerous control.

On Dok's lap was a white duffel bag full of chemical bombs. At the Federal Building, he would heave them through every open door and place them outside every vent they passed on the way to the cache of weapons the first team had discovered. Then he was to quickly scan the inventory with his cameras until the Whites saw something that might work against the beetles, then grab it, and run out again. They could figure out how effective it would be once he was back outside.

Considering the circumstances and his age, Robi was doing a pretty good job of driving, following the directions the Whites were providing electronically. The other teen girl, Lora, and her ten year-old sister, Petra, were back with Lawrence guarding the *Agnes*. Petra, who had been too young for an EI back at the time the world broke, was the only other member of the team without one. They had given her one of the suits like Dok's, with screens built into the head. The bulky headpiece made her small body seem even tinier.

They were nearing the end of the trek across the desert. The sprawling Federal Building now took up most of the horizon.

"Location data indicate that all surviving members of Team 1 are still together in the underground room," Li'l Ed said. "You should have visual on the Federal Building any moment now."

"Whoa! Stop! Stop!" Dok shouted. The machine lurched to a halt. "Lawrence, are you seeing this?"

"Get out of there, Dok!" Lawrence said. "Just turn it around!"

The Federal Building itself was about ten stories tall, stretching off in three directions. Two Amelix structures, each roughly as tall as the Federal Building, crouched outside it.

"Keep your head in that position, Dok," Li'l Ed cut in. "I'm zooming your camera on that connection between the two of them."

Robi locked one tread in place and kept the other going at full throttle so that the machine pivoted. He let off the brake and they jerked forward, following the tracks they'd left in the desert grit.

"What is that?" Lawrence asked. Dok tried to find the proper screen to follow along, grateful that he was still too far away to clearly see the feature with his naked eye.

"A bridge of some kind?" 547 speculated.

"What's going on?" Dok asked. "Where's my screen for my own view?" He scanned the various images projected in the lower left corner of his visual field, but by the time he found his own camera, the mining machine had moved behind a hill and the Amelix structures were out of sight. "Dok," Lawrence said. "There is a translucent, flexible tube running between the two beetles. We could see something moving through it from one structure to another—it might have been people, but hard to say for sure."

"Team 1 is in motion," 547 said. "422, find a heading and get the Team 1 cameras back on."

For a while Dok heard nothing but the throbbing growl of the biocat.

"Team 1 cameras are back on, sir," 422 said. "Feed is now available. Team 1 has exited the building and appears to be approaching the structures."

"Dok," Lawrence said. "Have you found Team 1's camera views? The structures have disconnected from each other, and one of the structures is starting to walk. It's slowly stalking away from the Federal building."

"Toward us?" Dok asked.

"Not clear," 547 said. "But not directly at you. Team 1 is running, now…right toward the stationary structure. The tube is still hanging down from that one, almost touching the ground. Team 1 appears to be heading for it."

"Are they trying to enter the structure?" Lawrence asked. "How would they do that?"

"They are entering the tube now, packing shoulder to shoulder," 547 said. "Looks like they're seeking hand and foot holds among the ridges and other structural components."

"Climbing?" Lawrence asked.

"I don't think so," 547 said. "They're just hanging on, bracing themselves."

"Sett, sir?" Robi cut in. "Can you see the controls through my camera? Is there any way to get more speed, sir?"

"Sorry, kid," Lawrence said. "That's the full open throttle position. It can't go any faster."

"The tube is lifting. Team 1 is about three meters above the ground," 547 said. "Both Amelix structures are moving now. This one's path is apparently a mirror image of the first. They are both arcing in your direction; it's a pincer maneuver. They are on course to intersect with the mining machine in a few minutes."

Camera lab aboard Agnes

"Okay, Team 2A," 547 said. "Be alert. Those things are nimble. We're going to try and guide you away from them. Make a forty-five degree turn to the right and head for the dry riverbed there. Then just follow it on down. Hopefully the banks will keep you hidden.

"Won't that take us farther away from you?" Dok asked. "Shouldn't we be heading back to where Lawrence has the gun?"

"Sorry, Dok. Our first priority has to be keeping those things away from the *Agnes*, protecting the seven hundred sixty lives still aboard. I think I can help you navigate away from them and hide, though. You should be far enough ahead of the one on that side that you can pass it unseen in the riverbed."

"Great."

The various cameras showed the machine's progress as it crept along, following the winding course of what had apparently once been a substantial river.

"Distance to the Amelix craft with Team 1 is holding steady between four hundred twenty and four hundred fifty meters," 422 said.

"Wait!" 547 said. "Dok, hold completely still. I saw something move."

547 changed the main projection from the rear camera to one of Dok's right side cameras. He scanned over hills, looking for what he assumed would be an edge of the Amelix beetle poking up from behind, but there was nothing there.

"Cock your head to the side for me," 547 said. "No, other side. Yes, like that." One camera captured an angle where the movement might have been. 547 manipulated it to zoom in. There, poking out from a little hole in the bank, was a single rat, watching them. Several three-shot bursts fired, impacting all around the animal before a hit broke the rat's head open.

"I'm sorry, sir," Gen-li said. "I couldn't help it. I couldn't think. I saw the rat there and…I…It made me sick, and I got angrier and angrier, and I had to kill it. I couldn't think of anything, sir. I only knew that it had to die."

"Continue on down the riverbed, Team 2A," 547 said.

The cameras bobbed as the machine lurched and resumed its course down the river.

"Light, sir," 422 said. "I have full daylight again on Team 1's cameras. All of the remaining five are outside, sir. Data shows they're moving quickly, probably running."

"Switch it now. Give me visual from any forward-facing camera."

They could see nothing in the camera's view except empty desert ground, with sand and billows of dust blowing over the barren terrain.

"Are they headed for 2A?"

"Yes, sir."

"2A, Team 1 is approaching you at a run. They look set to intercept you at the next bend ahead. You don't have time to turn that thing around, but this would be a good time to put it in reverse."

Outside the Williams Gypsum mine

"We have to go help my friend," Sett said. "We'll get a truck from inside the mine. C'mon."

"Team 2B has been directed to stay here and guard the *Agnes*," the older girl, Lora, said. She drew her gun out of its pouch on the front of her orange suit. "We're going to stay here and guard the *Agnes*."

Great.

Sett made sure the communication link was set for person-to-person rather than broadcast through the White workstation aboard the ship. "Look, Lora. We both know you don't actually work for Amelix. I'm going to help my friend, and I would like you to come with me. This is an emergency. Don't screw it all up out of some sense of loyalty to a company that just literally shat you out."

"I should be loyal to you instead?" Lora asked.

"You always wanted to work for a company someday, right? We all did. It's all we ever learned to want." Lawrence pointed up at the hulking *Agnes*. "That company didn't want you. You are unemployed. You are *Departed*." He paused, letting the word sink in.

He gestured toward the mine. "But this gypsum mine is *my* company. As sole heir, I'm now offering you and your sister positions within my organization. "Do you accept my offer?"

The dry riverbed

"Oh!" Gen Li said. Her voice sounded panicked.

Dok ducked down behind the mining machine, running hunched over as the first shots fired. All of the mining machine's devices were now spinning and shuddering as it rumbled backward.

Next to him, Gen-li's HAZMAT suit crumpled, empty, its former owner obviously succumbing to the Slatewiper long before a bullet in the shoulder would have done her in. The suit, and the gun she'd been holding, disappeared beneath the retreating machine.

Shots rang constantly, though most of them seemed wildly off target.

The mining machine traced its earlier path, leading with its rattling conveyor belt, its massive wheels of teeth whirring threateningly at the other end. The edge of the toolbox Dok had been sitting on was taller than his shoulder, providing some minimal cover as he ran in front of it. The seat from which Robi was driving was sunk low enough as to be partially protected, so there was a good chance he was still alive.

"Robi?" Dok asked over the com-link. "Are you still there?"

"Yes," the boy said, barely audible over the machinery. Dok had no idea how to turn up the volume in his speakers. "I can't climb out. Too many shots going just over my head."

"Can you see them?"

"There's at least one, maybe two on this side, but they keep disappearing behind the dunes."

"Listen," Dok said. "We're coming up on a bend in the riverbed. Can you see behind you to turn?"

"Yes. There's a camera."

"You're going to need to slow down a lot to navigate that turn. Don't risk plowing into the riverbank and getting stuck. When you slow, Team 1 will catch up. Just stay where you are, okay? Concentrate on making the turn. It's okay to slow down for it." Dok unzipped the white duffel bag and removed some of the chemical bombs, lining them up on top of the machine for easy access. The machine's movement over the smooth dry sediment was slow enough that they didn't even wobble. "At about twenty meters, I can start throwing the bombs and take out the rats, and hopefully free Team 1. Just stay down as much as you can."

"Okay."

Lawrence's voice came over the link. "Dok? Can you hear me? I'm coming to help you. Just hold on."

"Yes, I can hear you. That is most welcome news. Thanks, Lawrence."

Dok set the bomb and grabbed the duffel bag, moving off to the side for a better angle. He lobbed the bomb as far as he could, but because it was quite heavy and he was still spindly and weak, it landed just beyond the machine's treads as they rolled backward away from it.

The machine's pace had seemed so slow when he'd been riding, but now he struggled to stay ahead of it. He was short of breath and felt a stitch in his gut. He tried to swallow but his mouth was too dry. The dizziness and exhaustion he was experiencing would have made carrying the heavy bag feel impossible even at half the speed. He reached up to one of the bombs he'd set on the machine, arming and setting it. It went off, spraying deadly toxins through little openings that aimed in every direction, with enough force that it blew a clean spot in the gypsum dust on the conveyor belt housing. There was a pretty strong wind coming from behind him that would move the stuff twenty meters pretty fast.

"Hang in there, Robi," Dok said, his labored breathing making it difficult to get the words out. "Hopefully the range of these chemical bombs is wider than the range of the rats' effectiveness. If so, Team 1 should soon be released, armed and ready to fight for the humans again."

Dok jumped up and clung on to the back edge of the machine so he could look between its shovel and spinning disks to where Team 1 was approaching the chemical bomb. His arms quaked but he held tight, watching, sheltered under the conveyor belt track.

"All right!" Dok said. "Team 1, prepare to be rescued!"

The members of Team 1 turned toward each other and fired their weapons. Five suits collapsed to the clay.

Dok's fingers lost their hold and he dropped back to the ground. He turned, but before he could take a step the mining machine hit him, knocking him to his knees. The underside of the vehicle shoved against him as it rumbled onward, his HAZMAT suit scraping against the roughened surface between the treads as the machine's weight pressed him into the dusty sediment. The material of his suit wouldn't withstand much of this, but the machine was moving too fast for him to do anything but crouch and hope.

A shadow fell across the ground as insectile jaws rose above the riverbank. They tilted down at a sharp angle from the Amelix craft and seized the mining vehicle, untouched by its wheels of spinning teeth. Robi screamed. The jaws angled upward again and squeezed tightly together, crushing the machine and silencing Robi. Dok was left exposed, knees still embedded in the dirt. As he struggled to stand, the Amelix craft's jaws opened, dropping the wreckage to the dry riverbed, where its impact caused a tremor that nearly knocked him down again. An even stronger shockwave shook the ground as the Amelix structure brought one of its feet down to crush what was left.

The Amelix craft stopped. For a moment, the only sound was the wind ruffling the HAZMAT suit and whipping dust against it.

Then the giant beetle shifted. Dok gasped and stumbled backward as it raised an enormous leg above his head. He fought to suppress his panic and summon a rational thought.

Don't just stand here and let it kill you. Overcome the anxiety. Be someone else again! Kel. What would Kel do? Be Kel.

Dok imagined it was Kel in this situation instead of himself, overriding his instinct to run away. As the enormous foot shot down toward him, Dok ran forward at the beetle as fast as he could. The beetle tried to compensate but could not bend enough to catch him. Its foot sank deep into the dusty sediment as Dok darted beneath the structure and out again. He raised both middle fingers at the machine. "Bitch!" he said.

Dok smiled to himself. Imagining he was Kel was a lot more fun than imagining he was the Prophet. By resurrecting his old associates, he could understand and adapt to circumstances to which he was ill suited on his own. Through him, they lived again, if only in his mind.

The riverbed was the only hiding place in many square kilometers of desert. Dok ran for a bend as the structure turned again. Its leg movements were startlingly quick and agile, while the hull remained balanced and stable. Dok dove around the curving sandy bank, clenching his teeth as the suit scraped across the grit.

In seconds, the machine was above him again, straddling the riverbed and angling its jaws toward him.

Dok's own personality had retreated in terror and now even Kel was inaccessible. He stood staring up at the beetle, paralyzed and insensible.

But the beetle was no longer moving. A man-sized piece of the machine fell off and disappeared behind the riverbank, out of Dok's line of sight. He heard it crash to the ground.

Lawrence's voice came through the speakers. "Dok, I'll be right there. The other beetle is retreating and we're chasing it now. At least that one won't be giving you any more trouble, huh?"

The rail gun had opened a small entry hole several stories above the ground, which now looked to be dripping something. As Dok watched, a tiny speck became slightly bigger and then impacted the dry riverbed a few meters in front of him. More and more specks appeared, like droplets in a building thunderstorm.

They were too big to be droplets.

Rats!

The dropping things were rats, leaping from the hole five stories above and falling onto a growing pile. The first ones to fall remained there, either dead or badly injured, but soon some of them began to crawl off the pile and limp toward him.

He took one of the chemical bombs out of the white duffel bag he still carried and armed it, watching as the pile grew bigger and rats that survived the fall approached him in greater numbers.

The newest ones bounced from the pile and ran at him full force. Dok triggered the bomb and threw it, running backwards until he reached the bank. He triggered another and tossed it halfway across, filling the riverbed with haze. Careful to avoid scraping the suit any more than necessary, he gingerly climbed up the bank, watching behind him for any rats that might have gotten through. He prepared another chemical bomb, keeping his eyes on the pile and the drifting mist of the bomb he'd lobbed at the descending rats. The wind was blowing toward the dead structure so the cloud had moved in that direction, now looking like a tornado on its side as it jetted out and expanded. Every rat landed in the same spot and immediately rolled upwind, in exactly the same way.

Dok felt suddenly, irrationally furious, dizzy, and sick. He reeled, then tripped over something. Several wild rats had come up from behind. They had already made contact with the suit but not punctured it yet. Even earlier today when he'd finally been angered enough to kill a man, he'd not felt anything like the utter compulsion he had to destroy these animals. He activated the bomb he was holding and kept it in his hand as he stomped, twisted, and jumped, being careful to stay within the toxic cloud.

"Lawrence?" Dok said. "Where are you now?"

"Probably about ten kilometers away, Dok," Lawrence said. "The other beetle's doing a good job of hiding. I only see it in flashes, and it keeps vanishing behind the hills again before I can pull the trigger."

"Rats are pouring out of the Amelix craft, Lawrence. More all the time. The chemical bombs drift in the wind. I have this one and one more after that, but they don't last long out in the open like this. I can't hold them much longer."

"I'll be right there."

The wind was pushing on the HAZMAT suit, rippling and folding it against him, feeling very much like the rats had as they'd climbed. Dok set the chemical bomb on the ground upwind of him and put both his feet together so that the stream of chemicals was blasting his ankles. It impacted the suit and dissipated, expanding up and around him. As long as he stayed still, the rats couldn't make contact with the suit.

A few meters farther upwind, a rat stood on its hind legs, watching him. Another joined it, and another. Soon there were between twenty and thirty of them.

The dead Amelix beetle

"Dok? I'm here!" Sett said.

Dok was easy to spot, at the tip of a plume of white chemical fog. Upwind of him was a mass of rats, running away at top speed.

Dok ran up, carrying the still spewing bomb. "Look at that!" he said, pointing at the rats. "They weren't afraid of chemical bombs or leaping to their deaths, but your truck terrified them!" He placed the chemical bomb into a little tool compartment on the truck's exterior and climbed into the passenger area.

"Maybe that's a weakness we can exploit," Sett said.

Aboard the Agnes, site of the dead Amelix beetle

547 watched as the *Agnes* extended saws and other tools to break up the dead beetle. The advanced Amelix technology was lost, but at least the *Agnes* was claiming most of its organic recyclables. A long tube carried the various pieces up to where they were smashed, broken down with acid, and processed for use and storage.

Together, Dok, Sett, and the two sisters had returned to the Williams mine to collect its two best trucks. 547's most recent contact with them had been a few brief words of encouragement through Sett's EI as he'd taught the others to drive. Now, two to a truck, the surviving members of Team 2 were trailing the Agnes.

A pleasant chime alerted him to a request for intercom communication. As commander of the ship, 547 had opted to change his settings back to less intrusive forms of communication than he'd endured as an underling. A text notification appeared at the edge of his vision:

Kevin Bashar, Marketing Dept.
Requesting Voice Communication

"Proceed," he said aloud.

"Hello, sir," Bashar said. "The video you asked me to compile is now complete."

"Great. I'll watch it and let you know what I think."

"Yes, sir."

547 terminated the connection and opened the file. It was only about a minute long, assembled from camera footage of the two missions.

First there were shots from different cameras outside the mine, showing an edited and dialogue-free version of the driving lesson Sett had given the girls. In this context and at the front of the compilation, it appeared to be the beginning phase of a mission. Footage from Dok's camera showed the two linked Amelix beetles outside the Federal Building as he approached. The next shot was from Team 1 when it discovered the weapons underground, giving the impression that a single, small team had infiltrated the Federal Building right underneath the Amelix beetles. The scenes shifted quickly after that. Dok swatted and stomped rats and then appeared next to a huge pile of dead ones. Sett gave chase, with the Amelix beetle skittering over hills and eluding him, then the Amelix beetle dead, felled by a single shot. Finally there was a still shot of Sett's face framed by the white HAZMAT suit. White letters appeared over it, slightly difficult to read at first but becoming clearer as the picture faded to black, with an announcer reading the words: "Andro-Heathcliffe humbly thanks the heroic Williams

Gypsum Corporation, through whose sacrifice we fight on."

This would work well.

547 opened communication with Sett.

"Hey, 547," his old friend said.

"It's ready," 547 said. "Take a look. If you agree, we'll send it out around the world. Once there's enough chatter about your heroism, we'll announce the merger of our firms, to be managed under your company's leadership."

"Heh," Sett said. "As it should be."

Outside the Williams Gypsum mine

"Five minutes, Sett," Li'l Ed's voice said, over the speakers in Dok's HAZMAT hood.

"Thanks, Ed," Lawrence said. He was speaking faster than normal and breathing shallowly.

"Hey, Lawrence," Dok said. "How are you doing?"

Lawrence nodded at Dok from inside his white suit, but the nod was as quick as his breathing.

Dok made sure the communication setting was private just between them. "Nervous, huh?"

"I'm addressing the whole world in five minutes, Dok. Yeah, I'm a bit nervous."

"I can help if you want."

"Sure."

"All right. We're going to let you imagine someone else is facing this for you. It'll be your face and your words, but you can pretend that another person is actually doing it. Now I want you to take a deep breath and hold it. Close your eyes. Now let out that breath, and feel your whole body just relax completely. Now do it again. Hold it, now exhale and relax, sinking down. Again. Now, this time when you exhale, I want you to count down slowly from ten to one, all the way down with one strong breath."

"Ten, nine, eight, seven, six, five, four, three, two, one."

"Good. Again. Hold it, then exhale. We're going to keep doing this until you're deeply relaxed. Then I want you to think of someone with charisma, someone with the power and presence to address the whole world in a live broadcast. We're going to relax you completely, and then I want you to adopt that other persona, that magnetism, as your own. Let that person live in you, let that person play your role in the broadcast."

Lawrence followed along and did as Dok instructed.

"Have you identified that person?" Dok asked.

"Yes."

"Have you adopted that persona to play you in this broadcast?"

"Yes."

"Then open your eyes and prepare to address the world."

Dok smiled. "I recognize the steel in those eyes," he said. "Hello, Eadie."

Every human-controlled EI in the world

The face and body were sealed inside a white HAZMAT suit, but the person speaking commanded attention like no one else alive.

"This is Lawrence Williams the Seventh, Chairman of the reinstated Williams Gypsum Corporation, addressing you, the world's remaining free corporations. We are seeking merger partners. Williams Gypsum has a plan for the future of human-controlled humanity, and we want you to join us. Here in the former Des Moines area we were able to slay an Amelix beetle and chase another one away. We can show you how to do the same.

"As the world's final surviving terrestrial corporation, and as the one who has sacrificed itself to save all of you, Williams Gypsum hereby claims title to all land area on this planet. Those not participating in our offer of merger will be trespassing.

"The mergers have already begun. Andro-Heathcliffe is our latest partner in our mutual struggle against Amelix. At this time, we are seeking to merge with any and all other free corporations. Individual organizations will maintain control over all their existing assets, subject to Williams Gypsum authority for combat, coordination, and resolution of any disputes with other merged firms. My company and everyone in it have made the ultimate sacrifice to benefit our merger partners; I must demand that those partners submit to our direction in these matters.

"If you feel that your firm is worthy of this merger, contact me before it's too late."

A northbound Williams Gypsum truck, towed with three others behind the Agnes

The calls were stacked one after the other, and Sett had already been talking for hours. Still, each of these mergers had to be done right, or at least as rightly as they could manage, under these circumstances. He ended one conversation and left the others holding for a moment, needing to talk about something else—anything else but the same merger stuff again—even if just for a minute.

"Thanks for teaching me that trick, Dok," he said, turning to make eye contact through the two plastic hoods. "Looks like my alter ego might have saved the world."

"*You* did it, Lawrence," Dok said. "She lived again only in your mind. It was really you speaking, and you leading."

"You and I both know I'm just a figurehead. What can I do, really? And for how long?"

"You're Chairman of the world's second-largest corporation," Dok said. "That's something, anyway."

"I suppose. Okay, back to absorbing the world's surviving industries." Sett opened the channel to the next caller. "Hello, this is Lawrence Williams the Seventh, of Williams Gypsum."

"Mr. Williams, sir?" It was the voice of a young woman. "This is W-6e80xh of the *Odette*, outside Toulouse, France. We would like to accept your offer of merger, for the purpose of defending against Amelix."

"Good," Sett said. "And you understand that while you'll maintain your own assets, my firm is bringing you in as a subsidiary, subject to my firm's final discretion in terms of combat, coordination, and dispute resolution?"

"Yes, sir."

"I'm glad to hear it," Sett said. "We'll store a copy of this conversation as proof of our binding arrangement. *Odette*, here's the information you need and the plan you'll be following:

"The Amelix ships are afraid of trucks. We shot one from a truck, and now we are able to chase Amelix from trucks, without firing a shot. It's likely that your best chance at survival is to find volunteer drivers and send them out as soon as possible. We have no idea how long this pattern of behavior will last. While it does, we need to come together as much as possible, in the safest place possible. Head north, and meet others as close as you can get to the Arctic Circle."

"Very good, sir. And if I may ask, sir, what is our long-term goal after gathering there?"

"I think the area is small enough to be defendable. Through this merger we've learned there are a few structures that can navigate on the ocean, so hopefully they can keep us all in contact. It's unlikely there are many Amelix beetles that far north as of yet, so I'm hoping we can form and hold a perimeter at the sixty-six degree, thirty-three minute mark. I'm going to transfer you to a staff member aboard the Andro-Heathcliffe *Agnes* who can work with you to coordinate your approach. We hope to connect you with others making the journey so you can all watch each other's backs. Welcome to Williams Gypsum, *Odette*. We'll see you at the top of the world."

"Thank you, sir. It's an honor to be part of such an heroic organization, sir."

Sett terminated the conversation and answered another call.

Another voice responded. "This is the *May Wah*, of Nanjing, China."

Sett formed the merger and gave the same instructions.

"This is *La Línea*, of Buenos Aires," said another voice.

Sett formed the merger and gave the same instructions. He did it sixteen more times, merging each new corporation into the fold, from places like Pakistan and Cameroon. Some, like the *Dryandra* and the *Morlina*, both of Australia, had to receive different instructions since they'd never crawl to the Arctic Circle from there. Instead, they coordinated moves to a suitably defendable edge of their own continent.

A text appeared in the lower left corner of his vision.

??

It was 547, wondering how the merger was going. Sett replied.

29

547 answered right away.

Contratulations, Sett!
You are leader of the free world.

The *Agnes* slowly lumbered north.

ACKNOWLEDGMENTS

Thanks to my wife Jennifer, upon whose love and support I depend for absolutely everything. Thanks also to Alan Irving, Andy Snyder, Kari Sanders, and Heather Payson.

I have no words to adequately express my gratitude to Jill Ward for her painstaking and masterful edit of this book. Thank you so very much, Jill. You brought magic to every page.

ABOUT THE AUTHOR

Mark D. Diehl writes novels about power dynamics and the way people and organizations influence each other. He believes that obedience and conformity are becoming humanity's most important survival skills, and that we are thus evolving into a corporate species.

Diehl has: been homeless in Japan, practiced law with a major multinational firm in Chicago, studied in Singapore, fled South Korea as a fugitive, and been stranded in Hong Kong.

After spending most of his youth running around with hoods and thugs, he eventually earned his doctorate in law at the University of Iowa and did graduate work in creative writing at the University of Chicago. He currently lives and writes in Cape Elizabeth, Maine.

Website: www.ArmyOfTheDoomed.com
Facebook: https://www.facebook.com/dark.mark.diehl
Twitter: https://twitter.com/MarkDDiehl

CPSIA information can be obtained
at www.ICGtesting.com
Printed in the USA
BVHW072113131118
532961BV00002B/317/P